IF AT FIRST YOU DON'T SUCCEED...

Nile heard a series of clanging metallic sounds, partly muffled by the wind. Somebody was down there, perhaps engaged in forcing open her aircar's doors.

She waited, upper lip clamped between her teeth, heard no more. Then one end of the aircar edged into view, turning slowly as if it were being pushed about. A moment later all of it suddenly appeared in the open area—and on the canopy—

Nile's thoughts blurred in shock.

Parahuans. . . .

Some seventy years ago, they'd come out of space to launch almost simultaneous attacks against Nandy-Cline and a dozen other water worlds of the Hub. They'd done considerable damage, but in the end their forces were pulled back; and it was believed that by the time the Federation's warships finished hunting them through space, only insignificant remnants had survived to return to their *discovered* home worlds. It had been the la__ ___ ___ttack by an alien civilization against a F_____—even planets as far out from ___ ___ andy-Cline.

And we beca_____ ___ ___ ___ ___ ___ felt we were so big no ___ ___ ___ ___ ___ ___ gain. . . .

THE HUB:
DANGEROUS TERRITORY

The Complete Federation
of the Hub

Volume IV

JAMES H. SCHMITZ

EDITED BY ERIC FLINT

co-edited by Guy Gordon

"Grandpa" was first published in *Astounding*, February 1955; "The Other Likeness" was first published in *Analog*, July 1962; "The Winds of Time" was first published in *Analog*, September 1962; "The Machmen" was first published in *Analog*, September 1964; "A Nice Day for Screaming" was first published in *Analog*, January 1965; "Balanced Ecology" was first published in *Analog*, March 1965; "Trouble Tide" was first published in *Analog*, May 1965; "The Searcher" was first published in *Analog*, February 1966; "Attitudes" was first published in *Magazine of F&SF*, February 1969; *The Demon Breed* was originally published as a two-part serial in *Analog* (September-October, 1968), under the title "The Tuvela." It was first published in book form by Ace Books in 1968.

Afterword, © 2001 by Eric Flint.

A Baen Books Original

Baen Publishing Enterprises
P.O. Box 1403
Riverdale, NY 10471
www.baen.com

ISBN: 0-671-31984-1

Cover art by Bob Eggleton

First printing, April 2001

Distributed by Simon & Schuster
1230 Avenue of the Americas
New York, NY 10020

Production by Windhaven Press, Auburn, NH
Printed in the United States of America

CONTENTS

The Searcher

～❦～

It was night in that part of the world of Mezmiali—deep night, for much of the sky was obscured by the dense cosmic cloud called the Pit, little more than two light-years away. Overhead, only a scattering of nearby stars twinkled against the sullen gloom of the cloud. Far to the east, its curving edges were limned in brilliance, for beyond it, still just below the horizon, blazed the central sun clusters of the Hub.

The landscaped private spaceport was well lit but almost deserted. A number of small ships stood about in their individual stations, and two watchmen on a pair of float scooters were making a tour of the grounds, moving along unhurriedly twenty feet up in the air. They weren't too concerned about intruders—the ships were locked and there was little else of value around to steal. But their duties included inspecting the area every two hours, and they were doing it.

One of them checked his scooter suddenly, said through his mike, "Take a look at Twenty-two, will you!"

His companion turned his head in the indicated direction. The ship at Station Twenty-two was the largest one here at present, an interstellar yacht which had berthed late in the afternoon, following an extensive pleasure cruise. He stared in surprise, asked, "Nobody on board, is there?"

The first watchman was checking his list. "Not supposed to be until tomorrow. She's getting a standard overhaul then. What do you suppose that stuff is?"

The stuff he referred to looked like a stream of pale, purple fire welling silently out of the solid hull of the yacht, about halfway up its side. It flowed down along the side of the ship, vanishing as it touched the ground— appeared actually to be pouring on unchecked through the base of Station Twenty-two into the earth. Both men had glanced automatically at the radiation indicators on the scooters and found them reassuringly inactive. But it was a puzzling, eerie sight.

"It's new to me!" the other man said uneasily. "Better report it right away! There might be somebody on board, maybe messing around with the engines. Wait a moment. It's stopping!"

They looked on in silence as the last of the fiery flow slid down the yacht, disappeared soundlessly into the station's foundation.

The first watchman shook his head.

"I'll call the super," he said. "He'll—"

A sharp whistling rose simultaneously from the two radiation indicators. Pale fire surged out of the ground beneath the scooters, curved over them, enclosing the men and their vehicles. For a moment, the figures of the watchmen moved convulsively in a shifting purple glow; then they appeared to melt, and vanished. The fire sank back to the ground, flowed down into it. The piercing clamor of the radiation indicators faded quickly to a whisper and ended.

The scooters hung in the air, motionless, apparently undamaged. But the watchmen were gone.

Eighty yards underground, the goyal lay quiet while the section it had detached to assimilate the two humans who had observed it as it left the ship returned and again became a part of it. It was a composite of billions of units, an entity now energy, now matter, vastly extensible and mobile in space, comparatively limited in the heavy mediums of a planet. At the moment, it was close to its densest material form, a sheet of unseen luminescence in the ground, sensor groups probing the spaceport area to make sure there had been no other witnesses to its arrival on Mezmiali.

There appeared to have been none. The goyal began to drift underground toward a point on the surface of the planet about a thousand miles away from the spaceport. . . .

And, about a thousand miles away, in the direction the goyal was heading, Danestar Gems raked dark-green fingernails through her matching dark-green hair, and swore nervously at the little spy-screen she'd been manipulating.

Danestar was alone at the moment, in a small room of the University League's Unclassified Specimens Depot on Mezmiali. The Depot was composed of a group of large, heavily structured, rather ugly buildings, covering about the area of an average village, which stood in the countryside far from any major residential sections. The buildings were over three centuries old and enclosed as a unit by a permanent energy barrier, presenting to the world outside the appearance of a somewhat flattened black dome which completely concealed the structures.

Originally, there had been a fortress on this site, constructed during a period when Mezmiali was subject to periodic attacks by space raiders, human and alien. The ponderous armament of the fortress, designed to deal with such enemies, had long since been dismantled; but the basic buildings remained, and the old energy barrier was the one still in use—a thing of monstrous power, retained only because it had been simpler and less expensive to leave it in place than to remove it.

Nowadays, the complex was essentially a warehouse area with automatic maintenance facilities, an untidy giant museum of current and extinct galactic life and its artifacts. It stored mineral, soil, and atmosphere samples, almost anything, in fact, that scientific expeditions, government exploration groups, prospectors, colonial workers, or adventuring private parties were likely to pick up in space or on strange worlds and hand over to the University League as being perhaps of sufficient interest to warrant detailed analysis of its nature and properties. For over a century, the League had struggled—and never quite managed—to keep up with the material provided it for study in this manner. Meanwhile, the specimens continued to come in and were routed into special depots for preliminary cataloging and storage. Most of them would turn out to be without interest, or of interest only to the followers of some esoteric branch of science. A relatively very small number of items, however, eventually might become very valuable, indeed, either because of the new scientific information they would provide or because they could be commercially exploited, or both. Such items had a correspondingly high immediate sales value as soon as their potential qualities were recognized.

Hence the Unclassified Specimens Depots were, in one way or another, well protected areas; none of them more impressively so than the Mezmiali Depot. The lowering black barrier enclosing it also served to reassure the citizenry of the planet when rumors arose, as they did periodically, that the Depot's Life Bank vaults contained dormant alien monstrosities such as human eyes rarely looked upon.

But mainly the barrier was there because the University League did not want some perhaps priceless specimens to be stolen.

That was also why Danestar Gems was there.

Danestar was a long-waisted, lithe, beautiful girl, dressed severely in a fitted black coverall suit and loose short white jacket, the latter containing numerous concealed pockets for the tools and snooping devices with which she worked. The wide ornamental belt enclosing the suit under the jacket similarly carried almost indetectable batteries of tiny control switches. Her apparently frivolous penchant for monocolor make-up—dark-green at the moment: green hair and lashes, green eyes, lips, nails, all precisely the same shade—was part of the same professional pattern. The hair was a wig, like a large flowing helmet, designed for Danestar personally, with exquisite artistry, by a stylist of interstellar fame; but beneath its waves was a mass of miniature gadgetry, installed with no less artistry by Danestar herself. On another day, or another job, depending on the purpose she was pursuing, the wig and other items might be sea-blue, scarlet, or a somewhat appalling pale-pink. Her own hair was dark brown, cut short. In most respects, Danestar actually was a rather conservative girl.

For the past ten minutes, she had been trying unsuccessfully to contact her colleague, Corvin Wergard. Wergard's last report, terminated abruptly, had reached her from another section of the Depot. He'd warned her that a number of armed men were trying to close in on him there and that it would be necessary for him to take prompt evasive action.

Danestar Gems and Corvin Wergard were employees of the Kyth Interstellar Detective Agency, working in the Depot on a secret assignment for University League authorities. Officially, they had been sent here two weeks before as communications technicians who were to modernize the Depot's antiquated systems. Danestar was, as a matter of fact, a communications expert, holding an advanced degree in the subject. Corvin Wergard had a fair working knowledge of communication systems; but they were not his specialty. He was a picklock in the widest sense. Keeping him out of a place he wanted to get into or look into was a remarkably difficult thing to do.

Their working methods differed considerably. Danestar was an instrument girl. The instruments she favored were cobwebby miniatures; disassembled, all fitted comfortably into a single flat valise which went wherever Danestar did. Most of them she had built herself, painstakingly and with loving care like a fly fisherman creating the gossamer tools of his hobby. Next to them, their finest commercial equivalents looked crude and heavy—not too surprisingly, since Danestar's instruments were designed to be handled only by her own slender, extremely deft fingers. On an operation, she went about, putting out ten, twenty, fifty or a hundred eyes and ears, along with such other sensors, telltales, and recorders of utterly inhuman type as were required by the circumstances, cutting in on established communication lines and setting up her own, masked by anti-antispying devices. In many cases, of course, her touch had to be imperceptible; and it almost always was. She was a confirmed snoop, liked her work, and was very good at it.

Wergard's use of tools, on the other hand, was restricted to half a dozen general-utility items, not particularly superior to what might be expected of the equipment of any enterprising and experienced burglar. He simply knew locks and the methods used to protect them against tampering or to turn them into deadly traps inside and out; and, by what might have been in part an intuitive process of which he was unaware, he knew what to do about them, whether they were of a type with which he was familiar or not, almost in the instant he encountered them. To observers, he sometimes appeared to pass through the ordinary run of locked doors without pausing. Concealed alarms and the like might delay him a minute or two; but he rarely ran into any contrivance of the sort that could stop him completely.

The two had been on a number of previous assignments together and made a good team. Between them, the Unclassified Specimens Depot became equipped with a satisfactorily comprehensive network of Danestar's espionage devices within twenty-four hours after their arrival.

At that point, a number of complications made themselves evident.

Their principal target here was the director of the Depot, Dr. Hishkan. The University League had reason to believe—though it lacked proof—that several items which should have been in the Depot at present were no longer there. It was possible that the fault lay with the automatic storage, recording, and shipping equipment; in other words, that the apparently missing items were simply not in their proper place and would eventually be found. The probability, however, was that they had been clandestinely removed from the Depot and disposed of for profit.

In spite of the Depot's size, only twenty-eight permanent employees worked there, all of whom were housed in the Depot itself. If any stealing was going on, a number of these people must be involved in it. Among them, Dr. Hishkan alone appeared capable of selecting out of the vast hodgepodge of specimens those which would have a genuine value to interested persons outside the University League. The finger of suspicion was definitely pointed at him.

That made it a difficult and delicate situation. Dr. Hishkan had a considerable reputation as a man of science and friends in high positions within the League. Unquestionable proof of his guilt must be provided before accusations could be made. . . .

Danestar and Corvin Wergard went at the matter unhurriedly, feeling their way. They would have outside assistance available if needed but had limited means of getting information out of the Depot. Their private transmitter could not drive a message through the energy barrier, hence could be used at most for a short period several times a day when airtrucks or space shuttles passed through the entrance lock. The Depot's communicators were set up to work through the barrier, but they were in the main control station near the entrance lock and under observation around the clock.

Two things became clear almost immediately. The nature of their assignment here was suspected, if not definitely known; and every U-League employee in the Depot, from Dr. Hishkan on down, was involved in the thefts. It was not random pilfering but a well-organized operation with established outside contacts and with connections in the League to tip them off against investigators.

Except for Wergard's uncanny ability to move unnoticed about an area with which he had familiarized himself almost as he chose, and Danestar's detection-proof instrument system, their usefulness in the Depot would have been over before they got started. But within a few days, they were picking up significant scraps of information. Dr. Hishkan did not intend to let their presence interfere with his activities; he had something going on too big to postpone until the supposed communications technicians gave up here and left. In fact, the investigation was forcing him to rush his plans through, since he might now be relieved of his position as head of the Depot at any time, on general suspicions alone.

They continued with the modernization of the communications systems, and made respectable progress there. It was a three months' job, so there was no danger they would get done too quickly with it. During and between work periods, Danestar watched, listened, recorded; and Wergard prowled. The conspirators remained on guard. Dr. Hishkan left the Depot for several hours three times in two weeks. He was not trailed outside, to avoid the chance of a slip which might sharpen his suspicions. The plan was to let him make his arrangements, then catch him in the act of transferring University League property out of the Depot and into the hands of his contacts. In other respects, he was carrying out his duties as scientific director in an irreproachable manner.

They presently identified the specimen which Dr. Hishkan appeared to be intending to sell this time. It seemed an unpromising choice, by its looks a lump of asteroid material which might weigh around half a ton. But Dr. Hishkan evidently saw something in it, for it had been taken out of storage and was being kept in a special vault near his office in the main Depot building. The vault was left unguarded—presumably so as not to lead to speculations about its contents—but had an impressive series of locks, which Wergard studied reflectively one night for several minutes before opening them in turn in a little less than forty seconds. He planted a number of Danestar's observation devices in the vault, locked it up again and went away.

The devices, in their various ways, presently took note of the fact that Dr. Hishkan, following his third trip outside the Depot, came into the vault and remained occupied for over an hour with the specimen. His activities revealed that the thing was an artifact, that the thick shell of the apparent asteroid chunk could be opened in layers within which nestled a variety of instruments. Hishkan did something with the instruments which created a brief but monstrous blast of static in Danestar's listening recorders.

As the next supplies truck left the Depot, Danestar beamed a shortcode message through the open barrier locks to their confederates outside, alerting them for possibly impending action and describing the object which would be smuggled out. Next day, she received an acknowledgment by the same route, including a summary of two recent news reports. The static blast she had described apparently had been picked up at the same instant by widely scattered instruments as much as a third of the way through the nearest Hub cluster. There was some speculation about its source, particularly—this was the subject of the earlier report—because a similar disturbance had been noted approximately three weeks before, showing the same mysteriously widespread pattern of simultaneous occurrence.

Wergard, meanwhile, had dug out and copied the Depot record of the item's history. It had been picked up in the fringes of the cosmic dust cloud of the Pit several years earlier by the only surviving ship of a three-vessel U-League expedition, brought back because it was emitting a very faint, irregular trickle of radiation, and stored in the Unclassified Specimens Depot pending further investigation. The possibility that the radiation might be coming from instruments had not occurred to anybody until Dr. Hishkan took a closer look at the asteroid from the Pit.

"Floating in space," Danestar said thoughtfully. "So it's a signaling device. An alien signaling device. Probably belonging to whatever's been knocking off Hub ships in the Pit."

"Apparently," Wergard said. He added, "Our business here, of course, is to nail Hishkan and stop the thieving. . . . "

"Of course," Danestar said. "But we can't take a chance on this thing's getting lost. The Federation has to have it. It will tell them more about who built it, what they're like, than they've ever found out since they began to suspect there's something actively hostile in the Pit."

Wergard looked at her consideringly. Over two hundred ships, most of them Federation naval vessels, had disappeared during the past eighty years in attempts to explore the dense cosmic dust cloud near Mezmiali. Navigational conditions in the Pit were among the worst known. Its subspace was a seething turmoil of energies into which no ship could venture. Progress in normal space was a matter of creeping blindly through a murky medium stretching out for twelve light-years ahead where contact with other ships and with stations beyond the cloud was almost instantly lost. A number of expeditions had worked without mishap in the outer fringes of the Pit, but ships attempting penetration in depth simply did not return. A few fragmentary reports indicated the Pit concealed inimical intelligent forces along with natural hazards.

Wergard said, "I remember now . . . you had a brother on one of the last Navy ships lost there, didn't you?"

"I did," Danestar said. "Eight years ago. I was wild about him—I thought I'd never get over it. The ship sent out a report that its personnel was being wiped out by what might be a radiation weapon. That's the most definite word they've ever had about what happens there. And that's the last they heard of the ship."

"All right," Wergard said. "That makes it a personal matter. I understand that. And it makes sense to have the thing wind up in the hands of the military scientists. But I don't want to louse up our operation."

"It needn't be loused up," Danestar said. "You've got to get me into the vault, Wergard. Tonight, if possible. I'll need around two hours to study the thing."

"Two hours?" Wergard looked doubtful.

"Yes. I want a look at what it's using for power to cut through standard static shielding, not to mention the Depot's force barrier. And I probably should make duplos of at least part of the system."

"The section patrol goes past there every hour," Wergard said. "You'll be running a chance of getting caught."

"Well, you see to it that I don't," Danestar told him.

Wergard grunted. "All right," he said. "Can do."

She spent her two hours in Dr. Hishkan's special vault that night, told Wergard afterwards, "It's a temporal distorter, of course. A long-range communicator in the most simple form—downright primitive. At a guess, a route marker for ships. A signaling device. . . . It picks up impulses, can respond with any one of fourteen signal patterns. Hishkan apparently tripped the lot of them in those blasts. I don't think he really knew what he was doing."

"That should be really big stuff commercially, then," Wergard remarked.

"Decidedly! On the power side, it's forty percent more efficient than the best transmitters I've heard about. Nothing primitive there! Whoever got his hands on the thing should be able to give the ComWeb system the first real competition it's had. . . . "

She added, "But this is the most interesting part. Wergard, that thing is *old!* It's an antique. At a guess, it hasn't been used or serviced within the past five centuries. Obviously, it's still operational—the central sections are so well shielded they haven't been affected much. Other parts have begun to fall apart or have vanished. That's a little bit sinister, wouldn't you say?"

Wergard looked startled. "Yes, I would. If they had stuff five hundred years ago better in some respects than the most sophisticated systems we have today . . . "

"In some rather important respects, too," Danestar said. "I didn't get any clues to it, but there's obviously a principle embodied designed to punch an impulse through all the disturbances of the Pit. If our ships had that . . . "

"All right," Wergard said. "I see it. But let's set it up to play Dr. Hishkan into our hands besides. How about this—you put out a shortcode description at the first opportunity of what you've found and what it seems to indicate. Tell the boys to get the information to Federation agents at once."

Danestar nodded. "Adding that we'll go ahead with our plans as they are, but they're to stand by outside to make sure the gadget doesn't get away if there's a slip-up?"

"That's what I had in mind," Wergard agreed. "The Feds should cooperate—we're handing them the thing on a platter."

He left, and Danestar settled down to prepare the message for transmission. It was fifteen minutes later, just before she'd finished with it, that Wergard's voice informed her over their private intercom that the entry lock in the energy barrier had been opened briefly to let in a space shuttle and closed again.

"I wouldn't bet," he said, "that this one's bringing in specimens or supplies. . . . " He paused, added suddenly, "Look out for yourself! There're boys with guns sneaking into this section from several sides. I'll have to move. Looks like the word's been given to pick us up!"

Danestar heard his instrument snap off. She swore softly, turned on a screen showing the area of the lock. The shuttle stood there, a sizable one. Men were coming out of it. It clearly hadn't been bringing in supplies or specimens.

Danestar stared at it, biting her lip. In another few hours, they would have been completely prepared for this! The airtruck which brought supplies from the city every two days would have come and left during that time; and as the lock opened for it, her signal to set up the trap for the specimen smugglers would have been received by the Kyth Agency men waiting within observation range of the Depot. Thirty minutes later, any vehicle leaving the Depot without being given a simultaneous shortcode clearance by her would be promptly intercepted and searched.

But now, suddenly, they had a problem. Not only were the smugglers here, they had come prepared to take care of the two supposed technicians the U-League had planted in the Depot to spy on Dr. Hishkan. She and Corvin Wergard could make themselves very difficult to find; but if they couldn't be located, the instrument from the Pit would be loaded on the shuttle and the thieves would be gone again with it, probably taking Dr. Hishkan and one or two of his principal U-League confederates along. Danestar's warning message would go out as they left, but that was cutting it much too fine! A space shuttle of that type was fast and maneuverable, and this one probably carried effective armament. There was a chance the Kyth operators outside would be able to capture it before it rejoined its mother ship and vanished from the Mezmiali System—but the chance was not at all a good one.

No, she decided, Dr. Hishkan's visitors had to be persuaded to stay around a while, or the entire operation would go down the drain. Switching on half a dozen other screens, she set recorders to cover them, went quickly about the room making various preparations to meet the emergency, came back to her worktable, completed the message to their confederates and fed it into a small shortcode transmitter. The transmitter vanished into a deep wall recess it shared with a few other essential devices. Danestar settled down to study the screens, in which various matters of interest could now be observed, while she waited with increasing impatience for Wergard to call in again.

More minutes passed before he did, and she'd started checking over areas in the Depot where he might have gone with the spy-screen. Then his face suddenly appeared in the instrument.

"Clear of them now," he said. "They got rather close for a while. Nobody's tried to bother you yet?"

"No," said Danestar. "But our Depot manager and three men from the shuttle came skulking along the hall a minute or two ago. They're waiting outside the *door.*"

"Waiting for what?"

"For you to show up."

"They know you're in the room?" Wergard asked.

"Yes. One of them has a life detector."

"The group that's looking around for me has another

of the gadgets," Wergard said. "That's why it took so long to shake them. I'm in a sneaksuit now. You intend to let them take you?"

"That's the indicated move," Danestar said. "Everything's set up for it. Let me brief you. . . . "

The eight men who had come off the shuttle belonged to a smuggling ring which would act as middleman in the purchase of the signaling device from the Pit. They'd gone directly to Dr. Hishkan's office in the Depot's main building, and Danestar had a view of the office in one of her wall screens when they arrived. The specimen already had been brought out of the vault, and she'd been following their conversation about it.

Volcheme, the chief of the smugglers, and his assistant, Galester, who appeared to have had scientific training, showed the manner of crack professionals. They were efficient businessmen who operated outside the law as a calculated risk because it paid off. This made dealing with them a less uncertain matter than if they had been men of Dr. Hishkan's caliber—intelligent, amoral, but relatively inexperienced amateurs in crime. Amateurs with a big-money glint in their eyes and guns in their hands were unpredictable, took very careful handling. Volcheme and Galester, on the other hand, while not easy to bluff, could be counted on to think and act logically under pressure.

Danestar was planning to put on considerable pressure.

"They aren't sure about us," she said. "Hishkan thinks we're U-League spies but that we haven't found out anything. Volcheme wants to be certain. That's why he sent in word to have us picked up before he got here. Hishkan is nervous about getting involved in outright murder but will go along with it."

Wergard nodded. "He hasn't much choice at this stage. Well, play it straight then—or nearly straight. I'll listen but won't show unless there's a reason. While I'm at large, you have life insurance. I suppose you're quizproofed. . . . "

"Right." Danestar checked her watch. "Doped to the eyebrows. I took it twenty minutes ago, so the stuff should be in full effect now. I'll make the contact at once."

Wergard's face vanished from the spy-screen. Danestar turned the sound volume on the wall screen showing the group in Dr. Hishkan's office back up. Two sets of recorders were taking down what went on in there and already had stored away enough evidence to convict Dr. Hishkan on a number of counts. One of the sets was a decoy; it was concealed in the wall, cleverly enough but not so cleverly that the smugglers wouldn't find it when they searched the room. The duplicate set was extremely well concealed. Danestar had made similar arrangements concerning the handful of other instruments she couldn't allow them to discover. When they took stock of the vast array of miniature espionage devices they'd dig up here, it should seem inconceivable to them that anything else might still be hidden.

She sent a final glance around the room. Everything was as ready as she could make it. She licked her lips lightly, twisted a tiny knob on her control belt, shifted her fingers a quarter-inch, turned down a switch. Her eyes went back to the view in Dr. Hishkan's office.

Dr. Hishkan, Volcheme, and Galester were alone in it at the moment. Three of Volcheme's men waited with Tornull, the Depot manager, in the hall outside of Danestar's room; the remaining three had been sent to join the search for Wergard. The craggy lump of the asteroid which wasn't an asteroid stood in one corner. Several of its sections had been opened, and Galester was making a careful examination of a number of instruments he'd removed from them.

Dr. Hishkan, showing signs of nervousness, evidently had protested that this was an unnecessary delay because Galester was now saying to Volcheme, "Perhaps he doesn't understand that when our clients pay for this specimen, they're buying the exclusive privilege of studying it and making use of what they learn."

"Naturally I understand that!" Dr. Hishkan snapped.

"Then," Galester went on, "I think we should have an explanation for the fact that copies have been made of several of these subassemblies."

"Copies?" Dr. Hishkan's eyes went wide with amazed suspicion. "Ridiculous! I—"

"You're certain?" Volcheme interrupted.

"Absolutely," Galester told him. "There's measurable duplo radiation coming from four of the devices I've checked so far. There's no point in denying that, Doctor. We simply want to know why you made the duplicates and what you've done with them."

"Excuse me!" Danestar said crisply as Dr. Hishkan began to splutter an indignant denial. "I can explain the matter. The duplos are here."

In the office, a brief silence followed her announcement. Eyes switched right and left, then, as if obeying a common impulse, swung suddenly around to the wall screen in which Danestar's image had appeared.

Dr. Hishkan gasped, "Why—why that's—"

"Miss Gems, the communications technician, no doubt," Volcheme said dryly.

"Of course, it is," Danestar said. "Volcheme, I've listened to this discussion. You put yourself in a jam by coming here. But, under the circumstances, we can make a deal."

The smuggler studied her. He was a lean, blond man, no longer young, with a hard, wise face. He smiled briefly, said, "A deal I'll like?"

"If you like an out. That's what you're being offered."

Dr. Hishkan's eyes had swiveled with growing incredulity between the screen and Volcheme's face. He said angrily, "What nonsense is this? Have her picked up and brought here at once! We must find out what—"

"I suggest," Volcheme interrupted gently, "you let me

handle the matter. Miss Gems, I assume your primary purpose here is to obtain evidence against Dr. Hishkan?"

"Yes," said Danestar.

"You and your associate—Mr. Wergard—are U-League detectives?"

She shook her head.

"No such luck, Volcheme! We're private agency, full-privilege, Federation charter."

"I suspected it." Volcheme's lips pulled back from his teeth in a grimace of hostility. "You show the attributes of the breed. Do I know the agency?"

"Kyth Interstellar."

He was silent a moment, said, "I see. . . . Is Mr. Wergard available for negotiations?"

"No. You'll talk to me."

"That will be satisfactory. You realize, of course, that I don't propose to buy your deal blind. . . . "

"You aren't expected to," Danestar said.

"Then let's get the preliminaries out of the way." The smuggler's face was bleak and watchful. "I have men guarding your room. Unlock the door for them."

"Of course." Danestar turned toward the door's lock control in the wall on her left. Volcheme pulled a speaker from his pocket.

They understood each other perfectly. One of the last things a man of Volcheme's sort cared to do was get a major private detective agency on his neck. It was a mistake, frequently a fatal one. As a matter of principle and good business, the agencies didn't get off again.

But if he saw a chance to go free with the loot, leaving no witnesses to point a finger at him, he'd take it. Danestar would remain personally safe so long as Volcheme's men didn't catch up with Wergard. After that, she'd be safe only if she kept the smuggler convinced he was in a trap from which there was no escape. Within a few hours he would be in such a trap, but he wasn't in it at present. Her arrangements were designed to keep him from discovering that.

The door clicked open and four men came quickly and cautiously into the room. Three of them were smugglers; the fourth was Tornull, the U-League depot manager. The one who'd entered first stayed at the door, pointing a gun at Danestar. Volcheme's other two men separated, moved toward her watchfully from right and left. They were competent professionals who had just heard that Danestar was also one. The gun aimed at her from the door wasn't there for display.

"As a start, Decrain," Volcheme's voice said from the screen, "have Miss Gems give you the control belt she's wearing."

Danestar unsnapped the belt, making no unnecessary motions, and handed it to the big man named Decrain. They were pulling her teeth, or thought they were, which was sensible from their point of view and made no immediate difference from hers; the belt could be of no use at present. Decrain drew out a chair, told her to sit down and keep her hands in sight. She complied, and the man with the gun came up and stood eight feet to her left. Decrain and his companion began a quick, expert search of her living quarters with detectors. Tornull, Dr. Hishkan's accomplice in amateur crime, watched them, now and then giving Danestar and her guard a puzzled look which indicated the girl didn't appear very dangerous to him and that he couldn't understand why they were taking such elaborate precautions with her.

Within six minutes, Decrain discovered as much as Danestar had wanted them to find of her equipment and records. Whenever the detector beams approached the rest of it, other beams reached out gently and blended with them until they'd slid without a quiver past the shielded areas. The collection of gadgetry Decrain laid out on Danestar's worktable was impressive and exotic enough to still suspicions, as she had expected. When he announced yet another discovery, Galester observed thoughtfully from the screen, "That's a dangerously powerful anti-interrogation drug you use, Miss Gems!"

"It is," Danestar acknowledged. "But it's dependable. I'm conditioned to it."

"How much have you taken?"

"My limit. A ten-hour dose . . . sixty-five units."

She was telling the truth—her developed ability to absorb massive dosages of quizproof without permanent ill effects had pulled her out of more than one difficult situation. But a third of the amount she'd mentioned was considered potentially lethal. Decrain studied her dubiously a moment as if pondering the degree of her humanity. Decrain appeared to be a stolid type, but the uncovering of successive batteries of spidery instruments unlike anything he had encountered in his professional career had caused him mental discomfort; and when he brought Danestar's set of gimmicked wigs—to which the green one she'd been wearing was now added—out of a shrinkcase and watched them unfold on the table, he'd seemed shaken.

"You'll be brought over here now, Miss Gems," Volcheme said, his face sour. "We want a relaxed atmosphere for our discussion, so Decrain will search you thoroughly first. As far as possible, he'll be a gentleman about it, of course,"

"I'm sure he will be," Danestar said agreeably. "Because if he isn't, his hide becomes part of the deal."

The muscles along Decrain's jaw tightened, but he continued packaging the sections of Danestar's instruments Galester wanted to examine without comment. Tornull began to laugh, caught sight of the big man's expression, and sobered abruptly, looking startled.

The semi-material composite body of the goyal flowed below the solid surface of the world of Mezmiali toward the Unclassified Specimens Depot, swerving from its course occasionally to avoid the confusing turbulences of radiation about the larger cities. Its myriad units hummed with coordinating communal impulses of direction and purpose.

Before this, in all its thousand years of existence, the goyal had known only the planets of the Pit, murkily lit by stars which swam like patches of glowing fog in the dark. Once those worlds had supported the civilization of an inventive race which called itself the Builders.

The Builders developed spaceships capable of sliding unharmed through the cosmic dust at a speed above that of light, and a location system to guide them infallibly through the formless gloom where ordinary communication methods were useless. Eventually they reached the edges of the Pit . . . and shrank back. They had assumed the dust cloud stretched on to the end of the universe, were appalled when they realized it was limited, seemed suspended in some awesome, gleaming, impossibly *open* void.

To venture into that terrible alien emptiness themselves was unthinkable. But the urge to explore it by other means grew strong. The means they presently selected was a lowly form of energy life, at home both in the space and on the planets of the Pit. The ingenuity of the Builders produced in it the impulse to combine with its kind into increasingly large, more coherent and more purposeful groups; and the final result of their manipulations was the goyal, a superbeing which thought and acted as an individual, while its essential structure was still that of a gigantic swarm of the minor uncomplicated prototypes of energy life with which the Builders had begun. The goyal was intended to be their galactic explorer, an intelligent, superbly adaptable servant, capable of existing and sustaining itself as readily in space as on the worlds it encountered.

In its way, the goyal was an ultimate achievement of the Builders' skills. But it was to become also the monument to an irredeemable act of stupidity. They had endowed it with great and varied powers and with keen, specialized intelligence, but not with gratitude. When it discovered it was stronger than its creators and swifter than their ships, it turned on the Builders and made war on them, exterminating them on planet after planet until, within not much more than a century, it became sole master of the Pit.

For a long time, it remained unchallenged there. It shifted about the great dust cloud at will, guided by the Builders' locator system, feeding on the life of the dim worlds. During that period, it had no concept of intelligence other than its own and that of the Builders. Then a signal which had not come into use since the last of the Builders vanished alerted the locator system. A ship again had appeared within its range.

The goyal flashed through the cloud on the locator impulses like a great spider darting along the strands of its web. At the point of disturbance, it found an alien ship groping slowly and blindly through the gloom. Without hesitation, it flowed aboard and swept through the ship, destroying all life inside.

It had been given an understanding of instruments, and it studied the ship in detail, then studied the dead beings. They were not Builders though they showed some resemblance to them. Their ship was not designed to respond to the locator system; it had come probing into the Pit from the surrounding void.

Other ships presently followed it, singly and in groups. They came cautiously, scanning the smothering haze for peril, minds and instruments alert behind a variety of protective devices which seemed adequate until the moment the goyal struck. The enveloping protective screens simply were too light to hamper it seriously; and once it was through the screens, the alien crew was at its mercy. But the persistence these beings showed in intruding on its domain was disturbing to it. It let some of them live for a time on the ships it captured while it watched and studied them, manipulated them, experimented with them. Gradually, it formed a picture of an enemy race in the void which must be destroyed as it had destroyed the Builders if its supremacy was to be maintained.

It did not intend to venture into the void alone. It had planted sections of its body on a number of the worlds of the Pit. The sections were as yet immature. They could not move about in space as the parent body did, possessed barely enough communal mind to know how to nourish themselves from the planetary life about them. But they were growing and developing. In time the goyal would have others of its kind to support it. Until then, it planned to hold the Pit against the blind intruders from the void without letting the enemy race become aware of its existence.

Then the unforeseeable happened. An entire section of the locator system suddenly went dead, leaving the remainder functioning erratically. For the first time in its long existence, the goyal was made aware of the extent of its dependence on the work of the Builders. After a long difficult search, it discovered the source of the trouble. A key locator near the edge of the dust cloud had disappeared. Its loss threatened to make the entire system unusable.

There was no way of replacing it. The goyal's mind was not that of a Builder. It had learned readily to use instruments, but it could not construct them. Now it realized its mistake in exterminating the only civilized race in the Pit. It should have kept the Builders in subservience to itself so that their skills would always be at its disposal. It could no longer be certain even of detecting the intruding aliens when they came again and preventing them from discovering the secrets of the cloud. Suddenly, the end of its reign seemed near.

Unable to develop a solution to the problem, the goyal

settled into a kind of apathy, drifted with dimming energies aimlessly about the Pit . . . until, unmistakably, the lost locator called it! Alert at once, the goyal sped to other units of the system, found they had recorded and pinpointed the distant blast. It had come from beyond the cloud, out of the void! Raging, the goyal set off in the indicated direction. It had no doubt of what had happened—one of the alien ships had discovered the locator and carried it away. But now it could be and would be recovered.

Extended into a needle of attenuated energy over a million miles in length, the goyal flashed out into the starlit void, its sensor units straining. There was a sun dead ahead; the stolen instrument must be within that system. The goyal discovered a spaceship of the aliens moving in the same direction, closed with it and drew itself on board. For a time, its presence unsuspected, it remained there, forming its plans. It could use the ship's energies to build up its reserves, but while the ship continued toward Mezmiali, it made no move.

Presently it noted a course shift which would take the ship past the Mezmiali system but close enough to it to make the transfer to any of the sun's four planets an almost effortless step. The goyal remained quiet. Not long afterwards, its sensors recorded a second blast from the lost locator. Now it knew not only to which planet it should go but, within a few hundred miles, at what point of that planet the instrument was to be found.

Purple fire lashed out from the ship's bulkheads to engulf every human being on board simultaneously. Within moments, the crew was absorbed. The goyal drank energy from the drive generators to the point of surfeit, left the ship and vanished in the direction of Mezmiali. Within the system, it again closed in on a ship and rode down with it to the planet.

It had reached its destination undetected and at the peak of power, its reserves intact. But this was unknown

enemy territory, and it remained cautious. For hours, its
sensors had known precisely where the locator was to be
found. The goyal waited until the humans had disem-
barked from the ship, until the engines were quiet and
it could detect no significant activity in the area immediately about it. Then it flowed out of the ship and into
the ground. The two humans who saw it emerge were
absorbed before they could make a report.

There was no reason to hesitate longer. Moving
through the dense solid matter of the planet was a tedious
process by the goyal's standards; but, in fact, only a short
time passed before it reached the University League's
isolated Depot.

There it was brought to a very abrupt stop.

It had flowed up to the energy barrier surrounding
the old fortress site and partly into it. Hostile forces
crashed through it instantly with hideous, destructive
power. A quarter of its units died in that moment. The
remaining units whipped back out of the boiling fury of
the field, reassembled painfully underground near the
Depot. The body was reduced and its energy depleted,
but it had suffered no lasting damage.

The communal mind remained badly shocked for
minutes; then it, too, began to function again. There was
not the slightest possibility of breaking through that
terrible barrier! In all its experience, the goyal had never
encountered anything similar to it. The defensive ship
screens it had driven through in its secretive murders in
the Pit had been fragile webs by comparison, and the
Builders' stoutest planetary energy shields had been
hardly more effective. It began searching cautiously along
the perimeter of the barrier. Presently it discovered the
entrance lock.

It was closed, but the goyal knew about locks and their
uses. The missing locator was so close that the sensors'
reports on it were blurred, but it was somewhere within
this monstrously guarded structure. The goyal decided

it needed only to wait. In time, the lock would open and it would enter. It would destroy the humans inside, and be back on its way to the Pit with the locator before the alien world realized that anything was amiss. . . .

Approximately an hour later, a slow bulky vehicle came gliding down from the sky toward the Depot. Messages were exchanged between it and a small building on the outside of the barrier in the language employed on the ships which had come into the Pit. A section of the communal mind interpreted the exchange without difficulty, reported:

The vehicle was bringing supplies, was expected, and would be passed through the barrier lock.

At the lock, just below the surface of the ground, the goyal waited, its form compressed to near-solidity, to accompany the vehicle inside.

In Dr. Hishkan's office in the central building of the Depot, the arrival of the supplies truck was being awaited with a similar degree of interest by the group assembled there. Their feelings about it varied. Danestar's feeling— in part—was vast relief. Volcheme was a very tough character, and there was a streak of gambler's recklessness in him which might have ruined her plan.

"Any time anything big enough to have that apparatus on board leaves the Depot now, we clear it by shortcode before the lock closes," she'd said. "You don't know what message to send. You can't get it from me, and you can't get it from Wergard. The next truck or shuttle that leaves won't get cleared. And it will get stopped almost as soon as it's outside."

That was it—the basic lie! If they'd been willing to take the chance, they could have established in five minutes that it was a lie.

"You're bluffing," Volcheme had said, icily hating her. "The bluff won't stop us from leaving when we're ready to go. We won't have to run any risks. We'll simply go out with the shuttle to check your story before we load the thing on."

"Then why don't you do it? Why wait?" She'd laughed, a little high, a little feverish, with the drugs cooking in her—her own and the stuff Galester had given her in an attempt to counteract the quizproof effect. She'd told them it wasn't going to work; and now, almost two hours later, they knew it wasn't going to work.

They couldn't make her feel physical pain, they couldn't intimidate her, they couldn't touch her mind. They'd tried all that in the first fifteen minutes when she came into the office, escorted by Decrain and Tornull, and told Volcheme bluntly what the situation was, what he had to do. They could, of course, as they suggested, kill her, maim her, disfigure her. Danestar shrugged it off. They could, but she didn't have to mention the price tag it would saddle them with. Volcheme was all too aware of it.

The threats soon stopped. Volcheme either was in a trap, or he wasn't. If the Kyth Agency had him boxed in here, he would have to accept Danestar's offer, leave with his group and without the specimen. He could see her point—they had an airtight case against Dr. Hishkan and his accomplices now. The specimen, whatever its nature, was a very valuable one; if it had to be recaptured in a running fight with the shuttle, it might be damaged or destroyed. That was the extent of the agency's responsibility to the U-League. They had no interest in Volcheme.

The smuggler was being given an out, as Danestar had indicated. But he'd had the biggest, most profitable transaction of his career set up, and he was being told he couldn't go through with it. He didn't know whether Danestar was lying or not, and he was savage with indecision. If the Depot was being watched—Volcheme didn't much doubt that part of the story—sending the shuttle out to check around and come back could arouse the suspicions of the observers enough to make them halt it when it emerged the second time. That, in fact, might be precisely what Danestar wanted him to do.

He was forced to conclude he couldn't take the chance. To wait for the scheduled arrival of the supplies truck was the smaller risk. Volcheme didn't like waiting, either. Wergard hadn't been found; and he didn't know what other tricks the Kyth agents could have prepared. But, at any rate, the truck was the answer to part of his problem. It would be let in, unloaded routinely, allowed to depart, its men unaware that anything out of the ordinary was going on in the Depot. They would watch then to see if the truck was stopped outside and searched. If that happened, Volcheme would be obliged to agree to Danestar's proposal.

If it didn't happen, he would know she'd been lying on one point; but that would not be the end of his difficulties. Until Wergard was captured or killed, he still couldn't leave with the specimen. The Kyth agents knew enough about him to make the success of the enterprise depend on whether he could silence both of them permanently. If it was possible, he would do it. With stakes as high as they were, Volcheme was not inclined to be squeamish. But that would put an interstellar organization of experienced man-hunters on an unrelenting search for the murderers of two of its members. . . .

Whatever the outcome, Volcheme wasn't going to be happy. What had looked like the haul of a lifetime, sweetly clean and simple, would wind up either in failure or as a dangerously messy partial success. Galester and Decrain, seeing the same prospects, shared their chief's feelings. And while nobody mentioned that the situation looked even less promising for Dr. Hishkan and Tornull, those two had at least begun to suspect that if the smugglers succeeded in escaping with the specimen, they would not want to leave informed witnesses behind.

When the voice of an attendant in the control building

near the lock entry finally announced from the wall screen communicator that the supplies truck had arrived and was about to be let into the Depot, Danestar therefore was the most composed of the group. Even Decrain, who had been detailed to keep his attention on her at all times, stood staring with the others at the screen where Dr. Hishkan was switching on a view of the interior lock area.

Danestar made a mental note of Decrain's momentary lapse of alertness, though it could make no difference to her at present. The only thing she needed to do, or could do, now was wait. Her gaze shifted to the table where assorted instruments Galester had taken out of the alien signaling device still stood. At the other side of the table was the gadgetry Decrain had brought here from her room, a toy-sized shortcode transmitter among it. Volcheme had wanted to be sure nobody would send out messages while the lock was open.

And neither she nor Wergard would be sending any messages. But automatically, as the lock switches were thrown, the duplicate transmitter concealed in the wall of her room would start flicking its coded alert out of the Depot, repeating it over and over until the lock closed.

And twenty or thirty minutes later, when the supplies truck slid back out through the lock and lifted into the air, it would be challenged and stopped.

Then Volcheme would give up, buy his pass to liberty on her terms. There was nothing else he could do.

It wasn't the kind of stunt she'd care to repeat too often—her nerves were still quivering with unresolved tensions. But she'd carried it off without letting matters get to a point where Wergard might have had to help her out with some of his fast-action gunplay. Danestar told herself to relax, that nothing at all was likely to go wrong now.

Her gaze slipped over to Volcheme and the others, silently watching the wall screen, which was filled with the dead, light-drinking black of the energy barrier, except at the far left where the edge of the control building blocked the barrier from view. A great glowing circle, marking the opened lock in the barrier, was centered on the screen. As Danestar looked at it, it was turning a brilliant white.

Some seconds passed. Then a big airtruck glided out of the whiteness and settled to the ground. The lock faded behind it, became reabsorbed by the dull black of the barrier. Several men climbed unhurriedly out of the truck, began walking over to the control building.

Danestar started upright in her chair, went rigid.

A wave of ghostly purple fire had lifted suddenly out of the ground about the truck, about the walking men, enclosing them.

There was a general gasp from the watching group in Hishkan's office. Then, before anyone moved or spoke, a voice roared from the communicator:

"Control office, attention! Radiation attack! Close internal barrier fields at once! *Close all internal Depot barrier fields at once!*"

Volcheme, whatever else might be said of him, was a man of action. Perhaps, after two hours of growing frustration, he was ready to welcome action. Apparently, a radiation weapon of unidentified type had been used inside the Depot. Why it had been turned on the men who had got off the supplies truck was unexplained. But it had consumed them completely in an instant, though the truck itself appeared undamaged.

Coming on top of the tensions already seething in the office, the shock of such an attack might have brought on complete confusion. But Volcheme immediately was snapping out very practical orders. The four smugglers detailed to help find Corvin Wergard were working through the Depot's underground passage system within a few hundred yards of the main building. They

joined the group in the office minutes later. The last
of Volcheme's men was stationed in the control section.
He confirmed that the defensive force fields enclosing
the individual sections of the Depot inside the main barrier
had been activated. Something occurred to Volcheme
then. "Who gave that order?"

"Wergard did," said Danestar.

They stared at her. "That *was* Wergard," Tornull
agreed. "I didn't realize it, but that was his voice."

Volcheme asked Danestar. "Do you know where he is?"

She shook her head. She didn't know, as a matter of
fact. Wergard might have been watching the lock from
any one of half a hundred screens in the Depot. He could
have been in one of the structures adjacent to the control
building . . . too close to that weird fiery phenomenon for
comfort. Radiation attack? What had he really made of
it? Probably, Danestar thought, the same fantastic thing
she'd made of it. His reaction, the general warning
shouted into the communications system, implied that;
very likely had been intended to imply it to her. She was
badly frightened, very much aware of it, trying to decide
how to handle the incredibly bad turn the situation might
have taken.

Volcheme, having hurried Tornull off to make sure the
space shuttle, which had been left beside the building's
landing dock, was within the section's barrier field, was
asking Galester and Dr. Hishkan, "Have you decided what
happened out there?"

Galester shrugged. "It appears to be a selective antipersonnel weapon. The truck presumably was enclosed by the
charge because there was somebody still on it. But it shows
no sign of damage, while the clothing the men outside were
wearing disappeared with them. It's possible the weapon
is stationed outside the Depot and fired the charge through
the open lock. But my opinion is that it's being operated
from some concealed point within the Depot."

Volcheme looked at Hishkan. "Well? Could it have

been something that was among your specimens here? Something Miss Gems and Wergard discovered and that Wergard put to use just now?"

The scientist gave Danestar a startled glance.

Danestar said evenly, "Forget that notion, Volcheme. It doesn't make sense."

"Doesn't it? What else makes sense?" the smuggler demanded. "You've been here two weeks. You're clever people, as you've demonstrated. Clever enough to recognize a really big deal when Hishkan shoved it under your noses. Clever enough to try to frighten competitors away. You know what I think, Miss Gems? I think that when I showed up here today, it loused up the private plans you and Wergard had for Hishkan's specimen."

"We do have plans for it," said Danestar. "It goes to the Federation. And now you'd better help us see it gets there."

Volcheme almost laughed. "I should?"

Danestar said, "You asked what else makes sense. There's one thing that does. You might have thought of it. That U-League specimen didn't just happen to be drifting around in the Pit where it was found. *Somebody made it and put it there!*"

She had the full attention of everyone in the office now, went on quickly. It was a space-signaling device which could tell human scientists a nearly complete story of how its unknown designers were able to move about freely in the dust cloud and how they communicated within it. And recently Dr. Hishkan had twice broadcast the information that human beings had the space instrument. The static bursts he'd produced had been recorded a great deal farther away from Mezmiali than the Pit.

Volcheme interrupted with angry incredulity. "So you're suggesting aliens from the Pit have come here for it!"

"I'm suggesting just that," Danestar said. "And Dr. Hishkan, at least, must be aware that a ship which vanished in the Pit a few years ago reported it was being attacked with what appeared to be radiation weapons."

"That's true! That's true!" Dr. Hishkan's face was white.

"I think," Danestar told them, "that when that airtruck came into the Depot, something came in with it the truckers didn't know was there. Something that had a radiation weapon of a kind we don't know about. Volcheme, if you people have a single functioning brain cell left between you, you'll tell the control building right now to put out a call for help! We're going to need it. We want the heaviest Navy ships near Mezmiali to get down here to handle this, and—"

"Volcheme!" a voice cut in urgently from the screen communicator.

The smuggler's head turned. "Go ahead, Yee!" His voice was harsh with impatience.

"The U-League group that's been hunting for this Wergard fellow doesn't answer!" Yee announced. He was the man Volcheme had stationed in the control building. "Seven men—two wearing communicators. We've been trying to contact them for eight minutes. Looks like they might have got wiped out somewhere in the Depot the same way as the truck crew!"

There was an uneasy stir among the men in the office. Volcheme said sharply, "Don't jump to conclusions! Have the operators keep calling them. They may have some reason for staying quiet at the moment. The others have checked in?"

"Yes," said Yee. "Everyone else who isn't in the control building is sitting tight behind defense screens somewhere."

"They've been told to stay where they are and report anything they observe?"

"Yes. But nobody's reported anything yet."

"Let me know as soon as someone does. And, Yee, make very sure everyone in the control building is aware that until this matter is settled, the control building takes orders only from me."

"They're *real* aware of that, Volcheme," said Yee.

The smuggler turned back to the group in the office. "Of course, we're not going to be stupid enough to take Miss Gems's advice!" he said. If he felt any uncertainty, it didn't show in his voice or face. "Somebody has pulled a surprise trick with some radiation device and killed a number of people. But we're on guard now, and we're very far from helpless! Decrain will stay here to make sure Miss Gems does not attempt to interfere in any way. The rest of us will act as a group."

He indicated the men who had been searching for Wergard. "There are four high-powered energy rifles on the shuttle. You four will handle them. Galester, Dr. Hishkan, Tornull, and I will have handguns. Dr. Hishkan tells me that the radiation suits used for dangerous inspection work in the Depot are stored on the ground level of this building.

"Remember, this device is an antipersonnel weapon. We'll be in the suits, which will block its effect on us at least temporarily; we'll be armed, and we'll be in the shuttle. There's a barrier exit at the building loading dock, through which we can get the shuttle out into the Depot. Scanscreens are being used in the control building to locate the device or its operator. When they're found—"

The communicator clicked. Wergard's voice said, "Volcheme, this is Wergard. Better listen!"

Volcheme's head swung around. "What do you want?" It was almost a snarl.

"If you'd like a look at that antipersonnel weapon," Wergard's voice told him drily, "switch your screen to Section Thirty-six. You may change your mind about chasing it around in the shuttle."

A few seconds later, the wall screen flickered and cleared. For an instant, they all stared in silence.

Like a sheet of living purple fire, the thing flowed with eerie swiftness along the surface of one of the

Depot's side streets toward a looming warehouse. Its size, Danestar thought, was the immediately startling factor—it spread across the full width of the street and was a hundred and fifty, perhaps two hundred, yards long. As it reached the warehouse, the big building's defense field flared into activity. Instantly, the fiery apparition veered sideways, whipped around the corner of the street and was gone from sight.

Shifting views of the Depot flicked through the screen as Dr. Hishkan hurriedly manipulated the controls. He glanced around, eyes wide and excited. "I've lost it! It appears to be nowhere in the area."

"I wouldn't worry," Volcheme said grimly. "It will show up again." He asked Galester, "What did you make of that? What *is* it?"

Galester said, "It's identical, of course, with what we saw engulfing the truck and the men at the lock. We saw only one section of it there. It emerged partly above the surface of the Depot and withdrew into it again. As to what it is . . . " He shrugged. "I know of nothing to compare it to precisely!" He hesitated again, went on. "My impression was that it was moving purposefully— directing itself. Conceivably an energy weapon could control a mobile charge in such a manner that it would present that appearance."

Dr. Hishkan added, "Whatever this is, Volcheme, I believe it would be very unwise to attempt to oppose it with standard weapons!"

The smuggler gave him a tight grin. "Since there's no immediate need to make the attempt, we'll postpone it, at any rate, Doctor. To me, the significant part of what we just saw was that the thing avoided contact with the defense field of that building . . . or was turned away from it, if it's the mobile guided charge Galester was talking about. In either case, our enemy can't reach us until we decide what we're dealing with and how we should deal with it."

Danestar said sharply, "Volcheme, don't be a fool—don't count on that! The ships that disappeared in the Pit carried defense fields, too."

Volcheme gave her a venomous glance but didn't answer. Dr. Hishkan said thoughtfully, "What Miss Gems says is technically true. But even if we are being subjected to a similar attack, this is a very different situation! This complex was once a fort designed to defend a quarter of the continent against the heaviest of spaceborne weapons. And while the interior fields do not compare with the external barrier in strength, they are still far denser than anything that would or could be carried by even the largest exploration ships. I believe we can depend on the field about this building to protect us while we consider means to extricate ourselves from the situation." He added, "I feel far more optimistic now! When we have determined the nature of the attacking entity, we should find a method of combating it available to us in the Depot. There is no need to appeal to the authorities for help, as Miss Gems suggested, and thereby have our personal plans exposed to them—which was, of course, what she intended!"

Wergard's voice said from the communicator, "If you want to continue your studies, Dr. Hishkan, you'll get the chance immediately! The thing is now approaching the main building from the north, and it's coming fast."

Dr. Hishkan turned quickly back to the screen controls.

There was a wide square enclosed by large buildings directly north of the main one. The current of fire was half across the square as it came to view in the screen. As Wergard had said, it was approaching very swiftly and there was a suggestion of purposeful malevolence in that rushing motion which sent a chill down Danestar's spine. In an instant, it seemed, it reached the main building and the energy field shielding it; and now, instead of veering off to the side as it had done before, the tip of the fiery body curved upwards. It flowed vertically up along the wall of the building, inches away from the flickering defense field. For seconds, the wall screen showed nothing but pale purple flame streaming across it. Then the flame was gone; and the empty square again filled the screen.

From the communicator, Wergard's voice said quickly, "It crossed the top of the building, went down the other side and disappeared below the ground level surface—"

The voice broke off. Almost immediately, it resumed. "I've had more luck keeping it in view than you. It's been half around the Depot by now, and my impression is it's been looking things over before it makes its next move—whatever that's going to be.

"But one thing I've noticed makes me feel much less secure behind a section energy field than some of you people think you are. The thing has kept carefully away from the outer Depot barrier—a hundred yards or so at all times—and it cuts its speed down sharply when it gets anywhere near that limit. On the other hand, as you saw just now, it shows very little respect for the sectional building fields. I haven't seen it attempt to penetrate one of them, but it's actually contacted them a number of times without apparent harm to itself, as it did again in passing over the main building a moment ago."

Volcheme snapped, "What's that supposed to tell us?"

"I think," Wergard said, "that, among other things, our visitor has been testing the strength of those barriers. I wouldn't care to bet my life on what it's concluded, as you seem willing to do. Another point—it may be developing a particular interest in the building you're in. I suggest you take a close look at the square on the north again."

At first glance, the square still seemed empty. Then one noticed that its flat surface was alive with tiny sparks, with flickers and ripplings of pale light. The thing was there, almost completely submerged beneath the Depot's ground level, apparently unmoving.

Tornull said, staring fascinatedly, "Perhaps it knows we have that specimen in here!"

Nobody answered. But in the square, as if aware its presence had been discovered, the fire shape rose slowly to the surface of the ground until it lay in full view, flat and monstrous, sideways to the main building. The silence in the office was broken suddenly by a chattering sound. It had not been a loud noise, but everyone started nervously and looked over at the table where the pile of instruments had been assembled.

"What was that?" Volcheme demanded.

"My shortcode transmitter," Danestar told him.

"It's recorded a message?"

"Obviously."

"From whom?"

"I'm not sure," said Danestar evenly. "But let's guess. It's not from outside the Depot because shortcode won't go through the barrier. It's not from Wergard, and it's not from one of your people. What's left?"

The smuggler stared at her. "That's an insane suggestion!"

"Perhaps," Danestar said. "Why don't we listen to the translation?"

"We will!" Volcheme jerked his head at Decrain. "Go over to the table with her. She isn't to touch anything but the transmitter!"

He watched, mouth twisted unpleasantly, as Decrain followed Danestar to the table. She picked up the miniature transmitter, slid a fingernail quickly along a groove to the phonetic translator switch. As she set the instrument back on the table, the words began.

"Who . . . has . . . it . . . where . . . is . . . it . . . I . . . want . . . it . . . who . . . has . . . it . . . where . . ."

It went on for perhaps a minute and a half, three sentences repeated monotonously over and over, then stopped with a click. Danestar wasn't immediately aware of the effect on the others. She'd listened in a mixture of fear, grief, hatred, and sick revulsion. Shortcode was speech, transmitted in an economical flash, restored to phonetic speech in the translator at the reception point. Each of the words which made up the three sentences had been pronounced at one time by a human being, were so faithfully reproduced one could tell the sentences had, in fact, been patched together with words taken individually from the speech of three or four different human beings. Human beings captured by the enemy in the Pit, Danestar thought, long dead now, but allowed to live while the enemy learned human speech from them, recorded their voices for future use. . . .

She looked around. The others seemed as shaken as she was. Volcheme's face showed he no longer doubted that the owner of the alien instrument had come to claim it.

Dr. Hishkan remarked carefully, "If it should turn out that we are unable to destroy or control this creature, it is possible we can get rid of it simply by reassembling the device it's looking for and placing it outside the defense screen. If it picks it up, we can open the barrier lock as an indication of our willingness to let it depart in peace with its property."

Volcheme looked at him. "Doctor," he said, "don't panic just because you've heard the thing talk to you! What this does seem to prove is that the specimen you're selling through us is at least as valuable as it appeared to be—and I for one don't intend to be cheated out of my profit."

"Nor I," Dr. Hishkan said hastily. "But the creature's ability to utilize shortcode to address us indicates a dangerous level of intelligence. Do you have any thoughts on how it might be handled now?"

Galester interrupted, indicating the screen. "I believe it's beginning to move. . . ."

There was silence again as they watched the fire body in the square. Its purple luminescence deepened and paled in slowly pulsing waves; then the tip swung about, swift as a flicking tongue, first toward the building, then away from it; and the thing flowed in a darting curve across the square and into a side street.

"Going to nose around for its treasure somewhere else!" Volcheme said after it had vanished. "So, while it may suspect it's here, it isn't sure. I'm less impressed by its apparent intelligence than you are, Doctor. A stupid man can learn to use a complicated instrument, if somebody shows him how to do it. This may be a stupid alien . . . a soldier type sent here from the Pit to carry out a specific, limited mission."

Galester nodded. "Possibly a robot."

"Possibly a robot," Volcheme agreed. "And, to answer your question of a moment ago, Doctor—yes, I have thought of a way to get it off our necks."

"What's that?" Dr. Hishkan inquired eagerly.

"No need to discuss it here!" Volcheme gave Danestar a glance of mingled malevolence and triumph. She understood its meaning well enough. If Wergard could be located, Volcheme could now rid himself of the Kyth operators with impunity. There were plenty of witnesses to testify that the monstrous creature which had invaded the Depot had destroyed over a dozen men. She and Wergard would be put down as two more of its victims.

"We won't use the shuttle at present," Volcheme went on. "But we want the portable guns, and we'll get ourselves into antiradiation suits immediately. Decrain, watch the lady until we get back—use any methods necessary to make sure she stays where she is and behaves herself. We'll bring a suit back up for you. The rest of you come along. Hurry!"

Decrain started to say something, then stood silent and scowling as the others filed quickly out of the office and started down the hall to the right. The big man looked uneasy. With a gigantic fiery alien around, he might not appreciate being left alone to guard the prisoner while his companions climbed into the security of antiradiation suits. As the last of the group disappeared, he sighed heavily, shifted his attention back to Danestar.

His eyes went huge with shocked surprise. The chair in which she had been sitting was empty. Decrain's hand flashed to his gun holster, stopped as it touched it. He stood perfectly still.

Something hard was pushing against the center of his back below his shoulder blades.

"Yes, I've got it," Danestar whispered behind him. "Not a sound, Decrain! If you even breathe louder than I like, I'll split your spine!"

They waited in silence. Decrain breathed cautiously while the voices and footsteps in the hall grew fainter, became inaudible. Then the gun muzzle stopped pressing against his back.

"All right," Danestar said softly—she'd moved off but was still close behind him—"just stand there now!"

Decrain moistened his lips.

"Miss Gems," he said, speaking with some difficulty, "I was, you remember, a gentleman!"

"So you were, buster," her voice agreed. "And a very fortunate thing that is for you at the moment. But—"

Decrain dropped forward, turning in the air, lashing out savagely with both feet in the direction of the voice. It was a trick that worked about half the time. A blurred glimpse of Danestar flashing a white smile above him and of her arm swinging down told him it hadn't worked here. The butt of the gun caught the side of his head a solid wallop, and Decrain closed his eyes and drifted far, far away.

She bent over him an instant, half minded to give him a second rap for insurance, decided it wasn't necessary, shoved the gun into a pocket of her coveralls and went quickly to the big table in the center of the office. Her control belt was there among the jumble of things they'd brought over from her room. Danestar fastened it about her waist, slipped on the white jacket lying beside it, rummaged hurriedly among the rest, storing the shortcode transmitter and half a dozen other items into various pockets before she picked up her emptied instrument valise and moved to the opposite end of the table where Galester had arranged the mechanisms he'd removed for examination from the false asteroid.

She'd had her eye on one of those devices since she'd been brought to the office. It was enclosed in some brassy pseudometal, about the size of a goose egg and shaped like one. Galester hadn't known what to make of it in his brief investigation, and Dr. Hishkan had offered only vague conjectures; but she had studied it and its relationship to a number of other instruments very carefully on the night she'd been in Dr. Hishkan's vault, and knew exactly what to make of it. She placed it inside her valise, went back to the collection of her own instruments, turned on the spy-screen and fingered a switch on the control belt. The spy-screen made a staccato chirping noise.

"I'm alone here," she told it quickly. "Decrain's out cold. Now, how do I get out of this building and to some rendezvous point—fastest? Volcheme's gone berserk, as you heard. I don't want to be anywhere near them when they start playing games with that animated slice of sheet lightning!"

"Turn left when you leave the office," Wergard's voice said from the blank screen. "Take the first elevator two levels down and get out."

"And then?"

"I'll be waiting for you there."

"How long have you been in the building?" she asked, startled.

"About five minutes. Came over to pick up a couple of those antiradiation suits for us, which I have. The way things were going then, I thought I'd better hang around and wait for a chance to get you away from our friends."

"I was about to start upstairs when Volcheme and the others left. Then I heard a little commotion in the office and decided you were doing something about Decrain. So I waited."

"Bless you, boy!" Danestar said gratefully. "Be with you in a minute!"

She switched off the spy-screen, went out of the office, skirting Decrain's harshly snoring form on the carpet, and turned left down the quiet hall.

The hideaway from which Corvin Wergard had been keeping an observer's eye on events in the Depot was one of a number he'd set up for emergency use shortly after their arrival. He'd selected it for operations today because it was only a few steps from an exit door in the building, and less than a hundred and twenty yards from both the control section and the outer barrier lock—potential critical points in whatever action would develop. Guiding Danestar back to it took minutes longer than either of them liked, but the route Wergard had worked out led almost entirely through structures shielded from the alien visitor by section defense screens.

She sat across the tiny room from him, enclosed in one of the bulky antiradiation suits, the shortcode transmitter on a wall shelf before her, fingers delicately, minutely, adjusting another of the instruments she had brought back from Hishkan's office. Her eyes were fixed on the projection field above the instrument. Occasional squigglings and ripples of light flashed through it—meaningless static. But she'd had glimpses of light patterns which seemed far from meaningless here, was tracking them now through the commband detector to establish the settings which would fix them in the visual projection field for study. That was a nearly automatic process—her hands knew what to do and were doing it. Her thoughts kept turning in nightmare fascination about other aspects of the gigantic raider.

What did they know about it? And what did it know about them?

That living, deadly energy body, or its kind, had not built the signaling device. If it was not acting for itself, if it had hidden masters in the Pit, the masters had not built the device, either. Regardless of its origin, the instrument, though centuries old, still had been in use; and in the dust cloud its value in establishing location, in permitting free purposeful action, must be immense. But whoever was using it evidently had lacked even the ability to keep it in repair. Much less would they have been able to replace it after it disappeared—and they must be in mortal fear that mankind would discover the secrets of the instrument and return to meet them on even terms in the cloud. . . .

So this creature had traversed deep space to reach Mezmiali and recover it.

Volcheme, conditioned to success in dealing with human opponents, still believed his resourcefulness was sufficient to permit him to handle the emissary from the Pit. To Danestar it seemed approximately like attempting to handle an animated warship. The thing was complex, not simply an elemental force directed by a limited robotic mind. It had demonstrated it could use its energies to duplicate the human shortcode system, and the glimpse she'd had in the detector's field of one of its patterns implied it was capable of much more than had been shown so far. And it might not have come here alone. There could be others of its kind undetected beyond the Depot's barrier with whom it was in communication.

In the face of such possibilities, Volcheme's determination amounted to lunacy. They might have convinced the others of the need to call for outside help; but the intercom system had been shut off, evidently on the smuggler's orders, when Danestar's escape was discovered. Through various spy devices they knew he was coordinating the activities of his men with personal communicators, and that a sectional force barrier was being set up across the center of the main building, connected to the external ones. Completed, the barrier system would transform half the building into a box trap, open at the end. The men and the specimen from the Pit would be in the other half. When the monster flowed into the trap to get at them, observers in the control building would snap a barrier shut across the open end. The thing would be safely inside . . . assuming that barriers of sectional strength were impassable to it.

Volcheme's calculations were based entirely on that assumption. So far, nothing had happened to prove him wrong. The alien creature was still moving about the Depot. Wergard, before the multiple-view screen through which he had followed the earlier events of the day, reported glimpses of it every minute or two. And there were increasing indications of purpose in its motions. It had passed along this building once, paused briefly. But it had shown itself three times about the control section, three times at the main building. Its interest appeared to be centering on those points.

Until it ended its swift and unpredictable prowling, they could only wait here. Wergard was ready to slip over to a personnel lock in the barrier about the control building when an opportunity came. A gas charge would knock out the men inside, and the main barrier would open long enough then to let out their prepared short-code warning. Their main concern after that would be to stay alive until help arrived.

Their heads turned sharply as the shortcode trans-mitter on the shelf before Danestar gave its chattering pickup signal. She stood up, snapped the headpiece of her radiation suit into position, collapsed the other instruments on the shelf, slid them into the suit's pockets, and picked up the valise she'd brought back from Dr. Hishkan's office.

" . . . where . . . is . . . it . . . I . . . want . . . it . . ." whispered the transmitter.

"Pickup range still set at thirty yards?" Wergard asked.

"Yes," she said.

"There's nothing in sight around here."

Danestar glanced over at him. He'd encased himself in the other radiation suit. A small high-power energy carbine lay across a chair beside him. His eyes were on the viewscreen which now showed only the area immediately around the building. She didn't answer. The transmitter continued to whisper.

It wasn't in sight, but it was nearby. Very near. Within thirty yards of the transmitter, of their hideout, of them. And pausing now much longer than it had the first time it passed the building.

" . . . who . . . has . . . it . . . where . . . is . . . it . . ."

Her skin crawled, icy and uncontrollable. If it had any way of sensing what she held concealed inside the valise, it would want it. She didn't think it could. No spying device she knew of could pierce the covering of the valise. But the egg-shaped alien instrument within—no bigger than her two fists placed together—was the heart and core of the specimen from the Pit, its black box, the part which must hold all significant clues to the range and penetrating power of its signals. Without it, the rest of the contents of that great boulder-shaped thing would be of no use now—to Volcheme or to the alien.

They waited, eyes on the viewscreen, ready to move. If the building was attacked and the creature showed it could force its way through the enclosing energy barrier, there was an unlocked door behind them. An elevator lay seconds beyond the door; and two levels down, they would be in the underground tunnel system where a transport shell waited. If they were followed, they could continue

along the escape route Wergard had marked out, moving
from barrier to barrier to slow the pursuer. Unless it over-
took them, they would eventually reach the eastern section of the Depot, known as the Keep, where ancient
defense screens formed so dense a honeycomb that they
should be safe for hours from even the most persistent
attacks.

But retreat would cost them their chance to make use
of the control section. . . .

The transmitter's whisper faded suddenly. For some
seconds, neither stirred. Then Wergard said, relief sharp
in his voice: "It may have moved off!"

He shifted the screen mechanisms. A pattern of half
a dozen simultaneous views appeared. "There it is!"

On the far side of the control building, flowing
purple fire lifted into view along fifty yards of one of
the Depot's streets like the back of a great surfacing
sea beast, sank from sight again. Danestar hesitated, took
the commband detector quickly out of her suit pocket,
placed it on the wall shelf. She pressed a button on
the little instrument and the projection field sprang into
semi-visibility above it.

Wergard, eyes shifting about the viewscreen, said, "It's
still only seconds away from us. Don't get too absorbed
in whatever you're trying to do."

"I won't."

Danestar released the bulky radiation headpiece,
turned it back out of her way. Her fingertips slipped along
the side of the detector, touched a tiny adjustment knob,
began a fractional turn, froze.

The visual projection she'd been hunting had appeared
in the field before her.

A flickering, shifting, glowing galaxy of tiny momentary
sparks and lines of light . . . the combined communication
systems of a megacity might have presented approximately
such a picture if the projector had presented them
simultaneously. She licked her lips, breath still, as her

fingers shifted cautiously, locking the settings into place.

When she drew her hand away, Wergard's voice asked quietly, "What's that?"

"The thing's intercom system. It's . . . let me think—Wergard! What's it doing now?"

"It's beside the control building." Wergard paused. He hadn't asked what her manipulations with the detector were about; she seemed to be on the trail of something, and he hadn't wanted to distract her.

But now he added, "Its behavior indicates . . . yes! Apparently it is going to try to pass through the section barrier there!"

The viewscreen showed the ghostly, reddish glittering of an activated defense barrier along most of the solid front wall of the control building. Two deep-rose glowing patches, perhaps a yard across, marked points where the alien had come into direct contact with the barrier's energies.

It hadn't, Danestar thought, liked the experience, though in each case it had maintained the contact for seconds, evidently in a deliberate test of the barrier's strength. Her eyes shifted in a brief glance to the viewscreen, returned to the patterns of swarming lights in the projector field.

The reaction of the creature could be observed better there. As it touched the barrier, dark stains had appeared in the patterns, spread, then faded quickly after it withdrew. There was a shock effect of sorts. But not a lasting one. Danestar's breathing seemed constricted. She was badly frightened now. The section barriers did hurt this thing, but they wouldn't stop it if it was determined to force its way through their energies. Perhaps the men in the control building weren't yet aware of the fact. She didn't want to think of that—

She heard a brief exclamation from Wergard, glanced over again at the screen.

And here it comes, she thought.

The thing was rising unhurriedly out of the street surface before the control building, yards from the wall. When it tested the barrier, it had extruded a fiery pointed tentacle and touched it to the building. Now it surged into view as a rounded luminous column twenty feet across, widening as it lifted higher. The top of the column began to lean slowly forward like a ponderous cresting wave, reached the wall, passed shuddering into it. The force field blazed in red brilliance about it and its own purple radiance flared, but the great mass continued to flow steadily through the barrier.

And throughout the galaxy of dancing, scintillating, tiny lights in the projector field, Danestar watched long shock shadows sweep, darken, and spread . . . then gradually lighten and commence to fade.

When she looked again at the viewscreen, the defense barrier still blazed wildly. But the street was empty. The alien had vanished into the control building.

"It isn't one being," Danestar said. "It's probably several billion. Like a city at work, an army on the march. An organization. A system. The force field did hurt it—but at most it lost one half of one percent of the entities that make it up in going through the barrier."

Wergard glanced at the projection field, then at her.

"Nobody in the control building had access to a radiation suit," he said. "So they must have been dead in an instant when the thing reached them. If it can move through a section barrier with no more damage than you feel it took, why hasn't it come out again? It's been in there for over five minutes now."

Danestar, eyes on the pattern in the projection field, said, "It may have been damaged in another way. I don't know. . . ."

"What do you mean?"

She nodded at the pattern. "It's difficult to describe.

But there's a change there! And it's becoming more distinct. I'm not sure what it means."

Wergard looked at the field a moment, shrugged. "I'll take your word for it. It's a jumble to me. I don't see any changes in it."

Danestar hesitated. She had almost intuitive sensitivity for the significance of her instruments' indications; and that something was being altered now, moment by moment, in the millionfold interplay of signals in the pattern seemed certain.

She said suddenly, "There's a directing center to the thing, of course, or it couldn't function as it does. Before it went through the force field, every part of it was oriented to that center. There was a kind of rhythm to the whole which showed that. Now, there's a section that's going out of phase with the general rhythm."

"What does that add up to?"

Danestar shook her head. "I can't tell that yet. But if the shock it got from the barrier disrupted part of its internal communication system, it might be, in our terms, at least partly paralyzed now. A percentage of the individual entities—say about one-tenth—are no longer coordinating with the whole, are disconnected from it. . . . Of course, we can't count on it, but it would explain why it hasn't reappeared."

Both were silent a moment. Then Wergard said, "If it is immobilized, it killed everyone in the control building before the shock got through to it. Otherwise we would have had indications of action by Volcheme by now."

She nodded. The intercom switch on the viewscreen was open, but the system remained dead. And whatever the smuggler and the group in the main building were engaged in, they were not at present in an area covered by her spy devices. But the space shuttle had not left the building, so they were still there. If the creature from the Pit was no longer a menace and Volcheme knew it, every survivor of the gang would be combing the Depot for traces of Wergard and herself. Since they weren't, Volcheme had received no such report from the control building. Whatever else had happened, the men stationed there had died as the alien poured in through the barrier.

Her breath caught suddenly. She said, "Wergard, I think . . . it's trying to come out again!"

"The barrier's flickering," he acknowledged from the viewscreen. An instant later: "Full on now! Afraid you're right! Watch for signs of damage. If it isn't crippled, and if it suspects someone is here, it may hit this building next, immediately! It isn't in sight . . . must be moving out below ground level."

Danestar snapped the radiation headpiece back in position without taking her eyes from the projection field. Shock darkness crisscrossed the pattern of massed twinkling pinpoints of brightness again, deepened. She could judge the thing's rate of progress through the barrier by that now. There were no indications of paralysis; if anything, its passage seemed swifter. Within seconds, the darkness stopped spreading, began to fade. "It's outside," she said. "It doesn't seem seriously injured."

"And it's still not in sight," said Wergard. "Stay ready to move!"

They were both on their feet. The shortcode transmitter on the shelf was silent, but this time the creature might not be announcing its approach. Danestar's eyes kept returning to the projection field. Again the barrier had achieved minor destruction, but she could make out no further significant changes. The cold probability was now that there was no practical limit to the number of such passages the creature could risk if it chose. But something about the pattern kept nagging at her mind. What was it?

A minute passed in a humming silence that stretched her nerves, another . . . and now, Danestar told herself, it was no longer likely that the monster's attention would turn next to this building, to them. The barrier had remained quiet, and there had been no other sign of it. Perhaps it wasn't certain humans were hiding here; at any rate, it must have shifted by now to some other section of the Depot.

Almost with the thought, she saw Wergard's hand move on the viewscreen controls, and in the screen the area about them was replaced by a multiple-view pattern.

Nothing stirred in the various panels; no defense field was ablaze about any of the buildings shown. The entire great Depot seemed empty and quiet.

"At a guess," Wergard remarked thoughtfully, "it's hanging around the main building again now." He moved back a step from the screen, still watching it, began to unfasten his antiradiation suit.

"What are you doing?" she asked.

He glanced over at her. "Getting out of it. One thing these suits weren't made for is fast running. I expect to be doing some of the fastest running in my career in perhaps another minute or two."

"Running? You're not—"

"Our alien," Wergard said, "should take action concerning Volcheme's boys next. But whatever it does, the instant we see it involved somewhere else, I'll sprint for the control building. It may be the last chance we get to yell for help from outside. And I don't want to be slowed down by twenty pounds of suit while I'm about it."

Danestar swallowed hard. He was right. But there was something, a feeling. . . .

"No! Don't go there!" she said sharply, surprising herself.

He looked around in bewilderment. "Don't go there? What are you—watch that!"

His eyes had shifted back to the screen. For an instant, she couldn't tell what he had seen. Then, just as the view began to blur into another, she found it.

Volcheme's space shuttle had darted out of the cover

of the main building, swung right, was flashing up a wide street toward the eastern section of the Depot.

"Making a run for the Keep!" Wergard said harshly. He fingered the controls, following the shuttle from view section to view section. "They might just—no, there it is!"

The great fire body—flattened, elongated—whipped past between two warehouse complexes, a rushing brightness fifty feet above the ground, vanished beyond the buildings.

"Too fast for them!" Wergard shook his head. "It knows what they're doing and is cutting them off. Perhaps their guns can check it! You watch what happens—I'm going now."

"No! I . . ."

Then at last the realization surged up. Danestar stared at him, completely dismayed.

"It's a trap," she said evenly. "Of course!"

"What is? What are you talking about?"

"The control building! Don't you see?" She jerked her head at the projection field. "I *said* a section of the thing was splitting off from the main body! When it came out through the barrier again, *that* section wasn't showing any shock effects. I saw it but didn't understand what it meant. Of course! It didn't come through the barrier at all. It's still *in there*, Wergard! In the control building. Waiting for any of us to show up. There're two of them now. . . ."

She watched stunned comprehension grow in his face as she spoke.

The smugglers' shuttle was caught not much more than a minute later. It had discovered the enemy between it and the Keep section, turned back. When the space thing followed, tiny bursts of dazzling white light showed the shuttle's energy guns were in action. The fire body jerked aside and paused . . . and now the shuttle turned again, flashed straight at its pursuer, guns blazing full out.

For a moment, it seemed a successful maneuver. The

great creature swept up out of the path of the machine, slipped over the top of a building, disappeared. The shuttle rushed on toward the Keep—and at the next corner a loop of purple radiance snared it, drove it smashing into a building front. The fire giant flowed down, sent the shuttle hurtling against the building again, closed over it. For seconds, the radiance pulsed about the engulfed vehicle, then lifted into the air, moved off. There was no sign of the shuttle until, some hundreds of yards away, the fire body opened to let the shattered machine slide out, drop to the surface of the Depot. Its lock door was half twisted away; and Volcheme and his companions clearly were no longer within it.

To Danestar, watching in sick fascination, it had seemed as if a great beast of prey had picked up some shelled, stinging creature, disarmed it, cracked it to draw out the living contents, and flung aside the empty shell.

The alien swung west, toward the central section of the Depot, seemed to be returning to the main building complex, but then flowed down to the surface, sank into it and vanished.

Minutes passed and it did not reappear. Again the Depot's sections stood quiet and lifeless in the viewscreen.

"It may be waiting for somebody else to break from cover," Wergard said suddenly. "But you'd think the first thing it would do now is push into the main building and get its gadget! Volcheme must have left it there—the thing wouldn't have slammed the shuttle around like that if it hadn't been sure the contraption wasn't inside."

Danestar didn't reply. Their nerves were on edge, and Wergard was simply thinking aloud. They had no immediate explanation for the thing's behavior. But it had been acting purposefully throughout, and there must be purpose in its disappearance.

All they could do at present was wait, alert for signs of an approach on any level. She had discarded her antiradiation suit, as Wergard had done previously. The

men in the shuttle might have gained a second or two
of life because of the protection the suits gave them;
but against so overwhelmingly powerful a creature they
obviously had made no real difference. And they were
cumbersome enough to be a serious disadvantage in other
respects. If there were indications that the second
energy body, the smaller one in the control building,
had left it, Wergard would still attempt a dash over
there.

There were no such indications. There were, in fact,
no indications of any kind of activity whatever until,
approximately ten minutes after it vanished, the big space
creature showed itself again.

It was rising slowly from the ground into the square
before the deserted main building when Wergard
detected it in the screen. Then, while they watched, it
flowed deliberately up to the building and into it.

And no defending force fields flared into action.

As it disappeared, they exchanged startled looks.
Wergard said quickly, "Volcheme must have had the
barriers shut off just before they left by the lock—so the
thing could pick up its device. . . ."

"And let them get away?" Danestar hesitated. There'd
been talk of that before she escaped from Volcheme's
group. But she was not at all certain that the smuggler,
even under such intense immediate pressures, would
abandon his prize completely. The flight might even have
been designed in part to draw the raider away from it.

"Otherwise—" Wergard scowled, chewed his lip. "Has
there been anything in the projection pattern to show
it's split again?"

She shook her head. "No. But if you're thinking it
could detach a section small enough to get in through
a personnel lock and turn off the building's barrier—"

"That's what I'm thinking."

Danestar shrugged, said, "I wouldn't be able to tell
that, Wergard. I've been watching the projection. But it

would be too minor a difference to be noticeable. It may have done it."

He was silent a moment. "Well," he said then, "it has the gadget it came for now. We'll see what it does next." He added, without change of tone, "Incidentally, it doesn't have all of it, does it?"

Danestar gave him a startled glance.

"How did you guess?" she asked.

A half-grin flicked over Wergard's tense face. "It's the sort of thing you'd do. You've been hanging on to that valise as if there were something very precious inside."

"There is," Danestar agreed. "It's not very big, but the specimen won't work without it. And when those things in the Pit realize it's gone, they won't be able to replace it."

"Very dirty trick!" Wergard said approvingly. He glanced at the valise. "Supposing we manage to get out of this alive—how useful could the item become?"

"Extremely useful, if it gets to really capable people. As far as I could make out, it must embody all the essentials of that system."

Wergard nodded. "We'll hang on to it, then. As long as we can, anyway. We may have to destroy it, of course. Think the thing could spot there's a part missing?"

"It could if it has a way of testing it," said Danestar. "But if the specimen's been reassembled and resealed, nothing will show. . . . There the creature comes now!"

They watched its emergence from the main building. It poured out of the landing lock area, swung west across the central square, moving swiftly. It might be carrying the specimen with it, as it had carried the shuttle.

"Coming back here!" Wergard remarked some seconds later. "And if it can open sectional barriers, it can open the main Depot lock in the control building. . . . "

Danestar knew what he meant. The Pit creature might believe it had achieved its objective in regaining the lost signaling instrument and simply leave now. She began to feel almost feverish with hope, warned herself it was much more probable it did not intend to let any human being in the Depot remain alive to tell about it.

Her gaze shifted again to the patterns in the projection field. No further changes had been apparent, but a sense of dissatisfaction, of missing some hidden significance, still stirred in her each time she studied them. I'm not seeing everything they should tell me, she thought. She shook her head tiredly. Too much had happened these hours! Now her thinking seemed dulled.

She heard Wergard say, "It's stopped for something!"

It had come to an intersection, paused. Then suddenly it veered to the right, moved swiftly past three buildings, checked again before a fourth. A probing fire tentacle reached toward the building, and defense barriers promptly blazed into activity.

The creature withdrew the tentacle, remained where it was, half submerged in the street. Activated by its proximity, the defense field continued to flare while one or two minutes passed. Then the field subsided, vanished. The creature moved forward until some two-thirds of it appeared to be within the building. Barely seconds later, it drew back again, swung away. . . .

"It caught somebody inside there!" Wergard said. "It couldn't have been looking for anything else. How did it know some poor devils had holed up in that particular section?"

The intercom signal on the viewscreen burred sharply with his last words, then stopped. They stared at it, glanced at each other. Neither attempted to move toward the switch.

The intercom began ringing again. It rang, insistently, jarringly, with brief pauses, for a full minute now before it went silent.

"So that's how!" Wergard said heavily. He shrugged.

"Well, if it—or a section of it—can manipulate a barrier lock and reproduce shortcode impulses, it can grasp and manipulate an intercom system. Not a bad way to locate survivors. If we don't answer—"

"We can't stay here, anyway," Danestar told him, frowning at the projection field. She had spoken in an oddly flat, detached manner.

"No. It's mopping up before it heads home—and now it can apparently cut off every sectional barrier that isn't locally maintained directly from the control building. It won't be long before it discovers that—if it hasn't already done it." Wergard picked up the energy gun. "Grab what you need and let's move! I've thought of something better than trying to make it to the Keep and playing hide-and-seek with it there. With the tricks it's developed, we wouldn't last—" He looked over, said quickly, sharply, "Danestar!"

Danestar glanced around at him, bemused, lips parted. "Yes? I . . ."

"Wake up!" Wergard's voice was edged with nervous impatience. "I think I can work us over to the section the thing just cleared out. If we leave the barrier off, there's a good chance it won't check that building again. Let's not hang around here!"

"No." She shook her head, turned to the instruments on the shelf. "You've got to get me to our quarters, Wergard—immediately!"

"From here? Impossible! There're several stretches—over three hundred yards in all—where we'd be in the open without the slightest cover. It's suicide! We—" Wergard checked himself, staring at her. "You've thought up something? Is it going to work?"

"It might, if we can get there."

He swore, blinked in scowling reflection.

"All right!" he said suddenly. "Can do—I hope! Tell me on the way or when we're there what you're after. We'll make a short detour. There's something I could do to keep our friend occupied for a while. It may buy us an additional twenty, thirty minutes. . . . "

Hurrying up a narrow dim passage behind Wergard, Danestar felt clusters of eerie fears hurry along with her. Wergard swung on at a fast walking pace. Now and then she broke into a run to keep up with him; and when she did, he slowed instantly to let her walk again. It was sensible—they might have running enough to do shortly. But staying sensible wasn't easy. Her legs *wanted* to run.

They were blind here, she thought. Her awareness of it was what had built up the feeling of frightened helplessness during the past minutes to the point where it seemed hardly bearable. She couldn't use her instruments, and the sectional barriers in this area were turned off; they were also deprived of that partial protection. As Wergard had suspected, the alien had discovered the force fields could be operated from the central control office. The Depot was open to it now except in sections where human beings had taken refuge and cut in defense barriers under local control. Such points, of course, were the ones it would investigate.

And they might encounter it at any moment, with no warning at all. Whether they got through to their quarters had become a matter of luck—good luck or bad— and Danestar, who always prepared, always planned, found herself unable to accept that condition.

Wergard halted ahead of her; and she stopped, watched him cautiously edge a door open, glance out. He looked back, slid the energy carbine from his shoulder, held it in one hand, made a beckoning motion with the other. Danestar followed him through the door and he eased it back into its lock. They had come out into one of the Depot's side streets. It stretched away on either side between unbroken building fronts, a strip of the dull black dome of the main barrier arching high above.

They darted across the street, ran fifty feet along the building on the far side before Wergard stopped at another door. This one opened on a pitch-dark passage; and, a moment later, the darkness closed in about them.

Wergard produced a light, said quietly, "Watch your step here! The section was sealed off officially fifty years ago and apparently hasn't been inspected since."

He moved ahead, rapidly but carefully, holding the light down for her. They were some five minutes from their starting point. Beyond that, Danestar did not know what part of the Depot they'd come to, but Wergard had told her about this building. It had been part of the old fortress system, cheaper to seal off than remove, an emergency unit station which operated the barrier defenses of the complexes surrounding it. If the equipment was still in working order, Wergard would turn on those barriers. Approximately a tenth of Depot would again be shielded then, beyond manipulation by the control office. That should draw the creature's attention to the area, while they moved on. Their living quarters were in a building a considerable distance away.

Eyes shifting about, Danestar followed the pool of light dancing ahead of her feet. The flooring was decayed here and there; little piles of undefinable litter lay about, and the air was stale and musty. Wergard, in his prowling, might in fact have been the first to enter the building in fifty years. They turned a corner of the passage, came to a dark doorspace. There he stopped.

"You'd better wait here," he told her. "There's a mess of machinery inside, and some of it's broken. I'll have to climb around and over it. If the barrier system is operating, I'll have it going within three or four minutes."

He vanished through the door. Danestar watched the receding light as it moved jerkily deeper into a forest of

ancient machines, lost it when it went suddenly around
a corner. There was complete darkness about her then.
She fingered a lighter in her pocket but left it there. No
need to nourish the swirling tide of apprehensions within
her by peering about at shadows. Darkness wasn't the
enemy. After a minute or two, she heard a succession of
metallic sounds in the distance. Presently they ended, and
a little later Wergard returned. He was breathing hard
and his face was covered with dirt-streaked sweat.

"As far as I can make out, the barriers are on," he
said briefly. "Now we'd better get out of the neighbor-
hood fast!"

But they made slower over-all progress than before,
because now they had to use the personnel locks in the
force fields as they moved from one complex section to
the next. In between, they ran where they could. They
crossed two more side streets. After the second one,
Wergard said, "At the end of this building we'll be out
of the screened area."

"How far beyond that?" Danestar asked.

"Three blocks. Two big sprints in the open!" He grimaced. "We *could* use the underground systems along part
of the stretch. But they won't get us across the main
streets unless we follow them all the way to the Keep
and back down."

She shook her head. "Let's stick to your route." A
transport shell of the underground system could have
taken them to the Keep and into the far side of the
Depot in minutes. But its use would register on betraying
instruments in the control building, and might too easily
draw the alien to the moving shell.

The personnel lock at the other end of the building
let them into a narrow alley. Across it was the flank of
one of the Depot's giant warehouses. As they started along
the alley, there was a crackling, spitting, explosive sound—
the snarl of a defense field flashing into action.

Wergard reached out, snatched the valise from Danestar's hand.

"*Run!*"

They raced up the alley. The furious crackle of the force field came from behind them, from some other building. It was not far away, and it was continuing. A hundred yards on, Wergard halted abruptly, caught Danestar as she plowed into him, thrust the valise at her.

"Here—!" he gasped. She saw they'd reached a door to the warehouse; now Wergard was turning to open it. Clutching the valise, thoughts a roiling confusion of terror, she looked back, half expecting to see a wave of purple fire sweeping up the alley toward them.

But the alley was empty, though the building front along which the barrier blazed was only a few hundred yards away. Then, as Wergard caught her arm, hauled her in through the door, a closer section—the building from which they had emerged a moment before—erupted in glittering fury. The door slammed in back of her, and they were running again, through a great hall, along aisles between high-stacked rows of packing cases. And—*where was the valise?* Then she realized Wergard had taken it.

She followed him into a cross-aisle. Another turn to the right, and the end of the hall was ahead, a wide passage leading off it. She had a glimpse of Wergard's strained face looking back for her; then, suddenly, he swerved aside against the line of cases, crouched, his free arm making a violent gesture, motioning her to the floor.

Danestar dropped instantly. A moment later, he was next to her.

"Keep . . . down!" he warned. "*Way* . . . down!"

Sobbing for breath, flattened against the cases, she twisted her head around, saw what he was staring at over the stacked rows behind them. A pale purple reflection went gliding silently along the ceiling at the far end of the hall, seemed to strengthen for an instant, abruptly faded out.

They scrambled to their feet, ran on into the passage.

Even after they'd slowed to a walk again, had reached a structure beyond the warehouse, they didn't talk about it much. Both were badly winded and shaken. It had been difficult to believe that the thing could have failed to detect them. Its attention must have been wholly on the force fields it was skirting, even as a section of it flowed through the warehouse within a few hundred feet of them.

If they'd been a few seconds later reaching the alley. . . .

Danestar reached into her white jacket, turning up its cooling unit. Wergard glanced at her. His face was dripping sweat. He wiped at it with his sleeve.

She asked, "You're still wearing the sneaksuit?"

Wergard lifted a strand of transparent webbing from under his collar, let it snap back. "Think it might have helped?"

"I don't know." But the creature might have the equivalent of a life detector unit as part of its sensory equipment, and a sneaksuit, distorting and blurring the energy patterns of a living body, would perhaps afford some protection. She said, "I'll get into one as soon as we reach our quarters. It may have known somebody was around but didn't want to waste time picking up another human until it found out why the defense barriers were turned on again in that area."

Wergard remarked dubiously, "It seems to me it's got picking up humans at the top of its priority list!" After a moment, he added, "The long sprint comes next. Feel up to it?"

Danestar looked at him. "I'd better feel up to it! If we see that thing again—I'm one inch this side of pure panic right now!"

He grunted. "Quit bragging!" He slid the carbine from his shoulder. "It's that door ahead. Let me have a look out first."

As he began to unlock the door, Danestar found

herself glancing back automatically once more at the long, lit, empty corridor through which they had come, their hurried steps echoing in the silence of the building. Then she saw Wergard had paused, half crouched and motionless, at the barely opened door.

"What is it?" she asked quickly.

"I don't know!" The face he turned to her was puzzled and apprehensive. "Come up and take a look!"

She moved to where she could look out past him. After a moment, she said, "There are adjustment instruments for the Depot lighting somewhere in the control section."

"Uh-huh," said Wergard. "Another item that's been sealed away for a hundred years or so. But our Number Two Thing in the control building seems to have got to them. I'd like to know what it means."

He opened the door wider. Both moved forward carefully, glancing along the street outside.

This was one of the main streets of the Depot. Across from them, a hundred and fifty yards away, was the massive white front of the structure which housed the central generators. Approximately two hundred yards to the left, it was pierced by a small entrance door which was the next step on Wergard's route to their quarters. To west and east, the street stretched away for half a mile before rows of buildings crossed it.

But all this was in semi-darkness now; too dim to let them make out the door in the wall of the generator building from where they stood. A hazy brightness above the line of buildings across the street indicated the rest of the Depot was still flooded by the projection lighting system which was that of the old fortress—wear-proof and ageless. If not deliberately tampered with, it would go on filling the Depot with eternal day-brightness for millennia.

But something had tampered with it and was still tampering with it. As they looked, the gloom along the street deepened perceptibly, then, slowly, lightened to its previous level.

"There can't be much light in the Pit, of course," Wergard said, staring up the street to the west. The control section, Danestar realized suddenly, lay in that direction. "It may be trying to improve visibility in the Depot for its perceptions."

"Or," said Danestar, "ruin visibility for ours."

Wergard looked at her. "We don't have the time left to try another route," he said. "Whatever it's doing, we may make a mistake in crossing the street while it's experimenting. But waiting here makes no sense."

She shook her head. "The intention might be to keep us waiting here."

"Yes, I thought of that. So let's go. Right now. Top speed across. I'll stay behind you."

For an instant, Danestar hesitated. Her feeling that the uncertain darkness of the wide street was under the scrutiny of alien senses, that they would be observed and tracked, like small scuttling animals, as soon as they left the shelter of the doorway, became almost a conviction in that moment. The fact remained that they could not stay where they were. She tightened her grip on the handle of the valise, drew a deep breath, darted out.

They were half across when the darkness thickened so completely that they might have moved in mid-stride into a black universe. Blind, she thought. It was an abrupt mental shock. She faltered, almost stumbled, felt she had swerved from the line she was following, tried to turn back to it . . . suddenly didn't know at all in which direction to move. Now panic closed in.

"Wergard!"

"That way!" His voice, hoarse and strained, was on her right, rather than behind her. As she turned toward it, his light flicked on, narrowed to a pale thread, marking a small circle on the wall of the generator building ahead of Danestar. She was hurrying toward the wall again as the thread of light cut out ... and seconds later, the wall and the street began to reappear, dim and vague as before, but tangibly present. They reached the wall together, turned left along it. Again the street darkened, became lost in absolute blackness.

Wergard's hand caught her arm. "Just walk." He added something, muttered and indistinct, which might have been a curse. They went on, breathing raggedly. Wergard's hand remained on Danestar's arm. The darkness lightened a trifle, grew dense again. "Hold on a moment!" Wergard said, very softly.

She stopped instantly, stood unmoving, let her breath out slowly. Wergard's hand left her arm. She had an impression of cautious motion from him, decided he'd raised the carbine to fire-ready position. Then he, too, was still.

He'd speak when he thought he could. Danestar's eyes shifted quickly, scanning the unrelieved dark about them. The only sound was a dim faint hum of machinery from within the structure on their right.

Then she realized something had appeared in her field of vision.

It was ahead and to the left. A small pale patch of purple luminescence, moving swiftly but in an oddly jerky manner, its outline shifting and wavering, as it approached their path at what might be a right angle. How far away? If it was touching the ground, Danestar thought, or just above it, it must be at least two hundred yards farther up the street. That would make it a considerably larger thing than her first impression had suggested.

As these calculations flicked through her mind, their object passed by ahead, moved on to the right, abruptly vanished.

"You saw it?" Wergard whispered.

"Yes."

"Went in between a couple of buildings. Not so good—

but it was some distance off. We don't seem to have been noticed. Let's go on."

Wergard had glimpsed another of the minor fire shapes just before they stopped. That one had been smaller—or farther away—and had been in sight for only an instant, on the left side of the street.

"They shouldn't be too large to get through a personnel lock and switch off a barrier for Thing Number One," he said as they hurried along a catwalk in the generator building. "But that doesn't necessarily mean Number One is in this area."

"Scouts?" Danestar suggested.

That had been Wergard's thought. The Pit creature could have split off several dozen autonomous sections of itself of the size they had observed without noticeably reducing its main bulk, and scattered them about the Depot to speed up the search for any humans still hiding out. The carbine couldn't have done significant damage to the alien giant but should have the power to disrupt essential force patterns in these lesser replicas. "They don't make things easier for us," Wergard said, "but we'll have to show ourselves only once more. After that, we'll have cover. And we can change our tactics a little. . . ."

At the end of the generator building was the central street of the Depot, slightly wider than the last one they had crossed. It was almost startling to find it normally lit. Directly opposite was the entrance recess to another building. This was the final open stretch on the way to their quarters. Wergard mopped his forehead, asked, "Ready to try it?"

Danestar nodded. She felt lightly tensed, not at all tired. Dread had its uses—her body had recognized an ultimate emergency and responded. She thought it would go on running now when she called on it until it fell dead. Wergard was wearing a sneaksuit; she wasn't. It was possible they were being followed, that the light-shapes they'd seen were casting about in the area for the source of the life energy they'd detected here, of which she was the focus. In that case, getting across the central street might be the point of greatest danger. They'd decided she should go first while Wergard covered her with the carbine. He would follow as soon as she was within the other building.

She slipped out the door ahead of him, drew a deep breath, ran straight across the too-silent, bright-lit street toward the entrance recess.

And nothing happened. The carbine stayed quiet. The paving flowed by, and it seemed only an instant then before the building front swayed close before her. Danestar flung herself into the recess, came up gasping against the wall.

A door on the left, Wergard had said. Where?—she discovered it next to her, pulled it open.

For a moment, her mind seemed about to spin into insanity. Then she was backing away from the door, screaming with all her strength, while two shapes of pale fire glided out through it toward her. Somewhere, she heard the distant sharp snarl of the carbine. A blizzard of darting, writhing lines of purple light enveloped her suddenly, boiled in wild turmoil about the recess. The closer of the shapes had vanished, and the carbine was snarling again.

Abruptly, her awareness was wiped out.

"Got your third setting now, I think!" Wergard announced.

Danestar glanced at him. He sat at a table a few feet to her left, hunched forward, elbows planted on the table, face twisted in concentration as he peered at the tiny paper-flat instrument in his left hand.

"Uh-huh, that's it!" He sighed heavily. "Four to go." His right forefinger and thumb closed cautiously down on the device, shifted minutely, shifted back again. It was an attachment taken from Danestar's commband detector. She had designed it, used it on occasion to intrude on covert communications in which she had a professional interest, sometimes blanking a band out gently at a critical moment, sometimes injecting misinformation.

But it was an instrument designed for her fingers, magical instruments themselves in their sensitized skill, deftness, and experience. It had not been designed for Wergard's fingers, or anyone else's; and the only help she could give him with it was to tell him what must be done. Both hands were needed to operate the settings, and at present she couldn't use her left hand. What had knocked her out in the building entrance, an instant before Wergard's gun disrupted the second of the two Pit things that surprised her there, seemed to have been the approximate equivalent of a near miss from a bolt of lightning. Wergard had carried her two Depot blocks to their quarters, was working a sneaksuit over her, before she regained consciousness. Then she woke up suddenly, muscles knotted, trying to scream, voice thick and slurred when she started to answer Wergard's questions. They discovered her left side was almost completely paralyzed, her tongue partly affected. As soon as he could make out what she wanted, what her plan had been, Wergard hauled her down to the ground-level barrier room of the building, along with an assortment of hastily selected gadgetry, settled her in a chair next to the barrier control panel, arranged the various instruments on a table before her where she could reach them with her right hand. Then he went to work on the attachment's miniature dials to adjust them to the seven settings she'd told him were needed.

He swore suddenly, in a gust of savage impatience, asked without looking up, "How long have I been playing around with this midget monster of yours?"

"Sixteen minutes," Danestar told him. The paralysis

had begun to lift; she could enunciate well enough, though the left side of her face remained numb. But she still couldn't force meaningful motion into her left hand. If she had been able to use it, she wouldn't have needed half a minute to flick in the dial readings, slap the attachment back into the detector. It was a job no more involved than threading a series of miniature needles. The problem was simply that Wergard's hands weren't made for work on that scale, weren't trained to it.

"Sixteen minutes!" He groaned. His face was beaded with the sweat of effort. "Well, I seem to be getting the hang of it. Our luck may hold up."

It might, she thought. It was still a matter of luck. They'd had good luck and bad luck both during the past half hour. Until now, the main alien body had been engaged in the cluster of activated defense barriers on the north side of the Depot. The viewscreen on the table showed her the intermittent flickering of force fields there; now and then, a section blazed brightly. And sometimes she'd seen the great purple glow passing among the buildings. While it remained in that area, they had time left. But the barriers were being shut off, one by one. Detached work segments of the thing would be able to enter by a personnel lock and cut the controls. And—perhaps when the locks could not be immediately found—the main body was again driving directly through the force fields and absorbing what damage it must to get into a protected building.

During the past four minutes alone, it appeared to have passed through three such sectional barriers. Changes in the detector's visual pattern revealed the damage. The accumulated effect was not inconsiderable.

Danestar's gaze went to the locked instrument valise, lying on the table between the detector and the shortcode transmitter, in immediate reach of her right hand. Within it was still the alien instrument she'd taken from Dr.

Hishkan's office, the small, all-essential coordinating device without which the artificial asteroid from the cosmic cloud was a nonoperative, useless, meaningless lump of deteriorating machinery.

Had the alien mind discovered it wouldn't function, that the humans here had removed a section of it?

She thought it had. The repeated acceptance, during these last minutes, of the destruction of whole layers of its units in the raging force fields, to allow it to reach the barrier controls more quickly, suggested a new urgency in its search for human survivors. It would have been logical for it to assume that whoever had the missing instrument had sought refuge in the one area still shielded by multiple barriers.

But when the last of those defense fields was shut off and the last of the northern buildings hunted through, the creature would turn here. In that, their luck had been bad—very bad! To avoid attracting attention to the building, they'd planned to leave its barrier off as long as possible. They were in sneaksuits, perhaps untraceable. They might have remained undetected indefinitely.

But they had been in the barrier room only a few minutes before one of the prowling segments found them. Danestar had the streets along two sides of the building under observation, and nothing had been in sight there. Evidently, the thing had approached through an adjacent building. Without warning, it erupted from an upper corner of the room, swept down toward them. Danestar barely glimpsed it before Wergard scooped up the carbine placed across the table beside him and triggered it one-handed.

The segment vanished, as its counterparts in the building entry had done, in an exploding swirl of darting, purple-gleaming lines of light. The individual energy entities which had survived the gun's shock-charge seemed as mindless and purposeless as an insect swarm whirled away on a sudden gust of wind. Danestar had slapped

on the building's defense fields almost as Wergard fired;
and in seconds, the indicators showed the fields flickering momentarily at thousands of points as the glittering
purple threads flashed against them and were absorbed.
Within a minute, the building was clear again.

But almost immediately afterwards, the barrier was
impacted in a far more solid manner; and now the
viewscreen showed a sudden shifting and weaving of fire
shapes in one of the streets beside the building. Four or
five segments had appeared together; one had attempted
to slip into the building and encountered the force field.
Lacking the protective bulk of the main body, it was
instantly destroyed. The others obviously had become
aware of the danger.

"If they can find the personnel lock here, they should
try that!" Wergard remarked.

He laid Danestar's instrument carefully to one side,
stood waiting with the gun. The entry surface of the lock
was in the wall across from them, ringed in warning light
to show the field was active. Danestar kept her eyes on
the control panel. After a moment, she said sharply, "They
have found the lock!" A yellow light had begun to flash
beside the field indicators, signaling that the lock was in
use. As it began to open on the room, the carbine flicked
a charge into it, and the purple glow within exploded in
glittering frenzies.

The attempt to use the lock wasn't repeated. The
scouting segments were not in themselves an immediate
danger here. But in the open, away from the building,
where they could bring their destructive powers into play,
a few of them should be more than a match for the
carbine. To retreat again to some other point of the
Depot had become impossible. The things remained in
the vicinity and were on guard, and other segments began
to join them.

That made it simply a question of how many minutes
it still would be before the main body appeared to deal

with the humans pinned down in this building. Neither
Wergard nor Danestar mentioned it. They'd had good
luck and bad, lasted longer than there had been any real
reason to expect; now they'd run out of alternative moves.
Nothing was left to discuss. Wergard had laid the carbine
down, resumed his carefully deliberate groping with the
spidery dials of Danestar's device. Danestar watched the
instruments; and the instruments, in their various ways,
watched the enemy. A tic began working in the corner
of Wergard's jaw; sweat ran down his face. But his hands
remained steady. After a time, he announced he had
locked in the first setting. Then the second, and the
third. . . .

There were developments in the instruments Danestar
didn't tell him about. That the main body of the alien
was absorbing savage punishment in its onslaught on the
force fields became increasingly evident. The detector's
projection field pattern almost might have been that of
a city undergoing an intermittent brutal barrage. Blacked-
out sections remained lifeless now, and there were
indications of an erratically spreading breakdown in
general organization.

But it should know, she thought, how much of that
it could tolerate. Meanwhile it was achieving its purpose
with frightening quickness. Barrier after barrier blazed
in sudden bright fury along the line of search through
the northern complex, subsided again. The viewscreen
panels kept shifting as Danestar followed the thing's
progress. Then she cut in one more panel, and knew it
was the last. The alien had very little farther to go.

She switched the screen back momentarily to the local
area, the streets immediately around their building.
There was evidence here, she thought, in the steadily
increasing number of ghostly darting light shapes beyond
the barrier, that alien control of the Depot was almost
complete. The segments had been sent through it like

minor detachments of an invading army to make sure
no humans were left in hiding anywhere. They were
massing about this building now because the composite
mind knew that within the building were the only
survivors outside of the northern complex.

The thing was intelligent by any standards, had used
its resources methodically and calculatingly. The major
section which had been detached from it after it captured
the control building apparently had remained there
throughout, taking no part in other action. That eliminated
the possibility that humans might escape from the Depot
or obtain outside help. Only during the past few minutes,
after the alien mind was assured that the last survivors
were pinned down, had there been a change in that part
of the pattern in the projector field. The thing seemed
to be on the move now, filling some other role in the
over-all plan. Perhaps, Danestar thought, it would rejoin
the main body as a reserve force, to make up for the
losses suffered in the barriers. Or it might be on its way
here.

Wergard said absently, as if it had occurred to him
to mention in passing something that was of no great
interest to either of them, "Got that fourth setting
now. . . ."

Less than a minute later, in the same flat, perfunctory
tone, he announced the fifth setting was locked in; and
hope flared in Danestar so suddenly it was like a shock
of hot fright.

She glanced quickly at him. Staring down at the instrument he fingered with infinite two-handed deliberation,
Wergard looked drugged, in a white-faced trance. She
didn't dare address him, do anything that might break into
that complete absorption.

But mentally she found herself screaming at him to
hurry. There was so little time left. The last barrier in the
northern complex had flared, gone dead, minutes before.
The giant main body of the alien seemed quiescent then.

There were indications of deep continuing disturbances in
the scintillating signal swarms in the projector, and briefly
Danestar had thought that the last tearing shock of force
field energies could have left the great mass finally disor-
ganized, crippled and stunned.

But then evidence grew that the component which
had remained in the control station was, in fact, rejoin-
ing the main body. And its role became clear. As the
two merged, the erratic disturbances in the major section dimmed, smoothed out. A suggestion of swift, mul-
titudinous rhythms coordinating the whole gradually
returned.

The Pit thing was the equivalent of an army of billions
of individuals. And that entity had a directing intelligence—centered in the section which had held itself out
of action until the energy defenses of the Depot were
neutralized. Now it had reappeared, unaffected by the
damage the main body had suffered, to resume control,
restore order. Quantitatively, the composite monster was
reduced, shrunken. But its efficiency remained unimpaired;
and as far as she and Wergard were concerned, the loss
in sheer mass made no difference at all.

And where was it now? She'd kept the panels of the
viewscreen shifting about along the line of approach it
should take between the northern complex and this
building. She did not catch sight of it. But, of course,
if it was in motion again, it could as easily be flowing
toward them below ground level where the screen
wouldn't show it. . . .

Danestar paused, right hand on the screen mechanism.

Had there been the lightest, most momentary,
betraying quiver in a section of the defense barrier
indicator: just then? The screen was turned to the area
about the building; and only the swift gliding ghost
shapes of the segments were visible in the streets
outside.

But that meant nothing. She kept her eyes on the

barrier panel. Seconds passed; then a brief quivering ran through the indicators and subsided.

The thing was here, beneath the building, barely beyond range of its force field.

Danestar drew the instrument valise quietly toward her, opened its dial lock and took out the ovoid alien device and a small gun lying in the valise beside it. She laid the device on the table, placed the gun's muzzle against it. A slight pull of her trigger finger would drive a shattering charge into the instrument. . . .

Her eyes went back to the viewscreen. The swirling mass of light shapes out there abruptly had stopped moving.

She and Wergard had discussed this. The alien had traced the U-League's asteroid specimen from the Pit to Mezmiali, and to the Depot. While the instrument now missing from the specimen had been enclosed by the spyproof screens of Danestar's valise, the alien's senses evidently had not detected it. But it should register on them as soon as it was removed again from the valise.

One question had been then whether the alien would be aware of the device's importance to it. Danestar thought now that it was. The other question was whether it had learned enough from its contacts with humans to realize that, cornered and facing death, they might destroy such an instrument to keep it from an enemy.

If the alien knew that, it might, in the final situation, gain them a little more time.

She would not have been surprised if the barrier indicators had blazed red the instant after she opened the valise. And she would, in that moment, which certainly must be the last of her life and Wergard's, have pulled the gun trigger.

But nothing happened immediately, except that the segments in the streets outside the building went motionless. That, of course, should have some significance.

Danestar waited now as motionlessly. Perhaps half a minute passed. Then the rattling pickup signal of the shortcode transmitter on the table suddenly jarred the stillness of the room.

Some seconds later, three spaced words, stolen from living human voices, patched together by the alien's cunning, came from the transmitter:

"I . . . want . . . it. . . . "

There was a pause. On Danestar's left, Wergard made a harsh laughing sound. She watched the barrier panel. The indicators there remained quiet.

"I . . . want . . . it. . . ." repeated the transmitter suddenly. It paused again.

"Six, Danestar!" Wergard's voice told her. He added something in a mutter, went silent.

"I . . . want—"

The transmitter cut off abruptly. The force field indicators flickered very slightly and then were still. But in the viewscreen there was renewed motion.

The segments in the street to the left of the building lifted like burning leaves caught by the breath of an approaching storm, swirled up together, streamed into and across the building beyond. In an instant, the street was empty of them. In the street on the right, ghostly fire shapes also were moving off, more slowly, gliding away to the east, while the others began pouring out of building fronts and down through the air again to join the withdrawal. Some four hundred yards away, the swarm came to a stop, massing together. Seconds later, the paving about them showed the familiar purple glitter and the gleaming mass of the Pit creature lifted slowly into view from below, its minor emissaries merging into it and vanishing as it arose. It lay there quietly then, filling the width of the street.

The situation had been presented in a manner which could not be misunderstood. The alien mind wanted the instrument. It knew the humans in this building had it.

It had communicated the fact to them, then drawn back from the building, drawn its segments with it.

The humans, it implied, were free to go now, leaving the instrument behind. . . .

But, of course, that was not the real situation. There was no possible compromise. The insignificant-looking device against which Danestar's gun was held was the key to the Pit. To abandon it to the alien at this final moment was out of the question. And the act, in any case, would not have extended their lives by more than a few minutes.

So the muzzle of the gun remained where it was, and Danestar made no other move. Revealing they had here what the creature wanted had gained them a trifling addition in time. Until she heard Wergard tell her he had locked in the seventh and final setting on the diabolically tiny instrument with which he had been struggling for almost twenty minutes, she could do nothing else.

But Wergard stayed silent while the seconds slipped away. When some two minutes had passed, Danestar realized the giant fire shape was settling back beneath the surface of the street. Within seconds then it disappeared.

A leaden hopelessness settled on her at last. When they saw the thing again, it would be coming in for the final attack. And if it rose against the force fields from below the building, they would not see it then. She must remember to pull the trigger the instant the barrier indicators flashed their warning. Then it would be over.

She looked around at Wergard, saw he had placed the instrument on the table before him and was scowling down at it, lost in the black abstraction that somehow had enabled his fingers to do what normally must have been impossible to them. Only a few more minutes, Danestar thought, and he might have completed it. She parted her lips to warn him of what was about to happen, then shook her head silently. Why disturb him now? There was nothing more Wergard could do, either.

As she looked back at the viewscreen, the Pit creature began to rise through the street level a hundred yards away. It lifted smoothly, monstrously, a flowing mountain of purple brilliance, poured toward them.

Seconds left. . . . Her finger went taut on the trigger.

A bemused, slow voice seemed to say heavily, "My eyes keep blurring now. Want to check this, Danestar? I think I have the setting, but—"

"No time!" She screamed it out, as the gun dropped to the table. She twisted awkwardly around on the chair, right hand reaching. "Let me have it!"

Then Wergard, shocked free of whatever trance had closed on him, was there, slapping the device into her hand, steadying her as she twisted back toward the detector and fitted it in. He swung away from her. Danestar locked the attachment down, glanced over her shoulder, saw him standing again at the other table, eyes fixed on her, hand lifted above the plunger of the power pack beside the carbine.

"Now!" she whispered.

Wergard couldn't possibly have beard it. But his palm came down in a hard slap on the plunger as the indicators of the entire eastern section of the barrier flared red.

Danestar was a girl who preferred subtle methods in her work when possible. She had designed the detector's interference attachment primarily to permit careful, unnoticeable manipulations of messages passing over supposedly untappable communication lines; and it worked very well for that purpose.

On this occasion, however, with the peak thrust of the power pack surging into it, there was nothing subtle about its action. A storm of static howled through the Depot along the Pit creature's internal communication band. In reaction to it, the composite body quite literally shattered. The viewscreen filled with boiling geysers of purple light.

Under the dull black dome of the main barrier, the rising mass expanded into a writhing, glowing cloud. Ripped by continuing torrents of static, it faded further, dissipated into billions of flashing lines of light, mindlessly seeking escape. In their billions, they poured upon the defense globe of the ancient fortress.

For three or four minutes, the great barrier drank them in greedily.

Then the U-League Depot stood quiet again.

Grandpa

⚬❦⚬

A green-winged, downy thing as big as a hen fluttered along the hillside to a point directly above Cord's head and hovered there, twenty feet above him. Cord, a fifteen-year-old human being, leaned back against a skipboat parked on the equator of a world that had known human beings for only the past four Earth years, and eyed the thing speculatively. The thing was, in the free and easy terminology of the Sutang Colonial Team, a swamp bug. Concealed in the downy fur back of the bug's head was a second, smaller, semiparasitical thing, classed as a bug rider.

The bug itself looked like a new species to Cord. Its parasite might or might not turn out to be another unknown. Cord was a natural research man; his first glimpse of the odd flying team had sent endless curiosities thrilling through him. How did that particular phenomenon tick, and why? What fascinating things, once you'd learned about it, could you get it to do?

Normally, he was hampered by circumstances in

carrying out any such investigation. The Colonial Team was a practical, hardworking outfit—two thousand people who'd been given twenty years to size up and tame down the brand-new world of Sutang to the point where a hundred thousand colonists could be settled on it, in reasonable safety and comfort. Even junior colonial students like Cord were expected to confine their curiosity to the pattern of research set up by the station to which they were attached. Cord's inclination toward independent experiments had got him into disfavor with his immediate superiors before this.

He sent a casual glance in the direction of the Yoger Bay Colonial Station behind him. No signs of human activity about that low, fortresslike bulk in the hill. Its central lock was still closed. In fifteen minutes, it was scheduled to be opened to let out the Planetary Regent, who was inspecting the Yoger Bay Station and its principal activities today.

Fifteen minutes was time enough to find out something about the new bug, Cord decided.

But he'd have to collect it first.

He slid out one of the two handguns holstered at his side. This one was his own property: a Vanadian projectile weapon. Cord thumbed it to position for anesthetic small-game missiles and brought the hovering swamp bug down, drilled neatly and microscopically through the head.

As the bug hit the ground, the rider left its back. A tiny scarlet demon, round and bouncy as a rubber ball, it shot toward Cord in three long hops, mouth wide to sink home inch-long, venom-dripping fangs. Rather breathlessly, Cord triggered the gun again and knocked it out in mid-leap. A new species, all right! Most bug riders were harmless plant-eaters, mere suckers of vegetable juice—

"Cord!" A feminine voice.

Cord swore softly. He hadn't heard the central lock click open. She must have come around from the other side of the station.

"Hi, Grayan!" he shouted innocently without looking around. "Come see what I got! New species!"

Grayan Mahoney, a slender, black-haired girl two years older than himself, came trotting down the hillside toward him. She was Sutang's star colonial student, and the station manager, Nirmond, indicated from time to time that she was a fine example for Cord to pattern his own behavior on. In spite of that, she and Cord were good friends, but she bossed him around considerably.

"Cord, you dope!" she scowled as she came up. "Quit acting like a collector! If the Regent came out now, you'd be sunk. Nirmond's been telling her about you!"

"Telling her what?" Cord asked, startled.

"For one," Grayan reported, "that you don't keep up on your assigned work. Two, that you sneak off on one-man expeditions of your own at least once a month and have to be rescued—"

"Nobody," Cord interrupted hotly, "has had to rescue me yet!"

"How's Nirmond to know you're alive and healthy when you just drop out of sight for a week?" Grayan countered. "Three," she resumed checking the items off on slim fingertips, "he complained that you keep private zoological gardens of unidentified and possibly deadly vermin in the woods back of the station. And four . . . well, Nirmond simply doesn't want the responsibility for you any more!" She held up the four fingers significantly.

"Golly!" gulped Cord, dismayed. Summed up tersely like that, his record *didn't* look too good.

"Golly is right! I keep warning you! Now Nirmond wants the Regent to send you back to Vanadia—and there's a starship coming in to New Venus forty-eight hours from now!" New Venus was the Colonial Team's main settlement on the opposite side of Sutang.

"What'll I do?"

"Start acting like you had good sense mainly." Grayan grinned suddenly. "I talked to the Regent, too—Nirmond isn't rid of you yet! But if you louse up on our tour of the Bay Farms today, you'll be off the Team for good!"

She turned to go. "You might as well put the skipboat back; we're not using it. Nirmond's driving us down to the edge of the Bay in a treadcar, and we'll take a raft from there. Don't let them know I warned you!"

Cord looked after her, slightly stunned. He hadn't realized his reputation had become as bad as all that! To Grayan, whose family had served on Colonial Teams for the past four generations, nothing worse was imaginable than to be dismissed and sent back ignominiously to one's own homeworld. Much to his surprise, Cord was discovering now that he felt exactly the same way about it!

Leaving his newly bagged specimens to revive by themselves and flutter off again, he hurriedly flew the skipboat around the station and rolled it back into its stall.

Three rafts lay moored just offshore in the marshy cove, at the edge of which Nirmond had stopped the treadcar. They looked somewhat like exceptionally broad-brimmed, well-worn sugarloaf hats floating out there, green and leathery. Or like lily pads twenty-five feet across, with the upper section of a big, gray-green pineapple growing from the center of each. Plant animals of some sort. Sutang was too new to have had its phyla sorted out into anything remotely like an orderly classification. The rafts were a local oddity which had been investigated and could be regarded as harmless and moderately useful. Their usefulness lay in the fact that they were employed as a rather slow means of transportation about the shallow, swampy waters of the Yoger Bay. That was as far as the Team's interest in them went at present.

The Regent had stood up from the back seat of the car, where she was sitting next to Cord. There were only four in the party; Grayan was up front with Nirmond.

"Are those our vehicles?" The Regent sounded amused.

Nirmond grinned, a little sourly. "Don't underestimate them, Dane! They could become an important economic factor in this region in time. But, as a matter of fact, these three are smaller than I like to use." He was peering about the reedy edges of the cove. "There's a regular monster parked here usually—"

Grayan turned to Cord. "Maybe Cord knows where Grandpa is hiding."

It was well-meant, but Cord had been hoping nobody would ask him about Grandpa. Now they all looked at him.

"Oh, you want Grandpa?" he said, somewhat flustered. "Well, I left him . . . I mean I saw him a couple of weeks ago about a mile south from here—"

Grayan sighed. Nirmond grunted and told the Regent, "The rafts tend to stay wherever they're left, providing it's shallow and muddy. They use a hair-root system to draw chemicals and microscopic nourishment directly from the bottom of the bay. Well—Grayan, would you like to drive us there?"

Cord settled back unhappily as the treadcar lurched into motion. Nirmond suspected he'd used Grandpa for one of his unauthorized tours of the area, and Nirmond was quite right.

"I understand you're an expert with these rafts, Cord," Dane said from beside him. "Grayan told me we couldn't find a better steersman, or pilot, or whatever you call it, for our trip today."

"I can handle them," Cord said, perspiring. "They don't give you any trouble!" He didn't feel he'd made a good impression on the Regent so far. Dane was a young, handsome-looking woman with an easy way of talking and laughing, but she wasn't the head of the Sutang Colonial Team for nothing. She looked quite capable of shipping out anybody whose record wasn't up to par.

"There's one big advantage our beasties have over a

skipboat, too," Nirmond remarked from the front seat. "You don't have to worry about a snapper trying to climb on board with you!" He went on to describe the stinging ribbon-tentacles the rafts spread around them under water to discourage creatures that might make a meal off their tender underparts. The snappers and two or three other active and aggressive species of the Bay hadn't yet learned it was foolish to attack armed human beings in a boat, but they would skitter hurriedly out of the path of a leisurely perambulating raft.

Cord was happy to be ignored for the moment. The Regent, Nirmond, and Grayan were all Earth people, which was true of most of the members of the Team; and Earth people made him uncomfortable, particularly in groups. Vanadia, his own homeworld, had barely graduated from the status of Earth colony itself, which might explain the difference. All the Earth people he'd met so far seemed dedicated to what Grayan Mahoney called the Big Picture, while Nirmond usually spoke of it as "Our Purpose Here." They acted strictly in accordance with their Team Regulations—sometimes, in Cord's opinion, quite insanely. Because now and then the Regulations didn't quite cover a new situation and then somebody was likely to get killed. In which case, the Regulations would be modified promptly, but Earth people didn't seem otherwise disturbed by such events.

Grayan had tried to explain it to Cord:

"We can't really ever *know* in advance what a new world is going to be like! And once we're there, there's too much to do, in the time we've got, to study it inch by inch. You get your job done, and you take a chance. But if you stick by the Regulations you've got the best chances of surviving anybody's been able to figure out for you—"

Cord felt he preferred to just use good sense and not let Regulations or the job get him into a situation he couldn't figure out for himself.

To which Grayan replied impatiently that he hadn't yet got the Big Picture—

The treadcar swung around and stopped, and Grayan stood up in the front seat, pointing. "That's Grandpa, over there!"

Dane also stood up and whistled softly, apparently impressed by Grandpa's fifty-foot spread. Cord looked around in surprise. He was pretty sure this was several hundred yards from the spot where he'd left the big raft two weeks ago; and as Nirmond said, they didn't usually move about by themselves.

Puzzled, he followed the others down a narrow path to the water, hemmed in by tree-sized reeds. Now and then he got a glimpse of Grandpa's swimming platform, the rim of which just touched the shore. Then the path opened out, and he saw the whole raft lying in sunlit, shallow water; and he stopped short, startled.

Nirmond was about to step up on the platform, ahead of Dane.

"Wait!" Cord shouted. His voice sounded squeaky with alarm. "Stop!"

He came running forward.

They had frozen where they stood, looked around swiftly. Then glanced back at Cord coming up. They were well trained.

"What's the matter, Cord?" Nirmond's voice was quiet and urgent.

"Don't get on that raft—it's changed!" Cord's voice sounded wobbly, even to himself. "Maybe it's not even Grandpa—"

He saw he was wrong on the last point before he'd finished the sentence. Scattered along the rim of the raft were discolored spots left by a variety of heat-guns, one of which had been his own. It was the way you goaded the sluggish and mindless things into motion. Cord pointed at the cone-shaped central projection. "There— his head! He's sprouting!"

"Sprouting?" the station manager repeated uncomprehendingly. Grandpa's head, as befitted his girth, was almost twelve feet high and equally wide. It was armor-plated like the back of a saurian to keep off plant-suckers, but two weeks ago it had been an otherwise featureless knob, like those on all other rafts. Now scores of long, kinky, leafless vines had grown out from all surfaces of the cone, like green wires. Some were drawn up like tightly coiled springs, others trailed limply to the platform and over it. The top of the cone was dotted with angry red buds, rather like pimples, which hadn't been there before either. Grandpa looked unhealthy.

"Well," Nirmond said, "so it is. Sprouting!" Grayan made a choked sound. Nirmond glanced at Cord as if puzzled. "Is that all that was bothering you, Cord?"

"Well, sure!" Cord began excitedly. He hadn't caught the significance of the word "all"; his hackles were still up, and he was shaking. "None of them ever—"

Then he stopped. He could tell by their faces that they hadn't got it. Or rather, that they'd got it all right but simply weren't going to let it change their plans. The rafts were classified as harmless, according to the Regulations. Until proved otherwise, they would continue to be regarded as harmless. You didn't waste time quibbling with the Regulations—apparently even if you were the Planetary Regent. You didn't feel you had the time to waste.

He tried again. "Look—" he began. What he wanted to tell them was that Grandpa with one unknown factor added wasn't Grandpa any more. He was an unpredictable, oversized lifeform, to be investigated with cautious thoroughness till you knew what the unknown factor meant.

But it was no use. They knew all that. He stared at them helplessly. "I—"

Dane turned to Nirmond. "Perhaps you'd better check," she said. She didn't add,—"to reassure the boy!" but that was what she meant.

Cord felt himself flushing terribly. They thought he
was scared—which he was—and they were feeling sorry
for him, which they had no right to do. But there was
nothing he could say or do now except watch Nirmond
walk steadily across the platform. Grandpa shivered
slightly a few times, but the rafts always did that when
someone first stepped on them. The station manager
stopped before one of the kinky sprouts, touched it, and
then gave it a tug. He reached up and poked at the
lowest of the budlike growths. "Odd-looking things!" he
called back. He gave Cord another glance. "Well,
everything seems harmless enough, Cord. Coming
aboard, everyone?"

It was like dreaming a dream in which you yelled and
yelled at people and couldn't make them hear you! Cord
stepped up stiff-legged on the platform behind Dane and
Grayan. He knew exactly what would have happened if
he'd hesitated even a moment. One of them would have
said in a friendly voice, careful not to let it sound too
contemptuous: "You don't have to come along if you don't
want to, Cord!"

Grayan had unholstered her heat-gun and was ready
to start Grandpa moving out into the channels of the
Yoger Bay.

Cord hauled out his own heat-gun and said roughly,
"I was to do that!"

"All right, Cord." She gave him a brief, impersonal
smile, as if he were someone she'd met for the first time
that day, and stood aside.

They were so infuriatingly polite! He was, Cord decided,
as good as on his way back to Vanadia right now.

For a while, Cord almost hoped that something awesome
and catastrophic would happen promptly to teach the
Team people a lesson. But nothing did. As always,
Grandpa shook himself vaguely and experimentally when
he felt the heat on one edge of the platform and then
decided to withdraw from it, all of which was standard

procedure. Under the water, out of sight, were the raft's working sections: short, thick leaf-structures shaped like paddles and designed to work as such, along with the slimy nettle-streamers which kept the vegetarians of the Yoger Bay away, and a jungle of hair roots through which Grandpa sucked nourishments from the mud and the sluggish waters of the Bay, and with which he also anchored himself.

The paddles started churning, the platform quivered, the hair roots were hauled out of the mud; and Grandpa was on his ponderous way.

Cord switched off the heat, reholstered his gun, and stood up. Once in motion, the rafts tended to keep traveling unhurriedly for quite a while. To stop them, you gave them a touch of heat along their leading edge; and they could be turned in any direction by using the gun lightly on the opposite side of the platform.

It was simple enough. Cord didn't look at the others. He was still burning inside. He watched the reed beds move past and open out, giving him glimpses of the misty, yellow and green and blue expanse of the brackish Bay ahead. Behind the mist, to the west, were the Yoger Straits, tricky and ugly water when the tides were running; and beyond the Straits lay the open sea, the great Zlanti Deep, which was another world entirely and one of which he hadn't seen much as yet.

Suddenly he was sick with the full realization that he wasn't likely to see any more of it now! Vanadia was a pleasant enough planet; but the wildness and strangeness were long gone from it. It wasn't Sutang.

Grayan called from beside Dane, "What's the best route from here into the farms, Cord?"

"The big channel to the right," he answered. He added somewhat sullenly, "We're headed for it!"

Grayan came over to him. "The Regent doesn't want to see all of it," she said, lowering her voice. "The algae and plankton beds first. Then as much of the mutated grains as we can show her in about three hours. Steer for the ones that have been doing best, and you'll keep Nirmond happy!"

She gave him a conspiratorial wink. Cord looked after her uncertainly. You couldn't tell from her behavior that anything was wrong. Maybe—

He had a flare of hope. It was hard not to like the Team people, even when they were being rock-headed about their Regulations. Perhaps it was that purpose that gave them their vitality and drive, even though it made them remorseless about themselves and everyone else. Anyway, the day wasn't over yet. He might still redeem himself in the Regent's opinion. Something might happen—

Cord had a sudden cheerful, if improbable, vision of some Bay monster plunging up on the raft with snapping jaws, and of himself alertly blowing out what passed for the monster's brains before anyone else—Nirmond, in particular—was even aware of the threat. The Bay monsters shunned Grandpa, of course, but there might be ways of tempting one of them.

So far, Cord realized, he'd been letting his feelings control him. It was time to start thinking!

Grandpa first. So he'd sprouted—green vines and red buds, purpose unknown, but with no change observable in his behavior-patterns otherwise. He was the biggest raft in this end of the Bay, though all of them had been growing steadily in the two years since Cord had first seen one. Sutang's seasons changed slowly; its year was somewhat more than five Earth years long. The first Team members to land here hadn't yet seen a full year pass.

Grandpa then was showing a seasonal change. The other rafts, not quite so far developed, would be reacting similarly a little later. Plant animals—they might be blossoming, preparing to propagate.

"Grayan," he called, "how do the rafts get started? When they're small, I mean."

Grayan looked pleased; and Cord's hopes went up a little more. Grayan was on his side again anyway!

"Nobody knows yet," she said. "We were just talking about it. About half of the coastal marsh-fauna of the continent seems to go through a preliminary larval stage in the sea." She nodded at the red buds on the raft's cone. "It looks as if Grandpa is going to produce flowers and let the wind or tide take the seeds out through the Straits."

It made sense. It also knocked out Cord's still half-held hope that the change in Grandpa might turn out to be drastic enough, in some way, to justify his reluctance to get on board. Cord studied Grandpa's armored head carefully once more—unwilling to give up that hope entirely. There were a series of vertical gummy black slits between the armor plates, which hadn't been in evidence two weeks ago either. It looked as if Grandpa were beginning to come apart at the seams. Which might indicate that the rafts, big as they grew to be, didn't outlive a full seasonal cycle, but came to flower at about this time of Sutang's year and died. However, it was a safe bet that Grandpa wasn't going to collapse into senile decay before they completed their trip today.

Cord gave up on Grandpa. The other notion returned to him— Perhaps he *could* coax an obliging Bay monster into action that would show the Regent he was no sissy!

Because the monsters were there, all right.

Kneeling at the edge of the platform and peering down into the wine-colored, clear water of the deep channel they were moving through, Cord could see a fair selection of them at almost any moment.

Some five or six snappers, for one thing. Like big, flattened crayfish, chocolate-brown mostly, with green and red spots on their carapaced backs. In some areas they were so thick you'd wonder what they found to live on, except that they ate almost anything, down to chewing up the mud in which they squatted. However, they preferred their food in large chunks and alive, which was one reason you didn't go swimming in the Bay. They would attack a boat on occasion; but the excited manner in which the ones he saw were scuttling off toward the edges of the channel showed they wanted to have nothing to do with a big moving raft.

Dotted across the bottom were two-foot round holes which looked vacant at the moment. Normally, Cord knew, there would be a head filling each of those holes. The heads consisted mainly of triple sets of jaws, held open patiently like so many traps to grab at anything that came within range of the long, wormlike bodies behind the heads. But Grandpa's passage, waving his stingers like transparent pennants through the water, had scared the worms out of sight, too.

Otherwise, mostly schools of small stuff—and then a flash of wicked scarlet, off to the left behind the raft, darting out from the reeds! Turning its needle-nose into their wake.

Cord watched it without moving. He knew that creature, though it was rare in the Bay and hadn't been classified. Swift, vicious—alert enough to snap swamp bugs out of the air as they fluttered across the surface. And he'd tantalized one with fishing tackle once into leaping up on a moored raft, where it had flung itself about furiously until he was able to shoot it.

No fishing tackle. A handkerchief might just do it, if he cared to risk an arm—

"What fantastic creatures!" Dane's voice just behind him.

"Yellowheads," said Nirmond. "They've got a high utility rating. Keep down the bugs."

Cord stood up casually. It was no time for tricks! The reed bed to their right was thick with yellowheads, a colony of them. Vaguely froggy things, man-sized and better. Of all the creatures he'd discovered in the Bay, Cord liked them least. The flabby, sacklike bodies clung with four thin limbs to the upper sections of the twenty-foot reeds that lined the channel. They hardly ever moved, but their huge, bulging eyes seemed to take in everything that went on about them. Every so often, a downy swamp bug came close enough; and a yellowhead would open its vertical, enormous, tooth-lined slash of a mouth, extend the whole front of its face like a bellows in a flashing strike; and the bug would be gone. They might be useful, but Cord hated them.

"Ten years from now we should know what the cycle of coastal life is like," Nirmond said. "When we set up the Yoger Bay Station there were no yellowheads here. They came the following year. Still with traces of the oceanic larval form; but the metamorphosis was almost complete. About twelve inches long—"

Dane remarked that the same pattern was duplicated endlessly elsewhere. The Regent was inspecting the yellowhead colony with field glasses; she put them down now, looked at Cord, and smiled. "How far to the farms?"

"About twenty minutes."

"The key," Nirmond said, "seems to be the Zlanti Basin. It must be almost a soup of life in spring."

"It is," nodded Dane, who had been here in Sutang's spring, four Earth years ago. "It's beginning to look as if the Basin alone might justify colonization. The question is still—" she gestured towards the yellowheads— "how do creatures like that get there?"

They walked off toward the other side of the raft, arguing about ocean currents. Cord might have followed. But something splashed back of them, off to the left and not too far back. He stayed, watching.

After a moment, he saw the big yellowhead. It had slipped down from its reedy perch, which was what had caused the splash. Almost submerged at the water line, it stared after the raft with huge pale-green eyes. To Cord, it seemed to look directly at him. In that moment, he knew for the first time why he didn't like yellowheads.

There was something very like intelligence in that look, an alien calculation. In creatures like that, intelligence seemed out of place. What use could they have for it?

A little shiver went over him when it sank completely under the water and he realized it intended to swim after the raft. But it was mostly excitement. He had never seen a yellowhead come down out of the reeds before. The obliging monster he'd been looking for might be presenting itself in an unexpected way.

Half a minute later, he watched it again, swimming awkwardly far down. It had no immediate intention of boarding, at any rate. Cord saw it come into the area of the raft's trailing stingers. It maneuvered its way between them with curiously human swimming motions, and went out of sight under the platform.

He stood up, wondering what it meant. The yellow-head had appeared to know about the stingers; there had been an air of purpose in every move of its approach. He was tempted to tell the others about it, but there was the moment of triumph he could have if it suddenly came slobbering up over the edge of the platform and he nailed it before their eyes.

It was almost time anyway to turn the raft in toward the farms. If nothing happened before then—

He watched. Almost five minutes, but no sign of the yellowhead. Still wondering, a little uneasy, he gave Grandpa a calculated needling of heat.

After a moment, he repeated it. Then he drew a deep breath and forgot all about the yellowhead.

"Nirmond!" he called sharply.

The three of them were standing near the center of the platform, next to the big armored cone, looking ahead at the farms. They glanced around.

"What's the matter now, Cord?"

Cord couldn't say it for a moment. He was suddenly, terribly scared again. Something *had* gone wrong!

"The raft won't turn!" he told them.

"Give it a real burn this time!" Nirmond said.

Cord glanced up at him. Nirmond, standing a few steps in front of Dane and Grayan as if he wanted to protect them, had begun to look a little strained, and no wonder. Cord already had pressed the gun to three different points on the platform; but Grandpa appeared to have developed a sudden anesthesia for heat. They kept moving out steadily toward the center of the Bay.

Now Cord held his breath, switched the heat on full, and let Grandpa have it. A six-inch patch on the platform blistered up instantly, turned brown, then black—

Grandpa stopped dead. Just like that.

"That's right! Keep burn—" Nirmond didn't finish his order.

A giant shudder. Cord staggered back toward the water. Then the whole edge of the raft came curling up behind him and went down again, smacking the Bay with a sound like a cannon shot. He flew forward off his feet, hit the platform face down, and flattened himself against it. It swelled up beneath him. Two more enormous slaps and joltings. Then quiet. He looked round for the others.

He lay within twelve feet of the central cone. Some twenty or thirty of the mysterious new vines the cone had sprouted were stretched out stiffly toward him now, like so many thin green fingers. They couldn't quite reach him. The nearest tip was still ten inches from his shoes.

But Grandpa had caught the others, all three of them. They were tumbled together at the foot of the cone, wrapped in a stiff network of green vegetable ropes, and they didn't move.

Cord drew his feet up cautiously, prepared for another earthquake reaction. But nothing happened. Then he discovered that Grandpa was back in motion on his previous course. The heat-gun had vanished. Gently, he took out the Vanadian gun.

A voice, thin and pain-filled, spoke to him from one of the three huddled bodies.

"Cord? It didn't get you?" It was the Regent.

"No," he said, keeping his voice low. He realized suddenly he'd simply assumed they were all dead. Now he felt sick and shaky.

"What are you doing?"

Cord looked at Grandpa's big armor-plated head with a certain hunger. The cones were hollowed out inside; the station's lab had decided their chief function was to keep enough air trapped under the rafts to float them. But in that central section was also the organ that controlled Grandpa's overall reactions.

He said softly, "I've got a gun and twelve heavy-duty explosive bullets. Two of them will blow that cone apart."

"No good, Cord!" the pain-racked voice told him. "If the thing sinks, we'll die anyway. You have anesthetic charges for that gun of yours?"

He stared at her back. "Yes."

"Give Nirmond and the girl a shot each, before you do anything else. Directly into the spine, if you can. But don't come any closer—"

Somehow, Cord couldn't argue with that voice. He stood up carefully. The gun made two soft spitting sounds.

"All right," he said hoarsely. "What do I do now?"

Dane was silent a moment. "I'm sorry, Cord. I can't tell you that. I'll tell you what I can—"

She paused for some seconds again. "This thing didn't try to kill us, Cord. It could have easily. It's incredibly strong. I saw it break Nirmond's legs. But as soon as we stopped moving, it just held us. They were both unconscious then—"

"You've got that to go on. It was trying to pitch you within reach of its vines or tendrils, or whatever they are, too, wasn't it?"

"I think so," Cord said shakily. That was what had happened, of course; and at any moment Grandpa might try again.

"Now it's feeding us some sort of anesthetic of its own

through those vines. Tiny thorns. A sort of numbness—"
Dane's voice trailed off a moment. Then she said clearly,
"Look, Cord—it seems we're food it's storing up! You get
that?"

"Yes," he said.

"Seeding time for the rafts. There are analogues. Live
food for its seed probably; not for the raft. One couldn't
have counted on that. Cord?"

"Yes. I'm here."

"I want," said Dane, "to stay awake as long as I can.
But there's really just one other thing—this raft's going
somewhere. To some particularly favorable location. And
that might be very near shore. You might make it in then;
otherwise it's up to you. But keep your head and wait
for a chance. No heroics, understand?"

"Sure, I understand," Cord told her. He realized
then that he was talking reassuringly, as if it weren't
the Planetary Regent but someone like Grayan.

"Nirmond's the worst," Dane said. "The girl was
knocked unconscious at once. If it weren't for my arm—
But, if we can get help in five hours or so, everything
should be all right. Let me know if anything happens,
Cord."

"I will," Cord said gently again. Then he sighted his
gun carefully at a point between Dane's shoulder blades,
and the anesthetic chamber made its soft, spitting sound
once more. Dane's taut body relaxed slowly, and that
was all.

There was no point Cord could see in letting her stay
awake; because they weren't going anywhere near shore.
The reed beds and the channels were already behind
them, and Grandpa hadn't changed direction by the
fraction of a degree. He was moving out into the open
Bay—and he was picking up company!

So far, Cord could count seven big rafts within two
miles of them; and on the three that were closest he
could make out a sprouting of new green vines. All of

them were traveling in a straight direction; and the common point they were all headed for appeared to be the roaring center of the Yoger Straits, now some three miles away!

Behind the Straits, the cold Zlanti Deep—the rolling fogs, and the open sea! It might be seeding time for the rafts, but it looked as if they weren't going to distribute their seeds in the Bay—

For a human being, Cord was a fine swimmer. He had a gun and he had a knife; in spite of what Dane had said, he might have stood a chance among the killers of the Bay. But it would be a very small chance, at best. And it wasn't, he thought, as if there weren't still other possibilities. He was going to keep his head.

Except by accident, of course, nobody was going to come looking for them in time to do any good. If anyone did look, it would be around the Bay Farms. There were a number of rafts moored there; and it would be assumed they'd used one of them. Now and then something unexpected happened and somebody simply vanished—by the time it was figured out just what had happened on this occasion, it would be much too late.

Neither was anybody likely to notice within the next few hours that the rafts had started migrating out of the swamps through the Yoger Straits. There was a small weather station a little inland, on the north side of the Straits, which used a helicopter occasionally. It was about as improbable, Cord decided dismally, that they'd use it in the right spot just now as it would be for a jet transport to happen to come in low enough to spot them.

The fact that it was up to him, as the Regent had said, sank in a little more after that! Cord had never felt so lonely.

Simply because he was going to try it sooner or later, he carried out an experiment next that he knew couldn't work. He opened the gun's anesthetic chamber and counted out fifty pellets—rather hurriedly because he didn't particularly want to think of what he might be using them for eventually. There were around three hundred charges left in the chamber then; and in the next few minutes Cord carefully planted a third of them in Grandpa's head.

He stopped after that. A whale might have showed signs of somnolence under a lesser load. Grandpa paddled on undisturbed. Perhaps he had become a little numb in spots, but his cells weren't equipped to distribute the soporific effect of that type of drug.

There wasn't anything else Cord could think of doing before they reached the Straits. At the rate they were moving, he calculated that would happen in something less than an hour; and if they did pass through the Straits, he was going to risk a swim. He didn't think Dane would have disapproved, under the circumstances. If the raft simply carried them all out into the foggy vastness of the Zlanti Deep, there would be no practical chance of survival left at all.

Meanwhile, Grandpa was definitely picking up speed. And there were other changes going on—minor ones, but still a little awe-inspiring to Cord. The pimply-looking red buds that dotted the upper part of the cone were opening out gradually. From the center of most of them protruded now something like a thin, wet, scarlet worm: a worm that twisted weakly, extended itself by an inch or so, rested and twisted again, and stretched up a little farther, groping into the air. The vertical black slits between the armor plates looked somehow deeper and wider than they had been even some minutes ago; a dark, thick liquid dripped slowly from several of them.

Under other circumstances Cord knew he would have been fascinated by these developments in Grandpa. As it was, they drew his suspicious attention only because he didn't know what they meant.

Then something quite horrible happened suddenly. Grayan started moaning loudly and terribly and twisted almost completely around. Afterwards, Cord knew it hadn't been a second before he stopped her struggles and the sounds together with another anesthetic pellet; but the vines had tightened their grip on her first, not flexibly but like the digging, bony green talons of some monstrous bird of prey. If Dane hadn't warned him—

White and sweating, Cord put his gun down slowly while the vines relaxed again. Grayan didn't seem to have suffered any additional harm; and she would certainly have been the first to point out that his murderous rage might have been as intelligently directed against a machine. But for some moments Cord continued to luxuriate furiously in the thought that, at any instant he chose, he could still turn the raft very quickly into a ripped and exploded mess of sinking vegetation.

Instead, and more sensibly, he gave both Dane and Nirmond another shot, to prevent a similar occurrence with them. The contents of two such pellets, he knew, would keep any human being torpid for at least four hours. Five shots—

Cord withdrew his mind hastily from the direction it was turning into; but it wouldn't stay withdrawn. The thought kept coming up again, until at last he had to recognize it:

Five shots would leave the three of them completely unconscious, whatever else might happen to them, until they either died from other causes or were given a counteracting agent.

Shocked, he told himself he couldn't do it. It was exactly like killing them.

But then, quite steadily, he found himself raising the gun once more, to bring the total charge for each of the three Team people up to five. And if it was the first time in the last four years Cord had felt like crying, it also seemed to him that he had begun to understand what was meant by using your head—along with other things.

Barely thirty minutes later, he watched a raft as big

as the one he rode go sliding into the foaming white waters of the Straits a few hundred yards ahead, and dart off abruptly at an angle, caught by one of the swirling currents. It pitched and spun, made some headway, and was swept aside again. And then it righted itself once more. Not like some blindly animated vegetable, Cord thought, but like a creature that struggled with intelligent purpose to maintain its chosen direction.

At least, they seemed practically unsinkable—

Knife in hand, he flattened himself against the platform as the Straits roared just ahead. When the platform jolted and tilted up beneath him, he rammed the knife all the way into it and hung on. Cold water rushed suddenly over him, and Grandpa shuddered like a laboring engine. In the middle of it all, Cord had the horrified notion that the raft might release its unconscious human prisoners in its struggle with the Straits. But he underestimated Grandpa in that. Grandpa also hung on.

Abruptly, it was over. They were riding a long swell, and there were three other rafts not far away. The Straits had swept them together, but they seemed to have no interest in one another's company. As Cord stood up shakily and began to strip off his clothes, they were visibly drawing apart again. The platform of one of them was half-submerged; it must have lost too much of the air that held it afloat and, like a small ship, it was foundering.

From this point, it was only a two-mile swim to the shore north of the Straits, and another mile inland from there to the Straits Head Station. He didn't know about the current; but the distance didn't seem too much, and he couldn't bring himself to leave knife and gun behind. The Bay creatures loved warmth and mud, they didn't venture beyond the Straits. But Zlanti Deep bred its own killers, though they weren't often observed so close to shore.

Things were beginning to look rather hopeful.

Thin, crying voices drifted overhead, like the voices of curious cats, as Cord knotted his clothes into a tight bundle, shoes inside. He looked up. There were four of them circling there; magnified seagoing swamp bugs, each carrying an unseen rider. Probably harmless scavengers— but the ten-foot wingspread was impressive. Uneasily, Cord remembered the venomously carnivorous rider he'd left lying beside the station.

One of them dipped lazily and came sliding down toward him. It soared overhead and came back, to hover about the raft's cone.

The bug rider that directed the mindless flier hadn't been interested in him at all! Grandpa was baiting it!

Cord stared in fascination. The top of the cone was alive now with a softly wriggling mass of the scarlet, wormlike extrusions that had started sprouting before the raft left the Bay. Presumably, they looked enticingly edible to the bug rider.

The flier settled with an airy fluttering and touched the cone. Like a trap springing shut, the green vines flashed up and around it, crumpling the brittle wings, almost vanishing into the long soft body—

Barely a second later, Grandpa made another catch, this one from the sea itself. Cord had a fleeting glimpse of something like a small, rubbery seal that flung itself out of the water upon the edge of the raft, with a suggestion of desperate haste—and was flipped on instantly against the cone, where the vines clamped it down beside the flier's body.

It wasn't the enormous ease with which the unexpected kill was accomplished that left Cord standing there, completely shocked. It was the shattering of his hopes to swim to shore from here. Fifty yards away, the creature from which the rubbery thing had been fleeing showed briefly on the surface, as it turned away from the raft; and the glance was all he needed. The ivory-white body and gaping jaws were similar enough to those of the shark of Earth to indicate the pursuer's nature. The important difference was that, wherever the white hunters of the Zlanti Deep went, they went by the thousands.

Stunned by that incredible piece of bad luck, still clutching his bundled clothes, Cord stared toward shore. Knowing what to look for, he could spot the telltale roilings of the surface now—the long, ivory gleams that flashed through the swells and vanished again. Shoals of smaller things burst into the air in sprays of glittering desperation and fell back.

He would have been snapped up like a drowning fly before he'd covered a twentieth of that distance!

But almost another full minute passed before the realization of the finality of his defeat really sank in.

Grandpa was beginning to eat!

Each of the dark slits down the sides of the cone was a mouth. So far only one of them was in operating condition, and the raft wasn't able to open that one very wide as yet. The first morsel had been fed into it, however: the bug rider the vines had plucked out of the flier's downy neck fur. It took Grandpa several minutes to work it out of sight, small as it was. But it was a start.

Cord didn't feel quite sane any more. He sat there, clutching his bundle of clothes and only vaguely aware of the fact that he was shivering steadily under the cold spray that touched him now and then, while he followed Grandpa's activities attentively. He decided it would be at least some hours before one of that black set of mouths grew flexible and vigorous enough to dispose of a human being. Under the circumstances, it couldn't make much difference to the other human beings here; but the moment Grandpa reached for the first of them would also be the moment he finally blew the raft to pieces. The white hunters were cleaner eaters, at any rate; and that was about the extent to which he could still control what was going to happen.

Meanwhile, there was the very faint chance that the weather station's helicopter might spot them—

Meanwhile also, in a weary and horrified fascination, he kept debating the mystery of what could have produced such a nightmarish change in the rafts. He could guess where they were going by now; there were scattered strings of them stretching back to the Straits or roughly parallel to their own course, and the direction was that of the plankton-swarming pool of the Zlanti Basin, a thousand miles to the north. Given time, even mobile lily pads like the rafts had been could make that trip for the benefit of their seedlings. But nothing in their structure explained the sudden change into alert and capable carnivores.

He watched the rubbery little seal-thing being hauled up to a mouth next. The vines broke its neck; and the mouth took it in up to the shoulders and then went on working patiently at what was still a trifle too large a bite. Meanwhile, there were more thin cat-cries overhead; and a few minutes later, two more sea bugs were trapped almost simultaneously and added to the larder. Grandpa dropped the dead seal-thing and fed himself another bug rider. The second rider left its mount with a sudden hop, sank its teeth viciously into one of the vines that caught it again, and was promptly battered to death against the platform.

Cord felt a resurge of unreasoning hatred against Grandpa. Killing a bug was about equal to cutting a branch from a tree; they had almost no life-awareness. But the rider had aroused his partisanship because of its appearance of intelligent action—and it was in fact closer to the human scale in that feature than to the monstrous life-form that had, mechanically, but quite successfully, trapped both it and the human beings. Then his thoughts had drifted again; and he found himself speculating vaguely on the curious symbiosis in which the nerve systems of two creatures as dissimilar as the bugs and their riders could be linked so closely that they functioned as one organism.

Suddenly an expression of vast and stunned surprise appeared on his face.

Why—now he knew!

Cord stood up hurriedly, shaking with excitement, the whole plan complete in his mind. And a dozen long vines snaked instantly in the direction of his sudden motion, and groped for him, taut and stretching. They couldn't reach him, but their savagely alert reaction froze Cord briefly where he was. The platform was shuddering under his feet, as if in irritation at his inaccessibility; but it couldn't be tilted up suddenly here to throw him within the grasp of the vines, as it could around the edges.

Still, it was a warning! Cord sidled gingerly around the cone till he had gained the position he wanted, which was on the forward half of the raft. And then he waited. Waited long minutes, quite motionless, until his heart stopped pounding and the irregular angry shivering of the surface of the raft-thing died away, and the last vine tendril had stopped its blind groping. It might help a lot if, for a second or two after he next started moving, Grandpa wasn't too aware of his exact whereabouts!

He looked back once to check how far they had gone by now beyond the Straits Head Station. It couldn't, he decided, be even an hour behind them. Which was close enough, by the most pessimistic count—if everything else worked out all right! He didn't try to think out in detail what that "everything else" could include, because there were factors that simply couldn't be calculated in advance. And he had an uneasy feeling that speculating too vividly about them might make him almost incapable of carrying out his plan.

At last, moving carefully, Cord took the knife in his left hand but left the gun holstered. He raised the tightly knotted bundle of clothes slowly over his head, balanced in his right hand. With a long, smooth motion he tossed the bundle back across the cone, almost to the opposite edge of the platform.

It hit with a soggy thump. Almost immediately, the whole far edge of the raft buckled and flapped up to toss the strange object to the reaching vines.

Simultaneously, Cord was racing forward. For a moment, his attempt to divert Grandpa's attention seemed completely successful—then he was pitched to his knees as the platform came up.

He was within eight feet of the edge. As it slapped down again, he threw himself desperately forward.

An instant later, he was knifing down through cold, clear water, just ahead of the raft, then twisting and coming up again.

The raft was passing over him. Clouds of tiny sea creatures scattered through its dark jungle of feeding roots. Cord jerked back from a broad, wavering streak of glassy greenness, which was a stinger, and felt a burning jolt on his side, which meant he'd been touched lightly by another. He bumped on blindly through the slimy black tangles of hair roots that covered the bottom of the raft; then green half-light passed over him, and he burst up into the central bubble under the cone.

Half-light and foul, hot air. Water slapped around him, dragging him away again—nothing to hang on to here! Then above him, to his right, molded against the interior curve of the cone as if it had grown there from the start, the froglike, man-sized shape of the yellowhead.

The raft rider—

Cord reached up and caught Grandpa's symbiotic partner and guide by a flabby hind leg, pulled himself half out of the water, and struck twice with the knife, fast while the pale-green eyes were still opening.

He'd thought the yellowhead might need a second or so to detach itself from its host, as the bug riders usually did, before it tried to defend itself. This one merely turned its head; the mouth slashed down and clamped on Cord's left arm above the elbow. His right hand sank the knife through one staring eye, and the yellowhead jerked away, pulling the knife from his grasp.

Sliding down, he wrapped both hands around the slimy leg and hauled with all his weight. For a moment more, the yellowhead hung on. Then the countless neural extensions that connected it now with the raft came free in a succession of sucking, tearing sounds; and Cord and the yellowhead splashed into the water together.

Black tangle of roots again—and two more electric burns suddenly across his back and legs! Strangling, Cord let go. Below him, for a moment, a body was turning over and over with oddly human motions; then a solid wall of water thrust him up and aside, as something big and white struck the turning body and went on.

Cord broke the surface twelve feet behind the raft. And that would have been that, if Grandpa hadn't already been slowing down.

After two tries, he floundered back up on the platform and lay there gasping and coughing a while. There were no indications that his presence was resented now. A few vine tips twitched uneasily, as if trying to remember previous functions, when he came limping up presently to make sure his three companions were still breathing; but Cord never noticed that.

They were still breathing; and he knew better than to waste time trying to help them himself. He took Grayan's heat-gun from its holster. Grandpa had come to a full stop.

Cord hadn't had time to become completely sane again, or he might have worried now whether Grandpa, violently sundered from his controlling partner, was still capable of motion on his own. Instead, he determined the approximate direction of the Straits Head Station, selected a corresponding spot on the platform, and gave Grandpa a light tap of heat.

Nothing happened immediately. Cord sighed patiently and stepped up the heat a little.

Grandpa shuddered gently. Cord stood up.

Slowly and hesitatingly at first, then with steadfast—though now again brainless—purpose, Grandpa began paddling back toward the Straits Head Station.

Balanced Ecology

❧

The diamondwood tree farm was restless this morning. Ilf Cholm had been aware of it for about an hour but had said nothing to Auris, thinking he might be getting a summer fever or a stomach upset and imagining things, and that Auris would decide they should go back to the house so Ilf's grandmother could dose him. But the feeling continued to grow, and by now Ilf knew it was the farm.

Outwardly, everyone in the forest appeared to be going about their usual business. There had been a rainfall earlier in the day; and the tumbleweeds had uprooted themselves and were moving about in the bushes, lapping water off the leaves. Ilf had noticed a small one rolling straight towards a waiting slurp and stopped for a moment to watch the slurp catch it. The slurp was of average size, which gave it a tongue-reach of between twelve and fourteen feet, and the tumbleweed was already within range.

The tongue shot out suddenly, a thin, yellow flash. Its

tip flicked twice around the tumbleweed, jerked it off the ground and back to the feed opening in the imitation tree stump within which the rest of the slurp was concealed. The tumbleweed said "Oof!" in the surprised way they always did when something caught them, and went in through the opening. After a moment, the slurp's tongue tip appeared in the opening again and waved gently around, ready for somebody else of the right size to come within reach.

Ilf, just turned eleven and rather small for his age, was the right size for this slurp, though barely. But, being a human boy, he was in no danger. The slurps of the diamondwood farms on Wrake didn't attack humans. For a moment, he was tempted to tease the creature into a brief fencing match. If he picked up a stick and banged on the stump with it a few times, the slurp would become annoyed and dart its tongue out and try to knock the stick from his hand.

But it wasn't the day for entertainment of that kind. Ilf couldn't shake off his crawly, uncomfortable feeling, and while he had been standing there, Auris and Sam had moved a couple of hundred feet farther uphill, in the direction of the Queen Grove, and home. He turned and sprinted after them, caught up with them as they came out into one of the stretches of grassland which lay between the individual groves of diamondwood trees.

Auris, who was two years, two months, and two days older than Ilf, stood on top of Sam's semiglobular shell, looking off to the right towards the valley where the diamondwood factory was. Most of the world of Wrake was on the hot side, either rather dry or rather steamy; but this was cool mountain country. Far to the south, below the valley and the foothills behind it, lay the continental plain, shimmering like a flat, green brown sea. To the north and east were higher plateaus, above the level where the diamondwood liked to grow. Ilf ran past Sam's steadily moving bulk to the point where the forward

rim of the shell made a flat upward curve, close enough
to the ground so he could reach it.

Sam rolled a somber brown eye back for an instant
as Ilf caught the shell and swung up on it, but his huge
beaked head didn't turn. He was a mossback, Wrake's
version of the turtle pattern, and, except for the full-grown
trees and perhaps some members of the clean-up squad,
the biggest thing on the farm. His corrugated shell was
overgrown with a plant which had the appearance of long
green fur; and occasionally when Sam fed, he would
extend and use a pair of heavy arms with three-fingered
hands, normally held folded up against the lower rim of
the shell.

Auris had paid no attention to Ilf's arrival. She still
seemed to be watching the factory in the valley. She and
Ilf were cousins but didn't resemble each other. Ilf was
small and wiry, with tight-curled red hair. Auris was slim
and blond, and stood a good head taller than he did. He
thought she looked as if she owned everything she could
see from the top of Sam's shell; and she did, as a matter
of fact, own a good deal of it—nine tenths of the
diamondwood farm and nine tenths of the factory. Ilf
owned the remaining tenth of both.

He scrambled up the shell, grabbing the moss-fur to
haul himself along, until he stood beside her. Sam,
awkward as he looked when walking, was moving at a
good ten miles an hour, clearly headed for the Queen
Grove. Ilf didn't know whether it was Sam or Auris who
had decided to go back to the house. Whichever it had
been, he could feel the purpose of going there.

"They're nervous about something," he told Auris,
meaning the whole farm. "Think there's a big storm
coming?"

"Doesn't look like a storm," Auris said.

Ilf glanced about the sky, agreed silently. "Earthquake,
maybe?"

Auris shook her head. "It doesn't feel like earthquake."

She hadn't turned her gaze from the factory. Ilf asked, "Something going on down there?"

Auris shrugged. "They're cutting a lot today," she said. "They got in a limit order."

Sam swayed on into the next grove while Ilf considered the information. Limit orders were fairly unusual; but it hardly explained the general uneasiness. He sighed, sat down, crossed his legs, and looked about. This was a grove of young trees, fifteen years and less. There was plenty of open space left between them. Ahead, a huge tumbleweed was dying, making happy, chuckling sounds as it pitched its scarlet seed pellets far out from its slowly unfolding leaves. The pellets rolled hurriedly farther away from the old weed as soon as they touched the ground. In a twelve-foot circle about their parent, the earth was being disturbed, churned, shifted steadily about. The clean-up squad had arrived to dispose of the dying tumbleweed; as Ilf looked, it suddenly settled six or seven inches deeper into the softened dirt. The pellets were hurrying to get beyond the reach of the clean-up squad so they wouldn't get hauled down, too. But half-grown tumbleweeds, speckled yellow-green and ready to start their rooted period, were rolling through the grove towards the disturbed area. They would wait around the edge of the circle until the clean-up squad finished, then move in and put down their roots. The ground where the squad had worked recently was always richer than any other spot in the forest.

Ilf wondered, as he had many times before, what the clean-up squad looked like. Nobody ever caught so much as a glimpse of them. Riquol Cholm, his grandfather, had told him of attempts made by scientists to catch a member of the squad with digging machines. Even the smallest ones could dig much faster than the machines could dig after them, so the scientists always gave up finally and went away.

✧   ✧   ✧

"Ilf, come in for lunch!" called Ilf's grandmother's voice.

Ilf filled his lungs, shouted, "Coming, grand—"

He broke off, looked up at Auris. She was smirking. "Caught me again," Ilf admitted. "Dumb humbugs!" He yelled, "Come out, Lying Lou! I know who it was."

Meldy Cholm laughed her low, sweet laugh, a silverbell called the giant greenweb of the Queen Grove sounded its deep harp note, more or less all together. Then Lying Lou and Gabby darted into sight, leaped up on the mossback's hump. The humbugs were small, brown, bobtailed animals, built with spider lean-ness and very quick. They had round skulls, monkey faces, and the pointed teeth of animals who lived by catching and killing other animals. Gabby sat down beside Ilf, inflating and deflating his voice pouch, while Lou burst into a series of rattling, clicking, spitting sounds.

"They've been down at the factory?" Ilf asked.

"Yes," Auris said. "Hush now. I'm listening."

Lou was jabbering along at the rate at which the humbugs chattered among themselves, but this sounded like, and was, a recording of human voices played back at high speed. When Auris wanted to know what people somewhere were talking about, she sent the humbugs off to listen. They remembered everything they heard, came back and repeated it to her at their own speed, which saved time. Ilf, if he tried hard, could understand scraps of it. Auris understood it all. She was hearing now what the people at the factory had been saying during the morning.

Gabby inflated his voice pouch part way, remarked in Grandfather Riquol's strong, rich voice, "My, my! We're not being quite on our best behavior today, are we, Ilf?"

"Shut up," said Ilf.

"Hush now," Gabby said in Auris' voice. "I'm listening."
He added in Ilf's voice, sounding crestfallen, "Caught me
again!" then chuckled nastily.

Ilf made a fist of his left hand and swung fast. Gabby
became a momentary brown blur, and was sitting again
on Ilf's other side. He looked at Ilf with round, innocent
eyes, said in a solemn tone. "We must pay more attention
to details, men. Mistakes can be expensive!"

He'd probably picked that up at the factory. Ilf ignored
him. Trying to hit a humbug was a waste of effort. So
was talking back to them. He shifted his attention to
catching what Lou was saying; but Lou had finished up
at that moment. She and Gabby took off instantly in a
leap from Sam's back and were gone in the bushes. Ilf
thought they were a little jittery and erratic in their
motions today, as if they, too, were keyed up even more
than usual. Auris walked down to the front lip of the shell
and sat on it, dangling her legs. Ilf joined her there.

"What were they talking about at the factory?" he
asked.

"They did get in a limit order yesterday," Auris said.
"And another one this morning. They're not taking any
more orders until they've filled those two."

"That's good, isn't it?" Ilf asked.

"I guess so."

After a moment, Ilf asked, "Is that what *they're*
worrying about?"

"I don't know," Auris said. But she frowned.

Sam came lumbering up to another stretch of open
ground, stopped while he was still well back among the
trees. Auris slipped down from the shell, said, "Come on
but don't let them see you," and moved ahead through
the trees until she could look into the open. Ilf followed
her as quietly as he could.

"What's the matter?" he inquired. A hundred and fifty
yards away, on the other side of the open area, towered

the Queen Grove, its tops dancing gently like armies of slender green spears against the blue sky. The house wasn't visible from here; it was a big one-story bungalow built around the trunks of a number of trees deep within the grove. Ahead of them lay the road which came up from the valley and wound on through the mountains to the west.

Auris said, "An aircar came down here a while ago . . . There it is!"

They looked at the aircar parked at the side of the road on their left, a little distance away. Opposite the car was an opening in the Queen Grove where a path led to the house. Ilf couldn't see anything very interesting about the car. It was neither new nor old, looked like any ordinary aircar. The man sitting inside it was nobody they knew.

"Somebody's here on a visit," Ilf said.

"Yes," Auris said. "Uncle Kugus has come back."

Ilf had to reflect an instant to remember who Uncle Kugus was. Then it came to his mind in a flash. It had been some while ago, a year or so. Uncle Kugus was a big, handsome man with thick, black eyebrows, who always smiled. He wasn't Ilf's uncle but Auris'; but he'd had presents for both of them when he arrived. He had told Ilf a great many jokes. He and Grandfather Riquol had argued on one occasion for almost two hours about something or other; Ilf couldn't remember now what it had been. Uncle Kugus had come and gone in a tiny, beautiful, bright yellow aircar, had taken Ilf for a couple of rides in it, and told him about winning races with it. Ilf hadn't had too bad an impression of him.

"That isn't him," he said, "and that isn't his car."

"I know. He's in the house," Auris said. "He's got a couple of people with him. They're talking with Riquol and Meldy."

A sound rose slowly from the Queen Grove as she spoke, deep and resonant, like the stroke of a big, old clock or the hum of a harp. The man in the aircar turned his head towards the grove to listen. The sound was repeated twice. It came from the giant greenweb at the far end of the grove and could be heard all over the farm, even, faintly, down in the valley when the wind was favorable. Ilf said, "Lying Lou and Gabby were up here?"

"Yes. They went down to the factory first, then up to the house."

"What are they talking about in the house?" Ilf inquired.

"Oh, a lot of things." Auris frowned again. "We'll go and find out, but we won't let them see us right away."

Something stirred beside Ilf. He looked down and saw Lying Lou and Gabby had joined them again. The humbugs peered for a moment at the man in the aircar, then flicked out into the open, on across the road, and into the Queen Grove, like small, flying shadows, almost impossible to keep in sight. The man in the aircar looked about in a puzzled way, apparently uncertain whether he'd seen something move or not.

"Come on," Auris said.

Ilf followed her back to Sam. Sam lifted his head and extended his neck. Auris swung herself upon the edge of the undershell beside the neck, crept on hands and knees into the hollow between the upper and lower shells. Ilf climbed in after her. The shell-cave was a familiar place. He'd scuttled in there many times when they'd been caught outdoors in one of the violent electric storms which came down through the mountains from the north or when the ground began to shudder in an earthquake's first rumbling. With the massive curved shell above him and the equally massive flat shell below, the angle formed by the cool, leathery wall which was the side of Sam's neck and the front of his shoulder seemed like the safest place in the world to be on such occasions.

The undershell tilted and swayed beneath Ilf now as the mossback started forward. He squirmed around and looked out through the opening between the shells. They moved out of the grove, headed towards the road at Sam's steady walking pace. Ilf couldn't see the aircar and wondered why Auris didn't want the man in the car to see them. He wriggled uncomfortably. It was a strange, uneasy-making morning in every way.

They crossed the road, went swishing through high grass with Sam's ponderous side-to-side sway like a big ship sailing over dry land, and came to the Queen Grove. Sam moved on into the green-tinted shade under the Queen Trees. The air grew cooler. Presently he turned to the right, and Ilf saw a flash of blue ahead. That was the great thicket of flower bushes, in the center of which was Sam's sleeping pit.

Sam pushed through the thicket, stopped when he reached the open space in the center to let Ilf and Auris climb out of the shell-cave. Sam then lowered his fore-legs, one after the other, into the pit, which was lined so solidly with tree roots that almost no earth showed between them, shaped like a mold to fit the lower half of his body, tilted forward, drawing neck and head back under his shell, slid slowly into the pit, straightened out and settled down. The edge of his upper shell was now level with the edge of the pit, and what still could be seen of him looked simply like a big, moss-grown boulder. If nobody came to disturb him, he might stay there unmoving the rest of the year. There were mossbacks in other groves of the farm which had never come out of their sleeping pits or given any indication of being awake since Ilf could remember. They lived an enormous length of time and a nap of half a dozen years apparently meant nothing to them.

Ilf looked questioningly at Auris. She said, "We'll go up to the house and listen to what Uncle Kugus is talking about."

They turned into a path which led from Sam's place to the house. It had been made by six generations of human

children, all of whom had used Sam for transportation
about the diamondwood farm. He was half again as big as
any other mossback around and the only one whose sleeping pit was in the Queen Grove. Everything about the
Queen Grove was special, from the trees themselves, which
were never cut and twice as thick and almost twice as tall
as the trees of other groves, to Sam and his blue flower
thicket, the huge stump of the Grandfather Slurp not far
away, and the giant greenweb at the other end of the grove.
It was quieter here; there were fewer of the other animals.
The Queen Grove, from what Riquol Cholm had told Ilf,
was the point from which the whole diamondwood forest
had started a long time ago.

Auris said, "We'll go around and come in from the back.
They don't have to know right away that we're here . . . "

"Mr. Terokaw," said Riquol Cholm, "I'm sorry Kugus
Ovin persuaded you and Mr. Bliman to accompany him
to Wrake on this business. You've simply wasted your
time. Kugus should have known better. I've discussed the
situation quite thoroughly with him on other occasions."

"I'm afraid I don't follow you, Mr. Cholm," Mr. Terokaw
said stiffly. "I'm making you a businesslike proposition
in regard to this farm of diamondwood trees—a proposition which will be very much to your advantage as well
as to that of the children whose property the Diamondwood is. Certainly you should at least be willing to listen
to my terms!"

Riquol shook his head. It was clear that he was angry
with Kugus but attempting to control his anger.

"Your terms, whatever they may be, are not a factor
in this," he said. "The maintenance of a diamondwood
forest is not entirely a business proposition. Let me
explain that to you—as Kugus should have done.

"No doubt you're aware that there are less than forty
such forests on the world of Wrake and that attempts to
grow the trees elsewhere have been uniformly unsuccessful.

That and the unique beauty of diamondwood products, which has never been duplicated by artificial means, is, of course, the reason that such products command a price which compares with that of precious stones and similar items."

Mr. Terokaw regarded Riquol with a bleak blue eye, nodded briefly. "Please continue, Mr. Cholm."

"A diamondwood forest," said Riquol, "is a great deal more than an assemblage of trees. The trees are a basic factor, but still only a factor, of a closely integrated, balanced natural ecology. The manner of interdependence of the plants and animals that make up a diamondwood forest is not clear in all details, but the interdependence is a very pronounced one. None of the involved species seem able to survive in any other environment. On the other hand, plants and animals not naturally a part of this ecology will not thrive if brought into it. They move out or vanish quickly. Human beings appear to be the only exception to that rule."

"Very interesting," Mr. Terokaw said dryly.

"It is," said Riquol. "It is a very interesting natural situation and many people, including Mrs. Cholm and myself, feel it should be preserved. The studied, limited cutting practiced on the diamondwood farms at present acts towards its preservation. That degree of harvesting actually is beneficial to the forests, keeps them moving through an optimum cycle of growth and maturity. They are flourishing under the hand of man to an extent which was not usually attained in their natural, untouched state. The people who are at present responsible for them—the farm owners and their associates—have been working for some time to have all diamondwood forests turned into Federation preserves, with the right to harvest them retained by the present owners and their heirs under the same carefully supervised conditions. When Auris and Ilf come of age and can sign an agreement to that effect, the farms will in fact become

Federation preserves. All other steps to that end have been taken by now.

"That, Mr. Terokaw, is why we're not interested in your business proposition. You'll discover, if you wish to sound them out on it, that the other diamondwood farmers are not interested in it either. We are all of one mind in that matter. If we weren't, we would long since have accepted propositions essentially similar to yours."

There was silence for a moment. Then Kugus Ovin said pleasantly, "I know you're annoyed with me, Riquol, but I'm thinking of Auris and Ilf in this. Perhaps in your concern for the preservation of a natural phenomenon, you aren't sufficiently considering their interests."

Riquol looked at him, said, "When Auris reaches maturity, she'll be an extremely wealthy young woman, even if this farm never sells another cubic foot of diamondwood from this day on. Ilf would be sufficiently well-to-do to make it unnecessary for him ever to work a stroke in his life—though I doubt very much he would make such a choice."

Kugus smiled. "There are degrees even to the state of being extremely wealthy," he remarked. "What my niece can expect to gain in her lifetime from this careful harvesting you talk about can't begin to compare with what she would get at one stroke through Mr. Terokaw's offer. The same, of course, holds true of Ilf."

"Quite right," Mr. Terokaw said heavily. "I'm generous in my business dealings, Mr. Cholm. I have a reputation for it. And I can afford to be generous because I profit well from my investments. Let me bring another point to your attention. Interest in diamondwood products throughout the Federation waxes and wanes, as you must be aware. It rises and falls. There are fashions and fads. At present, we are approaching the crest of a new wave of interest in these products. This interest can be properly stimulated and exploited, but in any event we must expect it will have passed its peak in another few months. The next interest peak might develop six years from now, or twelve years from now. Or it might never develop since there are very few natural products which cannot eventually be duplicated and usually surpassed by artificial methods, and there is no good reason to assume that diamondwood will remain an exception indefinitely.

"We should be prepared, therefore, to make the fullest use of this bonanza while it lasts. I am prepared to do just that, Mr. Cholm. A cargo ship full of cutting equipment is at present stationed a few hours' flight from Wrake. This machinery can be landed and in operation here within a day after the contract I am offering you is signed. Within a week, the forest can be leveled. We shall make no use of your factory here, which would be entirely inadequate for my purpose. The diamondwood will be shipped at express speeds to another world where I have adequate processing facilities set up. And we can hit the Federation's main markets with the finished products the following month."

Riquol Cholm said, icily polite now, "And what would be the reason for all that haste, Mr. Terokaw?"

Mr. Terokaw looked surprised. "To insure that we have no competition, Mr. Cholm. What else? When the other diamondwood farmers here discover what has happened, they may be tempted to follow our example. But we'll be so far ahead of them that the diamondwood boom will be almost entirely to our exclusive advantage. We have taken every precaution to see that. Mr. Bliman, Mr. Ovin and I arrived here in the utmost secrecy today. No one so much as suspects that we are on Wrake, much less what our purpose is. I make no mistakes in such matters, Mr. Cholm!"

He broke off and looked around as Meldy Cholm said in a troubled voice, "Come in, children. Sit down over there. We're discussing a matter which concerns you."

"Hello, Auris!" Kugus said heartily. "Hello, Ilf! Remember old Uncle Kugus?"

"Yes," Ilf said. He sat down on the bench by the wall beside Auris, feeling scared.

"Auris," Riquol Cholm said, "did you happen to overhear anything of what was being said before you came into the room?"

Auris nodded. "Yes." She glanced at Mr. Terokaw, looked at Riquol again. "He wants to cut down the forest."

"It's your forest and Ilf's, you know. Do you want him to do it?"

"Mr. Cholm, please!" Mr. Terokaw protested. "We must approach this properly. Kugus, show Mr. Cholm what I'm offering."

Riquol took the document Kugus held out to him, looked over it. After a moment, he gave it back to Kugus. "Auris," he said, "Mr. Terokaw, as he's indicated, is offering you more money than you would ever be able to spend in your life for the right to cut down your share of the forest. Now . . . do you want him to do it?"

"No," Auris said.

Riquol glanced at Ilf, who shook his head. Riquol turned back to Mr. Terokaw.

"Well, Mr. Terokaw," he said, "there's your answer. My wife and I don't want you to do it, and Auris and Ilf don't want you to do it. Now . . . "

"Oh, come now, Riquol!" Kugus said, smiling. "No one can expect either Auris or Ilf to really understand what's involved here. When they come of age—"

"When they come of age," Riquol said, "they'll again have the opportunity to decide what they wish to do." He made a gesture of distaste. "Gentlemen, let's conclude this discussion. Mr. Terokaw, we thank you for your offer, but it's been rejected."

Mr. Terokaw frowned, pursed his lips.

"Well, not so fast, Mr. Cholm," he said. "As I told

you, I make no mistakes in business matters. You suggested a few minutes ago that I might contact the other diamondwood farmers on the planet on the subject but predicted that I would have no better luck with them."

"So I did," Riquol agreed. He looked puzzled.

"As a matter of fact," Mr. Terokaw went on, "I already have contacted a number of these people. Not in person, you understand, since I did not want to tip off certain possible competitors that I was interested in diamondwood at present. The offer was rejected, as you indicated it would be. In fact, I learned that the owners of the Wrake diamondwood farms are so involved in legally binding agreements with one another that it would be very difficult for them to accept such an offer even if they wished to do it."

Riquol nodded, smiled briefly. "We realized that the temptation to sell out to commercial interests who would not be willing to act in accordance with our accepted policies could be made very strong," he said. "So we've made it as nearly impossible as we could for any of us to yield to temptation."

"Well," Mr. Terokaw continued, "I am not a man who is easily put off. I ascertained that you and Mrs. Cholm are also bound by such an agreement to the other diamondwood owners of Wrake not to be the first to sell either the farm or its cutting rights to outside interests, or to exceed the established limits of cutting. But you are not the owners of this farm. These two children own it between them."

Riquol frowned. "What difference does that make?" he demanded. "Ilf is our grandson. Auris is related to us and our adopted daughter."

Mr. Terokaw rubbed his chin.

"Mr. Bliman," he said, "please explain to these people what the legal situation is."

✦   ✦   ✦

Mr. Bliman cleared his throat. He was a tall, thin man with fierce dark eyes, like a bird of prey. "Mr. and Mrs. Cholm," he began, "I work for the Federation Government and am a specialist in adoptive procedures. I will make this short. Some months ago, Mr. Kugus Ovin filed the necessary papers to adopt his niece, Auris Luteel, citizen of Wrake. I conducted the investigation which is standard in such cases and can assure you that no official record exists that you have at any time gone through the steps of adopting Auris."

"What?" Riquol came half to his feet. Then he froze in position for a moment, settled slowly back in his chair. "What is this? Just what kind of trick are you trying to play?" he said. His face had gone white.

Ilf had lost sight of Mr. Terokaw for a few seconds, because Uncle Kugus had suddenly moved over in front of the bench on which he and Auris were sitting. But now he saw him again and he had a jolt of fright. There was a large blue and silver gun in Mr. Terokaw's hand, and the muzzle of it was pointed very steadily at Riquol Cholm.

"Mr. Cholm," Mr. Terokaw said, "before Mr. Bliman concludes his explanation, allow me to caution you! I do not wish to kill you. This gun, in fact, is not designed to kill. But if I pull the trigger, you will be in excruciating pain for some minutes. You are an elderly man and it is possible that you would not survive the experience. This would not inconvenience us very seriously. Therefore, stay seated and give up any thoughts of summoning help . . . Kugus, watch the children. Mr. Bliman, let me speak to Mr. Het before you resume."

He put his left hand up to his face, and Ilf saw he was wearing a wrist-talker. "Het," Mr. Terokaw said to the talker without taking his eyes off Riquol Cholm, "you are aware, I believe, that the children are with us in the house?"

The wrist-talker made murmuring sounds for a few seconds, then stopped.

"Yes," Mr. Terokaw said. "There should be no problem about it. But let me know if you see somebody approaching the area . . . " He put his hand back down on the table. "Mr. Bliman, please continue."

Mr. Bliman cleared his throat again.

"Mr. Kugus Ovin," he said, "is now officially recorded as the parent by adoption of his niece, Auris Luteel. Since Auris has not yet reached the age where her formal consent to this action would be required, the matter is settled."

"Meaning," Mr. Terokaw added, "that Kugus can act for Auris in such affairs as selling the cutting rights on this tree farm. Mr. Cholm, if you are thinking of taking legal action against us, forget it. You may have had certain papers purporting to show that the girl was your adopted child filed away in the deposit vault of a bank. If so, those papers have been destroyed. With enough money, many things become possible. Neither you nor Mrs. Cholm nor the two children will do or say anything that might cause trouble to me. Since you have made no rash moves, Mr. Bliman will now use an instrument to put you and Mrs. Cholm painlessly to sleep for the few hours required to get you off this planet. Later, if you should be questioned in connection with this situation, you will say about it only what certain psychological experts will have impressed on you to say, and within a few months, nobody will be taking any further interest whatever in what is happening here today.

"Please do not think that I am a cruel man. I am not. I merely take what steps are required to carry out my purpose. Mr. Bliman, please proceed!"

Ilf felt a quiver of terror. Uncle Kugus was holding his wrist with one hand and Auris' wrist with the other, smiling reassuringly down at them. Ilf darted a glance over to Auris' face. She looked as white as his grandparents but she was making no attempt to squirm away from Kugus, so Ilf stayed quiet, too. Mr. Bliman stood up, looking more like a fierce bird of prey than ever, and stalked over to Riquol Cholm, holding something in his hand that looked unpleasantly like another gun. Ilf shut his eyes. There was a moment of silence, then Mr. Terokaw said, "Catch him before he falls out of the chair. Mrs. Cholm, if you will just settle back comfortably . . ."

There was another moment of silence. Then, from beside him, Ilf heard Auris speak.

It wasn't regular speech but a quick burst of thin, rattling gabble, like human speech speeded up twenty times or so. It ended almost immediately.

"What's that? What's that?" Mr. Terokaw said, surprised.

Ilf's eyes flew open as something came in through the window with a whistling shriek. The two humbugs were in the room, brown blurs flicking here and there, screeching like demons. Mr. Terokaw exclaimed something in a loud voice and jumped up from the chair, his gun swinging this way and that. Something scuttled up Mr. Bliman's back like a big spider, and he yelled and spun away from Meldy Cholm lying slumped back in her chair. Something ran up Uncle Kugus' back. He yelled, letting go of Ilf and Auris, and pulled out a gun of his own. "Wide aperture!" roared Mr. Terokaw, whose gun was making loud, thumping noises. A brown shadow swirled suddenly about his knees. Uncle Kugus cursed, took aim at the shadow and fired.

"Stop that, you fool!" Mr. Terokaw shouted. "You nearly hit me."

"Come," whispered Auris, grabbing Ilf's arm. They sprang up from the bench and darted out the door behind Uncle Kugus' broad back.

"Het!" Mr. Terokaw's voice came bellowing down the hall behind them. "Up in the air and look out for those children! They're trying to get away. If you see them start to cross the road, knock 'em out. Kugus—after them! They may try to hide in the house."

Then he yowled angrily, and his gun began making the thumping noises again. The humbugs were too small to harm people, but their sharp little teeth could hurt and they seemed to be using them now.

"In here," Auris whispered, opening a door. Ilf ducked into the room with her, and she closed the door softly behind them. Ilf looked at her, his heart pounding wildly.

Auris nodded at the barred window. "Through there! Run and hide in the grove. I'll be right behind you . . . "

"Auris! Ilf!" Uncle Kugus called in the hall. "Wait—don't be afraid. Where are you?" His voice still seemed to be smiling. Ilf heard his footsteps hurrying along the hall as he squirmed quickly sideways between two of the thick wooden bars over the window, dropped to the ground. He turned, darted off towards the nearest bushes.

He heard Auris gabble something to the humbugs again, high and shrill, looked back as he reached the bushes and saw her already outside, running towards the shrubbery on his right. There was a shout from the window. Uncle Kugus was peering out from behind the bars, pointing a gun at Auris. He fired. Auris swerved to the side, was gone among the shrubs. Ilf didn't think she had been hit.

"They're outside!" Uncle Kugus yelled. He was too big to get through the bars himself.

Mr. Terokaw and Mr. Bliman were also shouting within the house. Uncle Kugus turned around, disappeared from the window.

"Auris!" Ilf called, his voice shaking with fright.

"Run and hide, Ilf!" Auris seemed to be on the far side of the shrubbery, deeper in the Queen Grove.

Ilf hesitated, started running along the path that led to Sam's sleeping pit, glancing up at the open patches of sky among the treetops. He didn't see the aircar with the man Het in it. Het would be circling around the Queen Grove now, waiting for the other men to chase them into sight so he could knock them out with something. But they could hide inside Sam's shell and Sam would get them across the road. "Auris, where are you?" Ilf cried.

Her voice came low and clear from behind him. "Run and hide, Ilf!"

Ilf looked back. Auris wasn't there but the two humbugs were loping up the path a dozen feet away. They darted past Ilf without stopping, disappeared around the turn ahead. He could hear the three men yelling for him and Auris to come back. They were outside, looking around for them now, and they seemed to be coming closer.

Ilf ran on, reached Sam's sleeping place. Sam lay there unmoving, like a great mossy boulder filling the pit. Ilf picked up a stone and pounded on the front part of the shell.

"Wake up!" he said desperately. "Sam, wake up!"

Sam didn't stir. And the men were getting closer. Ilf looked this way and that, trying to decide what to do.

"Don't let them see you," Auris called suddenly.

"That was the girl over there," Mr. Terokaw's voice shouted. "Go after her, Bliman!"

"Auris, watch out!" Ilf screamed, terrified.

"Aha! And here's the boy, Kugus. This way! Het," Mr. Terokaw yelled triumphantly, "come down and help us catch them! We've got them spotted . . . "

Ilf dropped to hands and knees, crawled away quickly under the branches of the blue flower thicket and waited, crouched low. He heard Mr. Terokaw crashing through the bushes towards him and Mr. Bliman braying, "Hurry up, Het! Hurry up!" Then he heard something else. It was the sound the giant greenweb sometimes made to trick a flock of silverbells into fluttering straight towards it, a deep drone which suddenly seemed to be pouring down from the trees and rising up from the ground.

Ilf shook his head dizzily. The drone faded, grew up again. For a moment, he thought he heard his own voice call "Auris, where are you?" from the other side of the blue flower thicket. Mr. Terokaw veered off in that direction, yelling something to Mr. Bliman and Kugus. Ilf backed farther away through the thicket, came out on the other side, climbed to his feet and turned.

He stopped. For a stretch of twenty feet ahead of him, the forest floor was moving, shifting and churning with a slow, circular motion, turning lumps of deep brown mold over and over.

Mr. Terokaw came panting into Sam's sleeping place, red-faced, glaring about, the blue and silver gun in his hand. He shook his head to clear the resonance of the humming air from his brain. He saw a huge, moss-covered boulder tilted at a slant away from him but no sign of Ilf.

Then something shook the branches of the thicket behind the boulder. "Auris!" Ilf's frightened voice called.

Mr. Terokaw ran around the boulder, leveling the gun. The droning in the air suddenly swelled to a roar. Two big gray, three-fingered hands came out from the boulder on either side of Mr. Terokaw and picked him up.

"Awk!" he gasped, then dropped the gun as the hands folded him, once, twice, and lifted him towards Sam's descending head. Sam opened his large mouth, closed it, swallowed. His neck and head drew back under his shell and he settled slowly into the sleeping pit again.

The greenweb's roar ebbed and rose continuously now, like a thousand harps being struck together in a bewildering, quickening beat. Human voices danced and swirled through the din, crying, wailing, screeching. Ilf stood at the edge of the twenty-foot circle of churning earth outside the blue flower thicket, half stunned by it all. He heard Mr. Terokaw bellow to Mr. Bliman to go after Auris, and Mr. Bliman squalling to Het to hurry.

He heard his own voice nearby call Auris frantically
and then Mr. Terokaw's triumphant yell: "This way!
Here's the boy, Kugus!"

Uncle Kugus bounded out of some bushes thirty feet
away, eyes staring, mouth stretched in a wide grin. He
saw Ilf, shouted excitedly and ran towards him. Ilf
watched, suddenly unable to move. Uncle Kugus took
four long steps out over the shifting loam between them,
sank ankle-deep, knee-deep. Then the brown earth
leaped in cascades about him, and he went sliding
straight down into it as if it were water, still grinning,
and disappeared.

In the distance, Mr. Terokaw roared, "This way!"
and Mr. Bliman yelled to Het to hurry up. A loud,
slapping sound came from the direction of the stump
of the Grandfather Slurp. It was followed by a great
commotion in the bushes around there; but that only
lasted a moment. Then, a few seconds later, the
greenweb's drone rose and thinned to the wild shriek
it made when it had caught something big and faded
slowly away . . .

Ilf came walking shakily through the opening in the
thickets to Sam's sleeping place. His head still seemed
to hum inside with the greenweb's drone but the Queen
Grove was quiet again; no voices called anywhere. Sam
was settled into his pit. Ilf saw something gleam on the
ground near the front end of the pit. He went over and
looked at it, then at the big, moss-grown dome of Sam's
shell.

"Oh, Sam," he whispered, "I'm not sure we should
have done it . . ."

Sam didn't stir. Ilf picked up Mr. Terokaw's blue and
silver gun gingerly by the barrel and went off with it
to look for Auris. He found her at the edge of the
grove, watching Het's aircar on the other side of the
road. The aircar was turned on its side and about a
third of it was sunk in the ground. At work around and

below it was the biggest member of the clean-up squad Ilf had ever seen in action.

They went up to the side of the road together and looked on while the aircar continued to shudder and turn and sink deeper into the earth. Ilf suddenly remembered the gun he was holding and threw it over on the ground next to the aircar. It was swallowed up instantly there. Tumbleweeds came rolling up to join them and clustered around the edge of the circle, waiting. With a final jerk, the aircar disappeared. The disturbed section of earth began to smooth over. The tumbleweeds moved out into it.

There was a soft whistling in the air, and from a Queen Tree at the edge of the grove a hundred and fifty feet away, a diamondwood seedling came lancing down, struck at a slant into the center of the circle where the aircar had vanished, stood trembling a moment, then straightened up. The tumbleweeds nearest it moved respectfully aside to give it room. The seedling shuddered and unfolded its first five-fingered cluster of silver-green leaves. Then it stood still.

Ilf looked over at Auris. "Auris," he said, "should we have done it?"

Auris was silent a moment.

"Nobody did anything," she said then. "They've just gone away again." She took Ilf's hand. "Let's go back to the house and wait for Riquol and Meldy to wake up."

The organism that was the diamondwood forest grew quiet again. The quiet spread back to its central mind unit in the Queen Grove, and the unit began to relax towards somnolence. A crisis had been passed—perhaps the last of the many it had foreseen when human beings first arrived on the world of Wrake.

The only defense against Man was Man. Understanding that, it had laid its plans. On a world now owned by Man, it adopted Man, brought him into its ecology, and its ecology into a new and again successful balance.

This had been a final flurry. A dangerous attack by dangerous humans. But the period of danger was nearly over, would soon be for good a thing of the past.

It had planned well, the central mind unit told itself drowsily. But now, since there was no further need to think today, it would stop thinking . . .

Sam the mossback fell gratefully asleep.

A Nice Day for Screaming

As soon as the Marsar Shift began, Adacee newscaster Keth Deboll had the feeling that he wasn't going to like this assignment. In part, it might be simply a reaction to the pitch-blackness which closed down instantly on the pseudospace ship. He knew the lights in the personnel section around him were on. Yet not the faintest glow was visible anywhere—not even from Furnay's control console directly before him. It was the deadest, emptiest black he had ever experienced . . . the kind of black that might be left after the Universe ended. The thought came suddenly that, if he had to stay in it for any length of time, it would drain everything out of him and leave him sitting here, an empty, black shell, as dead as the rest of it.

However, the shift wouldn't last long. The Navy men with whom Keth Deboll had talked during his briefing the day before had emphasized the eerie aspects of Space Three, no doubt deliberately. Keth knew he wasn't welcome on board, and he couldn't have cared less. It had taken a great deal of maneuvering and string-pulling by the Adacee News Viewer System to get him the assignment on one of the fourteen pseudospace ships presently in operation. The Navy wanted more money for its enormously expensive Space Three projects; and in the end the argument had prevailed that the best way to get popular support for their wishes was to have a popular newscaster provide an enthusiastic, first-hand projected report on one of the sorties into pseudospace. And there were simply no more popular newscasters in the Federation that year than Keth Deboll.

But the men he would actually be on shipboard with hadn't liked the arrangement much, especially the provision that Keth was to have the run of the ship insofar as he didn't interfere with operations. And like many other people who dealt with him in person, they might not have cared much for Keth. He was undersized and thin, still on the young side but already—since he lived well— sporting a small, round paunch. A point which seemed to irk the Navy scientists in particular was that he hadn't bothered to take notes on the information they had given him for the telecast. Keth never did take notes, of course; he had nearly perfect recall. But they didn't know that.

There was a brief, sharp tingling in the palm of his right hand—a signal from Furnay, his technician, that the telecast, which would be transmitted to normspace by special Navy communicators, was beginning; and Keth automatically began to talk . . .

As usual, he didn't pay much attention to what he was saying. It wasn't necessary. The relevant material was stored in his mind, already arranged into a number of variant patterns. Depending on the circumstances, it would emerge in one sequence or another, always coherently, smoothly, effectively. He discovered he had started now with the statement that this was another milestone in newscasting history—the first direct report from pseudospace or Space Three. They were shifting at the moment into the field of an entirely new class of energies, a region where space appeared to exist only as a useful symbol, or as an illusionary medium in the recording instruments. The discovery of pseudospace five years ago had been a triumph of human ingenuity; its existence had been established by the calculations of Navy mathematicians, and the means of contacting it derived from those same calculations. Since then two new mathematical systems already had been developed to provide even a theoretical understanding of the problems encountered in the further exploration of this weird new stratum of the Universe.

He turned briefly to technicalities. They would remain in pseudospace for the period of one hour less a few minutes, in a Navy ship especially designed and constructed to permit even temporary existence there. Aside from the standard drives, it was equipped with an engine which made the shift possible. This engine would be shut off as soon as the shift was accomplished, would be turned on again ten minutes before the scheduled return because it took five minutes to build up the required power for the shift. One hour was at present the maximum period a ship could remain safely in Space Three.

The shift engine would be shut off for the curious reason that although motion *in* Space Three was impossible, motion relative to normal space and subspace *while* in Space Three was not only possible but greatly augmented. What produced it was any use of energy by the intruding vessel. The result was that a pseudospace ship always emerged into normspace again at a point removed from its point of entry—and at a distance far greater than it could otherwise have covered by the full use of standard drive engines in the same period of time. The potential value of this phenomenon for space travel was obvious; but at present there was no fixed ratio between the energy expended by a ship and the distance it moved, and the direction in which it would move was equally unpredictable. Many of the multiple studies programmed for today's one-hour shift were designed to yield additional information on precisely those points.

Their shift had been initiated in the vicinity of Orado. They would release an exceptional amount of energy because of a demonstration graciously prepared by the Navy to illustrate certain interesting qualities of pseudo-space to Adacee's billions of viewers. So all they knew definitely was that when they emerged again, they would find themselves somewhere within the space boundaries of the Federation. The exact location would be determined after they had arrived.

Keth Deboll came to that point at the instant the Marsar Shift ended and the ship lights reappeared. He hadn't consciously planned it that way; but he'd been told how long the shift would take, and the material stored in his mind had re-sorted itself so that he'd have the preliminary explanations cleared up when the moment came.

He went on without a break into the next part. In a moment the vision screens would go on. He and Furnay had been provided with a smaller duplicate of the main screen at the far end of the personnel section; and Adacee's viewers would get the first live look afforded the general public of the instruments' rendition of a nonspatial energy field. They would be seeing something no eyes had seen, or could have seen, before Man's supreme intelligence, determination and courage found a way to begin to map Space Three—perhaps eventually to make use of it.

The illusionary medium of Space Three appeared abruptly. Keth's stomach seemed to turn over twice. He had the feeling that he was being pulled painlessly but inexorably apart. His mouth went on talking but he hadn't the faintest idea now of what he said. The medium was a bright pink and white, gave the impression of vast but unstable depth. The colors shifted in slowly changing patterns. Something like a transparent vapor streamed by from right to left—Keth had the impression it was a considerable distance away—like clouds moving across a summer sky. Of course, "distance" had no actual meaning here.

And neither, his voice reminded the viewers, did the word "cold" retain its familiar meaning in Space Three. It was cold beyond any previous understanding of the term, not merely in the sense of an utter absence of heat, but cold on the ascending scale, so to speak—cold above cold above cold.

This was the great hazard of Space Three, the factor which would have made it impenetrable, if its existence had been known, to life before Man. For the reason Man could penetrate it was the great discovery of the Marsar Field . . .

This whole universe-of-the-moment, Keth decided, was being twisted slowly in two directions at once! Not only Space Three in the screen, but the pseudospace ship itself, and he and Furnay in the seat beside him. He couldn't actually see anything to tell him why he knew that, but he knew it, and it was an extraordinarily unpleasant thing to know. He heard Furnay swallowing noisily—no harm done, the filters would catch it—and began to wish he had eaten a less healthy breakfast an hour ago . . .

The Marsar Energy Field, his voice was continuing smoothly, coated the outer boxlike hull of the pseudospace ship. The personnel section in the center of the ship, where they now were, was another box, separated from the other compartments of the ship by gravity pressors. In other words, the personnel section was suspended, floating free within the ship; and it also was coated with the Field.

This was a very necessary precaution because the Marsar Field was the only thing which stood now between them and the ultimate cold of Space Three—and it would be demonstrated immediately what that ultracold did to objects from normal space which lacked the Field's protection . . .

Keth had come to his feet, still speaking, and was moving along an open aisle toward an adjoining part of the personnel section. He wasn't concerned about getting beyond the range of the instruments; it was Furnay's department to cover him wherever he was in the ship, and Furnay would do it. He stopped at another screen where two Navy technicians were sitting. The expectancy in their faces as he approached had told him they were hoping for signs that Space Three was churning the unwelcome guest's brain along with assorted other innards; so he flashed them the famous Keth Deboll grin without interrupting his easy flow of talk. They swung back disappointedly to their switches and buttons.

"And these are the two gentlemen selected to carry out the demonstration . . . " Keth gave their full names, which shook them a little, went on explaining each move they made as they made it, never at a loss, never hesitant, enjoying his control of the situation and of the continuing awful feeling of internal and external distortion . . .

The pseudospace ship had brought another vessel into Space Three with it—a chunky, old-fashioned siege boat, of no greater length than a destroyer but covered with armor of the densest, toughest workable material known, designed to move in against the fire of heavy planet-based guns and remain operational. Unmanned because it was to be sacrificed now for the benefit of Adacee's viewers, it hung in the screen, gradually increasing in size. The two ships were in motion relative both to normal space and to each other, Keth explained—the siege boat only because its Marsar Field and the shift engine with which it had been equipped were giving off energy while the pseudospace ship was additionally using its standard drives to maneuver closer to the intended victim . . . but not too close because any contact with another solid object would collapse its Marsar Field—

Two devices had appeared in the screen about midway between the two ships, and Keth's description slid over to them, quickening. Telecontrolled projectile guns, each balancing a detached four-inch steel sphere in its launching field, spheres and guns both shielded by the Marsar effect, of course . . . and now one had veered about, his voice announced, rising in excitement, had aimed at the doomed siege boat, and the sphere was launched.

Close-up of a steel ball seemingly motionless against the frozen pink and white of pseudospace, then the armored flank of the siege boat swinging into view, swinging in toward it. The four-inch missile struck and adhered.

The close-up flowed out, became the previous picture, now including the projected image of a huge transparent time dial, a second hand sweeping around through its ten marked sections. As the hand touched the tenth mark, the dial vanished, the other projectile gun swerved, and the second steel ball was launched. Keth abruptly stopped speaking.

This time, there was no close-up. A moment passed; and then the siege boat shattered.

It was not a violent process but an awesomely quiet one. Cracks flicked about the massively armored hull, joined and deepened. The boat began to drift apart in sections, each section splitting again and again as it came separate. For an instant, the shift engine showed, protected by its own Marsar and pressor fields from the debacle around it, then vanished, on its way back to normspace. Keth felt a stab of annoyance. The Navy had insisted on salvaging the engine, and its intact appearance meant a fractional loss in overall effect.

But otherwise the picture of absolute destruction was complete. Chunks of battle-armor capable of resisting the pounding of ultrabeams continued to crack into fragments, fragments splintered into dust, Keth's voice quietly accompanying the siege boat's destruction. For a moment, a glittering fog, which still retained a suggestion of the vessel's outlines, was visible; then Space Three was clear again. Probably not one in a million of Adacee's viewers had noticed the simultaneous dissolution of the projectile guns, triggered off from the pseudospace ship.

And this was the explanation for the dual protection given the personnel section, Keth continued. If, for any reason, their ship's outer Marsar Field should fail . . . and Marsar Fields had been known to fail for reasons never explained . . . the rest of the ship would, within seconds, become a homogenous, brittle-frozen mass. But the personnel section would remain intact within its own field, and since it contained the shift engine, it could be brought back by itself to normal space to await the arrival of rescue ships.

In spite of such precautions, one pseudospace ship not too long ago had simply stopped communicating and disappeared during a shift. Space Three remained a medium of both unfathomed opportunities and unfathomed dangers, and until . . .

Keth again stopped listening to what he was saying. It was familiar ground: a pitch for money. The Navy was getting what it had paid for by providing the stage for a Deboll newscast while Keth moved toward the instrument room at the far end of the section. There he would introduce several scientists, question them individually about their specialties, then switch back to a few minor demonstrations . . . and, blessedly, the gruesome hour would be over.

A sharp whisper suddenly beside his left ear. "Keth! Get back here!"

What did Furnay want? Keth turned, started back toward the technician, not too hurriedly, mind racing. His

commentary veered off from the interviews toward which
it had been leading, took a new tack which would provide
an opening for whatever had caught Furnay's attention.
Whatever had caused that interruption could be no minor
matter.

As he slid into his seat before the screen, Furnay's
filtered voice said hurriedly on his left, "That dot in the
upper right corner! It appeared just a moment ago and
it's getting larger fast—"

Keth's eyes flicked over the screen, found the dot.
More than a dot . . . an irregular little dark blotch against
the blazing white of Space Three, changing shape constantly and expanding visibly as he stared at it. For
an instant, he felt cold fury. They hadn't mentioned
anything like this in yesterday's briefing, and in seconds
he'd have to be talking about it, explaining it glibly! His
hand already had pressed a button on the little intercom
rod in his pocket which would connect him with one
of the observers at the big screen, the man who was
standing by to fill in if Keth felt unable to interpret
what the screens showed.

He hadn't expected to use that button . . . and now
the fool didn't respond! He pressed again, repeatedly,
ragingly.

A loud voice announced:

"Emergency stations! Repeat—emergency stations!
Unidentified object approaching . . . "

Keth drew a sharp breath. *They* didn't know what
it was! A new Space Three phenomenon in the middle
of the newscast—what a break! WHAT a break! He
swung into the situation instantly, opening the pickup
filters, which had been blurring out irrelevant sounds,
and every intercom, catching commands and responses
crossing the personnel section his voice running along with
them, expanding, improvising . . . The drive engines
came on with a muted roar; the pseudospace ship
moved away, out of the course of the unknown object

which had been headed directly towards them—and which, thirty seconds later, *again* was headed directly towards them. The ship suddenly picked up speed in dead earnest.

They had turned on the shift engine, Keth announced to Adacee's viewers, voice shaking with excitement; but of course, it would take five minutes for the engine to develop enough power to permit their return to normal space. Meanwhile the blob, the blotch—the unidentified object—now four or five inches across in the screen— was sliding sideways out of sight as the ship turned away from it. It was still vague . . . objects more than two miles apart in normspace terms could not be clearly defined in pseudospace; but there was a suggestion, more than a suggestion, of bunched tentacles trailing from that shifting shape. It definitely, almost definitely, was following them—

Furnay was stabbing buttons desperately, as the object vanished from the screen, to get them switched over to another one where it would be visible again. The Adacee feedback tinkle sounded in Keth's left ear; a jubilant voice whispered, "Terrific, Deboll! Terrific! None of us can imagine how you did it, but keep the thing running! The interest indicator jumped to absolute top in less than thirty seconds and is staying right there. You sound scared to death!"

He *was* scared to death, Keth discovered. His knees rattled together whenever they came within four inches of each other . . . And now the screen blinked twice and shifted to a slightly different view of pseudospace.

"AWK!" Furnay said hoarsely.

The pursuing object couldn't be much more than two *miles* behind them now because its details were trembling on the verge of becoming discernible. Only two miles, Keth repeated, stunned, to himself—with the ship roaring along on its space drive!

And with that, the personnel section went black.

❖   ❖   ❖

Keth heard a thump beside him, put out his hand and found Furnay collapsed forward on the control console. He wasn't sure whether the technician had fainted or not, and he started shaking him by the shoulder. The intercom was still full of voices and his own voice was continuing automatically. "We have begun the Marsar Shift! Apparently, we escaped with only seconds to spare! What this . . ."

"Mr. Deboll," the intercom told him sharply, "the newscast was cut off twenty seconds ago! Communications is pre-empting all channels until we have completed the shift to normspace and established our new location there."

Twenty seconds ago would have been the instant they entered the shift. Oh, not bad, Keth thought giddily. Not bad at all! The last impression Adacee's viewers had been given was of that horrific unknown pursuer closing in. And now minutes of silence before the ship's escape was confirmed—it would be the sensation of the month!

"Shift ending," the intercom said. "Remain at your stations . . ."

The lights came on. The screen before Keth remained black for an instant. Then something flickered in it, and he was looking out at clouds and rivers of blazing stars.

Somebody cheered. After that, there was a dead stillness for perhaps half a second . . .

Somebody else yelled hoarsely. Keth shot up half out of his seat, stayed crouched, bent forward, staring at the screen.

The stars on the right were being obscured by a darkness which came flowing out over them . . . a darkness which extended broad, whipping tendrils and grew, covering half the screen, two thirds of it. Voices were shouting, and at the last moment, before the screen was completely blanked out, Keth glimpsed something like a section of a huge, rubbery tube swinging down toward him through space.

The personnel section seemed to slue around. The deck came up under Keth, threw him stumbling half across Furnay. He grasped the technician's shoulders to right himself.

"Main drive dead!" the intercom bellowed incredulously.

There was the sluing motion again, this time in reversed direction. For a moment, stars reappeared in one corner of the screen, racing through it—as if, Keth thought, the ship were spinning wildly through space. The deck heaved. He staggered, pitched forward, then back, tripped and went down. Something hard slammed the side of his head, and his mind went blank.

"He's coming around now," Furnay's voice was saying. "Hey, Keth, wake up!"

Keth opened his eyes. He was lying in the seat before the screen, tilted backward. Furnay was on one side of him, somebody else stood on the other side. He jerked his head up to look at the screen. It was full of stars.

"What's happened?" he gasped.

"We're no longer in danger, Mr. Deboll," the other man said reassuringly. He was in his shirt sleeves and closing a flat container full of medical instruments. "Exactly what did happen isn't at all clear, but we should know shortly."

"Captain Roan," the intercom said, "please come to Station Three at once!"

The man smiled at Keth, said to Furnay: "He'll be all right now," and hurried off with his container.

"That's the doctor," Furnay said. "You cut your head pretty bad, but he sealed it." Furnay looked pale and shaken. "That thing, whatever it was, went back to Space Three. Or at least, it's gone. I came to in the middle of it all, while it was coming aboard . . ."

"Coming aboard?" Keth repeated blankly. "You were hallucinating, Furnay. That thing was a hundred times bigger than this ship! I saw part of it close up."

"Well, something came on board," Furnay said doggedly. "Ask anybody. First there was an awful banging over the intercom from somewhere else on the ship. Then somebody yelled that all three ship locks were being opened."

"From outside?"

Furnay looked at him. "Keth, nobody here was opening them, believe me! Then there was more banging here and there for a while. They were trying to find out what was going on out there, of course, but the intership screens were too blurred to make out anything. That went on for a while." Furnay wet his lips. "Then the lock to the personnel section began to open . . . "

"*Huh?*"

"That's right," Furnay said. "It came right in here."

"*What* came right in here?" Keth demanded savagely.

The technician spread his hands. "Nobody really got a look at it, Keth! The air sort of got thick—not to breathe; it was more like you were trying to look through syrup. Same thing that had been blurring the intership screens apparently. It only lasted about a minute. Then the air turned clear and the lock here closed. Maybe a minute later, the ship screens cleared, and the three big locks all closed together. Nobody had seen anything. Right after that, everything went black again."

"Marsar Shift black, you mean?"

Furnay nodded. "We were shifting to Space Three. That seems to be why it came in here—to start the shift engine. But somebody reversed the field right away and we came back to normspace. The thing was gone, and the main problem now seems to be that our space drive is almost out. We're barely able to move. But the transmitters started working again . . . "

"They were out?" Keth asked.

"They went blank about the time the drive engines stopped," Furnay said. "Then, as soon as the thing left, they started up again. The communication boys called for help, and there's a Space Scout squadron four days away headed toward us now . . . "

"Four *days* away?"

"Well, we're way outside of the Hub. That five-minute run on full drive, while the shift engine was warming up, brought on the biggest Space Three jump ever recorded . . . Where are you going?"

Keth was climbing to his feet. "Where do you think? We still have a newscast running. I'm going to get hold of the brass, find out exactly what they know, and get Communication to release a channel so we can start beaming it back. This is the biggest . . . "

"Wait a minute, Keth!" Furnay looked worried. "This is a Navy ship and we're operating under emergency regulations at the moment." He nodded at the open personnel section lock fifty feet away. "The brass is outside in the ship, checking things over. Everyone else has been ordered to remain at their stations. And they figure this is our station."

Keth grunted irritably, looked around. A gold-braided jacket and cap lay across a chair a few feet away. He went over, glanced around again, put them on.

"They're the doctor's," Furnay said.

"He won't miss them. Sit tight here."

Keth walked down the aisle toward a food dispenser fifteen feet from the open lock. The borrowed jacket and cap were decidedly too big for him, and from moment to moment he was in partial view of various groups in the section; but everyone was too involved in discussing recent events to pay him much attention. He paused at the dispenser, punched a button at random and received a tube of liquid vitamins. Half turning, he flicked a glance from under the cap brim about the part of the section he could see, moved on to the lock and stepped quietly through it.

There was no one in sight on the other side. He

turned to the right along the passage through which he and Furnay had been conducted to the personnel section a little over an hour ago. The main entrance lock was just beyond its far end, out of sight. He might find something there to tell him how to get to the engine room. Since they were having trouble with the drives, that was presumably where the investigating senior officers would be.

At the end of the passage, he stopped, startled. The lock room was almost entirely filled with an assortment of items he found himself unable to identify. One wall was lined to the ceiling with luminous hexagonal boxes arranged like a honeycomb. Against them leaned bundled extrusions which looked like steel with bubbles of light trickling slowly through it. Completely blocking the lock was a great mass of rainbow-colored globes two feet in diameter, which appeared to be stuck together. The weirdest item was stacked by the hundreds along the left wall . . . transparent plastic blocks, each containing something which looked partly like a long-haired gloomy monkey and partly like a caterpillar.

Keth blinked at the arrangement, mouth open, for a moment, went over and touched a finger gingerly against one of the globes. It felt warm—around a hundred and ten degrees, he decided. Scowling and muttering to himself, he went off down another passage.

He passed a closed door, hesitated, returned and opened it. The area beyond was filled about equally by transparent sacks, bulging with what looked like white diamonds, and large, dark-red cylinders. The cylinders were groaning softly. Keth closed the door, opened another one thirty feet farther on, glanced in and hurriedly slammed it shut. He walked on, shaking his head, his mouth working nervously.

A minute or two later, he saw a sign which said ENGINE ROOM—MAINTENANCE above an opened lock. Keth entered, found himself on the upper level of the engine room with a spider web of catwalks running here and there about the machinery. From below came the sound of voices.

He edged out on one of the catwalks, peered down. Half a dozen men, two of them in uniform, stood about an open hatch from which another uniformed man, the engineering officer, was just emerging. These were the ship's senior officers, and every one of them, Keth reminded himself, was also one of the Federation Navy's top scientists. They were too far off to let him understand what they were talking about, but if he got within hearing range without being discovered, he should gather information they wouldn't volunteer for the purposes of a newscast. He drew back out of sight, located a ladder along the wall and climbed down to the main level.

Guided by their voices, he threaded his way among the machines toward the group. There was a sudden, loud slam—the hatch being closed again. Then the voices were coming toward him on the other side of the massive steel bole along which he had been moving. Keth flattened himself quickly into a shallow niche of the machine, stayed still.

They came out into an intersection of passages on Keth's left and stopped there. He held his breath. If they looked over at him now, they couldn't miss seeing him. But the engineering officer was speaking and their attention was on him.

"Up to a point," he was saying, "the matter is now clear. It removed our fuel plates and replaced them with its own . . ."

Keth's ears seemed to flick forwards. What was that? His thoughts began to race.

"Those plates," the man went on, "are producing energy. In fact, they have a really monstrous output. But the energy doesn't do much for our drives. In some way, almost all of it is being diverted, dissipated, shunted off somewhere else."

"There's no immediate explanation for that, but it isn't a practical problem. We'll simply shut off the drives, pull out the plates and put our own back again. We'll be docking at the station in a week. If we had to use this stuff, it would take us half a dozen years to crawl back to the Hub under our own power."

"In normspace," another man said.

"Yes, in normspace. In pseudo, naturally, it would be a very different matter."

The ship captain scratched his chin, remarked, "In pseudo, if your figures on the output are correct, those plates might have carried us out of the galaxy in a matter of hours."

"Depending on the course we took," the engineering officer agreed.

There was a pause. Then somebody said, "When we were maneuvering to get the siege boat in range, we may have been moving along, or nearly along, one of the scheduled courses. That and our slow speed would have been the signal . . . "

"It seems to explain it," the engineering officer said. He added, "A point I still don't understand is why we didn't lose our atmosphere in the process! We're agreed that the fact we were aboard would have had no meaning for the thing—it was a detail it simply wouldn't register. Yet there has been no drop in pressure."

Another man said dryly, "But it isn't quite the same atmosphere! I've found a substantially higher oxygen reading. I think it will be discovered that some of the objects it left on board—I suspect those in the lock room in particular—contain life in one form or another, and that it's oxygen-breathing life."

"That may have been a very fortunate circumstance for us," the captain said. "And . . . " His eyes had shifted along the passage, stopped now on Keth. He paused.

"Well," he said mildly, "it seems we have company! It's the gentleman from the newscast system."

The others looked around in surprise.

"Mr. Deboll," the captain went on thoughtfully, "I take it you overheard our discussion just now."

Keth cleared his throat. "Yes," he said. He took off the medical officer's cap.

"You came down here by way of the main lock passage?"

"Yes."

There was silence for a moment. Then the engineering officer said, "As I see it, no harm has been done." He looked rather pleased.

"Quite the contrary, in my opinion!" said the captain. He smiled at Keth. "Mr. Deboll please join our group. In observing you during yesterday's briefing, I was struck by your quickness in grasping the essentials of a situation. No doubt, you already have realized what the explanation for this extraordinary series of events must be."

"Yes, I have," Keth said hoarsely.

"Excellent. Our instructions are that we must not interfere in any way with your report to the public. Now I have a feeling that what you will have to say may be a definite upset to those who have maintained the exploratory Space Three projects should be limited or abandoned because of their expense, and because no information of practical value could possibly be gained from them."

"My guess is you'll get anything you want for them now," Keth told him.

The captain grinned. "Then let's return to the personnel section and get that newscast going!"

They started back to the engine room entrance Keth mentally phrasing the manner in which he would explain to Adacee's waiting billions of viewers that the pseudospace ship—one of Man's great achievements—had been halted, engulfed, checked, fueled, loaded up and released by somebody else's automatic depot and service station for intergalactic robot cargo carriers.

The Winds of Time

Gefty Rammer came along the narrow passages between the *Silver Queen's* control compartment and the staterooms, trying to exchange the haggard look on his face for one of competent self-assurance. There was nothing to gain by letting his two passengers suspect that during the past few minutes their pilot, the owner of Rammer Spacelines, had been a bare step away from plain and fancy gibbering.

He opened the door to Mr. Maulbow's stateroom and went inside. Mr. Maulbow, face very pale, eyes closed, lay on his back on the couch, still unconscious. He'd been knocked out when some unknown forces suddenly started batting the *Silver Queen's* turnip shape around as the *Queen* had never been batted before in her eighteen years of spacefaring. Kerim Ruse, Maulbow's secretary, knelt beside her employer, checking his pulse. She looked anxiously up at Gefty.

"What did you find out?" she asked in a voice that was not very steady.

Gefty shrugged. "Nothing definite as yet. The ship hasn't been damaged—she's a tough tub. That's one good point. Otherwise . . . well, I climbed into a suit and took a look out the escape hatch. And I saw the same thing there that the screens show. Whatever that is."

"You've no idea then of what's happened to us, or where we are?" Miss Ruse persisted. She was a rather small girl with large, beautiful gray eyes and thick blue-black hair. At the moment, she was barefoot and in a sleeping outfit which consisted of something soft wrapped around her top, soft and floppy trousers below. The black hair was tousled and she looked around fifteen. She'd been asleep in her stateroom when something smacked the *Queen*, and she was sensible enough then not to climb out of the bunk's safety field until the ship finally stopped shuddering and bucking about. That made her the only one of the three persons aboard who had collected no bruises. She was scared, of course, but taking the situation very well.

Gefty said carefully, "There're a number of possibilities. It's obvious that the *Queen* has been knocked out of normspace, and it may take some time to find out how to get her back there. But the main thing is that the ship's intact. So far, it doesn't look too bad."

Miss Ruse seemed somewhat reassured. Gefty could hardly have said the same for himself. He was a qualified normspace and subspace pilot. He had put in a hitch with the Federation Navy, and for the past eight years he'd been ferrying his own two ships about the Hub and not infrequently beyond the Federation's space territories, but he had never heard of a situation like this. What he saw in the viewscreens when the ship steadied enough to let him pick himself off the instrument room floor, and again, a few minutes later and with much more immediacy, from the escape hatch, made no sense—seemed simply to have no meaning. The pressure meters said there was a vacuum outside the *Queen's* skin. That vacuum was dark, even pitch-black but here and there came momentary suggestions of vague light and color. Occasional pinpricks of brightness showed and were gone. And there had been one startling phenomenon like a distant, giant explosion, a sudden pallid glare in the dark, which appeared far ahead of the *Queen* and, for the instant it remained in sight, seemed to be rushing directly towards them. It had given Gefty the feeling that the ship itself was plowing at high speed through this eerie medium. But he had cut the *Queen's* drives to the merest idling pulse as soon as he staggered back to the control console and got his first look at the screens, so it must have been the light that had moved.

But such details were best not discussed with a passenger. Kerim Ruse would be arriving at enough disquieting speculations on her own; the less he told her, the better. There was the matter of the ship's location instruments. The only set Gefty had been able to obtain any reading on were the direction indicators. And what they appeared to indicate was that the *Silver Queen* was turning on a new heading something like twenty times a second.

Gefty asked, "Has Mr. Maulbow shown any signs of waking up?"

Kerim shook her head. "His breathing and pulse seem all right, and that bump on his head doesn't look really bad, but he hasn't moved at all. Can you think of anything else we might do for him, Gefty?"

"Not at the moment," Gefty said. "He hasn't broken any bones. We'll see how he feels when he comes out of it." He was wondering about Mr. Maulbow and the fact that this charter had showed some unusual features from the beginning.

Kerim was a friendly sort of girl; they'd got to calling each other by their first names within a day or two after the trip started. But after that, she seemed to be avoiding him; and Gefty guessed that Maulbow had spoken to her, probably to make sure that Kerim didn't let any of her employer's secrets slip out.

Maulbow himself was as aloof and taciturn a client as Rammer Spacelines ever had picked up. A lean, blond character of indeterminate age, with pale eyes, hard mouth. Why he had selected a bulky semi-freighter like the *Queen* for a mineralogical survey jaunt to a lifeless little sun system far beyond the outposts of civilization was a point he didn't discuss. Gefty, needing the charter money, had restrained his curiosity. If Maulbow wanted only a pilot and preferred to do all the rest of the work himself, that was certainly Maulbow's affair. And if he happened to be up to something illegal—though it was difficult to imagine what—Customs would nail him when they got back to the Hub.

But those facts looked a little different now.

Gefty scratched his chin, inquired, "Do you happen to know where Mr. Maulbow keeps the keys to the storage vault?"

Kerim looked startled. "Why, no! I couldn't permit you to take the keys anyway while he . . . while he's unconscious! You know that."

Gefty grunted. "Any idea of what he has locked up in the vault?"

"You shouldn't ask me—" Her eyes widened. "Why, that couldn't possibly have anything to do with what's happened!"

He might, Gefty thought, have reassured her a little too much. He said, "I wouldn't know. But I don't want to just sit here and wonder about it until Maulbow wakes up. Until we're back in normspace, we'd better not miss any bets. Because one thing's sure—if this has happened to anybody else, they didn't turn up again to report it. You see?"

Kerim apparently did. She went pale, then said

hesitantly, "Well . . . the sealed cases Mr. Maulbow brought out from the Hub with him had some very expensive instruments in them. That's all I know. He's always trusted me not to pry into his business any more than my secretarial duties required, and of course I haven't."

"You don't know then what it was he brought up from that moon a few hours ago—those two big cases he stowed away in the vault?"

"No, I don't, Gefty. You see, he hasn't told me what the purpose of this trip is. I only know that it's a matter of great importance to him." Kerim paused, added, "From the careful manner Mr. Maulbow handled the cases with the cranes, I had the impression that whatever was inside them must be quite heavy."

"I noticed that," Gefty said. It wasn't much help. "Well, I'll tell you something now," he went on. "I let your boss keep both sets of keys to the storage vault because he insisted on it when he signed the charter. What I didn't tell him was that I could make up a duplicate set any time in around half an hour."

"Oh! Have you—?"

"Not yet. But I intend to take a look at what Mr. Maulbow's got in that vault now, with or without his consent. You'd better run along and get dressed while I take him up to the instrument room."

"Why move him?" Kerim asked.

"The instrument room's got an overall safety field. I've turned it on now, and if something starts banging us around again, the room will be the safest place on the ship. I'll bring his personal luggage up too, and you can start looking through it for the keys. You may find them before I get a new set made. Or he may wake up and tell us where they are."

Kerim Ruse gave her employer a dubious glance, then nodded, said, "I imagine you're right, Gefty," and pattered hurriedly out of the stateroom. A few minutes later, she arrived, fully dressed, in the instrument room. Gefty looked around from the tableshelf where he had laid out his tools, and said, "He hasn't stirred. His suitcases are over there. I've unlocked them."

Kerim gazed at what showed in the screens about the control console and shivered slightly. She said, "I was thinking, Gefty . . . isn't there something they call Space Three?"

"Sure. Pseudospace. But that isn't where we are. There're some special-built Navy tubs that can operate in that stuff if they don't stay too long. A ship like the *Queen* . . . well, you and I and everything else in here would be frozen solid by now if we'd got sucked somehow into Space Three."

"I see," Kerim said uncomfortably. Gefty heard her move over to the suitcases. After a moment, she asked, "What do the vault keys look like?"

"You can't miss them if he's just thrown them in there. They're over six inches long. What kind of a guy is this Maulbow? A scientist?"

"I couldn't say, Gefty. He's never referred to himself as a scientist. I've had this job a year and a half. Mr. Maulbow is a very considerate employer . . . one of the nicest men I've known, really. But it was simply understood that I should ask no questions about the business beyond what I actually needed to know for my work."

"What's the business called?"

"Maulbow Engineering."

"Big help," Gefty observed, somewhat sourly. "Those instruments he brought along . . . he build those himself?"

"No, but I think he designed some of them— probably most of them. The companies he had doing the actual work appeared to have a terrible time getting everything exactly the way Mr. Maulbow wanted it. There's nothing that looks like a set of keys in those first two suitcases, Gefty."

"Well," Gefty said, "if you don't find them in the

others, you might start thumping around to see if he's got secret compartments in his luggage somewhere."

"I do wish," Kerim Ruse said uneasily, "that Mr. Maulbow would regain consciousness. It seems so . . . so underhanded to be doing these things behind his back!"

Gefty grunted noncommittally. He wasn't at all certain by now that he wanted his secretive client to wake up before he'd checked on the contents of the *Queen's* storage vault.

Fifteen minutes later, Gefty Rammer was climbing down to the storage deck in the *Queen's* broad stern, the newly fashioned set of vault keys clanking heavily in his coat pocket. Kerim had remained with her employer who was getting back his color but still hadn't opened his eyes. She hadn't found the original keys. Gefty wasn't sure she'd tried too hard, though she seemed to realize the seriousness of the situation now. But her loyalty to Mr. Maulbow could make no further difference, and she probably felt more comfortable for it.

Lights went on automatically in the wide passage leading from the cargo lock to the vault as Gefty turned into it. His steps echoed between the steel bulkheads on either side. He paused a moment before the big circular vault doors, listening to the purr of the *Queen's* idling engines in the next compartment. The familiar sound was somehow reassuring. He inserted the first key, turned it over twice, drew it out again and pressed one of the buttons in the control panel beside the door. The heavy slab of steel moved sideways with a soft, hissing sound, vanished into the wall. Gefty slid the other key into the lock of the inner door. A few seconds later, the vault entrance lay open before him.

He stood still again, wrinkling his nose. The area ahead was only dimly illuminated—the shaking-up the *Queen* had undergone had disturbed the lighting system here.

And what was that odor? Rather sharp, unpleasant; it might have been spilled ammonia. Gefty stepped through the door into the wide, short entrance passage beyond it, turned to the right and peered about in the semi-darkness of the vault.

Two great steel cases—the ones Maulbow had taken down to an airless moon surface, loaded up with something and brought back to the *Queen*—were jammed awkwardly into a corner, in a manner which suggested they'd slid into it when the ship was being knocked around. One of them was open and appeared to be empty. Gefty wasn't sure of the other. In the dimness beside them lay the loose coils of some very thick, dark cable—And standing near the center of the floor was a thing that at once riveted his attention on it completely. He sucked his breath in softly, feeling chilled.

He realized he hadn't really believed his own hunch. But, of course, if it hadn't been an unheard-of outside force that plucked the *Queen* out of normspace and threw her into this elsewhere, then it must be something Maulbow had put on board. And that something had to be a machine of some kind—

It was.

About it he could make out a thin gleaming of wires—a jury-rigged safety field. Within the flimsy-looking, protective cage was a double bank of instruments, some of them alive with the flicker and glow of lights. Those must be the very expensive and difficult-to-build items Maulbow had brought out from the Hub. Beside them stood the machine, squat and ponderous. In the vague light, it looked misshaped and discolored. A piece of equipment that had taken a bad beating of some kind. But it was functioning. As he stared, intermittent bursts of clicking noises rose from it, like the staccato of irregular gunfire.

For a moment, questions raced in disorder through his mind. What was it? Why had it been on that moon?

Part of another ship, wrecked now . . . a ship that had been at home *here?* Was it some sort of drive?

Maulbow must know. He'd known enough to design the instruments required to bring the battered monster back to life. On the other hand, he had not foreseen in all detail what could happen once the thing was in operation, because the *Queen*'s sudden buck-jumping act had surprised him and knocked him out.

The first step, in any event, was to get Maulbow awake now. To tamper with a device like this, before learning as much as one could about it, would be lunatic foolhardiness. It looked like too good a bet that the next serious mistake made by anybody would finish them all—

Perhaps it was only because Gefty's nerves were on edge that he grew aware at that point in his reflections of two minor signals from his senses. One was that the smell of ammonia, which he had almost stopped noticing, was becoming appreciably stronger. The other was the faintest of sounds—a whispering suggestion of motion somewhere behind him. But here in the storage vault nothing should have moved, and Gefty's muscles were tensing as his head came around. Almost in the same instant, he flung himself wildly to one side, stumbling and regaining his balance as something big and dark slapped heavily down on the floor at the point where he had stood. Then he was darting up through the entrance passage, turning, and knocking down the lock switches on the outside door panel.

It came flowing around the corner of the passage behind him as the vault doors began to slide together. He was aware mainly of swift, smooth, oiling motion like that of a big snake; then, for a fraction of a second, a strip of brighter light from the outside passage showed a long, heavy wedge of a head, a green metal-glint of staring eyes.

The doors closed silently into their frames and locked.

The thing was inside. But it was almost a minute then before Gefty could control his shaking legs enough to start moving back towards the main deck. In the half-dark of the vault, it had looked like a big coiled cable lying next to the packing cases. Like Maulbow, it might have been battered around and knocked out during the recent disturbance; and when it recovered, it had found Gefty in the vault with it. But it might also have been awake all the while, waiting cunningly until Gefty's attention seemed fixed elsewhere before launching its attack. It was big enough to have flattened him and smashed every bone in his body if the stroke had landed.

Some kind of guard animal—a snakelike watchdog? What other connection could it have with the mystery machine? Perhaps Maulbow had intended to leave it confined in one of the cases, and it had broken loose.

Too many questions by now, Gefty thought. But Maulbow had the answers.

He was hurrying up the main deck's central passage when Maulbow's voice addressed him sharply from a door he'd just passed.

"Stop right there, Rammer! Don't dare to move! I—"

The voice ended on a note of surprise. Gefty's reaction had not been too rational, but it was prompt. Maulbow's tone and phrasing implied he was armed. Gefty wasn't, but he kept a gun in the instrument room for emergencies. He'd been through a whole series of unnerving experiences, winding up with being shagged out of his storage vault by something that stank of ammonia and looked like a giant snake. To have one of the *Queen*'s passengers order him to stand where he was topped it off. Every other consideration was swept aside by a great urge to get his hands on his gun.

He glanced back, saw Maulbow coming out of the half-opened door, something like a twenty-inch, thin white rod in one hand. Then Gefty went bounding on along the passage, hunched forward and zigzagging from wall to wall to give Maulbow—if the thing he held was a weapon and he actually intended to use it—as small and erratic a target as possible. Maulbow shouted angrily behind him. Then, as Gefty came up to the next cross-passage, a line of white fire seared through the air across his shoulders and smashed off the passage wall.

With that, he was around the corner, and boiling mad. He had no great liking for gunfire, but it didn't shake him like the silently attacking beast in the dark storage had done. He reached the deserted instrument room not many seconds later, had his gun out and cocked, and was faced back towards the passage by which he had entered. Maulbow, if he had pursued without hesitation, should be arriving by now. But the passage stayed quiet. Gefty couldn't see into it from where he stood. He waited, trying to steady his breathing, wondering where Kerim Ruse was and what had got into Maulbow. After a moment, without taking his eyes from the passage entrance, he reached into the wall closet from which he had taken the gun and fished out another souvenir of his active service days, a thin-bladed knife in a slip-sheath. Gefty worked the fastenings of the sheath over his left wrist and up his forearm under his coat, tested the release to make sure it was functioning, and shook his coat sleeve back into place.

The passage was still quiet. Gefty moved softly over to one of the chairs, took a small cushion from it and pitched it out in front of the entrance.

There was a hiss. The cushion turned in midair into a puff of bright white fire. Gefty aimed his gun high at the far passage wall just beyond the entrance and pulled the trigger. It was a projectile gun. He heard the slug screech off the slick bulkhead and go slamming down the passage. Somebody out there made a startled, incoherent noise. But not the kind of a noise a man makes when he's just been hit.

"If you come in here armed," Gefty called, "I'll blow your head off. Want to stop this nonsense now?"

There was a moment's silence. Then Maulbow's voice replied shakily from the passage. He seemed to be standing about twenty feet back from the room.

"If you'll end your thoughtless attempts at interference, Rammer," he said, "there will be no trouble." He was speaking with the restraint of a man who is in a state of cold fury. "You're endangering us all. You must realize that you have no understanding of what you are doing."

Well, the last could be true enough. "We'll talk about it," Gefty said without friendliness. "I haven't done anything yet, but I'm not just handing the ship over to you. And what have you done with Miss Ruse?"

Maulbow hesitated again. "She's in the map room," he said then. "I . . . it was necessary to restrict her movements for a while. But you might as well let her out now. We must reach an agreement without loss of time."

Gefty glanced over his shoulder at the small closed door of the map room. There was no lock on the door, and he had heard no sound from inside; this might be some trick. But it wouldn't take long to find out. He backed up to the wall, pushed the door open and looked inside.

Kerim was there, sitting on a chair in one corner of the tiny room. The reason she hadn't made any noise became clear. She and the chair were covered by a rather closely fitting sack of transparent, glistening fabric. She stared out through it despairingly at Gefty, her lips moving urgently, But no sound came from the sack.

Gefty called angrily, "Maulbow—"

"Don't excite yourself, Rammer." There was a suggestion of what might be contempt in Maulbow's tone now. "The girl hasn't been harmed. She can breathe easily through the restrainer. And you can remove it by pulling at the material from outside."

Gefty's mouth tightened. "I'll keep my gun on the passage while I do it—"

Maulbow didn't answer. Gefty edged back into the map room, tentatively grasped the transparent stuff above Kerim's shoulder. To his surprise, it parted like wet tissue. He pulled sharply, and in a moment Kerim came peeling herself out of it, her face tear-stained, working desperately with hands, elbows and shoulders.

"Gefty," she gasped, "he . . . Mr. Maulbow—"

"He's out in the passage there," Gefty said. "He can hear you." His glance shifted for an instant to the wall where a second of the shroud-like transparencies was hanging. And who could that have been intended for, he thought, but Gefty Rammer? He added, "We've had a little trouble."

"Oh!" She looked out of the room towards the passage, then at the gun in Gefty's hand, then up at his face.

"Maulbow," Gefty went on, speaking distinctly enough to make sure Maulbow heard, "has a gun, too. He'll stay there in the passage and we'll stay in the instrument room until we agree on what should be done. He's responsible for what's happened and seems to know where we are."

He looked at Kerim's frightened eyes, dropped his voice to a whisper. "Don't let this worry you too much. I haven't found out just what he's up to, but so far his tricks have pretty much backfired. He was counting on taking us both by surprise, for one thing. That didn't work, so now he'd like us to co-operate."

"Are you going to?"

Gefty shrugged. "Depends on what he has in mind. I'm just interested in getting us out of this alive. Let's hear what Maulbow has to say—"

Some minutes later Gefty was trying to decide whether it was taking a worse risk to believe what Maulbow said than to keep things stalled on the chance that he was lying.

Kerim Ruse, perched stiffly erect on the edge of a chair, eyes big and round, face almost colorless, apparently believed Maulbow and was wishing she didn't. There was, of course, some supporting evidence . . . primarily the improbable appearance of their surroundings. The pencil-thin fire-spouter and the sleazy-looking "restrainer" had a sufficiently unfamiliar air to go with Maulbow's story; but as far as Gefty knew, either of them could have been manufactured in the Hub.

Then there was the janandra—the big, snakish thing in the storage which Maulbow had brought back up from the moon along with the battered machine. It had been, he said, his shipboard companion on another voyage. It wasn't ordinarily aggressive—Gefty's sudden appearance in the vault must have startled it into making an attack. It was not exactly a pet. There was a psychological relationship between it and Maulbow which Maulbow would not attempt to explain because Gefty and Kerim would be unable to grasp its significance. The janandra was essential, in this unexplained manner, to his wellbeing.

That item was almost curious enough to seem to substantiate his other statements; but it didn't really prove anything. The only point Gefty didn't question in the least was that they were in a bad spot which might be getting worse rapidly. His gaze shifted back to the screens. What he saw out there, surrounding the ship, was, according to Maulbow, an illusion of space created by the time flow in which they were moving.

Also according to Maulbow, there was a race of the future, human in appearance, with machines to sail the current of time through the universe—to run and tack with the winds of time, dipping in and out of the normspace of distant periods and galaxies as they chose. Maulbow, one of the explorers, had met disaster a million light-years from the home of his kind, centuries behind them, his vehicle wrecked on an airless moon with damaged control unit and shattered instruments. He had made his way to a human civilization to obtain the equipment he needed, and returned at last with the *Silver Queen* to where the time-sailer lay buried.

Gefty's lip curled. No, he wasn't buying all that just yet— but if Maulbow was *not* lying, then the unseen stars were racing past, the mass of the galaxy beginning to slide by, eventually to be lost forever beyond a black distance no space drive could span. The matter simply had to be settled quickly. But Maulbow was also strained and impatient, and if his impatience could be increased a little more, he might start telling the things that really mattered, the things Gefty had to know. Gefty asked slowly, as if hesitant to commit himself, "Why did you bring us along?"

The voice from the passage snapped, "Because my resources were nearly exhausted, Rammer! I couldn't obtain a new ship. Therefore I chartered yours; and you came with it. As for Miss Ruse—in spite of every precaution, my activities may have aroused suspicion and curiosity among your people. When I disappeared, Miss Ruse might have been questioned. I couldn't risk being followed to the wreck of the sailer, so I took her with me. And what does that mean against what I have offered you? The greatest adventure—followed, I give you my solemn word, by a safe return to your own place and time, and the most generous compensations for any inconvenience you may have suffered!"

Kerim, looking up at Gefty, shook her head violently. Gefty said, "We find it difficult to take you on trust now, Maulbow. Why do you want to get into the instrument room?"

Maulbow was silent for some seconds. Then he said, "As I told you, this ship would not have been buffeted about during the moments of transfer if the control unit were operating with complete efficiency. Certain adjustments will have to be made in the unit, and this should be done promptly."

"Where do the ship instruments come in?" Gefty asked.

"I can determine the nature of the problem from them. When I was . . . stranded . . . the unit was seriously damaged. My recent repairs were necessarily hasty. I—"

"What caused the crack-up?"

Maulbow said, tone taut with impatience, "Certain sections of the Great Current are infested with dangerous forces. I shall not attempt to describe them . . ."

"I wouldn't get it?"

"I don't pretend to understand them very well myself, Rammer. They are not life but show characteristics of life—even of intelligent life. If you can imagine radiant energy being capable of conscious hostility . . ."

There was a chill at the back of Gefty's neck. "A big, fast-moving light?"

"Yes!" Sharp concern showed suddenly in the voice from the passage. "You . . . when did you see that?"

Gefty glanced at the screens. "Twice since you've been talking. And once before—immediately after we got tumbled around."

"Then we can waste no more time, Rammer. Those forces are sensitive to the fluctuations of the control unit. If they were close enough to be seen, they're aware the ship is here. They were attempting to locate it."

"What could they do?"

Maulbow said, "A single attack was enough to put the control unit out of operation in my sailer. The Great Current then rejected us instantly. A ship of this size might afford more protection, which is the reason I chose it. But if the control unit is not adjusted immediately to enable it to take us out of this section, the attacks will continue until the ship—and we—have been destroyed."

Gefty drew a deep breath. "There's another solution to that problem, Maulbow. Miss Ruse and I prefer it, and if you meant what you said that you'd see to it we got back eventually—you shouldn't object either."

The voice asked sharply, "What do you mean?"

Gefty said, "Shut the control unit off. From what you were saying, that throws us automatically back into normspace, while we're still close enough to the Hub. You'll find plenty of people there who'll stake you to a trip to the future if they can go along and are convinced they'll return. Miss Ruse and I don't happen to be that adventurous."

There was silence from the passage. Gefty added, "Take your time to make up your mind about it, if you want to. I don't like the idea of those lights hitting us, but neither do you. And I think I can wait this out as well as you can . . ."

The silence stretched out. Presently Gefty said, "If you do accept, slide that fire-shooting device of yours into the room before you show up. We don't want accidents."

He paused again. Kerim was chewing her lips, hands clenched into small fists in her lap. Then Maulbow answered, voice flat and expressionless now.

"The worst thing we can do at present," he said, "is to prolong a dispute about possible courses of action. If I disarm, will you lay aside your gun?"

"Yes."

"Then I accept your conditions, disappointing as they are."

He was silent. After a moment, Gefty heard the white rod clatter lightly along the floor of the passage. It struck the passage wall, spun off it, and rolled into the instrument room, coming to rest a few feet away from him. Gefty hesitated, picked it up and laid it on the wall table. He placed his own gun beside it, moved a dozen steps away. Kerim's eyes followed him anxiously.

"Gefty," she whispered, "he might . . ."

Gefty looked at her, formed the words "It's all right"

with his mouth and called, "Guns have been put aside, Maulbow. Come on in, and let's keep it peaceable."

He waited, arms hanging loosely at his side, heart beating heavily, as quick footsteps came up the passage. Maulbow appeared in the entrance, glanced at Gefty and Kerim, then about the room. His gaze rested for a moment on the wall table, shifted back to Gefty. Maulbow came on into the room, turning towards Gefty, mouth twisting.

He said softly, "It is not our practice, Rammer, to share the secrets of the Great Current with other races. I hadn't foreseen that you might become a dangerous nuisance. But now—"

His right hand began to lift, half closed about some small golden instrument. Gefty's left arm moved back and quickly forwards.

The service knife slid out of its sheath and up from his palm as an arrow of smoky blackness burst from the thing in Maulbow's hand. The blackness came racing with a thin, snarling noise across the floor towards Gefty's feet. The knife flashed above it, turning, and stood hilt-deep in Maulbow's chest.

Gefty returned a few minutes later from the forward cabin which served as the *Queen's* sick bay, and said to Kerim, "He's still alive, though I don't know why. He may even recover. He's full of anesthetic, and that should keep him quiet till we're back in normspace. Then I'll see what we can do for him."

Kerim had lost some of her white, shocked look while he was gone. "You knew he would try to kill you?" she asked shakily.

"Suspected he had it in mind—he gave in too quick. But I thought I'd have a chance to take any gadget he was hiding away from him first. I was wrong about that. Now we'd better move fast . . . "

He switched the emergency check panel back on,

glanced over the familiar patterns of lights and numbers. A few minor damage spots were indicated, but the ship was still fully operational. One minor damage spot which did not appear on the panel was now to be found in the instrument room itself, in the corner on which the door of the map room opened. The door, the adjoining bulkheads and section of flooring were scarred, blackened, and as assortedly malodorous as burned things tend to become. That was where Gefty had stood when Maulbow entered the room, and if he had remained there an instant after letting go of the knife, he would have been in very much worse condition than the essentially fireproof furnishings.

Both Maulbow's weapons—the white rod lying innocently on the wall table and the round, golden device which had dropped from his hand spitting darts of smoking blackness—had blasted unnervingly away into that area for almost thirty seconds after Maulbow was down and twisting about on the floor. Then he went limp and the firing instantly stopped. Apparently, Maulbow's control of them had ended as he lost consciousness.

It seemed fortunate that the sick bay cabin's emergency treatment accessories, gentle as their action was, might have been designed for the specific purpose of keeping the most violent of prisoners immobilized—let alone one with a terrible knife wound in him. At the angle along which the knife had driven in and up below the ribs, an ordinary man would have been dead in seconds. But it was very evident now that Maulbow was no ordinary man, and even after the eerie weapons had been pitched out of the ship through the instrument room's disposal tube, Gefty couldn't rid himself of an uncomfortable suspicion that he wasn't done with Maulbow yet—wouldn't be done with him, in fact, until one or the other of them was dead.

He said to Kerim, "I thought the machine Maulbow set up in the storage vault would turn out to be some drive engine, but apparently it has an entirely different function. He connected it with the instruments he had made in the Hub, and together they form what he calls a control unit. The emergency panel would show if the unit were drawing juice from the ship. It isn't, and I don't know what powers it. But we do know now that the control unit is holding us in the time current, and it will go on holding us there as long as it's in operation.

"If we could shut it off, the *Queen* would be 'rejected' by the current, like Maulbow's sailer was. In other words, we'd get knocked back into normspace—which is what we want. And we want it to happen as soon as possible because, if Maulbow was telling the truth on that point, every minute that passes here is taking us farther away from the Hub, and farther from our own time towards his."

Kerim nodded, eyes intent on his face.

"Now I can't just go down there and start slapping switches around on the thing," Gefty went on. "He said it wasn't working right, and even if it were, I couldn't tell what would happen. But it doesn't seem to connect up with any ship systems—it just seems to be holding us in a field of its own. So I should be able to move the whole unit into the cargo lock and eject it from there. If we shift the *Queen* outside its field, that should have the same effect as shutting the control unit off. It should throw us back into normspace."

Kerim nodded again. "What about Mr. Maulbow's janandra animal?"

Gefty shrugged. "Depends on the mood I find it in. He said it wasn't usually aggressive. Maybe it isn't. I'll get into a spacesuit for protection and break out some of the mining equipment to move it along with. If I can maneuver it into an empty compartment where it will be out of the . . ."

He broke off, expression changing, eyes fastened on the emergency panel. Then he turned hurriedly, reached across the side of the console for the intership airseal controls. Kerim asked apprehensively, "What's the matter, Gefty?"

"Wish I knew . . . exactly." Gefty indicated the emergency panel. "Little red light there, on the storage deck section—it wasn't showing a minute ago. It means that the vault doors have been opened since then."

He saw the same half-superstitious fear appear in her face that had touched him. "You think *he* did it?"

"I don't know." Maulbow's control of the guns had seemed uncanny enough. But that was a different matter. The guns were a product of his own time and science. But the vault door mechanisms? There might have been sufficient opportunity for Maulbow to study them and alter them, for some purpose of his own, since he'd come aboard . . .

"I've got the ship compartments and decks sealed off from each other now," Gefty said slowly. "The only connecting points from one to the other are personnel hatches—they're small air locks. So the janandra's confined to the storage deck. If it's come out of the vault, it might be a nuisance until I can get equipment to handle it. But that isn't too serious. The spacesuits are on the second deck, and I'll get into one before I go on to the storage. You wait here a moment, I'll look in on Maulbow again before I start."

If Maulbow wasn't still unconscious, he was doing a good job of feigning it. Gefty looked at the pale, lax face, the half-shut eyes, shook his head and left the cabin, locking it behind him. It mightn't be Maulbow's doing, but having the big snake loose in the storage could, in fact, make things extremely awkward now. He didn't think his gun would make much impression on anything of that size, and while several of the ship's mining tools could be employed as very effective close-range weapons, they happened, unfortunately, to be stored away on the same deck.

He found Kerim standing in the center of the instrument room, waiting for him.

"Gefty," she said, "do you notice anything? An odd sort of smell . . ."

Then the odor was in Gefty's nostrils, too, and the back of his neck turned to ice as he recognized it. He glanced up at the ventilation outlet, looked back at Kerim.

He took her arm, said softly, "Come this way. Keep very quiet! I don't know how it happened, but the janandra's on the main deck now. That's what it smells like. The smell's coming through the ventilation system, so the thing's moving around in the port section. We'll go the other way."

Kerim whispered, "What will we do?"

"Get ourselves into spacesuits first, and then get Maulbow's control unit out of the ship. The janandra may be looking around for him. If it is, it won't bother us."

He hadn't wanted to remind Kerim that, from what Maulbow said, there might be more than one reason for getting rid of the control unit as quickly as possible. But it had been constantly in the back of his mind; and twice, in the few minutes that passed after Maulbow's strange weapons were silenced, he had seen a momentary pale glare appear in the unquiet flow of darkness reflecting in the viewscreens. Gefty had said nothing, because if it was true that hostile forces were alert and searching for them here, it added to their immediate danger but not at all to the absolute need to free themselves from the inexorable rush of the Great Current before they were carried beyond hope of return to their civilization.

But those brief glimpses did add to the sense of urgency throbbing in Gefty's nerves, while events, and the equally hard necessity to avoid a fatally mistaken move

in this welter of unknown factors, kept blocking him. Now
the mysterious manner in which Maulbow's unpleasant
traveling companion had appeared on the main deck
made it impossible to do anything but keep Kerim at his
side. If Maulbow was still capable of taking a hand in
matters, there was no reasonably safe place to leave her
aboard the *Queen*.

And Maulbow might be capable of it. Twice as they
hurried up the narrow, angled passages along the
Queen's curving hull towards an airseal leading to the
next compartment, Gefty caught a trace of the ammonia-
like animal odor coming over the ventilating system.
They reached the lock without incident; but then, as
they came along the second deck hall to the ship's
magazine, there was a sharp click in the stillness behind
them. Its meaning was disconcertingly apparent. Gefty
hesitated, turned Kerim into a side passage, guided her
along it.

She looked up at his face. "It's following us?"

"Seems to be." No time for the spacesuits in the
magazine now—something had just emerged from the
air lock through which they had entered the second
deck not many moments before. He helped the girl
quickly down a section of ladder-like stairs to the airseal
connecting the second deck with the storage, punched
a wall button there. As the lock door opened, there was
another noise from the passage they had just left, as
if something had thudded briefly and heavily against one
of the bulkheads. Kerim uttered a little gasp. Then they
were in the lock, and Gefty slapped down two other
buttons, stood watching the door behind them snap shut
and, a few seconds later, the one on the far side open
on the dark storage deck.

They scrambled down another twelve feet of ladder
to the floor of a side passage, hearing the lock snap shut
behind them. As it closed, they were in complete darkness. Gefty seized Kerim's arm, ran with her up the

passage to the left, guiding himself with his fingertips on the left bulkhead. When they came to a corner, he turned her to the left again. A few seconds later, he pulled open a small door, bundled the girl through, came in himself, and shut the door to a narrow slit behind them.

Kerim whispered shakily, "What will we do now, Gefty?"

"Stay here for the moment. It'll look for us in the vault first."

And it should go to the storage vault first where it had been guarding Maulbow's machine, to hunt for them there. But it might not. Gefty eased the gun from his pocket on the far side of Kerim. Across the dark compartment was another door. They could retreat a little farther here if it became necessary—but not very much farther.

They waited in a silence that was complete except for their unsteady breathing and the distant, deep pulse of the *Queen*'s throttled-down drives. He felt Kerim trembling against him. How did Maulbow's creature move through the airseal locks? The operating mechanisms were simple—a dog might have been taught to use them. But a dog had paws . . .

There came the soft hiss of the opening lock, the faintest shimmer of light to the right of the passage mouth he was watching through the door. A heavy thump on the floor below the locks followed, then a hard click as the lock closed and complete darkness returned.

The silence resumed. Seconds dragged on. Gefty's imagination pictured the thing waiting, its great, wedge-shaped head raised as its senses probed the dark about it for a sign of the two human beings. Then a vague rushing noise began, growing louder as it approached the passage mouth, crossing it, receding rapidly again to the left.

Gefty let his breath out slowly, eased the door open and stood listening again. Abruptly, there was reflected light in the lock passage, coming now from the left. He said in a whisper, "It's moving around in the main hall, Kerim. We can go on the other way now, but we'll have to be fast and keep quiet. I've thought of how we can get rid of that thing."

The cargo lock on the storage deck had two inner doors. The one which opened into the side of the vault hall was built to allow passage of the largest chunks of freight the *Queen* was likely to be burdened with; it was almost thirty feet wide and twenty high. The second door was just large enough to let a man in a spacesuit climb in and out of the side of the lock without using the freight door. It opened on a tiny control cubicle from which the lock's mechanisms were operated during loading processes.

Gefty let Kerim and himself into the cubicle from one of the passages, steered the girl through the pitch blackness of the little room to the chair before the control panel and told her to sit down. He groped for a moment at the side of the panel, found a knob and twisted it. There was a faint click. A scattering of pale lights appeared suddenly on the panel, a dark viewscreen, set at a tilt above them, reflecting their gleam.

Gefty explained in a low voice, "Left side of that screen covers the lock. Right one covers the big hall outside. No lights in either at the moment, so you don't see anything. Only way the cargo door to the hall can be opened or closed is with these switches right here. What I want to do is get the janandra into the lock, slam the door on it and lock down the control switches. Then we've got it trapped."

"But how are you going to get it to go in there?"

"No real problem—I'll be three jumps ahead of it. Then I duck back up into this cubicle, and lock both doors. And it'll be inside the lock. You have the picture now?"

Kerim said unsteadily, "I do. But it sounds awfully risky, Gefty."

"Well, I don't like it either," Gefty admitted. "So I'll start right now before I lose my nerve. As soon as I move out into the vault hall, the lighting will go on. That's automatic. You watch the right side of the screen. If you see the janandra coming before I do, yell as loud as you can."

He shifted the two inner door switches to the right. A red spark appeared in the dark viewscreen, high up near the center. A second red light showed on the cubicle bulkhead beside Gefty. Beneath it an oblong section of the bulkhead turned silently away on heavy hinges, became a door two feet in thickness, which stood jutting out at a right angle into the darkness of the cargo lock. A wave of cold air moved through it into the control cubicle.

On the screen, another red spark appeared beside the first one.

"Both doors are open now," Gefty murmured to the girl. "The janandra isn't in the vault hall or the lighting would have turned on, but it may have heard the door open and be on its way. So keep watching the screen."

"I certainly will!" she whispered shakily.

Gefty took an oversized wrench from the wall, climbed quickly and quietly down the three ladder steps to the floor of the lock, and walked across it to the sill of the giant freight door, which now had swung out and down into the vault hall, fitting itself into a depression of the flooring. He hesitated an instant on the sill, then stepped out into the big dark hall. Light filled it immediately in both directions.

He stood quiet, intent on the storage vault entrance far up the hall to his left. He could see the vault was open. The janandra might still be inside it. But the

seconds passed, and the dark entrance remained silent
and there was no suggestion of motion beyond it. Gefty
glanced to the right, moved a dozen steps farther out into
the hall, hefted the wrench and spun it through the air
towards the ventilator frame on the opposite bulkhead.

The heavy tool clanged loudly against the frame,
bounced off and thudded to the floor. Gefty started slowly
over to it, heart pounding, with the vault entrance still
at the edge of his vision.

Kerim's voice screamed, *"Gefty, it's—"*

He spun around, sprinted back to the cargo lock.
The janandra had come silently out of the nearest side
passage behind him, was approaching with the remembered oiling swiftness of motion, its great head lifted
a yard from the floor. Gefty plunged through the lock,
jumped for the top of the cubicle door steps, came
stumbling into the cubicle. Kerim was on her feet,
staring. He swung the cubicle door switch to the left,
slapping it flat to the panel. The door snapped back
into the wall behind him with a force that shook the
floor.

On the screen, the janandra's thick, dark worm-shape
was swinging around in the dim lock to regain the open
hall. It had seen the trap. But the freight door switch
went flat beside the other, and the freight door rose with
massive swiftness. The heavy body smashed against it,
went sliding back to the floor as the door slammed shut
and the screen section showing the cargo lock turned
dark.

"Got it—got it—got it!" Gefty heard himself whispering exultantly. He switched on the lock's interior lights.

Then he swore softly, and, beside, him, Kerim sucked
in her breath.

The screen showed the janandra in violent but
apparently purposeful motion inside the lock . . . and
it was also apparent now that it was a more complexly

constructed creature than the long worm-body and heavy head had indicated. The skin, to a distance of some eight feet back of the head, had spread out into a wide, flexible frill. From beneath the frill extended half a dozen jointed, bone-white arms, along with waving, ribbon-like appendages less easy to define. The thing was reared half up along the hall door, inspecting its surface with these members; then suddenly it flung itself around and flashed over to the outer lock door. Three arms shot out; wiry fingers caught the three spin locks simultaneously, began to whirl them.

Gefty said, staring, "Kerim, it's going to . . . "

The janandra didn't. The motion checked suddenly, was reversed. The locks drew tight again. The janandra swung back from the door, lifting half its length upwards, big head weaving about as it inspected the tool racks overhead. An arm reached suddenly, snatched something from one of the racks. Then the thing turned again; and in the next instant its head filled the viewscreen. Kerim made a choked sound of fright, jerking back against Gefty. The bulging, metal-green eyes seemed to stare directly at him. And the screen went black.

Kerim whispered, "Wha . . . what happened, Gefty?"

Gefty swallowed, said, "It smashed the view pickup. Must have guessed we were watching and didn't like it . . . " He added, "I was beginning to think Maulbow must be some kind of superman. But it wasn't any remote control magic of his that let the janandra out of the vault, and opened the intership locks when it came up to the main deck and followed us down again. It was doing all that for itself. It's Maulbow's partner, not his pet. And it's probably got at least as good a brain as anyone else on board behind that ugly face."

Kerim moistened her lips. "Can it . . . could it get out again?"

"Into the ship?" Gefty shook his head decidedly. "Uh-uh. It could dump itself out on the other side—and it almost did before it realized where it was and what it was about to do. But the inner lock doors won't open until someone opens them right on this panel. No, the thing's safely trapped. On the other hand . . ."

On the other hand, Gefty realized that he wouldn't now be able to bring himself to eject the janandra out of the cargo lock and into the Great Current. Its intentions obviously hadn't been friendly, but its level of intelligence was as good as his own, and perhaps somewhat better; and at present it was helpless. To dispose of it as he'd had in mind would therefore be the cold-blooded murder of an equal. But so long as that ugly and formidable shipmate of Maulbow's stayed in the cargo lock, the lock couldn't be used to get rid of the control unit in the vault.

A new solution presented itself while Gefty was making a rapid and rather desperate mental review of various heavy-duty tools which might be employed as weapons to force the janandra into submission and haul it off for confinement elsewhere in the ship. Not impossible, but a highly precarious and time-consuming operation at best. Then another thought occurred: the safety vault lay directly against the hull of the *Queen*—

How long to cut through the hull? The ship's mining equipment was on board, and the tools were self-powered. Climb into a spacesuit, empty the air from the entire storage deck, leaving the janandra imprisoned in the cargo lock . . . with Maulbow incapacitated in sick bay, and Kerim back in the control compartment and also in a suit, for additional protection. Then cut ship's power to this deck to avoid complications with the *Queen*'s involved circuitry and work under space conditions—half an hour if he hurried.

"Shouldn't take more than another ten minutes," he informed Kerim presently over the suit's intercom.

"I'm very glad to hear it, Gefty." She sounded shaky.

"Anything going on in the screens?" he asked.

She hesitated a little, said, "No. Not at the moment."

Gefty grunted, blinked sweat from his eyes, and took hold of the handgrips of the heavy mining cutter again, turning it nose down towards the vault floor. The guide light found the point he was working on, and the slice beam stabbed out, began nibbling delicately away to extend the curving line it had eaten through the *Queen*'s thick skin. He had drawn a twenty-five foot circle around Maulbow's battered control unit and the instruments attached to it, well outside the fragile-looking safety field. The circle was broken at four points where he would plant explosives. The explosives, going off together, should shatter the connecting links with the hull and throw the machine clear. If that didn't release them immediately from its influence, he would see what putting the *Queen*'s drives into action would do.

"Gefty?" Kerim's voice asked.

"Uh-huh?"

He could hear her swallow over the intercom. "Those lights are back now."

"How many?"

"Two," Kerim said. "I *think* they're only two. They keep crossing back and forth in front of us." She laughed nervously. "It's idiotic, of course, but I do get the feeling they're looking at us."

Gefty said hesitantly, "Everything's set but I need another minute or two to get this last connection whittled down a little more. If I blow the charge too soon, it mightn't take the gadget clean out of the ship."

Kerim said, "I know. I'll just watch . . . they just disappeared again." Her voice changed. "Now there's something else."

"What's that?"

"You know you said to watch the cargo lock lights on the emergency panel."

"Yes."

"The outer lock door has just been opened."

"What!"

"It must have been. The light started blinking red just now as I was looking at it."

Gefty was silent a moment, his mind racing. Why would the janandra open the lock? From what Maulbow had said, it could live for a while without air, but it still could gain nothing but eventual death from leaving the ship—

Unless, Gefty thought, the janandra had become aware in some way that he was about to blow their machine out of the *Queen*. There were grappling lines in the cargo lock, and if four or five of those lines were slapped to the circular section of the hull he'd loosened . . .

"Kerim," he said.

"Yes?"

"I'm going to blow the deal right now. Got your suit snapped to the wall braces like I showed you?"

"Yes, Gefty." Her voice was faint but clear.

He turned the cutter away from the line it had dug, sent it rolling off towards the far wall. He hurried around the circle, checking the four charges, lumbered over to the vault passage, stopped just around the corner. He took the firing box from his suit.

"Ready, Kerim?" He opened the box.

"Ready . . . "

"Here goes!" Gefty reached into the box, twisted the firing handle. Light flared in the vault. The deck shook below him. He came stumbling out from behind the wall.

Maulbow's machine and its stand of instruments had vanished. Where it had stood was a dark circular hole. Nothing else seemed to have happened. Gefty clumped hurriedly over to the mining cutter, swung it around, started more cautiously back towards the hole. He didn't have the faintest idea what would come next, but a definite possibility was that he would see the janandra's dark form flowing up over the rim of the hole. Letting it run into the cutter beam might be the best way to discourage it from reentering the *Queen*.

Instead, a dazzling brilliance suddenly blotted out everything. The cutter was plucked from Gefty's grasp; then he was picked up, suit and all, and slammed up towards the vault ceiling. He had a feeling that inaudible thunders were shaking the ship. He seemed to be rolling over and over along the ceiling. At last, the suit crashed into something which showed a total disinclination to yield, and Gefty blacked out.

The left side of his face felt pushed out of shape; his left eye wasn't functioning too well, and there was a severe pulsing ache throughout the top of his head. But Gefty felt happy.

There were a few qualifying considerations.

"Of course," he pointed out to Kerim, "all we can really say immediately is that we're back in normspace and somewhere in the galaxy."

She smiled shakily. "Isn't that saying quite a lot, Gefty?"

"It's something." Gefty glanced around the instrument room. He had placed an emergency light on the console, but except for that, the control compartment was in darkness. The renewed battering the *Queen* had absorbed had knocked out the power in the forward section. The viewscreens were black, every instrument dead. But he'd seen the stars of normspace through the torn vault floor. It was something . . .

"We might have the light that slugged us to thank for that," he said. "I'm not sure just what did happen there, but it could have been Maulbow's control unit it was attacking rather than the ship. Maulbow said the lights were sensitive to the unit. At any rate, we're here, and we're rid of the gadget—and of the janandra." He hesitated. "I just don't feel you should get your hopes too high. We may find out we're a very long way from the Hub."

Kerim's large eyes showed a degree of confidence which made him almost uncomfortable. "If we are," she said serenely, "you'll get us back somehow."

Gefty cleared his throat. "Well, we'll see. If the power shutoff is something the *Queen's* repair scanners can handle, the instruments will come back on any minute. Give the scanners ten minutes. If they haven't done it by that time, they can't do it and I'll have to play repairman. Then, with the instruments working, we can determine exactly where we are."

Unless, he told himself silently, they'd wound up in a distant cluster never penetrated by the Federation's mapping teams. And there was the other little question of where they now were in time. But Kerim looked rosy with relief, and those details could wait.

He took up another emergency light, switched it on and said, "I'll see how Maulbow is doing while we're waiting for power. If the first aid treatment has pulled him through so far, the autosurgeon probably can fix him up."

Kerim's face suddenly took on a guilty expression. "I forgot all about Mr. Maulbow!" She hesitated. "Should I come along?"

Gefty shook his head. "I won't need help. And if it's a case for the surgeon, you wouldn't like it. Those things work painlessly, but it gets to be a mess for awhile."

He shut off the light again when he reached the sick bay which was running on its independent power system. As he opened the cabin door from the dispensary, carrying the autosurgeon, it became evident that Maulbow was still alive, but that he might be in delirium. Gefty placed the surgeon on the table, went over to the bed and looked at Maulbow.

To the extent that the emergency treatment instruments' cautious restraints permitted, Maulbow was

twisting slowly about on the bed. He was speaking in
a low, rapid voice, his face distorted by emotion. The
words were not slurred, but they were in a language
Gefty didn't know. It seemed clear that Maulbow had
reverted mentally to his own time, and for some seconds he remained unaware that Gefty had entered the
room. Then, surprisingly, the slitted blue eyes opened
wider and focused on Gefty's face. And Maulbow
screamed with rage.

Gefty felt somewhat disconcerted. For the reason alone
that he was under anesthetic, Maulbow should not have
been conscious. But he was. The words were now ones
Gefty could understand, and Maulbow was telling him
things which would have been interesting enough under
different circumstances. Gefty broke in as soon as he could.

"Look," he said quietly, "I'm trying to help you, I . . ."

Maulbow interrupted him in turn, not at all quietly.
Gefty listened a moment longer, then shrugged. So
Maulbow didn't like him. He could say honestly that he'd
never liked Maulbow much, and what he was hearing
made him like Maulbow considerably less. But he would
keep the man from the future alive if he could.

He positioned the autosurgeon behind the head of the
bed to allow the device to begin its analysis, stood back
at its controls where he could both follow the progress
it made and watch Maulbow without exciting him further
by remaining within his range of vision. After a moment,
the surgeon shut off the first-aid instruments and made
unobtrusive use of a heavy tranquilizing drug. Then, it
waited.

Maulbow should have lapsed into passive somnolence
thirty seconds afterwards. But the drug seemed to
produce no more effect on him mentally than the
preceding anesthetic. He raged and screeched on. Gefty
watched him uneasily, knowing now that he was looking
at insanity. There was nothing more he could do at the
moment—the autosurgeon's decisions were safer than any

nonprofessional's guesswork. And the surgeon continued to wait.

Then, abruptly, Maulbow died. The taut body slumped against the bed and the contorted features relaxed. The eyes remained half open; and when Gefty came around to the side of the bed, they still seemed to be looking up at him, but they no longer moved. A thin trickle of blood started from the side of the slack mouth and stopped again.

The control compartment was still darkened and without power when Gefty returned to it. He told Kerim briefly what had happened, added, "I'm not at all sure now he was even human. I'd rather believe he wasn't."

"Why's that, Gefty?" She was studying his expression soberly.

Gefty hesitated, said, "I thought at first he was furious because we'd upset his plans. But they weren't his plans . . . they were the janandra's. He wasn't exactly its servant. I suppose you'd have to say he was something like a pet animal."

Kerim said incredulously, "But that isn't possible! Think of how intelligently Mr. Maulbow . . . "

"He was following instructions," Gefty said. "The janandra let him know whatever it wanted done. He was following instructions again when he tried to kill me after I'd got away from the thing in the vault. The real brain around here was the janandra . . . and it was a real brain. With a little luck it would have had the ship."

Kerim smiled briefly. "You handled that big brain rather well, I think."

"I was the one who got lucky," Gefty said. "Anyway, where Maulbow came from, it's the janandra's kind that gives the orders. And the thing is, Maulbow liked it that way. He didn't want it to be different. When the light hit us, it killed the janandra on the outside of the ship.

Maulbow felt it happen and it cracked him up. He wanted to kill us for it. But since he was helpless, he killed himself. He didn't want to be healed—not by us. At least, that's what it looks like."

He shrugged, checked his watch, climbed out of the chair. "Well," he said, "the ten minutes I gave the *Queen* to turn the power back on are up. Looks like the old girl couldn't do it. So I'll—"

The indirect lighting system in the instrument room went on silently. The emergency light flickered and went out. Gefty's head came around.

Kerim was staring past him at the screens, her face radiant.

"Oh, Gefty!" she cried softly. "Oh, Gefty! Our stars!"

"Green dot here is us," Gefty explained, somewhat hoarsely. He cleared his throat, went on, "Our true ship position, that is—" He stopped, realizing he was talking too much, almost babbling, in an attempt to take some of the tension out of the moment. The next few seconds might not tell them where they were, but it would show whether they had been carried beyond the regions of space charted by Federation instruments. Which would mean the difference between having a chance—whether a good chance or a bad one—of getting home eventually, and the alternative of being hopelessly lost.

There had been nothing recognizably familiar about the brilliantly dense star patterns in the viewscreens, but he gave no further thought to that. Unless the ship's exact position was known or one was on an established route, it was a waste of time looking for landmarks in a sizable cluster.

He turned on the basic star chart. Within the locator plate the green pinpoint of light reappeared, red-ringed and suspended now against the three-dimensional immensities of the Milky Way. It stayed still a moment, began a smooth drift towards Galactic East. Gefty let his breath out carefully. He sensed Kerim's eyes on him but kept his gaze fixed on the locator plate.

The green dot slowed, came to a stop. Gefty's finger tapped the same button four times. The big chart flicked out of existence, and in the plate three regional star maps appeared and vanished in quick succession behind it. The fourth map stayed. For a few seconds, the red-circled green spark was not visible here. Then it showed at the eastern margin of the map, came gliding forwards and to the left, slowed again and held steady. Now the star map began to glide through the locator plate, carrying the fixed green dot with it. It brought the dot up to dead center point in the locator plate and stopped.

Gefty slumped a little. He rubbed his hands slowly down his face and muttered a few words. Then he shook his head.

"Gefty," Kerim whispered, "what is it? Where are we?"

Gefty looked at her.

"After we got hauled into that time current," he said hoarsely, "I tried to find out which way in space we were headed. The direction indicators over there seemed to show we were trying to go everywhere at once. You remember. Maulbow's control unit wasn't working right, needed adjustments . . . Well, all those little impulses must have pretty well canceled out because we weren't taken really far. In the last hour and a half we've covered roughly the distance the *Queen* could have gone on her own in, say, thirty days."

"Then where . . . "

"Home," Gefty said simply. "It's ridiculous! Other side of the Hub from where we started." He nodded at the plate. "Eastern Hub Quadrant Section Six Eight. The G2 behind the green dot—that's the Evalee system. We could be putting down at Evalee Interstellar three hours from now if we wanted to."

Kerim was laughing and crying together. "Oh, Gefty! I knew you would . . ."

"A fat lot I had to do with it!" Gefty leaned forward suddenly, switched on the transmitter. "And now let's pick up a Evalee newscast. There's something else I . . ."

His voice trailed off. The transmitter screen lit up with a blurred jumble of print, colors, a muttering of voices, music and noises. Gefty twisted a dial. The screen cleared, showed a newscast headline sheet. Gefty blinked at it, glanced sideways at Kerim, grimaced.

"The something else," he said, his voice a little strained, "was something I was also worried about. Looks like I was more or less right."

"Why, what's wrong?"

"Nothing really bad," Gefty assured her. He added, "I think. But take a look at the Federation dateline."

Kerim peered at the screen, frowned. "But . . ."

"Uh-huh."

"Why, that . . . that's almost . . ."

"That," Gefty said, "or rather *this* is the day after we started out from the Hub, headed roughly Galactic west. Three weeks ago. We'd be just past Miam." He knuckled his chin. "Interesting thought, isn't it?"

Kerim was silent for long seconds. "Then they . . . or we . . ."

"Oh, they're us, all right," Gefty said. "They'd have to be, wouldn't they?"

"I suppose so. It seems a little confusing. But I was thinking. If you send them a transmitter call . . ."

Gefty shook his head. "The *Queen's* transmitter isn't too hot, but it might push a call as far as Evalee. Then we could arrange for a ComWeb link-up there, and in another ten minutes or so . . . but I don't think we'd better."

"Why not?" Kerim demanded.

"Because we got through it all safely, so we're going to get through it safely. But if we receive that message now and never go on to Maulbow's moon . . . you see? There's no way of knowing just what would happen."

Kerim looked hesitant, frowned. "I suppose you're right," she agreed reluctantly at last. "So Mr. Maulbow will have to stay dead now. And that janandra." After a moment she added pensively, "Of course, they weren't really very nice—"

Gefty shivered. One of the things he'd learned from Maulbow's ravings was the real reason he and Kerim had been taken along on the trip. He didn't feel like telling Kerim about it just yet, but it had been solely because of Maulbow's concern for his master's creature comforts. The janandra could go for a long time without food, but after fasting for several years on the moon, a couple of snacks on the homeward run would have been highly welcome.

And the janandra was a gourmet. It much preferred, as Maulbow well knew, to have its snacks still wriggling-fresh as it started them down its gullet.

"No," Gefty said, "I couldn't call either of them really nice."

The Machmen

The fauna traps set up the previous day in the grasslands east of the Planetary Survey Station on Lederet had made a number of catches; but all of them represented species with which the two biologists of the survey team already were sufficiently familiar. Jeslin removed the traps, revived the captured animals from a safe distance with a stimulant gun, and shifted to a point a hundred and eighty miles northwest of the station, where he set the traps up again, half a mile apart. Here a tall forest spread over rolling hills, with stretches of dense undergrowth below; and the animal population could be expected to be of a somewhat different type.

Around midday, Jeslin had completed his preparations. He checked the new location of the traps on his charts, and turned the Pointer back toward the station. He was a stocky, well-muscled man, the youngest member of the team, who combined the duties of wildlife collector with those of the team's psychologist. Privately, he preferred the former work, enjoying his frequent encounters with curious and beautiful beasts on his way to and from the trap areas. And if the beasts were of a new variety, there would be a quick, stimulating chase in the Pointer, a versatile vehicle equally capable of hunting down game through thickest growth and of flying up to five times its own weight in captured specimens back to the station in undamaged condition.

Today was uneventful in that respect. There was game afoot but Jeslin was in a reflective mood, inclined to observe rather than pursue it. The station's cages were well supplied, and the traps, in their new location, would fill them up again before the biologists had completed their studies of the present occupants. He covered much of the stretch skimming over the forest at treetop level, emerged from it finally at a point twelve miles north of the station.

This was arid bush country, the ground below dotted with thorny growth. The Pointer flew across it, small things darting away from its shadow, vanishing with a flick into the thickets. Presently, Jeslin turned on the communicator, tapped the station's call button. Lederet was nearly a month's travel away from the nearest, civilized world; and small groups working on such remote out-worlds observed certain precautions as a matter of course. One of them was having every incoming vehicle identify itself before it arrived.

The screen lit up and the round-cheeked, freckled face of a middle-aged woman appeared in it. It was Ald, the team's dietician. She smiled pleasantly, said in an even voice, "Hello, Jeslin," went on in the same quiet, unemphasized tone, "Crash, machmen—"

The screen went blank.

Jeslin instantly reached out, grasped the Pointer's chase controls, spun the machine about and sent it racing back toward the forest. Flicking on the full set of ground and air-search screens, he studied them briefly in turn. His heart was pounding.

There was nothing in sight at the moment to justify Ald's warning. But the word "crash," used under such circumstances, had only one meaning. The station had been taken . . . he was to keep away from it, avoid capture and do whatever he could to help.

Machmen—Ald had been able to bring in that one additional word before they shut her off. Jeslin knew the term. Human beings surgically modified, equipped with a variety of devices to permit them to function freely in environments which otherwise would be instantly deadly to a man lacking the protection of a spacesuit or ship. They were instrumented men: machine men—machmen. Jeslin had not heard of recent experiments of the kind, but there were fairly numerous records of transitions to the machman condition, carried out with varying degrees of success.

His mind shifted back for an instant to a report received several days before from the Navy patrol boat assigned to Lederet for the protection of the survey station and its personnel. The boat had been contacted by a small I-Fleet vessel, requesting permission to carry out limited mining operations on the planet. After checking with the station, permission had been given. The I-Fleets were space vagrants, ordinarily harmless; and the mining party might be able to provide valuable information about the planet, with which they were evidently quite familiar.

The mining ship had begun its operations in a dry lakebed approximately a thousand miles from the station. Presumably, if machmen had captured the station, they had come over from the ship. With a heavily armed patrol boat circling the planet, it seemed an incredibly bold thing to do. Unless—

At that moment, Jeslin saw the figure in the search screen. It was human, appeared naked at first glance. Stretched out horizontally in the air about a hundred feet above the ground, arms laid back along its sides like a diver, it was approaching from the right, evidently with the intention of heading off the Pointer before the machine reached the forest.

And it was moving fast enough to do it . . .

Jeslin stared at the apparition for an instant, more in amazement than alarm. He saw now that the fellow was wearing trunks and boots and held some dark object in his left hand. Possibly the last was a flight device of some kind. Jeslin could make out nothing else to explain this headlong rush through the air. What did seem explained, he thought, was the manner in which the station had been taken. A handful of half-naked I-Fleet miners approaching on foot, apparently not even armed, would have aroused no concern there. The visitors would have been invited inside.

Jeslin glanced at the forest ahead, checked the search screens again. In the air far to the left were three tiny dots, which might be similar figures approaching. If so, it would take them several minutes to get here, and the Pointer would be lost in the forest by then. The machman moving up on the right apparently intended to attack by himself to prevent the escape—and that, Jeslin thought, was something he might turn to his advantage.

He drew a pack of plastic contact fetters out of a compartment, peeled off an eighteen-inch length, thrust it into his pocket. He patted another pocket on the right side of his jacket to make sure the gun he carried for last-ditch protection against overly aggressive Lederet wildlife was inside, then switched on the Pointer's stungun and turned the vehicle in a wide, swift curve toward the approaching machman.

The figure shot up at a steep slant before the gun could straighten out on it. In the screens, Jeslin watched it dart by perhaps two hundred yards overhead, come arcing down again behind the machine. He swung the Pointer's nose back to the forest, not more than a quarter of a mile ahead now, went rushing toward it, watching the machman close the gap between them, coming level with the ground a hundred yards away . . . then eighty . . . sixty . . .

The machman brought his left hand sweeping forward, the dark object held out in it. Jeslin braked hard. The Pointer, designed to change direction instantly to match the tactics of elusive game, pivoted end for end within its own length. As the stungun came around to the left of the pursuing figure, Jeslin pulled the trigger.

Caught by the outer fringe of the stunfield, the machman swerved sideways. The dark object—not a flight mechanism, after all, but some weapon—dropped from his hand. He went rolling limply on through the air, settling toward the ground.

The Pointer picked him up before he got there.

"My name," the machman said presently, "is Hulida. I'm aware of yours. It's quite possible, incidentally, that we've met before."

Jeslin glanced over at him. He'd fastened the fellow in the seat next to his own, wrists locked behind his back by a contact fetter, another fetter clamping a cloth blindfold over his eyes, seat belt drawn tight. For the past minute or two, he had been giving indications of recovering from stunshock, and it was no surprise to hear him speak. But a casually polite introduction, Jeslin thought, was hardly what he'd expected to hear.

"If we have," he said dryly, "I don't remember the occasion."

The blindfolded head of the man who called himself Hulida turned briefly toward him. He was not large; beside Jeslin, he seemed almost slight. But the olive-skinned body was firmly muscled, gave an impression of disciplined strength.

"It's only a possibility," Hulida said. "We happen to

have been graduated from the University of Rangier in the same year. My degree was in medicine."

"It seems regrettable that you didn't continue your professional career," Jeslin told him.

"Oh, but I did. I'm one of the results of a machman experiment, but I also had a considerable part in bringing that experiment to its remarkably successful conclusion."

Jeslin grunted, returned his attention to the search screens. Successful the experiment certainly seemed to have been. When he went out to free Hulida from the Pointer's snaring tentacles, he had expected to find at least some indications of the profound changes worked on a human body to enable it to pursue him through the air. But whatever the changes might be, they weren't outwardly visible. A hasty search of the man's few articles of clothing had revealed no instrument to explain such an ability either; but until Hulida acknowledged the fact, Jeslin hadn't been certain that Ald's description of the nature of the station's attackers was correct. Earlier work of that kind had produced shapes in which functional plastic and metal was obviously united with the necessary proportion of living flesh.

He looked at the clock in the instrument panel, checked the screens once more, swung the Pointer around toward a chart section due west of his present location, some three hundred miles away. Not once during the past twenty minutes while he was pursuing a constantly changing, randomly erratic course through the forest had one of the flying men appeared in the search screens. He could assume that for the present he had lost them. Meanwhile he had a prisoner who seemed willing to give him at least part of the information he wanted.

He said, "How many machmen are there on Lederet?"

"At the moment, about forty," Hulida said promptly. "The rest of our group—there are a hundred and ninety-five of us in all—are on a spaceship which is approaching the planet and will reach it shortly."

"That hundred and ninety-five," Jeslin asked, "is the total number of those who were transformed into machmen in your experiment?"

"Not entirely. There were a number of deaths at first, before we learned to perfect our methods."

"What will the spaceship do when it runs into our patrol boat?"

Hulida laughed. "It will simply take the crew on board, Jeslin. What else? Naturally, we captured the boat before we attempted to capture the station."

Jeslin already had been almost sure of it. Three times during his flight through the forest he had attempted to signal the patrol boat, had received no response.

"How was it done?"

"We took the mining ship up and sent them a distress message," Hulida said. "There had been an accident— we had injured men on board. Obligingly, they came to our help at once. When they set up a locktube, we released gas bombs in both ships. We don't breathe normally, of course. It was very simple."

He added, "But you need feel no concern for either the crew or your colleagues at the station. None of them has been harmed. That was not our intention."

"Glad to hear it," Jeslin said. "Now what's the purpose of this business? Apparently, your experiment resulted in an important scientific achievement. If it had been conducted openly, I would have heard of it. Why the secrecy? And why—" He checked himself. "How many deaths were there in the first stage of the experiment, while you were still perfecting your methods?"

The machman hesitated, said, "Fifty-two."

"I see. You weren't working strictly with volunteers."

"Of course not," Hulida said. "We were—and are still—a small group. The work was obviously dangerous, and none of us could be spared as subjects until the element of danger had been removed. But that was not the reason we worked secretly, published nothing after results were assured, and eventually left civilization together. After all, we need not have recorded those early failures."

"Then what was the reason?" Jeslin asked.

"Our realization that the machmen we were creating and presently would become is a higher order of being than the merely human one. At one stroke, he is rid of four-fifths of the body's distresses and infirmities. He can expect a vastly lengthened life span. He thinks more clearly, is less subject to emotional disturbances. He is tremendously more efficient on the physical level . . . independent of environmental circumstances as no ordinary human ever could be. And we are only at the beginning of this, the pioneers . . .

"Jeslin, we did not become machmen in order to be better able to toil on airless worlds or in space for our benefit or that of others. We made the choice because it is the greater manner of living. We are Homo Superior, the mankind of the future. And the ranks of Homo Superior are not to be opened to any low-grade fool who can pay to have the transformation carried out on him. Neither do we intend to subject our plans to the manipulations of government. We are a select group and shall remain it. That is why we detached ourselves from the Federation."

"And that," Jeslin asked, "adds up to a justification of piracy? One would think a couple of hundred of machmen geniuses might find it no more difficult to make a living in space than an ordinary I-Fleet composed of ordinarily competent human beings."

Hulida said, "Our purpose goes beyond looting the survey station, Jeslin. Its equipment and personnel, of course, are valuable prizes in themselves, and so, to a lesser extent, are the patrol boat and its crew."

Jeslin looked over at him. "The personnel—"

"The personnel," Hulida explained, "and the crew will

be transformed into machmen, naturally. They have highly trained minds, experience and skills which we can use to good advantage. Their consent isn't required. Not all of those who are machmen now underwent the transformation willingly, but their objections vanished as their experiences made its advantages fully apparent to them. They are as loyal to the group and its goals now as any of the others. And so will you be."

Jeslin felt a surge of cold anger. Mind-conditioning, of course. And it could be done . . .

"But our plan goes much farther than that," the machman was continuing. "This is a matter which has been very carefully investigated and prepared, Jeslin. The immediate consequence of your transformation will be that you will resume your work here as if nothing had happened—and, in fact, nothing else will have happened. You will continue to return favorable reports on Lederet to your department in the Hub. Within a year, the decision will be made to open precolonial operations on the planet.

"That is what we want. Equipment and supplies will be moved out here on a scale otherwise unobtainable by a small group such as ours. And with it will come technicians and scientists from whom we can select further recruits to round out our ranks. We will work carefully and quietly, but when we leave the planet, it will be to go forever beyond the Federation's reach with everything we need to found our own machman colony."

Jeslin was silent a moment, asked, "Why are you telling me all this?"

"To make it clear," the machman said, "that we simply cannot allow someone who knows about us to remain at large here. The possibility that you would still be alive and in a position to interfere with our plans when the Hub shipments begin to arrive may be slight, but we aren't ignoring it. Every other member of the survey team was accounted for during the morning. If necessary, we could turn all our resources now for months on end to the single purpose of hunting you down."

"You're inviting me to surrender?"

Hulida said, "I'm appealing to your reason. You have the opportunity of participating voluntarily in one of mankind's greatest adventures. If you reject it, it may not be possible to avoid killing you."

"At the moment," Jeslin said mildly, "it seems that I have one of the group's more important members as my hostage."

Hulida shook his blindfolded head. "No one of us is important enough to stand in the way of the group's goals. The fact that I'm your prisoner will be given every consideration, of course. But if it becomes necessary, we will both die."

Jeslin's gaze shifted to the course chart above the panel. He studied it a moment.

"I won't argue," he remarked, "with your claim that being transformed into a machman is a better way to live or the coming way to live. Possibly it's both. It's your methods I object to."

"They are our methods out of necessity," Hulida said.

"Perhaps. I'll think about it. And since you seem to have presented your case completely now, I'll appreciate it if you keep quiet for a while."

The machman smiled, shrugged, remained silent. After some minutes, Jeslin slowed the Pointer's advance. There was a valley ahead, a wide, sandy riverbed winding along it. His route led across the river. At this point, there was forest again on the other side, but there was no way he could avoid coming out from under the shelter of the trees for a distance of at least half a mile.

He had been watching the search screens constantly and did not think he was being followed. It would have been almost impossible for even a single machman to keep the fleeing Pointer in sight in the forest without coming into view occasionally in the screens. The sky was a different matter. Jeslin could not check for them there without showing himself above the forest. For all he knew, there were machmen directly overhead at the moment.

But he had to get over the river before the hunt for him became organized, and this was his best opportunity to do it. Now he could see sunlit patches of the valley ahead, between the trunks and undergrowth and he slowed the Pointer again. Prowl up to the edge of the open ground, he thought; then if there were no pursuers immediately in sight, make a quick dash across. It would be too bad if he was seen, but once he reached the forest on the other side of the valley, he should be able to lose them again . . .

He heard a sound from Hulida, an abrupt, soft intake of breath, looked over at him and saw the knotted jaw muscles, the tight, fixed grin of the machman's mouth. Immediately, almost before he could form a conscious thought of why he should do it, Jeslin was spinning the Pointer away from the valley, back into the forest, and slamming on speed.

Behind him, the forest crashed. In the rear search screen, he saw the thing sweep after him . . . a vertical torrent, fifteen feet across, composed of earth, brush, uprooted and shattered trees rushing into the air, sucked up by a tractor beam. Beyond it, a group of flying figures darted into the forest, fanned out.

In thick growth, Jeslin turned the Pointer left again, raced on, hugging the ground, for a hundred yards, swung sharply to the right. For perhaps a minute, he saw nothing in the screens except the thickets the machine was slashing through. Then there was a glimpse of two machmen weaving around tree trunks above the undergrowth. The roar of the tractor beam had lessened, now grew stronger again. The Pointer flashed into another thicket.

"Useless, Jeslin!" Hulida was shouting. "They've found you and you can't shake them off!"

For a while, it seemed Hulida was right. The fliers couldn't match the Pointer's speed in the forest. They would be there for instants, coming down through the crowns, fall behind as Jeslin swerved off, and vanish again. But they could rise back up through the trees and overtake him in the open air, and were doing it. He didn't know how many they were in all, but half the time he seemed to be in momentary view of one or the other of them.

And the tractors followed the fliers. There must be at least two of the machines moving across the forest after him, guided by the flying scouts. Suddenly the roar of the beam would arise, shredding the growth as it rushed in towards him; sometimes a second one appeared almost simultaneously from the other side. Once he nearly ran the Pointer directly into one of the dark, hurtling columns of forest debris; as he slewed away from it, the vehicle shuddered as if it were being shaken apart, and Hulida uttered a short, hoarse cry.

And then everything was quiet again. The Pointer rushed on—a minute, two minutes, three, four; and no pursuer appeared in the screens. Jeslin saw a gully ahead, a narrow, dry water bed, dropped into it, moved along it a quarter of a mile until it turned into a deep, rocky ravine almost enclosed by dense undergrowth above. There he stopped the machine.

The time display in the instrument panel told him twelve minutes had passed since he reached the edge of the valley. He would have said he had been running from the tractors for nearly an hour.

He rubbed his sweating palms along his thighs, looked over at Hulida's slumped form. There was no particular satisfaction in knowing that the chase had unnerved the machman more than it had him.

"Now talk," he said unsteadily, "if you care to go on living. What happened?"

Hulida straightened slowly but did not answer at once. Then he said, speaking carefully and obviously struggling to recover his self-possession, "Several of the survey team members were given truth drugs and questioned as soon as we secured the station. They told us of the long-range transmitter which was to be used to call for help if the station was disabled or overwhelmed by a hostile force. When you were warned off and escaped, it was assumed that that was where you would try to go. The transmitter has been located and is, of course, being guarded. We ran into the group which was watching the route you were most likely to take."

Jeslin had a sense of heavy, incredulous dismay. He hadn't expected that particular piece of information to get to the machmen so quickly. It had been the one way left open now to defeat their plans.

After a moment, he asked, "Where did those tractors come from?"

"They are part of our ship's equipment. The machines were sent ahead to help in your capture."

Jeslin grunted. "If one of the beams had touched us," he said, "there's a good chance we would have been torn apart before they made a capture! You're right about your group not caring who stands in the way when they're out to do something." He saw Hulida's cheeks go gray below the blindfold, added, "Just before they jumped us, you knew it was coming. You machmen have a built-in communication system of some kind—"

Hulida hesitated, said, "Yes, we do."

"How does it operate?"

"I could attempt to describe it to you," Hulida said, "but the description would have meaning only to another machman. The use of the system cannot be taught until it can be experienced."

"At any rate," Jeslin said, "your friends know we have stopped running and have settled down somewhere."

Hulida shook his head.

"I have not told them that." He managed a brief, shaky grin. "After all, Jeslin, I prefer to go on living . . . and there is no reason why either of us should die. You can do nothing more, and you've had a demonstration of what your life as a fugitive would be like. The group won't give up the hunt until they have you. You can calculate your final odds for yourself. But surrender to me—now—and all will still be well."

There had been a growing urgency in his voice. Jeslin watched him, not answering. The machman's mouth worked. Fear, Jeslin thought. More fear than Hulida should be feeling at the moment. His own skin began to crawl. Here at the bottom of the ravine, the search screens showed him nothing.

He reached out quietly, switched on the Pointer's stungun.

"Jeslin . . . "

Jeslin remained silent.

"Jeslin, there is no time to lose!" Hulida's voice was harsh with desperation. "I did not tell you the truth just now. I can conceal nothing from the group. There are multiple direct connections between the brains, the nervous systems, of all of us. Our communication is not wholly a mechanical process—we function almost as units of a group mind. They know you are hiding in the area and have been searching for you. At any instant—"

Jeslin turned the Pointer's nose upward, triggered the gun. The stunfield smashed up out of the ravine, the machine following it. Man-shapes swirled about limply among the trees like drifting leaves, and something came thundering along the floor of the gully toward the place where the Pointer had been hiding.

Then the nightmare chase began again . . .

An endless period later, Jeslin realized he was clear of the pursuit for a second time. He kept the Pointer hurtling forward on a straight line, staying below the trees where he could, but flicking through open stretches and over streambeds without pausing. Once the screen showed him two figures wheeling high against the sky; he thought they were machmen but was under cover again before he could be sure.

Then something smashed against the Pointer's engine section in the rear. Jeslin swung the machine about, saw a figure gliding away behind a massive tree trunk, sent it spinning with the stungun, turned again and rushed on. A minute later, there was a distant crashing in the forest; then silence.

The Pointer began to vibrate heavily, and presently the speed indicator dropped. Jeslin looked at the location chart, chewing his lip. His arm muscles ached; he was trembling with tension and fatigue. He found himself trying to urge the machine onward mentally, made a snorting sound of self-derision.

Then there was warm, golden sunlight ahead among the trees. Jeslin brought a folded black hood out from under the instrument panel, laid it beside him. He reached over and unfastened Hulida's seat belt. The machman sagged sideways on the seat. His mouth moved as if he were speaking, but he seemed dazed.

Jeslin brought the Pointer to the ground, turned off the laboring engine. He picked up the black hood, dropped it over his head, its lower folds resting on his shoulders. From within, it seemed transparent, showing a glassy glitter around the edges of objects.

He took his gun from his pocket, hauled open the side door and stepped out. Ahead something slid quickly through a sunlit opening in the treetops. Jeslin sent two bolts ripping through the foliage behind it, reached back into the Pointer and hauled Hulida out by the arm. He swung the staggering machman around,

started at a half-run toward the area of open ground
fifty yards away, thrusting Hulida ahead of him.

"Jeslin—" It was a hoarse gasp.

"Keep moving! They'll have a tractor on our machine
in a moment." He felt the figure lighten suddenly,
warned, "Don't try to leave me! I'll blow your head off
before you're ten feet away."

"You're insane! You can't escape now!"

Tractor beams roared suddenly among the trees
behind them, and Hulida screamed. They stumbled
through a thicket, out into the sunlight of a wide glade.
Machman figures darted above the treetops of the far side,
two hundred yards away. Jeslin ripped the blindfold from
Hulida's face, seized his arm again, ran forward with him
into the glade.

From the center of the open area came a single deep
bell note, a curiously attention-binding sound. Jeslin
stopped, hurled Hulida forward, away from him. The
machman rolled over, came swaying almost weightlessly
to his feet. The bell note sounded again. Hulida's head
turned toward it. He went motionless.

Here it comes, Jeslin thought . . .

And it came. Under the shielding hood, he was
experiencing it, as he had many times before, as a pulsing, dizzying, visual blur. Outside, wave after wave of
radiation was rushing out from the animal trap concealed
in the center of the clearing, a pounding, numbing pattern
of confusion to any mind within its range, increasing
moment by moment in intensity.

After ten seconds, it stopped.

Hulida slumped sideways, settled slowly to the ground.

A man-shape streaked down out of the sky, turning
over and over, crashed into the treetops beyond the glade.

Something else passed through the thickets behind
Jeslin, sucking noisily at the earth, and moved off into
the distance, dirt and other debris cascading back down
into the trees behind it. A similar din was receding

through the forest to the south. The tractors were continuing on their course, uncontrolled.

Overhead, Jeslin saw other machman fliers drifting gradually down through the air.

He moved forward, picked up Hulida and drew back with him out of the trap's range. It would reset itself automatically now for any moving thing of sufficient size to trigger its mechanisms.

He wasn't sure he would find anything left of the Pointer, but the beams hadn't come within fifty feet of it. As he came up, he heard the communicator signal inside. He put Hulida down hastily, climbed in and switched on the instrument.

The face of Govant, the team's geophysicist, appeared in the screen.

"Jeslin, what the devil's happened?" he demanded. "The machmen who took over the station all collapsed at the same instant just now! Ald says she's sure you caused it in some manner. They're alive but unconscious."

"I know," Jeslin said. "I suggest you disarm them and dump them into one of the cages."

"That's being done, of course!" Govant said irritably. "We're not exactly stupid. But—"

"You're yelling for help from any navy units around?"

"Naturally." Govant looked aside, away from the screen, added, "Apparently, we've just had a response! But it may be weeks before help arrives, and the machmen said they had a spaceship which—"

"Their ship won't be a problem," Jeslin said. "Get a few airtrucks over here, will you? I'll give you my location. In a rather short time, I'm going to have a great many machmen around to transport back to the station's cages."

Govant stared at him. "What did you do to them?"

"Well," Jeslin said, "for all practical purposes, I've blown out their cortical fuses. I walked one of them into a hypnoshock trap here, and it hit the others through him. I'll give you the details when I get back. At present, they're simply paralyzed. In a few hours, they'll be able to move again; but for days after that, they won't make any move that somebody hasn't specifically told them to make. By that time, we should have the last of them locked up."

He stepped out of the Pointer after Govant had switched off and went back to Hulida, mentally shaping the compulsive suggestions which presently would shut off the wandering tractors, round up the tranced fliers, and bring the captured patrol boat and the machman spaceship gliding obediently down to the planet.

The Other Likeness

When he felt the sudden sharp tingling on his skin which came from the alarm device under his wrist watch, Dr. Halder Leorm turned unhurriedly from the culture tray he was studying, walked past the laboratory technician to the radiation room, entered it and closed the door behind him. He slipped the instrument from his wrist, removed its back plate, and held it up to his eye.

He was looking into the living room of his home, fifty miles away in another section of Orado's great city of Draise. A few steps from the entry, a man lay on his back on the carpeting, eyes shut, face deeply flushed, apparently unconscious. Halder Leorm's mouth tightened. The man on the carpet was Dr. Atteo, his new assistant, assigned to the laboratory earlier in the week. Beyond Atteo, the entry from the residence's delivery area and car port stood open.

Fingering the rim of the tiny scanner with practiced quickness, Halder Leorm shifted the view to other sections of the house, finally to the car port. An empty aircar stood in the port; there was no one in sight.

Halder sighed, replaced the instrument on his wrist, and glanced over at a wall mirror. His face was pale but looked sufficiently composed. Leaving the radiation room, he picked up his hat, said to the technician, "Forgot to mention it, Reef, but I'll have to head over to central laboratories again."

Reef, a large, red-headed young man, glanced around in mild surprise. "They've got a nerve, calling you across town every two days!" he observed. "Whose problem are you supposed to solve now?"

"I wasn't informed. Apparently, something urgent has come up and they want my opinion on it."

"Yeah, I bet!" Reef scratched his head, glanced along the rows of culture trays. "Well . . . nothing here at the moment I can't handle, even if Atteo doesn't show up. Will you be back before evening?"

"I wouldn't count on it," Halder said. "You know how those conferences tend to go."

"Uh-huh. Well, Dr. Leorm, if I don't see you before tomorrow, give my love to your beautiful wife."

Halder smiled back at him from the door. "Will do, Reef!" He let the door slide shut behind him, started towards the exit level of the huge pharmaceutical plant. Reef had acted in a completely normal manner. If, as seemed very probable, "Dr. Atteo" was a Federation agent engaged in investigating Dr. Halder Leorm, Halder's co-workers evidently had not been apprised of the fact. Still, Halder thought, he must warn Kilby instantly. It was quite possible that an attempt to arrest him would be made before he left the building.

He stepped into the first ComWeb booth on his route, and dialed Kilby's business number. His wife had a desk job in one of the major fashion stores in the residential section of Draise, and—which was fortunate just now— a private office. Her face appeared almost immediately on the screen before him, a young face, soft-looking, with large, gray eyes. She smiled in pleased surprise. " 'Lo Halder!"

" 'Lo, Kilby . . . Did you forget?"

Kilby's smile became inquiring. "Forget what?"

"That we're lunching together at Hasmin's today."

Halder paused, watching the color drain quickly from Kilby's cheeks.

"Of course!" she whispered. "I did forget. Got tied up in . . . and . . . I'll leave right now! All right?"

Halder smiled. She was past the first moment of shock and would be able to handle herself. After all, they had made very precise preparations against the day when they might discover that the Federation's suspicions had turned, however tentatively, in their direction.

"That'll be fine," he said. "I'm calling from the lab and will leave at once"—he paused almost imperceptibly—"if I'm not held up. Meet you at Hasmin's, in any case, in around twenty minutes."

Kilby's eyes flickered for an instant. If Halder didn't make it away? She was to carry out her own escape, as planned. That was the understanding. She gave him a tremulous smile. "And I'm forgiven?"

"Of course." Halder smiled back.

The guards at the check-out point were not men he knew, but Halder walked through the ID-scanning band without incident, apparently without arousing interest. Beyond, to the left, was a wide one-way portal to a tube station. His aircar was in the executive parking area on the building's roof, but the escape plan called for both of them to abandon their private cars, which were more than likely to be traps, and use the public transportation systems in starting out.

Halder entered the tube station, went to a rented locker, opened it and took out two packages, one containing a complete change of clothing and a mirror, the other half a dozen canned cultures of as many varieties of microlife—highly specialized strains of life, of which the pharmaceutical concern that employed Dr. Halder Leorm knew no more than it did of the methods by which they had been developed.

Halder carried the packages into a ComWeb booth which he locked and shielded for privacy. Then he opened both packages and quickly removed his clothing. Opening the first of the cultures, he dipped one of the needles into it and, watching himself in the mirror, made a carefully measured injection in each side of his face. He laid the needle down and opened the next container, aware of the enzyme reaction that had begun to race through him.

Three minutes later, the mirror showed him a dark-skinned stranger with high cheek bones, heavy jaw, thick nose, slightly slanted eyes, graying hair. Halder disposed of the mirror, the clothes he had been wearing and the remaining contents of the second package. Unchecked, the alien organisms swarming in his blood stream now would have gone on to destroy him in a variety of unpleasant ways. But with their work of disguise completed, they were being checked.

He emerged presently from a tube exit in uptown Draise, on the terrace of a hotel forty stories above the street level. He didn't look about for Kilby, or rather the woman Kilby would turn into on her way here. The plan called for him to arrive first, to make sure he hadn't been traced, and then to see whether she was being followed.

She appeared five minutes later, a slightly stocky lady now, perhaps ten years under Halder's present apparent age, dark-skinned as he was, showing similar racial characteristics. She flashed her teeth at him as she came up, sloe eyes flirting.

"Didn't keep you waiting, did I?" she asked.

Halder growled amiably, "What do you think? Let's

grab a cab and get going." Nobody had come out of the tube exit behind her.

Kilby nodded understandingly; she had remembered not to look back. She was talking volubly about some imaginary adventure as they started down the terrace stairs towards a line of aircabs, playing her part, high-piled golden hairdo bobbing about. A greater contrast to the slender, quiet, gray-eyed girl, brown hair falling softly to her shoulders, with whom Halder had talked not more than twenty minutes ago would have been difficult to devise. The disguises might have been good enough, he thought, to permit them to remain undetected in Draise itself.

But the plan didn't call for that. There were too many things at stake.

Kilby slipped into the cab ahead of him without a break in her chatter.

Her voice stopped abruptly as Halder closed the cab door behind him, activating the vehicle's one-way vision shield. Kilby was leaning across the front seat beside the driver, turning off the comm box. She straightened, dropped down into the back seat beside Halder, biting her lip. The driver's head sagged sideways as if he had fallen asleep; then he slid slowly down on the seat and vanished from Halder's sight.

"Got him instantly, eh?" Halder asked, switching on the passenger controls.

"Hm-m-m!" Kilby opened her purse, slipped the little gun which had been in the palm of her left hand into it, reached out and gripped Halder's hand for an instant. "You drive, Halder," she said. "I'm so nervous I could scream! I'm scared cold! What happened?"

Halder lifted the cab out from the terrace, swung it skywards. "We were right in wondering about Dr. Atteo," he said. "Half an hour ago, he attempted to go through our home in our absence. We'll have to assume he's a

Federation agent. The entry trap knocked him out, but the fat's probably in the fire now. The Federation may not have been ready to make an arrest yet, but after this there'll be no hesitation. We'll have to move fast if we intend to keep ahead of Atteo's colleagues."

Kilby drew in an unsteady breath. "You warned Rane and Santin?"

Halder nodded. "I sent the alert signal to their apartment ComWeb in the capital. Under the circumstances, I didn't think a person-to-person call would be advisable. They'll have time to pack and get out to the ranch before we arrive. We'll give them the details then."

"Did you reset the trap switch at the house entry?"

Halder slowed the cab, turning it into one of the cross-city traffic lines above Draise. "No," he said. "Knocking out a few more Federation agents wouldn't give us any advantage. It'll be eight or nine hours before Atteo will be able to talk; and, with any luck at all, we'll be clear of the planet by that time."

The dark woman who was Kilby and a controlled devil's swarm of microlife looked over at him and asked in Kilby's voice, "Halder, do you think we should still go on trying to find the others now?"

"Of course. Why stop?"

Kilby hesitated, said, "It took you three months to find me. Four months later, we located Rane Rellis . . . and Santin, at almost the same time. Since then we've drawn one blank after another. A year and a half gone, and a year and a half left."

She paused, and Halder said nothing, knowing she was fighting to keep her voice steady. After a few seconds, Kilby went on. "Almost twelve hundred still to find, scattered over a thousand worlds. Most of them probably in hiding, as we were. And with the Federation on our trail . . . even if we get away this time, what chance is there now of contacting the whole group before time runs out?"

Halder said patiently, "It's not an impossibility. We've been forced to spend most of the past year and a half gathering information, studying the intricate functioning of this gigantic civilization—so many things that our mentors on Kalechi either weren't aware of or chose not to tell us. And we haven't done too badly, Kilby. We're prepared now to conduct the search for the group in a methodical manner. Nineteen hours in space, and we'll be on another world, under cover again, with new identities. Why shouldn't we continue with the plan until . . ."

Kilby interrupted without change of expression. "Until we hear some day that billions of human beings are dying on the Federation's worlds?"

Halder kept his eyes fixed on the traffic pattern ahead. "It won't come to that," he said.

"Won't it? How can you be sure?" Kilby asked tonelessly.

"Well," Halder asked, "what else can we do? You aren't suggesting that we give ourselves up—"

"I've thought of it."

"And be picked apart mentally and physically in the Federation's laboratories?" Halder shook his head. "In their eyes we'd be Kalechi's creatures . . . monsters. Even if we turn ourselves in, they'll think it's some trick, that we'd realized we'd get caught anyway. We couldn't expect much mercy. No, if everything fails we'll see to it that the Federation gets adequate warning. But not, if we can avoid it, at the expense of our own lives." He glanced over at her, his eyes troubled. "We've been over this before, Kilby."

"I know." Kilby bit her lip. "You're right, I suppose."

Halder let the cab glide out of the traffic lane, swung it around towards the top of a tall building three miles to their left. "We'll be at the club in a couple of minutes," he said. "If you're too disturbed, it would be better if you stayed in the car. I'll pick up our flight-hiking outfits and we can take the cab on to the city limits before we dismiss it."

Kilby shook her head. "We agreed we shouldn't change any details of the escape plan unless it was absolutely necessary. I'll straighten out. I've just let this situation shake me too much."

They set the aircab to traffic-safe random cruise control before getting out of it at their club. It lifted quietly into the air again as soon as the door had closed, was out of sight beyond the building before they reached the club entrance. The driver's records had indicated that his shift would end in three hours. Until that time he would not be missed. More hours would pass after the cab was located before the man returned to consciousness. What he had to say then would make no difference.

In one of the club rooms, rented to a Mr. and Mrs. Anley, they changed to shorts and flight-hiking equipment, then took a tube to the outskirts of Draise where vehicleless flight became possible. Forest parks interspersed with small residential centers stretched away to the east. They set their flight harnesses to Draise's power broadcast system, moved up fifty feet and floated off into the woods, energizing drive and direction units with the measured stroking motion which made flight-hiking one of the most relaxing and enjoyable of sports. And one— so Halder had theorized—which would be considered an improbable occupation for a couple attempting to escape from the Federation's man-hunting systems.

For an hour and a half, they held a steady course eastwards, following the contours of the rolling forested ground, rarely emerging into the open. Other groups of vehicleless fliers passed occasionally; as members of a sporting fraternity, they exchanged waves and shouted greetings. At last, a long, wild valley opened ahead, showing no trace of human habitation; at its far end began open land, dotted with small tobacco farms where automatic cultivators moved unhurriedly about. Kilby, glancing back over her shoulder at Halder for a moment, swung around towards one of the farms, gliding down close to the ground, Halder twenty feet behind her. They settled down beside a hedge at the foot of a slope covered with tobacco plants. A small gate in the hedge immediately swung open.

"All clear here, folks!" a voice curiously similar to Halder's addressed them from the gate speaker.

Rane Rellis, a lanky, red-headed man with a wide-boned face, was striding down the slope towards them as they moved through the gate. "We got your alert," he said; "but as it happens, we'd already realized that something had gone wrong."

Kilby gave him a startled glance. "Somebody has been checking on you, too?"

"Not that . . . at least as far as we know. Come on up to the shed. Santin's already inside the mountain." As they started along the narrow path between the rows of plants, Rellis went on, "The first responses to our inquiries came in today. One of them looked very promising. Santin flew her car to Draise immediately to inform you about it. She scanned your home as usual before calling, discovered three strange men waiting inside."

"When was this?" Halder interrupted.

"A few minutes after one o'clock. Santin checked at once at your place of work and Kilby's, learned you both were absent, deduced you were still at large and probably on your way here. She called to tell me about it. Your alert signal sounded almost before she'd finished talking."

Halder glanced at Kilby. "We seem to have escaped arrest by something like five minutes," he remarked dryly. "Were you able to bring the records with you, Rane?"

"Yes, everything. If we get clear of Orado, we can pick up almost where we left off." Rane Rellis swung the door of the cultivator shed open and followed them in, closing and locking the door behind him. They crossed quickly through the small building to an open wall portal at the far end. Beyond the portal a large, brightly lit room was visible, comfortably furnished, windowless. Between that room and the shed the portal spanned a distance of seven miles, a vital point in the organization of their escape route. If they were traced this far, the trail would end—temporarily, at least—at the ranch.

They stepped over into the room, and Rane Rellis pulled down a switch. Behind them the portal entry vanished. Back in the deserted ranch building, its mechanisms were bursting into flames, would burn fiercely for a few seconds and fuse to dead slag.

Rane said tightly, "I feel a little better now . . . just a little! The Fed agents are good, but I haven't yet heard of detection devices that could drive through five hundred yards of solid rock to spot us inside a mountain." He paused as a tall girl with black hair, dark-brown eyes, came in from an adjoining room. Santin Rellis was the only one of the four who was not employing a biological disguise at the moment, In spite of the differences in their appearance, she might have been taken for Kilby's sister.

Halder told them what had occurred in Draise, concluded, "I'd believed that suspicion was more likely to center first on one of you. Particularly, of course, on Santin, working openly in Orado's Identification Center."

Santin grinned. "And, less openly, copying out identity-patterns!" she added. Her face sobered quickly again. "There's no indication of what did attract attention to you?"

Halder shook his head. "I can only think it's the microbiological work I've been doing. That, of course, would suggest that they already have an inkling of Kalechi's three-year plan to destroy the Federation."

Rane added, "And that at least one of the group already has been captured!"

"Probably."

There was silence for a moment. Santin said evenly, "That isn't a pleasant thought. Halder, everything we've learned recently at the Identification Center indicates that Rane's theory is correct . . . every one of the twelve hundred members of the Kalechi group probably can be analyzed down to the same three basic identity-patterns, reshuffled in endless variation. The Federation wouldn't have to capture many of us before discovering the fact. It will then start doing exactly what we're trying to do— use it to identify the rest of the group."

Halder nodded. "I've thought of that."

"You still intend to use the Senla Starlight Cruisers to get out into space?" Rane asked.

"Kilby and I will," Halder said. "But now, of course, you two had better select one of the alternate escape routes."

"Why's that?" Santin asked sharply.

Halder looked at her. "That's obvious, isn't it? There's a good chance you're still completely in the clear."

"That's possible. But it isn't a good enough reason for splitting up. We're a working team, and we should stay together, regardless of circumstances. What do you say, Rane?"

Her husband said, "I agree with you." He smiled briefly at Halder. "We'll be waiting for you on the north shore of Lake Senla ten minutes before the Starlight Cruise lifts. Now, is there anything else to discuss?"

"Not at the moment." Halder paused, dissatisfied, then went on. "All right. We still don't know just what the Federation is capable of . . . one move might as easily be wrong as the other. We'll pick you up, as arranged. Kilby and I are flight-hiking on to Senla, so we might as well start immediately."

They went into the second room of the underground

hideout. Rane turned to the exit portal's controls, asked, "Where shall I let you out?"

"We'll take the river exit," Halder said. "Six miles from here, nine from the ranch . . . that should be far enough. We'll be lost in an army of vacationers from Draise and the capital thirty seconds after we emerge."

It was dusk when Halder and Kilby turned into the crowded shore walk of the lake resort of Senla, moving unhurriedly towards a bungalow Halder had bought under another name some months before. Halder's thoughts went again over the details of the final stage of their escape from Orado. Essentially, the plan was simple. An hour from now they would slide their small star cruiser out of the bungalow's yacht stall, pick up Rane and Santin on the far shore of the lake, then join the group of thirty or so private yachts which left the resort area nightly for a two-hour flight to a casino ship stationed off the planet. A group cruise was unlikely to draw official scrutiny even tonight; and after reaching the casino, they should be able to slip on unobserved into space.

There was, however, no way of knowing with certainty that the plan . . . or any other plan . . . would work. It was only during the past few months that the four of them had begun to understand in detail the extent to which the vast, apparently loose complex of the Federation's worlds was actually organized. How long they had been under observation, how much the Federation suspected or knew about them—those questions were, at the moment, unanswerable. So Halder walked on in alert silence; giving his attention to anything which might be a first indication of danger in the crowds surging quietly past them along Senla's shore promenade in the summer evening. It was near the peak of the resort's season; a sense of ease and relaxation came from the people he passed, their voices seeming to blend into a single, low-pitched, friendly murmur. In time, Halder told himself, if everything went well, he and Kilby might be able to mingle undisguised, unafraid, with just such a crowd. But tonight they were hunted.

He laid his hand lightly on Kilby's arm, said, "Let's rest on that bench over there for a moment."

She smiled up at him, said, "All right," turned and led the way towards an unoccupied bench set back among the trees above the walk. They sat down, and Halder quickly slipped the watch off his wrist and removed the scanner's cover plate. The bungalow was a few hundred yards away now, on a side path which led down to the lake. It was showing no lights, but as the scanner reached into it, invisible radiation flooded the dark rooms and hallway, disclosing them to the instrument's inspection. For two or three minutes, Halder studied the bungalow's interior carefully; then he shifted the view to the grounds outside, finally to the yacht stall and the little star cruiser. Twice Kilby touched him warningly as somebody appeared about to approach the bench, and Halder put down his hand. But the strangers went by without pausing.

At last, he replaced the instrument on his wrist. He had discovered no signs of intrusion in the bungalow; and, at any rate, it was clear that no one was waiting there now, either in the little house itself or in the immediate vicinity. He stood up, and put out his hand to assist Kilby to her feet.

"We'll go on," he said.

A few minutes later, they came along a narrow garden path to the bungalow's dark side entrance. There was to be no indication tonight that the bungalow had occupants. Halder unlocked the door quietly, and after Kilby had slipped inside, he stepped in behind her and secured the door.

For an instant, as they moved along the short, lightless passage to the front rooms, a curious sensation touched Halder—a terrifying conviction that some undefinable thing had just gone wrong. And with that, his whole body was suddenly rigid, every muscle locking in mid-motion. He felt momentum topple him slowly forwards; then he was no longer falling but stopped, tilted off-balance at a grotesque angle, suspended in a web of forces he could not feel. Not the slightest sound had come from Kilby, invisible in the blackness ahead of him.

Halder threw all his will and strength into the effort to force motion back into his body. Instead, a wave of cold numbness washed slowly up through him. It welled into his brain, and for a time all thought and sensation ended.

His first new awareness was a feeling of being asleep and not knowing how to wake up. There was no disturbance associated with it. All about was darkness, complete and quiet.

With curious deliberation, Halder's senses now began bringing other things to his attention. He was seated, half reclining, in a deep and comfortable chair, his back against it. He seemed unable to move. His arms were secured in some manner to the chair's armrests; but, beyond that, he also found it impossible to lift his body forwards or, he discovered next, to turn his head in any direction. He was breathing normally and he could open and shut his eyes and glance about in unchanging darkness. But that was all.

Still with a dreamlike lack of concern, Halder began to ask himself what had happened; and in that instant, with a rush of hot terror, his memory opened out. They had been trapped . . . some undetectable trick of Federation science had waited for them in the bungalow at Lake Senla. He had been taken somewhere else.

What had they done with Kilby?

Immediately, almost as if in answer to his question, the darkness seemed to lighten. But the process was gradual; seconds passed before Halder gained the impression of a very large room of indefinite proportions. Twenty feet away was the rim of a black, circular depression in the flooring. At first, his chair seemed the only piece of furnishing here; then, as the area continued to brighten, Halder became aware of several objects at some distance on his right.

For an instant he strained violently to turn his head towards them. That was still impossible, but the objects were there, near the edge of his vision. Again the great room grew lighter, and for seconds Halder could distinguish three armchairs like his own, spaced perhaps twenty feet apart along the rim of the central pit. Each chair had an occupant; in the nearest was Kilby, restored to her natural appearance, motionless, pale face turned forwards, eyes open. Suddenly the light vanished.

Halder sat shocked, realizing he had tried to speak to Kilby and that no sound had come from his throat. Neither speech nor motion was allowed them here. But he didn't doubt that Kilby was awake, or that Santin and Rane Rellis were in the farther chairs, though he hadn't seen either of them clearly. Their captors had given them a brief glimpse of one another, perhaps to let them know all had been caught. Then, as the light disappeared, Halder's glance had shifted for an instant to his right hand lying on the armrest—long enough to see that the dark tinge was gone from his skin, as it was from Kilby's, that he, too, had been deprived of the organisms which disguised him.

And that, his studies in Draise had showed clearly, was something the Federation's science would be a century away from knowing how to do unless it learned about Kalechi's deadly skills.

Once more, it was almost as if the thought were being given an answer. In the darkness of the room a bright image appeared, three-dimensional, not quite a sphere in form, tiger-striped in orange and black, balanced on a broad, bifurcated swimming tail. Stalked eyes protruded from the top of the sphere; their slit pupils seemed to be staring directly at Halder. Down both sides ran a row of ropy arms.

Simultaneously with the appearance of this projection, a man's voice began to speak, not loudly but distinctly. Dreamlike again, the voice seemed to have no specific source, as if it were coming from every direction at once; and a numbing conviction arose in Halder that their minds were being destroyed in this room, that a methodical dissecting process had begun which would continue move by move and hour by hour until the Federation's scientists were satisfied that no further scraps of information could be drained from the prisoners. The investigation might be completely impersonal; but the fact that they were being ignored here as sentient beings, were not permitted to argue their case or offer an explanation, seemed more chilling than deliberate brutality. And yet, Halder told himself, he couldn't really blame anyone for the situation they were in. The Kalechi group represented an urgent and terrible threat. The Federation could not afford to make any mistakes in dealing with it.

"This image," the voice was saying, "represents a Great Satog, the oxygen-breathing, water-dwelling native of the world of Kalechi. There are numerous type-variations of the species. Shown here is the dominant form. It is highly intelligent; approximately a third of a Satog's body space is occupied by its brain.

"Kalechi's civilization is based on an understanding of biological processes and the means of their manipulation which is well in advance of our own. This specialized interest appears to have developed from the Satogs' genetic instability, a factor which they have learned to control and to use to their advantage. At present, they have established themselves on at least a dozen other worlds, existing on each in a modified form which is completely adapted to the new environment.

"Our occasional contacts with Kalechi and its colonies during the past two centuries have been superficially friendly, but it appears now that the Great Satogs have regarded our technological and numerical superiority with alarm and have cast about for a method to destroy the Federation without risk to themselves. A weapon was on hand—their great skill and experience in altering genetic patterns in established life forms to produce desired changes. They devised the plan of distributing Kalechi agents secretly throughout the Federation. These were to develop and store specific strains of primitive organisms which, at an indicated later date, would sweep our major worlds simultaneously with an unparalleled storm of plagues.

"The most audacious part of the Kalechi scheme follows. Ninety-two years ago, a Federation survey ship disappeared in that sector of the galaxy. Aboard it was a man named Ohl Cantrall, an outstanding scientist of the period. We know now that this ship was captured by the Great Satogs, and that Cantrall, his staff, and his crew, were subjected to extensive experimentation by them, and eventually were killed.

"The experimentation had been designed to provide Kalechi's master-biologists with models towards which to work. They proposed to utilize the high mutability of their species to develop a Satog type that would be the exact physical counterpart of a human being and could live undetected on our worlds for the several years required to prepare for the attack. They were amazingly successful. Each group of cells in the long series which began moving towards an approximation of the human pattern was developed only far enough to initiate the greatest favorable shift possible at that point in its genetic structure. Cell generations may have followed each other within hours in this manner, for over six decades.

"The goal of the experiment, the last generation issued in Kalechi's laboratories, were Satog copies of embryonic human beings. This stage was comprised of approximately twelve hundred individuals who were now permitted to mature and were schooled individually in complete isolation by Satog teachers. They were indoctrinated with their purpose in life . . . the destruction of our populations . . . and trained fully in the manner of accomplishing it.

"Eventually, each was shipped to a Federation world. Cover identities as obscure Federation citizens with backgrounds and records had been prepared. The final instructions given these agents were simple. They were to do nothing to draw attention to themselves, make no attempt to contact one another. They were to create their stocks of lethal organisms, provide methods of distribution and, on a selected day, three Federation years away, release the floods of death."

The voice paused briefly, went on. "It is a sobering reflection that this plan—an attack by a comparatively minor race with one specialized skill on the greatest human civilization in history—might very well have been appallingly successful. But the Great Satogs failed, in part because of the very perfection of their work.

"From the human beings on board Ohl Cantrall's captured survey ship the Satog scientists selected Cantrall himself and two female technicians on his staff as the models to be followed in developing Kalechi's pseudo-humanity. In the twelve hundred members of the group sent to the Federation ninety years later, these three identity patterns are recognizable. They appear in varying degrees of combination, but an occasional individual will show only one or the other of the three patterns involved.

"Ohl Cantrall was regarded as a great man in his time, and his identification pattern is on record. That was the detail which first revealed the plot. When three duplicates of that particular pattern—and a considerable number of approximate duplicates—turned up simultaneously in identification banks at widely separated points in the Federation, it aroused more than scientific curiosity. Our security system has learned to look with suspicion on apparent miracles. The unsuspecting 'Cantralls' were located and apprehended at once; the threat to the Federation was disclosed; and an intensive though unpublicized search for the scattered group of Kalechi agents began immediately . . . "

The voice paused again.

The Satog image above the pit vanished. A clear light sprang up in the big room. Simultaneously, Halder felt the nightmare immobility draining from him and the sensation of dreamlike unreality fade from his mind. He turned to the right, found Kilby's eyes already on him, saw the Rellis couple sitting beyond her . . . Rane, no longer disguised, looking like a mirror image of Halder.

They were still fastened to their chairs. Halder's gaze shifted back quickly to the center of the room. Where the pit had been, the flooring was now level, carrying a massive, polished table. Behind the table sat a heavily built, white-haired man with a strong face, harsh mouth, in the formal black and gold robes of a Councilman of the Federation.

"I am Councilman Mavig." The voice was the one that had spoken in the dark; it came now from the man at the table. "I am in charge of the operation against the Kalechi agents, and it is my duty to inform them, after their arrest and examination, of the disposition that must be made of them."

He hesitated, twisting his mouth thoughtfully, almost as if unwilling to continue. "You four have been thoroughly examined," he stated at last. "Most of the work has been done while you were still unconscious. A final check of your emotional reactions was being made throughout the stress situation just ended, in which you listened to a replay of a report on the Kalechi matter. That part is now concluded."

Mavig paused, scowled, cleared his throat. "I find," he went on, "that some aspects of this affair still strain my credulity! More than half of your group have been captured by now; the remainder are at large but under observation. The danger is past. The activities of the Great Satogs of Kalechi will receive our very close scrutiny for generations to come. They shall be given no opportunity to repeat such a trick; nor—after they have been made aware of the measures we are preparing against them—will they feel the slightest inclination to try it.

"Now, as to yourselves. After we had tracked down the first dozen or so of you, a startling pattern began to emerge. You were not following Kalechi's careful instructions. In one way and another—in often very ingenious ways—you were attempting primarily to establish contact with one another. When captured and examined while unconscious by the various interrogation instruments of our psychologists you told us your reasons for doing this."

Councilman Mavig shook his head. "The interrogation machines are supposed to be infallible," he remarked. "Possibly they are. But I am not a psychologist, and for a long time I refused to accept the reports they returned. But still . . . "

He sighed. "Well, as to what is to happen with you. You will be sent to join the previously arrested members of your group, and will remain with them until the last of you is in our hands, has been examined, and . . . "

Mavig paused again.

"You see, we can accuse you of no crime!" he said irritably. "As individuals and as a group, your intention from the beginning has been to prevent the crime against the Federation from being committed. The Great Satogs simply did too good a job. You have been given the most searching physical examinations possible. They show uniformly that your genetic pattern is stable, and that in no detail can it be distinguished from a wholly human one of high order.

"You appreciate, I imagine, where that leaves the Federation! When imitation is carried to the point of identity . . . " Federation Councilman Mavig shook his head once more, concluded, "It is utterly absurd, in direct contradiction to everything we have understood to date! You've regarded yourselves as human beings, and believed that your place was among us. And we can only agree."

Attitudes

❧

It was now six of *their* hours since the Federation escort ships had signaled that they had completed their assignment and were turning back. Soon, Azard told himself, it would be safe to act . . . to take the final steps in the great gamble which had seemed so dangerous and had been so necessary. Without the Malatlo Attitude, it would have been impossible. Malatlo had helped him in more ways than one.

He stared from the back of the big control compartment at the three Federation humans. They were turned away, intent on various instruments, as the giant cargo carrier made its unhurried approach to the planet. Sashien had said he would begin landing operations in an hour. It would seem unnatural if Azard wasn't with them to observe the process in the screens. Therefore the arrangements he had to make must be made now.

He turned, left the room silently. They mightn't miss him. If they did, it wouldn't matter. He'd established on the voyage out from the Hub that he was constantly preoccupied with the condition and security of the immeasurably precious cargo destiny had placed in his care. As in all other matters, they did nothing to interfere with him in this.

He stepped into a transfer drop and emerged five levels below in a dully gleaming passage studded by many doors. This ship was huge, greater than anything he could have imagined was possible before he came to the Hub. A large part of it contained the layered multitudes of artificially grown inert human bodies, each of which presently would be imprinted with a mature eld and thus come to conscious, intelligent life. A gift to lost Malatlo from the Federation of the Hub. Gifts, too, were the endless thousands of tools, machines, and instruments stored in shrink-containers elsewhere on the ship; the supplies and means of immediate colonial life. The Federation was rich and generous. And it had respected, if it did not share generally, the Malatlo Attitude. It respected Azard and his mission . . . the mission to let Malatlo come into renewed existence on the world which now lay ahead.

Azard hurried down the echoing passages to the sealed ship area to which, by agreement, he alone had the means of entry. He hadn't taken it for granted that the agreement would be kept. His responsibilities were far too great to permit himself the weakness of trust. Supposedly the two men and the woman in the control compartment were the only Federation humans on the ship. Yet in this vast vessel one couldn't be certain of it; so, in the section which was his greatest concern, he had set up many concealed traps and warnings. If anyone entered there, he surely must leave some indication for Azard to read. So far there had been no indications.

He opened a massive compartment lock, went through and sealed it behind him. He checked the hidden warning devices meticulously. They had registered no intrusion. He went down another level, opened a second lock.

This one he left open. In the room beyond were the culture cases. Eight of them. Two contained, between them, in the energies flowing through their microscopically honeycombed linings, over half a billion elds—over half a billion personalities, identities, selves. Azard was not trained in the eld sciences, and had been given no information about the forces which maintained and restricted the elds in the cases. But he knew they were there.

He stood, head half turned sideways, eyes partly closed, in an attitude of listening. Nothing detectable, he thought. Nothing that possibly could be detected here while the cases remained shut, by instruments of any kind, or even by sensitivities such as his own. He bent forward, went through the complicated series of manipulations which alone could open a culture case. The thick lid of the one he was handling presently lifted back, revealing the instruments on its underside. Azard didn't touch those. He waited. A moment passed; then, gradually, he grew aware of the confined personalities.

It was like the rising hum of an agitated cloud of tiny swarming creatures. His ears didn't hear it, but his mind did. They were awake, conscious, greedy—terribly greedy, terribly driven to move, sense, live again. He wondered whether Federation humans would be able to hear them as he did, and, if they could, whether they would understand what they heard.

Not long, he told the elds. Not long! But the hum of their urge to regain the trappings of life didn't abate.

He closed the case, then checked the security devices on all eight. There were no signs of attempted tampering. The last six cases did not contain elds but something almost as valuable. The Federation humans didn't know about that. At least, Azard could be nearly certain they didn't know.

He left the sealed ship compartment. It no longer

mattered, he told himself, whether or not he had avoided suspicion entirely. The gamble had succeeded this far, was close to complete success. His three ship companions in the control room soon would be dead. Then the ship and everything on it would be in his hands.

He went off to complete his arrangements.

Sashien, the engineer, had brought the ship down on the planet's nightside, to the area suggested by Hub colonization specialists as being one where all conditions favored Malatlo's new beginning. The giant vehicle settled so smoothly that Azard didn't realize the landing had been completed until Sashien began shutting down the engines.

"And now," Odun said presently to Azard, "let's go out and have a firsthand look at your world."

Azard hesitated. He didn't want to be away from the ship, even for a few of their hours, while one of the Federation humans stayed on it. But it turned out then that they were all going . . . Odun, Sashien and the woman Griliom Tantrey who represented the project which had mass-produced and mass-conditioned the stored zombie bodies for Malatlo. A small atmosphere cruiser lifted from the cargo ship's flank. Thirty minutes later they were floating in sunshine.

It was a world of pleasing appearance, verdant and varied, with drifting clouds and rolling oceans. They flew over great animal herds in the plains, skimmed the edges of towering mountains. Finally they turned back into the night.

"What's that?" Azard asked, indicating a great glowing yellow patch on the dark ocean surface below and to their left.

Sashien turned the cruiser in that direction.

"A sea creature which eventually should become a valuable source of food and chemicals," said Odun. He'd been involved in the study of the records of this world and its recommendation for the Malatlo revival.

"Individually it's tiny. But at various seasons it gathers in masses to spawn."

Sashien checked a reading on the screen, said, "That patch covers more than forty square miles. That's quite a mass!"

They flew across the blanket of living fire on the sea surface. Azard said, "This is a rich planet. The Federation is being very generous . . ."

"Not too generous, really," said Odun. "This is a world which was surveyed and earmarked for possible settlement a long while ago. But it's so very far from the Hub that it's quite possible it never would have been put to any use. There's no shortage of habitable planets much closer to us." He added, "Its remoteness from the Federation and from any civilization of which we know is, of course, one of the reasons this world was chosen for Malatlo."

"It is still an act of great generosity," said Azard.

"Well, you see," Odun explained, "there are many more of us in the Federation than Malatlo believed who cared for it and its ideals."

Griliom Tantrey nodded. "We loved Malatlo," she said. "That's why we three are here. . . ."

Malatlo. The Malatlo Attitude.

Turn back something like two centuries from the night the giant cargo carrier came down to an untouched world.

The Federation of the Hub had been forged at last. It was forged in blood and fire and fury, but that was over now. For the first time in many human generations no Cluster Wars were being fought. And a great many people everywhere had begun to look back with shock and something like growing incredulity on the destruction and violence and cruelties of the immediate past. They wanted no more of that. None whatever.

But, of course, the forming of the Federation did not end violence and cruelties. It did establish a working society and one with a good deal of promise in it, but it was not a perfect society and probably never would be perfect. And when these people realized they couldn't change that, they simply wanted no more to do with the Federation either.

That was Malatlo, the Malatlo Attitude. No one seemed able to say how the term originated. On a thousand worlds it was somehow in the air. There were no great leaders of this movement or cult or philosophy, whatever one wanted to call it. But there were very many minor leaders.

They put it to the Federation. They wanted to be away from the Federation, these people who shared the Malatlo Attitude, away from all people who did not fully share it; they wanted to be by themselves. They had no dislike for other human beings, but they did not want to have Malatlo disturbed by those whose thinking and actions weren't in accord with it.

The Federation accepted the demand. Perhaps the men in authority looked on it as an experiment. Possibly they approved individually of the Malatlo Attitude but considered it impractical for most human beings—certainly impractical for the Federation. At any rate, they did everything needed to bring the world of Malatlo into being.

The location of the world was never made public. But it was known that it lay at an immense distance from the Hub, beyond any probability of chance discovery. It had a neighbor planet on which lived a race of beings who called themselves Raceels and called their world Tiurs. They had a well-developed civilization but had not yet discovered space flight. The followers of the Malatlo Attitude had wanted such neighbors to demonstrate that man could live in peace with all other creatures. Some eighty million of them were transferred to the world Malatlo within the time of a few years. Thereafter almost all ties with the Federation were dissolved. The people of Malatlo were opposed to galactic travel and retained only spacecraft designed to let them move about the system of their new sun.

By agreement, one connection with the Federation was retained. Once every ten years a small ship traveled from the Hub to the Malatlo system. It had few people on board, and all of them were sufficiently sympathetic to the Malatlo Attitude to create no discord. Even so they remained on the planet only long enough to gather the information wanted by the Federation, and then returned to report.

The reports remained favorable. In something less than two centuries, Malatlo's population increased to two hundred million and stabilized at that level. They had developed new branches of science dealing with the human psyche but were unwilling to reveal their findings in that area to outsiders. They established increasingly friendly contacts with the Raceels of Tiurs, who looked with favor on the Malatlo Attitude. That had been the last report.

And then Azard arrived in the Federation in a small battered ship which had taken more than three years to make the voyage from the Malatlo System. The world of Malatlo had been destroyed. The Raceels of Tiurs had struck against it with matter conversion fields which within days made the planet uninhabitable, then consumed it completely. With the exception of Azard, the followers of the Malatlo Attitude no longer existed in the flesh. But the elds, the personalities, of over half of them had been preserved, in the eight cases Azard brought with him. The isolation of the eld, the ability to maintain it in independence of a physical body, had been the last of Malatlo's great discoveries.

Azard reported that Tiurs had destroyed itself in the process. Evidently at least one conversion field had gone out of control on the planet, and once a field became active, there was no way to check it. Whatever had been the cause, it was apparent that before the one ship which escaped from Malatlo left the system, the Raceel world also was undergoing rapid disintegration.

Azard came with the plea that the Federation should once more help Malatlo become established. Federation science knew how to construct human bodies which were physically functional but lacked self-awareness, lacked a developed personality. The elds of Malatlo could be transferred to such bodies and resume physical existence.

The Federation agreed. Zombie bodies were primarily research tools, there had been no previous occasion to produce them in large quantities. But given sufficient supervisory personnel, their mass production involved no significant problems, and forced growth processes could bring armies of them to the point of physical maturity in months. Concurrent mechanical exercise and programmed neuron stimulation completed the process. The result was a limited but viable human facsimile. If the discoveries of Malatlo's experimenters could turn the facsimile into a complete new human being, they were welcome to the material.

So the construction of the bodies began. Meanwhile a world was selected which would meet the requirements of the Malatlo Attitude, and presently the zombies and the basic tools of a simple civilization were stored away on the great cargo ship. Azard brought his precious cases aboard. The Federation had selected Sashien, Odun and Griliom as the three specialists who would ferry the ship to the planet, supervise the automatic unloading and construction equipment, and check the final conditioning of the zombies, before returning with the ship to the Hub.

From Azard's point of view, the thing basically wrong with this schedule was that a considerable number of people were aware of the new world's location. It made it inevitable that someone presently would come out to see how things fared with Malatlo. And that was not an acceptable situation.

Naturally he'd made no mention of this. But the cargo ship would neither return to the Hub after disgorging its contents, nor would it remain on this world. Azard planned to destroy his Federation aides within hours after the landing, then equip as many selected elds as would be required to handle the ship with their new bodies, and lift the ship back into space to search for another planet so far from the Federation that they could be sure it never would be found.

As soon as the atmosphere cruiser returned from the survey tour of the planet, he took steps to execute the plan.

He was somewhat afraid of the three specialists. They would not have been chosen for this mission if they hadn't been very competent people. During the trip he'd avoided their company as much as possible, for which they showed no offense. But he'd still had enough contact with them to know that they were alert and quick thinking. It was unlikely that anything would go wrong. But it was possible. His first move, therefore, was to make the ship transmitters inoperative. It was quickly done, and with that, they were temporarily cut off from any chance of summoning help. No doubt it wouldn't take them long to trace down and repair the damage, if they discovered it in time, but before that happened, Azard's maneuvers would engulf them in one way or another.

His immediate preparations for their death were complete. The control compartment was one place on the ship where they regularly could be found together. Another was an adjoining three-room area where they took their meals, worked on their records, sometimes relaxed with music and tapes. From various points on the ship, he could now release an odorless vapor which killed on contact into either of these sections, but it was necessary to do this at a time when the three of them would be destroyed simultaneously.

They were in the control compartment, engaged in calculations connected with the disembarking of the heavy automatic construction equipment, when Azard went down once more to the ship's sealed section. When he emerged from it, he was carrying one of the eld cases. A few minutes later, he locked himself into a storage area where thirty zombie bodies lay in individual full-stimulation containers.

He'd been instructed thoroughly by Griliom Tantrey and others in the methods required to bring these bodies out of the stage of almost totally quiescent metabolism used to store them and to the functional level normal for an active human body. These thirty had been approaching that level for the past shipday, and the instruments on the containers told Azard that they now had reached it. All that remained to be done was to give them consciousness—and the elds could handle that.

He opened the case and slowly and carefully began to adjust its settings. Most of the vast swarm of personalities in there could not be isolated or handled individually. But the members of certain key groups could be contacted individually by the combined use of a number of dials and released one by one, and that was all that was required. Azard set the case down before one of the opened zombie containers, directed the release needle at the inert body within and set an eld free. He sensed it hurtle forward and take possession. The others knew at once what was happening. He felt their body-greed surge up like a roaring pressure against his mind. Not yet, he thought.

But thirty in all he set free. They were disciplined entities. The zombie bodies remained still, unstirring, except for their deep regular breathing. Azard turned on a device, and his voice began to speak from it. As he left the section, it was telling the thirty elds, listening now through the bodies' senses, what they must do. And, elsewhere in the ship, Azard was switching on a small viewscreen. It showed him first the control compartment—empty now. He turned to a view of one of the living-area rooms. Griliom Tantrey was just coming in through a door, and Sashien turned from a table to speak to her. Their voices became audible, and Azard listened a moment to what they were saying. Then Sashien called off to Odun, and Odun came through the door.

Azard smiled briefly, reached back of the screen, uncovered a stud set flush into its surface, pressed the stud down and held it. The gas which drifted into the room towards the three Federation specialists was colorless, soundless, odorless. It touched them in seconds, and one after the other, they collapsed. Azard released the stud. They were already dead . . . and within an hour, the ship's ventilation system would have filtered the poisonous vapor out of the living area again and disposed of it.

And now his duties were nearly concluded! With a sense of vast relief and triumph, he told himself the moment had come when he could turn all responsibility back to others greater than himself. Almost running in his eagerness, he returned through the ship to the sealed section. This time he didn't bother to close its locks behind him; there was no need.

There were over two thousand widely varying genetic patterns represented in the zombie bodies provided by the Federation. One of them was truly outstanding, both in physical development and mental potential. Azard had brought a specimen of this group here the preceding day and activated the awakening mechanisms of its container. It was to receive the eld of the greatest of all those who had been in his charge so long. He now examined the zombie and its condition for the final time with great care. But it was clearly an excellent choice, the best he could have made in the circumstances.

As he was setting the last of the transfer dials, there was a touch of odd weakness, a heaviness. A feeling then as if, in an instant, all his strength had been drained from him.

With immeasurable effort, in total dismay and incredulity, he forced himself to turn his head.

And there they stood. Sashien and the woman Griliom—

The third?

The insane realization came that the third figure was himself.

"No," the figure said, "This isn't you, Azard. We've concocted a disguise which will lend me your physical appearance for a while." The voice was Odun's.

Staring, unable to do more than stare, Azard watched Sashien hand a device which had been pointed at him to Griliom. The two men approached, picked him up from the floor and set him in a chair.

Griliom told him, "I'm reducing the pressure. You'll be able to speak."

Azard drew a deep breath. Some hope flowed back into him. The elds he had provided with bodies and information should soon be arming themselves and coming here. He'd warned them to be cautious. If these three wanted him to talk, he would talk. He said hoarsely, "What do you want?"

Odun said, "Why did you try to kill us?"

"I didn't," Azard said. How could they possibly have escaped? "You should have been unconscious for a time, but unhurt."

They stared at him a moment. Sashien said, "What was your purpose in making the attempt?"

Azard sighed. "I needed this ship for Malatlo."

"Malatlo could have had the ship for the asking," said Odun. "You knew that."

"Yes. But we can't stay here. This world is still too close to the Federation, and too many people would know Malatlo was here. We owe renewed gratitude to the Federation. But now we must break all ties with its people. The new Malatlo must be born on a world no one knows about—and too far away to be discovered accidentally."

"Malatlo," said Griliom, "did not object to maintaining limited contacts with the Federation before this."

"Many did object to it," Azard assured her. "And at the end many believed that our trouble arose because the Raceels of Tiurs had learned through us about the Federation. They tried to exterminate us not because they were afraid of us but because they were afraid of the Federation where the Malatlo Attitude didn't prevail."

"You still needed the Federation to supply you with zombie bodies," Griliom remarked. "The number we were able to store on this ship were no more than a beginning."

"But they were sufficient," said Azard. "Naturally our best scientists would have been among those awakened first. Their study of the bodies and of what I recorded of the techniques involved in developing them would allow them to duplicate the process."

He went on earnestly. "You must believe that no harm would have come to you. You would have been left here on the planet with the atmosphere cruiser and supplies. As soon as the cargo carrier was far enough away so that it could no longer be traced, we would have transmitted word to the escort ships to return and pick you up."

Sashien and Odun looked at Griliom. She shook her head. "Analysis showed three lethal components in the gas he released," she said. She glanced at Azard. "We weren't in that room. What you saw and heard were programmed zombies. They died in moments—as we would have done in their place." She added to the other two, "So we have here an alleged Malatlo Follower who was willing to kill three human beings to attain his ends. That seems difficult to believe."

Azard said doggedly, "The fact that I am a Malatlo Follower must indicate to you that if the gas I used was in fact deadly, it could only have been a mistake! A mistake which, I must admit, might have had terrible consequences. . . . "

Odun said thoughtfully, "Perhaps we should question one of the others." He nodded at the case standing before the body container. "I'll take the paralyzer, Griliom. Will you see how far along he was with that."

Azard slowly tensed his muscles as the woman went to the eld case, stooped above it to inspect the pattern of dials inside. There was no hesitancy in her manner—did she understand what she saw?

She said, "He's selected a specific psyche for transfer to the body. Let me see . . . " She turned to the container, opened it, bent over the zombie. Her shoulders moved. Azard couldn't see what she was doing, but he could assume she was checking its condition on the various instruments. She straightened again presently, looked at Odun. "Total capacity," she said. "We can effect the transfer."

Azard made a straining effort to arise. But they were watchful; the paralyzer's pressure increased instantly—he could not move, and now he discovered he had also become unable to speak. A wave of dizziness passed through him, his vision blurred. He became aware next that Griliom and Sashien were moving about him; then clear sight gradually returned.

He found himself still immobilized in the chair, looking out into the room through something like a thin veil of darkness. He guessed it was an energy field of some kind. Odun stood in the center of the room. Some twenty feet from him the zombie body Azard had prepared lay on its back, on the floor. Azard realized then that Sashien and Griliom stood on either side of his chair, a little behind him.

The body stirred, opened its eyes, sat up.

It looked about the room but seemed unable to see Azard and the two on his right and left. The energy veil evidently blocked vision from that side. Its gaze fastened on Odun, who stood watching it with the face of Azard. It came to its feet.

There had been no uncertainty in any of its motions. This was a powerful eld, instantly capable of impressing its intentions on the full range of the zombie's physical and mental response patterns. Azard should have been able to sense its presence in the room, but he could force no eld contact through the energy barrier. There was no way to transmit a warning.

"Dom belke anda grom, Azard!" the body addressed Odun. It was a strong, self-assured voice.

"Gelan ra Azard," Odun said. "Ra diriog Federation. Sellen ra Raceel."

The body moved instantly. It sprang sideways to a table standing ten feet away. And Azard saw only now what it must have noted in its sweeping glance about the room—the gun which lay on the table. The body snatched it up, pointed the muzzle at Odun, pulled the trigger.

And dropped limply back to the floor, the gun spinning from its hand.

"This was a test," Odun told Azard. He no longer wore Azard's face; the false skin or whatever it was had been removed. "You heard what I said to him. I identified myself as a human of the Federation and told him he was a Raceel. He immediately attempted to destroy me. The weapon, of course, was rigged. If the trigger was pressed, it would kill the user."

Azard did not reply.

"So you are Raceels," Odun went on. "And you'd kill any of us—any human being—as readily as you destroyed the people of Malatlo. We should like to know how this came about. Are you willing to talk?"

"Yes. I'll tell you whatever you want to know." Azard made his voice dull, his expression listless and resigned. But there was savage anger in him—and the longer he held these three in talk, the more certain their death and eventual Raceel victory became. The thirty elds he'd released had been a select group of superb fighters, and they must be searching the ship by now, in strong new bodies and with weapons in their hands. The demonstration here confirmed that they'd know very quickly how to put those bodies to full use.

"We were desperate," he said, and went on, knowing the statement had gained him their full attention. Before the Malatlo settlers contacted it, Tiurs had faced the problem of a population constantly on the verge of expanding beyond the ability of the planet to support it, and had no adequate techniques of space travel, which might have helped alleviate the problem. A temporary and unsatisfactory solution had been the development of methods of preserving a conscious personality indefinitely without the support of a physical body. . . .

"So it was you and not Malatlo," said Sashien, "who originated the eld sciences."

"They were investigating the subject," Azard told him. "But we accomplished the eld separation a century before they began to make significant progress in that direction—"

The Malatlo Followers did not push their contacts with Tiurs, believing it best to let the relationship develop gradually and in a manner which would be satisfactory to the Raceels. And the Raceels, though hungry for the information they might get from the humans, remained equally cautious. For them the situation held both great promise and a great threat. There were means of practical interstellar space travel, and there were worlds upon worlds among the stars to which their kind might spread. That was the promise.

The threat was the prospect of encountering competitors in space more formidable than themselves. The Followers were harmless, but from what they had told the Raceels of the species to which they belonged, the species certainly was not. Evidently it already controlled an enormous sector of space. Further, there might be other species equally dangerous to those weaker than they.

The logical approach was to remain unnoticed until one became strong enough to meet any opposition.

The Raceels immersed themselves in research on many levels, including lines long since abandoned as being too immediately dangerous to themselves. Somewhat to their surprise, they found Malatlo completely willing to supply them with spaceships for study when they indicated an interest in them. Unfortunately, these craft were not designed to accomplish interstellar flights, but they advanced the scientists of Tiurs a long step in that direction. The Raceels kept this as well as their other hopes and fears a careful secret from Malatlo.

They were a race which had a naturally high rate of reproduction and which throughout a war-studded history had made a fetish of the expansion of its kind. That drive became a liability when Tiurs was united at last into a single rigidly controlled society confined to the surface of its planet. Now suddenly it might be turned into an asset again. When they burst upon the stars, it would be in no timid and tentative colonial probes, but in many thousands of ships, each capable of peopling a world in a single generation.

They worked towards that end with feverish determination. From Malatlo they learned of the eld-less zombie bodies Federation science knew how to produce in theoretically limitless quantities, and they took up that line of investigation. The disembodied elds in the storage vaults, for whom there had been no room for normal existence on Tiurs, would come to life again in new bodies on new worlds. Dormant fertile germ cells of selected strains were stockpiled by the millions. Weaponry research moved quickly forwards. The full interstellar drive seemed almost within reach.

And then—

"Malatlo Followers informed us they had become aware of our plans and were horrified by them," Azard said. "Apparently they believed they could persuade us to abandon them." He hesitated. "So we silenced them."

"You extinguished a living world," said Griliom.

Azard said, "We couldn't stop what we were doing. And Malatlo would reveal what it had learned to the Federation. We believed we had no choice."

"How was Tiurs destroyed?" Sashien asked.

"We had intended to destroy it with mass-converter fields after we left," said Azard. "To later investigators it would appear that Malatlo and Tiurs had been engulfed by the same unexplained disaster. We didn't realize then how dangerously unstable the fields were. There was a premature reaction among the ones being positioned on Tiurs. After that—"

He shrugged. For a moment a three-year old horror seemed to darken his mind again.

"We were totally unprepared, and we had only days left to act," he continued. Up to the last moment, the most valuable sections of the population were moved through eld separation centers. Only one ship equipped with an experimental interstellar drive had escaped the initial conversion burst. It was very small. But it could carry as many Raceel elds as there would be time to salvage. It could carry a relatively huge quantity of stored fertile germ cells. And supplies for one Raceel during a trip that must take years. Because there was now only one place where zombie bodies for the salvaged elds could be produced, and that place was the human Federation of the Hub.

Griliom remarked, "The body you use has been analyzed. It obviously is a human one. How did you obtain it?"

"There were a number of Followers on Tiurs when we destroyed Malatlo," Azard said. "I was one of a group who had the various qualifications required to take our survival ship to the Federation. My eld was transferred to the body of a Follower for the purpose. The method employed was to bring the human subject to the point of physical death. The death process dissolved the inhabiting eld. The Raceel eld was then injected and an attempt made to revive the body. The first forty-eight such attempts failed, and the Raceel elds involved also died before they could be detached again from the dying bodies which had absorbed them. I was the forty-ninth transfer. That body was successfully revived, and so I lived."

He added, "There is much valuable information we could exchange if, for example, the Raceel scientists in charge of the eld transfer methods and the ones who developed the mass-converter fields were restored to physical existence. We offer you what they have learned in return for the use of your zombie bodies."

He didn't expect them to respond to the offer. They must believe that if they wanted such information they could get it from the elds who were now in effect their prisoners, without giving anything in return. But if they continued to let him talk, the released elds would have more time to find them here and destroy them.

He added again, "You must not judge us too harshly. Our history and traditions made the continued expansion of our species a matter of driving necessity to us. Nothing could be allowed to block it. But your species and mine can now be of value to each other. You should consider that rather than the question of avenging Malatlo."

"Azard," Odun said, "you don't fully understand the situation. The story you told in the Federation was tentatively accepted, but you were under close observation. And certain incongruities gradually became evident. Even allowing for the shock of the disaster, you didn't speak and act quite as a Malatlo Follower might be expected to speak and act. Your demands were logical, in the light of the Malatlo Attitude. But they were a trifle too precisely logical and uncompromising.

"Then there is the matter of your mind. It presents automatic blocks to psychic probes. Human minds can demonstrate that ability in various forms. In your case, however, it is brought into action in a manner no human mind of record has employed to date. So there presently was the question of whether you were in fact, in spite of physical appearances, wholly human. Meanwhile it had been confirmed that, as you reported, the worlds of Malatlo and Tiurs had disappeared. If you weren't human then, it followed that you were in all probability a Raceel eld in a human body . . . and that you were trying to trick the Federation into helping you re-establish the Raceel species."

Azard stared at him. "If that was suspected, why—"

"It was a test."

"A test?" Azard repeated.

Odun sighed. "Even at second hand," he remarked, "the Malatlo Attitude seems to retain a curious power. It was decided that if some indication could be found that the destruction of Malatlo was an act of thoughtless panic, an act which you and your kind regretted not only because of the destruction it brought in turn on yourselves, we would then help bring the stored Raceel elds into physical existence. But everything you've done since this voyage began was continuing evidence of the implacable hostility your species entertains towards all others. And you've been kept under constant observation."

Azard said harshly, "That would have been impossible!"

"We employed certain safeguards, of course," Griliom

Tantrey told him. She nodded at the zombie body on the floor. "I gave that body a final stimulant before we transferred the eld of what was presumably one of your people's leaders to it. This was a step in the animation of zombies of which you had not been informed. The bodies to which you transferred elds an hour ago lacked that stimulant. They all died therefore within minutes after the elds brought them into full normal activity, and the elds, of course, died with them."

He tried for some seconds to make himself disbelieve her, but it was clear that she spoke the truth. He looked at their faces, addressed Odun. "You used our language. How did you learn it?"

"I've made a study of the Malatlo-Raceel relationship for some years," Odun said. "The last ship to return from the system provided me with language tapes." He looked at his companions. "I believe Azard has told us as much as we need or wish to know."

They nodded.

"Then," Odun resumed, "it's time to take the final steps in this."

His hand moved. And darkness closed in with a rush around Azard.

He came awake again presently and looked about in dimness. He was seated in another chair, again unable to move his limbs or body, and the three were busy with something not far from him.

After some seconds he realized they were in the atmosphere cruiser. The screen showed the surface of one of the planetary oceans. The two eld cases stood near it.

Azard discovered he could speak and asked aloud, "What are you doing?"

They looked around. Griliom said matter-of-factly, "We'll dispose of the elds here."

In spite of everything, Azard felt a shock of incredulous rage.

But at least, he thought, these three would also die! Released simultaneously, the eld hordes would struggle furiously for possession of their bodies as well as his own. And neither the inhabiting elds nor the physical bodies could survive such an onslaught.

He said, "You have no authority to make such a decision!"

"We do have that authority, Azard," said Odun. "That's why we're here."

"Then," Azard told him, "you're worse than we ever were. We destroyed only the population of a world. You're taking it on yourselves to destroy an intelligent species."

They didn't respond immediately. They were watching the screen now, and Azard was able to shift his head far enough to watch it too. After a moment the rim of a glowing yellow formation came drifting into the screen. He realized it was a spawning swarm of billions of tiny sea creatures such as the one they'd seen earlier that night.

Griliom said without looking around at him, "Down there is an endless supply of bodies which have neither elds nor intelligence. I've set the controls on these cases so that the Raceel elds will be released within a minute after the cases strike the surface of the water. They'll emerge and enter host bodies in which they can live for something less than a standard year—the life span of these creatures. And then they'll die with them. That's the way we're settling this."

Odun added, "But you're mistaken in one basic respect, Azard. We're preserving the stored Raceel ova, and a new generation will be raised from them under our supervision. Only some terrible necessity would force us to destroy a species. So your species will not die. Its history, its traditions and its attitudes will die."

Azard asked, "And what are we if not our history, our traditions, and our attitudes?"

The humans didn't reply, and he wasn't certain then

whether he'd asked the question aloud. He discovered he was indifferent about the matter, and that the question itself had been an indifferent one. Then he noticed that the cruiser had moved close to the surface of the sea, and that someone was opening a hatch. The eld cases were dropped out, and the hatch closed again.

It occurred to Azard that he had no emotional feeling about this or about anything else. By their skills, they'd drained his emotions from him. He realized next that his senses were dimming and that he was dying. But he remained indifferent to that, too. He decided that in their way they were merciful.

Then he died.

Down below, the open eld cases bobbed in the glowing water. The elds, conscious and terribly hungry for physical existence, discovered abruptly that they had been released. They flashed out of the cases and found life in abundance about them. They entered, took possession, affixed themselves. Perhaps for an instant some of them retained awareness enough to understand they had become joined to a form of life which provided no vehicle for consciousness. But then, with nothing to give it support, their own consciousness drained away.

However, they would live on for a while. For something less than a standard year.

Trouble Tide

I

When Danrich Parrol, general manager of the Giard Pharmaceutical Station on Nandy-Cline, stepped hurriedly out of an aircab before the executive offices, he found Dr. Nile Etland's blazing blue PanElemental already parked on the landing strip next to the building entrance.

Parrol pushed through the door, asked the receptionist, "When did she get here, and where is she now?"

The girl grinned, checked her watch. "She arrived four minutes ago and went straight into Mr. Weldrow's office. They called in Freasie immediately. Welcome home, Mr. Parrol! We've had a dull time since you left—at least until this thing came up."

Parrol smiled briefly, said, "Put any calls for me on Weldrow's extension, will you?" and went down the hall. At the far end, he opened the door to an office. The three people standing in front of a wall map looked around at him. Ilium Weldrow, the assistant manager, appeared relieved to see him.

"Glad you're here, Dan!" he said heartily. "It seems that . . . "

"Dan, it's a mess!" Dr. Nile Etland interrupted. The head of Giard's station laboratory appeared to have dressed hastily after Parrol called her at the spaceport hotel—she would have had to, to show up here within ten minutes. Her coppery hair was still piled high on her head; the intent face with its almost too perfectly chiseled features was innocent of make-up. She nodded at the heavily built woman beside Weldrow. "Apparently it isn't an epidemic. Freasie says there's been no trace of disease in the specimens and samples that came through the lab."

"Naturally not!" the lab's chief technician said sourly. "If the material hadn't been absolutely healthy, it would have been returned with a warning to the ranches that supplied it."

"Of course. And there've been no reports of sea beef carcasses seen floating around," Nile Etland went on.

Parrol asked, "Exactly what does seem to have happened? The news report I picked up at the hotel just now didn't tell much, but it didn't sound like an epidemic. The man talked of 'mysterious wholesale disappearances' among the herds in this area. The way he put it almost implied that one or the other of the local ranchers is suspected of rustling stock."

Nile turned to the wall map. "That's darn improbable, Dan! Here, let me show you. The trouble started there . . . a hundred and fifty miles up the coast. Eight days ago. Throughout the week the ranches south of that point have been hit progressively.

"The worst of it is that the estimated losses are going up fast! It was five to ten per cent in the first herds affected. But the report this morning was that Lipyear's Oceanic is missing almost sixty per cent of its stock."

"Lipyear's? Sixty per cent!" Parrol repeated incredulously. "The newscast said nothing of that."

"I called the Southeastern Ranchers Association on my way here," Nile told him. "That's the figure Machon gave me. They haven't put it out yet. It's a big jump over yesterday's estimate, and Machon seemed to be in a state of shock about it. There are plenty of wild rumors but no useful explanation of what's happening."

Parrol looked at Weldrow, asked, "What have you done so far, Weldrow?"

The assistant manager frowned. Nile Etland said impatiently, "Weldrow's done exactly nothing!" She turned to the door, added, "Come on, Freasie! Let's get things set up in the lab. Be back in ten minutes, Dan."

Ilium Weldrow was a chubby, pink-faced man, Parrol's senior by ten years, whose feelings were easily bruised. As an assistant manager on a world like Nandy-Cline he was pretty much of a dead loss; but a distant relative on Giard's board of directors had made it impossible to ship him quietly back to the Federation's megacities where he should have been more in his element.

He was disturbed now by Nile Etland's comment, and Parrol spent a few minutes explaining that the coastal ranchers—particularly the ones under contract to Giard—depended on the company's facilities and expensively trained trouble-shooters to help them out in emergencies . . . and that if anything serious should happen to the local sea beef herds, Giard would drop a fortune in the medicinal extracts obtained by its laboratory from the glands of the specific strain of sea beef grown on Nandy-Cline and obtainable nowhere else.

Weldrow seemed to get the last point; his expression shifted from petulance to concern.

"But, Dan, this problem . . . whatever it turns out to be . . . appears to affect only this area of the eastern coast! What is to keep us from getting the required materials from sea beef ranches on the other side of the continent?"

"Mainly," Parrol said, "the fact that those ranches are under contract to outfits like Agenes. Can you see Agenes loosening up on its contract rights to help out Giard?"

Again the point seemed to sink in. Even Weldrow couldn't help being aware that Agenes Laboratories was Giard's most prominent competitor and one with a reputation for complete ruthlessness.

"Well," he said defensively, "I haven't had an easy time of it during the two and a half months you and Dr. Etland were in the Hub, Dan! My duties at the station have absorbed me to the extent that I simply haven't been able to give much attention to extraneous matters."

Parrol told him not to worry about it. On the way out, he instructed the receptionist, "If there are any calls for me during the next few hours, I'll be either at the Southeastern Ranchers Association or in Dr. Etland's car. That's the new job she had shipped out from Orado with us. She's had its call number registered here."

A few minutes later, he was easing Nile Etland's PanElemental off the landing terrace and into the air, fingering the controls gingerly and not without misgivings, while the doctor took care of her makeup.

"Don't be timid with the thing," she advised Parrol, squinting into her compact. "There's nothing easier to handle, once you get the hang of it."

He grunted. "I don't want to cut in its spacedrive by mistake!"

"That's impossible, dope . . . unless you're *in* space. Put up the windscreen, will you? Fourth button, second row, left side. Agenes? Well, I don't know. If those beef things were dying instead of disappearing, I'd be wondering about Agenes, too, of course."

Parrol found the windscreen button and shoved at it. The air whistling about them was abruptly quiet. Somewhat reassured about the PanElemental's tractability—

nobody but Nile would sink two years' salary into a quadruple-threat racing car—Parrol stepped up their speed and swung to the right, towards the sea. A string of buildings rushed briefly towards them and dropped below, and the sun-bright blue rim of Nandy-Cline's world-spanning ocean came into view.

"Would there be chemical means of inducing a herd of sea beef to move out of a specific body of water?" Parrol asked.

"Naturally. But who's going to give that kind of treatment to a body of water a hundred and fifty miles long and up to eighty miles wide? Besides, they haven't *all* moved out." She loosened her hair, fluffed, shook and stroked it into place. "Better try another theory, Danny," she added.

"Do you have one?"

"No. We'll see what goes on at the ranchers' emergency meeting first." Nile motioned with her head towards the back of the car. "I dumped some testing equipment in there, in case we want to go for a dip afterwards."

There was silence for some seconds; then Parrol said, "Looks about normal down there, doesn't it?"

He had swung the PanElemental left again, slowing and dropping towards the shoreline of the continental shelf. Near low tide at present, the shelf stretched away for almost sixty miles to the east, a great saline swamp and, from this altitude, a palette of bilious pigments. A number of aircars cruised slowly over it, and power launches were picking their way through the vegetation of the tidal lakes.

"Lipyear's Oceanic," Nile observed, "seems to have about every man they employ out spot-counting what's left!" She hesitated, added, "You're right about the herds we can see showing no sign of disturbance. Of course, nothing *does* disturb sea beef much."

Parrol sighed, said, "Well, let's get on to the meeting."

❖   ❖   ❖

By midmorning the sun was getting hot on the shelf, turning the air heavy with mingled smells of salt water and luxuriating vegetation. Escorted by a scolding flock of scarlet and black buzzbirds, Danrich Parrol brought a water scooter showing the stamp of Lipyear's Oceanic down to the edge of an offshore tidal pool. The buzzbirds deserted him there. The scooter settled to the water, drifted slowly across the pool towards Nile's PanElemental, berthed on the surface between two stands of reeds.

Parrol looked thoughtfully about. Passing overhead through the area half an hour earlier, he had seen the slender, long-legged figure of Dr. Etland standing in swim-briefs and flippers on her car. At the moment she was nowhere in sight. An array of testing equipment lay helter-skelter about on the Pan's hood, and the murkily roiled water indicated sea beef was feeding below the surface.

Parrol stepped over into the big car and tethered the scooter to it. He was wearing trunks and flippers; attached to his belt were an underwater gun and knife. The shelf ranchers were rarely invaded by the big deep-water carnivores, but assorted minor vermin wasn't too uncommon. He reached back to the rack of the scooter, fished cigarettes out from among a recorder, a case of maps and charts, a telecamera, a breather and a pocket communicator. As he was lighting a cigarette, a flat, brown animal head, fiercely whiskered and carrying a ragged white scar-line diagonally across its skull, broke the surface twenty feet away and looked at him.

"Hi, Spiff," Parrol said conversationally, recognizing the larger of the two hunting otters Nile kept around as bodyguards when engaged in water work. "Where's the boss?"

The otter grunted, curved over and submerged his nine-foot length again with a motion like flowing dark oil. Parrol waited patiently. A minute or two later there was a splash on his left. The face that looked at him this time showed the patrician features of Dr. Nile Etland. She came stroking over to him, and Parrol held a hand down to her. She grasped it, swung herself smoothly up on the hood of the PanElemental, squeezed water out of her hair and pulled off the transparent breather which had covered her face and the front part of her head.

She glanced at the watch on her wrist, inquired, "Well, did you find out anything new during the past hour and a half?"

"I picked up a few items. Just how meaningful—" Parrol checked himself. Slowly and almost without sound, a vast, pinkish-gray bulk rose above the surface near the center of the tidal pool. A pair of bulging, morose eyes regarded the humans and their vehicles suspiciously. Terra's *hippopotamus amphibious*, adapted to a salt water life with its richer food and increased growth potential, enlarged, tenderized and reflavored, had become the sea beef which provided the worlds of the Federation with a considerable share of their protein staples. This specimen, Parrol saw, was an old breed bull, over thirty feet long, with a battle-scarred hide and Oceanic's three broad white stripes painted across its back.

"Is that ancient monster what you're messing around with here?" Parrol asked.

"Uh-huh." Nile was taking an outsized hypodermic from a flap in one of her flippers. She placed it on the hood. "He's a bit reluctant to let me have a blood sample."

"Why bother with him?"

She shrugged. "Just a hunch. What were you about to say?"

"Well, there's one detail about the big beef disappearance I can't see as a coincidence," Parrol told her. "The thing started at the north bend of the continent. It's taken it a week to move a hundred and fifty miles down the coast to Lipyear's Oceanic. That's almost the exact rate of speed with which the edge of the Meral Current passes along the shelf of the Continental Rift."

Nile nodded. "That's occurred to me. If it's only a coincidence, it's certainly an odd one. But deciding the Meral's involved doesn't answer the big question, does it?"

"Where have the stupid things gone? No, it doesn't." Parrol scowled. "None of the theories brought up at the meeting made sense to me. Animal predators can't have caused. I've checked with half the northern ranches, and they've noticed no unusual numbers of dead or wounded beef floating around—or obviously sick ones either. And nobody's been running them off. There'd be no place to hide them in quantities like that, even if they could be moved off the ranches without attracting attention.

"I did hear about one thing I intend to look into immediately. Somewhat over two months ago—almost immediately after we'd left for the Hub, as a matter of fact—the Tuskason Sleds reported to mainland authorities that something had killed off their entire fraya pack."

Nile whistled soundlessly. "That's bad news, Dan! I'm sorry to hear it. You think there's a connection?"

"I don't know. The authorities sent investigators who couldn't find anything to show the pack hadn't died of natural causes. The sledmen claimed the frayas were deliberately poisoned, but they had no significant evidence to offer. The feeling here is they were fishing for federal indemnification. I've asked Machon to find out where the Tuskason fleet is cruising at present. He'll let me know as soon as it's been located, and I'll fly out there."

He added, "Then something occurred to me that might help explain the problem on the ranches. There's a possibility that it's chiefly the spot-counts on the beef that are way off at the moment. The computers figure that beef which is feeding submerged or napping on the bottom will, on the average, surface every ten minutes to breathe.

"But say something's happened to poison them mildly, make them exceptionally sluggish. If every animal in the herds is now surfacing only when it absolutely *has* to breath, it might almost make up for the apparent drop in their numbers."

"That's an ingenious theory," Nile said. "You've suggested an underwater check?"

"Yes. It will be a monstrous job, of course, particularly in an area the size of Lipyear's, but some of the ranchers are going at it immediately. You didn't . . . "

She shook her head. "So far there's been nothing in the water and blood samples I've sent in to the lab to suggest poisoning of any kind as a causative agent in the disappearances. But, as a matter of fact, I have noticed something which supports your idea."

"What's that?"

"The old bull who showed up just now," Nile said. "I don't know if you were watching him, but he went down again almost immediately. And one reason I wanted a blood sample from him is that he did *not* surface to breathe in anything like ten minutes after I'd started checking the pool. When you arrived, he'd been under water for better than half an hour. However, he isn't acting sluggish down there. He's busy feeding his face. In fact, I don't remember seeing a beef stuff away with quite that much steady enthusiasm before."

"Now why," Parrol said, puzzled, "would that be?"

Nile shrugged. "I don't know—yet." She picked up the king-sized syringe again. "Like to come down and help me get that sample? He doesn't want to let me get behind him, and Spiff and Sweeting aren't much help in this case because he simply ignores them."

The bull was stubborn and belligerent, not unusual qualities in the old herd leaders. Parrol wasn't too concerned. He and Nile Etland were natives of Nandy-Cline, born in shallows settlements a thousand miles from the single continent, quite literally as much at home in the water as on land. Nile, if one could believe her, had been helping herd her settlement's sea beef by the time she was big enough to toddle. She slipped away from the bull's ponderous lunges now with almost the easy grace of her otters; then, while Parrol began to move about near the gigantic head, fixing the beef's attention on himself, she glided out of sight behind it.

She emerged a minute or two later, held the blood-filled hypodermic up for Parrol to see, and stroked up to the surface.

Parrol followed. They climbed back up on the Pan, leaving the sea beef to return to its surly feeding, and pulled off their breathers.

"I'm going to pack up here now, Dan, and move on," Nile said. She'd stored the hypodermic away, was arranging her equipment inside the car. "I'll drop this stuff off at the lab for Freasie to work over, then run eighty miles south and duplicate the samplings in an area where the herds don't seem to be affected yet. That might give us a few clues. Want to come along, or do you have other immediate plans?"

"I . . . just a moment!" The communicator on the rack of Parrol's borrowed scooter was tinkling. He reached over, picked up the instrument, said, "Parrol here. Go ahead!"

"Machon speaking." It was the voice of the secretary of the Ranchers Association. "We've contacted the Tuskason Sleds, Dan, and they very much want to see you! They've been waiting for you to get back from Orado. Here's their present location . . ."

Parrol scribbled a few notes on the communicator's pad, thanked Machon and switched off. "I'll fly out at once," he told Nile. "Typhoon season—I'd better take the Hunter. Give me a call if you hit on anything that looks interesting."

She nodded, said, "Throw your stuff in the back while I get in Sweeting and Spiff. I'll give you a ride to the station . . ."

II

The sun wasn't far from setting when Parrol took his Hunter up from the deck of the Tuskason headquarters sled and started it arrowing back towards the mainland. He was glad he hadn't decided on a flimsier vehicle. The Tuskason area lay well within the typhoon belt, and the horizon ahead of him was leaden gray and black, walls of racing cloud banks heavy with rain.

He had let himself be delayed longer than he'd intended by his discussions with the sledmen; and the information he'd gained did not seem to be of any immediate value. The probability was that he'd simply burdened himself with a new and unrelated problem now. The Tuskason Sleds handled a fleet of chemical harvesting machines for Giard Pharmaceuticals and in consequence regarded Parrol and Nile Etland as their only dependable mainland contacts. The destruction of their fraya pack was a very serious economic loss to them.

The frayas were Nandy-Cline's closest native approximation of rich red mammalian meat, ungainly beasts with a body chemistry and structure which almost paralleled that of some of Terra's sea-going mammals, but with a quite unmammalian life cycle. Their breeding grounds lay in ocean rifts and trenches half a mile to a mile deep, and each pack had its individual ground to which it returned annually. Here the fraya changed from an omnivorous, air-breathing surface swimmer to a bottom-feeder, dependent on a single deepwater plant form. Within a few weeks it had doubled its weight, had bred, and was ready to return to the surface.

Every pack was the property of one of the sledmen communities, and at the end of the breeding period as many frayas as were needed to keep the sleds' mobile storehouses filled were butchered. Then the annual cycle began again. The animals weren't the sledmen's only food source by any means, but they were the principal one, the staple.

The Tuskason Sleds were certain their pack had been killed deliberately by a mainland organization, either one of the sea-processing concerns or a big rancher, with the intention of forcing them out of their sea area and taking over the chemical harvesting work there. The frayas had been within a hundred miles of their breeding ground and hurrying toward it when the disaster occurred. The following herd sleds were unaware of trouble until they found themselves riding through a floating litter of the beasts. The entire pack appeared to have died within minutes. It was a genuine calamity because the breeding ground could not be restocked now from other fraya packs. There was a relationship of mutual dependency between the animals and the chalot, the food plant they subsisted on during the breeding season. Each was necessary in the other's life cycle. If the frayas failed to make their annual appearance, the chalot died; and it could not be re-established in the barren grounds.

If some mainland outfit was found to be responsible, the Tuskason Sleds could collect a staggering indemnification either from those who were guilty or from the Federation itself. But aside from the reported blips of what might have been two submersible vessels moving away from the area, they had no proof to offer. Parrol promised to do what he could in the matter, and the sledmen seemed satisfied with that.

Otherwise, the afternoon had not brought him noticeably closer to answering the question of what was happening to the coastal ranchers' sea beef. The frayas had died outright, either through human malice or through the eruption of some vast bubble of lethal gas from the depths of the ocean—which seemed to Parrol the more probable explanation at the moment. The beef, so far as anyone could tell, wasn't dying. It simply wasn't around any more.

Parrol battered his way through typhoon winds for a while, then made use of the first extensive quiet area to put calls through to the mainland. At the Southeastern Ranchers Association, he was routed at once to the secretary's office. Machon was still on duty; his voice indicated he was close to exhaustion. He had one favorable fact to report: Parrol's hunch that an underwater check might reveal some of the missing stock had been a good one. At Lipyear's Oceanic, the estimated loss might be cut by almost a quarter now, and some of the northern ranches were inclined to go above that figure. But that left approximately seventy-five per cent of the vanished animals to be accounted for; and reports of new disappearances were still coming in from farther down the coast.

Parrol called the Giard Pharmaceuticals Station next. Nile Etland had been in and out during the day; at the moment she was out. She had left no message for him, given no information about where she might be reached. Freasie, at the laboratory, told him the checks Nile had them running on the sea beef specimens had been consistently negative.

He switched off as fresh gusts of heavy wind started the Hunter bucking again, gave his full attention for a time to the business of getting home alive. He'd already buzzed Nile's PanElemental twice and received no response. She could have called the Hunter if she'd felt like it. The fact that she hadn't suggested she had made no progress and was in one of her irritable moods.

By the time the Hunter had butted through the last

of the typhoon belt, Parrol was becoming somewhat irritable himself. He reached for one of the sandwiches he'd brought along for the trip, realized he'd long ago finished the lot and settled back, stomach growling emptily, to do some more thinking, while the car sped along on its course. Except for scattered thunderheads, the sky was clear over the mainland to the west. He rode into the gathering night. Zetman, the inner moon, already had ducked below the horizon, while Duse rode, round, pale and placid, overhead.

An annoyingly vague feeling remained that there should be a logical connection between the two sets of events which had occupied him during the day. The disappearing herds of beef. The Tuskason Sleds' mysteriously stricken fraya pack...

Details of what the sledmen had told him kept drifting through Parrol's mind. He gave his visualization of the events they had reported free rein. Sometimes in that way—

The scowl cleared suddenly from his face. He sat still, reflective, then leaned forward, tapped the listings button on the communicator.

"ComWeb Service," said an operator's voice.

"Give me Central Library Information."

A few moments later, Parrol was saying, "I'd like to see charts of the ocean currents along the east coast, to a thousand miles out."

He switched on the viewscreen, waited for the requested material to be shown.

Another hunch! This one looked hot!

The location indicator showed a hundred and three miles to the Giard Station. Parrol was pushing the Hunter along. He was reasonably certain he had part of the problem boxed now, but he wanted to discuss it with Nile, and that annoying young woman still had not made herself available. The PanElemental did not respond to its call number, and it had been three hours since she last checked in at the station.

Mingled with his irritation was a growing concern he was somewhat reluctant to recognize. Nile was very good at taking care of herself, and the thing he had discovered with the help of Central Library made it seem less probable now that human criminality was directly responsible for what had happened to the herds. But still . . .

The communicator buzzed. Parrol turned it on, said, "Parrol speaking. Who is it?"

A man's voice told him pleasantly, "My mistake, sir! Wrong call number."

Parrol's eyes narrowed. He didn't reply—the voice was a recording, and a signal from Nile. He snapped a decoder into the communicator's outlet, slipped on its earphones and waited. The decoder was set to a system they had developed to employ in emergencies when there was a chance that unfriendly ears were tuned to the communicators they were using.

After some seconds the decoder's flat, toneless whisper began:

"Alert. Alert. Guns. Air. Water. Land. Nile. Water. East. Fifty-eight. North. Forty-six. Come. Caution. Caution. Call. Not."

After an instant the message was repeated. Then the decoder remained silent.

Parrol removed the earphones, glanced at the speed indicator which showed the Hunter already moving along at its best clip, chewed his lip speculatively.

That meant, rather definitely, that a human agency *was* involved in the sea beef problem! Which didn't in itself disprove his latest conclusions but added another angle to them. Nile liked to dramatize matters on occasion but wasn't given to sending out false alarms. Guns . . . the possibility of an attack by air, water, or land. By whom? She didn't know or she would have told him. She'd called from the surface of the sea, fifty-eight miles east of the Giard Station, forty-six miles to the north. That would put her due east of the upper edge of the Lipyear's Oceanic ranch, beyond the shallows of the shelf, well out above the half-mile-deep canyon of the Continental Rift.

Parrol slid out the Hunter's swivel-gun, turned on the detection screens, dropped to a water-skimming level, and sped on in a straight course for Lipyear's.

Fog banks lay above the Rift. Except for a slow swell, the sea was quiet. Half a mile from the location she had given him, Parrol settled the Hunter on the surface, rode the swells in to the approximate point where Nile should be waiting. He snapped the car's canopy back, waited another minute, then tapped the Hunter's siren. As the sound died away, there came an answering brief wail out of the eddying fog. Dead ahead, simultaneously, a spark of blurred light flared and vanished. Parrol grinned with relief, turned on the Hunter's running lights and came in on the PanElemental lying half submerged in the swells. Its canopy was down; an anchor engine murmured softly. The subdued glow of instrument lights showed Nile standing in her swim rig in the front section, hands on her hips, watching him move in.

Parrol cut his drive engine and lights, switched on the sea anchor as the cars nosed gently together.

"Everything all right here?" he asked.

"More or less."

"From whom are you hiding?"

"I'm not sure. At a guess, Agenes Laboratories is the villain in the act, as you suspected. Come into my car, Dan."

Parrol grunted, stepped across and down into the PanElemental. He asked, "What makes you think so?"

"The fact that around noon today somebody scorched my beautiful left ear lobe with a needle beam."

"Huh? Who?"

Nile shrugged. "I never saw him at all. I was checking

out ranch beef about a hundred miles south, and this character fired out of a bunch of reeds thirty feet away. He'd sneaked up under water obviously. I peppered the reed bed with the UW. Probably missed him, but he must have got discouraged and dived, because there was no more shooting."

"You reported it?"

She shook her head. "No."

Parrol looked at her suspiciously. "Where were the otters?"

"The otters? Well . . . they may have gone after him, I suppose. Matter of fact, I remember there was some little screeching and splashing back among the reeds. I didn't go look. Blood upsets me."

"Yes, I've noticed," Parrol said. "Where are the otters now?"

"Turned them loose in their sea run at Lipyear's before I came out here. I thought it would be best if whoever sent a needle-beam operator after me didn't find out for a while that the trick hadn't worked. It might keep them from trying something new immediately. But it's a cinch somebody *doesn't* want us to poke around too far into the mystery of the vanishing beef. You were right about that."

Parrol frowned. "Uh-huh. The fact is I'd just finished convincing myself I'd been wrong—that there was no human agency back of this."

"What gave you that idea?" Nile reached under the instrument shelf, brought out a sandwich, asked, "Have you eaten? I've a stack of these around."

"Glad to hear it," Parrol said gratefully, taking the sandwich. "I've been getting downright ravenous the past couple of hours."

She watched him reflectively while he told her about his visit to the Tuskason Sleds. "Now here's the point," he continued. "The sled-men think their animals were hit by a couple of subs which released something like a nerve gas beneath them. The gas killed the frayas, reached the surface and dissipated instantly into the air."

Nil nodded. "Could be done just like that, Dan."

"I don't doubt it," Parrol said. "But for the past half hour my theory has been that it wasn't done by something that dissipated instantly into the air."

"Why not?"

"Because the spot where this happened is near the northern edge of the Meral Current. The pack was destroyed around two and a half months ago, shortly after we'd left for the Hub. Anything drifting on from there with the Meral would reach the Continental Rift, and this section of the coast, in approximately that time."

Nile frowned, rubbed the tip of her nose. "Meaning that the trouble with the sea beef wasn't intended—that it was an accidental aftermath of poisoning the fraya pack?"

"That's what I was assuming," Parrol said. "That whatever hit the Tuskason pack two months or so ago has been hitting the local sea beef during the past week. It didn't have anything like the same instantaneously deadly effect here because it was widely dispersed by now. But suppose the stuff is brought into the shallows with the tides. Some of the beef absorbs enough of it to get very uncomfortable and starts moving out to sea to escape from what's bothering it. The nearest drift-weed beds are around a hundred and ten miles out. The tubs could make the trip if they got the notion, and until they were discovered there they would seem to have disappeared.

"But the fact that a direct attempt has been made to kill you changes the picture in one important respect. Somebody else evidently knows what's going on—and that makes it appear that Giard may have been the real target throughout. If the beef herds on our contract ranches can be destroyed and the sleds that work for us starved out of their area, our operations on Nandy-Cline would be shot, perhaps permanently. Agenes and a few others would have the field to themselves.

"My guess is now that the business with the Tuskason pack and the trouble with the sea beef were two different maneuvers, though carried out by the same people, and that the stuff that's affected the beef was scattered out over the Continental Rift not far north of the coastal ranches with the idea of letting the Meral carry it south."

Nile shook her head.

"I think you came closer with your other idea," she said.

"What makes you say so?"

"Two things I discovered while you were gone. I'll let you see for yourself." She nodded toward the rear of the car. "You'll find your trunks and diving gear back there. If you'll climb into them, we'll go for a dip."

"Here? Why?"

"To get your unprejudiced impression of something I noticed a few hours ago. Use the helmet instead of the breather so we can talk."

The water was comfortably warm. Quite dark, but the combined pulse of the two anchor engines made a beacon of sound behind them. A glimmer of phosphorescence came from the surface fifteen feet above. Nile Etland was a vague shadow on Parrol's left.

"All right, we're here," Parrol said. "Now what?"

"Let's circle around the cars at about this level," the helmet communicator told him.

Parrol turned to the left, aware that she was turning with him. He stroked along twenty or thirty yards was about to speak impatiently again when Nile asked, "You can hold your breath just under four minutes, can't you, Dan?"

"As you know."

"Just establishing the fact. Start holding it now and keep on swimming."

"What's the . . . " Parrol broke off. She seemed dead serious about this. He stopped breathing, stroked on, turning gradually to keep the sound of the sea anchors at the same distance to his left. The shadow-shape of Nile dropped back behind him.

Irritation was simmering in Parrol, but so was curiosity. He was quite certain—certain in a somehow unpleasant way—that Nile wasn't playing some game in order to be mysterious. He kept moving along, jumbled questions and surmises flashing through his mind. After a time, his lungs labored heavily for breath, became quiet again. The sea water suddenly seemed colder. He realized the double pulse of the anchor engines had receded somewhat, turned in more sharply towards them. How long had he been swimming by now? It must be—

"Dan?"

He opened his mouth, took in a lungful of air.

"Yes?" he said hoarsely.

"How do you feel?"

"Fine."

"Liar! You're scared spitless! I don't blame you. You've been holding your breath since I asked you to?"

"Yes—until now."

"That's been"—a pause—"eight minutes and fifteen seconds, Dan!"

For a moment it made no sense. Then it did. Parrol felt numbed. He said at last, "That was the unprejudiced observation you wanted me to make?"

"Yes. Let's go up and get back into the car."

She swung herself into the PanElemental ahead of him, turned as he started to follow her. "Better stay out till you're dry, Dan. You'd soak the upholstery. Climb on the hood and I'll toss you a towel."

Parrol inquired presently, drying himself, "Same thing with you?"

"It would have been if I'd been holding my breath."

"That old herd bull we were monkeying with this morning . . . "

"Uh-huh. He might come to the surface occasionally but not because he had to breathe. Same thing again with a lot of the other beef that's stayed on the ranches. *That's* why the spot checks were so far off. Something the matter?"

Parrol had sworn aloud in surprise. The towel in his hand was dripping wet now, while he didn't seem to be any drier. "Toss me another towel, will you?"

Nile made an odd, choking sound. "Here it is, Dan."

He caught it, looked over at her suspiciously, looked down again at himself. Water was trickling over every portion of his skin as freely as if he'd just climbed out of the sea.

"What the devil's going on?" he demanded.

She made the choked sound again. "I . . . don't worry about it, Dan! It'll stop in a minute or two. The same thing happened to me this afternoon. I'd probably have to dissect you under a microscope to be able to say exactly what's happening."

"An educated guess will do for now."

"An educated guess? Well—the thing that we, and the beef, picked up has developed some biological mechanism for drawing water in through our skin, extracting the oxygen from the water, and expelling the water again. We've become gills all over, so to speak. Did you feel your lungs start trying to work while you were holding your breath?"

Parrol reflected, nodded. "For just an instant."

"That," Nile said, "seems to be what brings the water-breathing mechanism into action—the first oxygen-shortage reflex. I think you can dry yourself and stay dry now, by the way. You noticed a feeling of cold immediately afterwards?"

Parrol asked distastefully, "That was the sea water coming through my skin?"

"Yes. As I say, I don't think it's anything to worry about. The mechanism should dissolve again in a day or two if we don't pick up any more of the stuff."

"No permanent changes?"

"At a guess again, no. If you hadn't held your breath while you were under water just now, you probably never would have known there had been any change in you. You look like you're going to stay dry now, so come on inside."

III

She held out a sandwich as he swung down into the car's interior. "Still hungry?"

"No. I—" Parrol broke off, looked surprised. "I certainly am! Like that bull beef stuffing himself, eh?"

"Yes. Whatever that breathing mechanism is, it eats up a lot of energy fast. Here, take it—I've been piling away calories all afternoon. And here's my other piece of evidence."

She thrust the sandwich into his hand, swung a camera recorder out of its compartment, settled it on the instrument shelf before Parrol. Her fingers spun the dial setting back a few turns, pushed the start button. The front surface of the recorder turned into a viewscreen.

"Fire forest," Parrol said, chewing. A flat stretch of sea floor had appeared in the screen, shot from a slight angle above it. Dotting the silt were clumps of shrublike and treelike growths, burning eerily with all the colors of the spectrum. Towards the background they blended into a single blanket of blazing white which forced the gloom of the abyss up a hundred feet above the floor. Parrol asked, "The local one?"

"Yes," Nile said. "The section immediately beneath

us. I put in the last couple of hours prowling around the floor of the Rift. Now watch!"

The pickup swung about to a point where a cluster of giant yellow blooms was being slowly agitated by something dark moving through them. The view blurred for an instant as magnification cut in, then cleared.

Parrol paused on a bite of the sandwich, swallowed, leaned forward.

"Oh, no!" he said. "The floor's over a half-mile down! That isn't . . . but it is, of course!"

"Sea beef down in the Rift, alive—and feeding!" Nile agreed. "That's where something like eighty per cent of the missing stock seems to be now. I can show you whole herds in a minute. They're thickest a little farther south. Here's a closer look at this specimen."

The magnification stepped up again. After a moment Parrol said, "You get the impression it's lost half its blubber! No wonder the thing's gorging on fire plants. Energy loss through adaptation again, I suppose?"

"Of course," Nile said. "There'd be rather drastic changes needed to let sea beef live even a minute down there."

"Lungs, ears, sinuses . . . yes, there would. It's almost unbelievable! But wait a second! Supposing we—"

"Apparently," Nile said, "the process is similar to that of the development of the underwater breathing mechanism. The outer stimulus is required. As the beef moved down into the Rift, it adapted to deep-water living. The ones that stayed in the ranches weren't subjected to the same succession of stimuli, therefore didn't change."

Parrol cleared his throat. "So you think that if we started swimming down without suits . . .

"Well, we might find ourselves starting to adapt. Care to try it?"

"Not for anything!"

"Nor I. The sea beef's taking it, evidently. What would

happen to a human body is something I don't care to discover in person. That's the end of the sequence. Want to see the herds to the south now?"

Parrol shook his head. "Skip that. I'll take your word that most of them are down there."

She turned the recorder off, swung it back into the compartment. "What do you make of it all, Dan?"

"Just what you're making of it, apparently," Parrol said. "When the Tuskason frayas turned belly up and died, they were around a hundred miles southwest of their breeding ground, headed there. And the breeding ground—the Tuskason Rift—lies inside the Meral Current. There's that symbiotic relationship between the frayas and the chalot, their food plant during the breeding period. The chalot produces mobile spores as the frayas start arriving. Spore enzymes produce reactions in the frayas to turn them into their deep-water breeding form—"

He paused, scowling. The frayas were living anachronisms among Nandy-Cline's present animal forms, the last of a class of pelagic browsers in whose life cycle certain luminants of the fire forests had been intricately involved. "The chalot spores are assumed to actively seek out the frayas when they appear in the breeding grounds," he went on slowly. "But this time, when the chalot released its spores into the Tuskason Rift the fraya pack didn't show up. Eventually the Meral carried the free spores off, and eventually it brought them along the Continental Rift and into the shore ranches. Terran mammals—sea beef and humans, in this case—are a much closer approximation to frayas than any of Nandy-Cline's modern life strains. So the chalot spores settled for us! And we've responded to their enzymes almost as the frayas did."

"That's what it looks like," Nile agreed.

After a moment Parrol asked, "What makes you so sure the changes won't be permanent?"

"Simply the fact that the chalot doesn't grow here. The frayas maintain their deep-water form as long as there is chalot around for them to feed on. By the time the seasonal supply is exhausted, they've bred and are ready to return to their pelagic shape. The spores bring about only the initial reaction. It's maintained by contact with the parent plants. Some of the sea beef that went down into the Rift here may already be losing the effect and coming back to the surface, for that matter."

"All right," Parrol said. "We know now that the trouble with the beef wasn't planned. It was an accidental result of wiping out the fraya pack. But we're still thinking of Agenes. If they killed the frayas, their biochemists would realize soon enough what's happening now—and that would be a good enough reason to send needle-beam men after us before we worked it out. But why kill the frayas in the first place?"

"That's what I'm wondering," Nile said. "Agenes has all the sea harvest territory it can use."

Parrol said, "So it does. But it occurs to me now that the Grenley Banks are about two hundred miles north of the Tuskason Rift."

"What's that got to do with it?"

"You may remember," Parrol said, "that a week or two before we left Orado there was a report that Giard had lost a submarine harvester here which was working along the Grenley Banks the last time it gave its position."

Nile's eyes widened an instant.

"I'd forgotten! That does look interesting. Agenes knocks off one of our harvesters roughly three hundred miles north of the point they knocked off the fraya pack. Why? They had something going in the area they didn't want the sub to stumble over—or maybe it *did* stumble over it. Why kill the pack before that, three hundred miles to the south?"

"To keep it from going on toward the breeding grounds," Parrol said.

"Of course! The Tuskason herd sleds were following the frayas. If somebody attacked the sleds, the whole planet would hear about it. But with the frayas dead, the sleds has no reason to go on to the breeding grounds, and didn't. Now . . . "

"The breeding grounds!" Parrol said. "A fire forest, Nile!"

She was silent a moment, said, "You're right, Dan! It has to be that. A new nidith bed Narcotics hasn't found out about!"

It was almost certainly the answer, Parrol thought. The luminant nidith plant was the source of a drug of unique medical properties when used with strict safeguards, viciously habit-forming when not. It could be harvested legally only under direct government supervision and in amounts limited to the actual medicinal demand. The nidith beds required for that purpose were patrolled; in the other fire forests on the planet Narcotics teams had painstakingly exterminated the plant.

But if a fresh bed had sprung up and been discovered by the wrong people . . .

"Agenes would take a chance on it!" he said. "Two or three seasonal hauls would be worth everything else they could expect to get out of the planet."

"That's what it is!" Nile said. She stared at him a moment, teeth worrying her upper lip. "How do we pin it on them, Dan?"

Parrol said, "This is about the peak of the nidith harvest season, isn't it?"

"Of course. They should be working there right now! Whom do we give it to? Fiawa and the cops? Narcotics? No, wait . . . "

"Uh-huh," Parrol agreed. "I just had that thought, too."

"They can harvest it on the quiet," Nile said, "at the expense of a few murders if somebody happens by. But they can't haul it off Nandy-Cline unless they've got people both in Narcotics and among the mainland police bought and paid for. This thing's organized to the hilt! If we blow our horn and nobody happens to be at the nidith bed at the moment, we'll never hang it on Agenes. We're got to be sure they're caught with the goods before we make another move."

Ilium Weldrow appeared disturbed. He had stared at Parrol and Nile with unconcealed disapproval when they called him into Parrol's office on their return to the station. By contrast with the assistant manager in his trimly proper business suit, the pair looked like criminally inclined beachcombers. Both wore their guns, and Parrol hadn't troubled to do more than pull his trousers back on over his swim trunks, while Nile had added only a short jacket to her swimming attire. But it was more than the lack of outer respectability in his colleagues that had upset Weldrow.

"I'm afraid I don't follow you, Dan," he said, frowning. "I'm to stay in your office, glued—as you say—to your private communicator, while the station is to remain darkened and locked after you leave. Why the latter?"

"Because if you indicate you're here during the next few hours, somebody might blow that pointed little head off your shoulders," Nile told him inelegantly.

Weldrow's face showed alarm. "But what is this desperate business all about?"

"If you don't know what it's about, you won't be involved in it," Parrol said. "And you'll be in no danger if you simply carry out your instructions and don't stick your neck out of the station before we get back. Let's go over the instructions now to make sure you've got them straight."

The assistant manager complied grudgingly. He was to wait here for a call from a Captain Mace, on the Giard cropper tender *Attris*. The call should come within three to six hours and would be an innocuous request to have certain spare parts flown out to the tender. This would be Weldrow's cue to dial two emergency call numbers on Parrol's communicator. One would put him in contact with Chief of Police Fiawa, the other with a Federation Narcotics man with whom Parrol had worked before. When they responded, he was to press the transmission button on the communicator's telewriter, which contained certain coded information Parrol had fed into it, and silently switch the machine off again.

Weldrow appeared to have absorbed the instructions well enough, Parrol decided. Even if he slipped up, it shouldn't do more than delay action by a few hours.

The night sky was clear above the Meral Current and Duse floodlighted the sky. "You're sure that's the *Attris* ahead?" Nile Etland asked.

Parrol said, "Uh-huh. Mace is around forty miles off his check point, but it's the *Attris*. I know that tub." The magnified image of the cropper tender eight thousand feet below was centered in the ground-view screen. Two flocks of pelagic cropping machines near it rose and sank slowly on the shimmer of the swells. The croppers were restless in the full moonlight, and the tender's chase-plane was circling beyond the farther of the two flocks, guiding a few runaways back to the fold.

"Then what are we waiting for?" Nile asked.

Parrol glanced over at her. "You've checked your position chart?"

"Of course. The ship's anchored above the north third of the Tuskason Rift. I see. You feel she'd be in danger if somebody spots the Pan snooping around the floor of the Rift?"

"She might be in danger, and in any case she's too close to where we want to operate," Parrol said. "If they're loading nidith down there, they're nervous people. They know a ship of that type can't spot them, but the mere fact the tender's at anchor here will make them that much more ready to dump the evidence and run at the first hint that something's wrong."

"So what do you want to do?"

"Go aboard, tell Mace to move his croppers fifty miles west and wait for us there. That will get him out of everybody's hair. He'll know something unusual is up, but he never asks questions. Give them the visual signal."

Nile's hand moved, and the Giard identification light . . . blue . . . blue . . . red . . . flashed out beneath the PanElemental. After a ten-second pause it was repeated. The communicator burred.

"Negative," Nile muttered. Her fingers shifted on the signal box; a purple glow appeared beneath them. As it faded, the communicator burr ended and Giard's blue-blue-red flickered up at them from the tender.

Nile said, "He's got the idea that we don't want conversation." She flashed the coming-in signal. A few moments later a clear green spark showed on the *Attris*.

Nile snapped off the signal box. "That's it! Let's go down." She shoved the car's nose over and fed it speed as Parrol switched off the ground-view plate. The sea was rising towards them, moonlit and stirring; then it tilted sharply up to the right, swung back and was level again just below. Water hissed under them as the Pan knifed lightly through the back of a swell. The tender's stern appeared ahead, its details outlined in Duse's light. Several men stood about the deck. Two of them . . .

"NILE! TURN—"

Parrol had no time to complete the warning. On the deck of the *Attris* a piece of shielding had dropped. Behind it stood a squat gun, nose pointed at them. Nile saw the trap in the moment he did, reacted instantly. The Pan shot down toward the water.

A blaze of light filled the screen and a giant fist rammed the car up and around. Nile was flung heavily over on Parrol, dropped away. He was struggling to reach the flight controls while the car flipped through the air, engine roaring wildly. In the screen, he had a flashing glimpse of the bow of the *Attris* receding from them, another of the tender's chase-plane darting past. A hail of steel rattled and tore at the PanElemental for an instant. Then the engine was dead. He had the car under partial control for the moment needed to straighten it out before it crashed into the sea.

The water was pitch-black all around. The PanElemental, sinking tail first now, ruined engine section flooded, settled heavily against some yielding obstruction, dropped again a few feet, was checked once more. It swayed over slowly into something close to a horizontal position, turned sideways and lay still in a grappling tangle of the vegetation that rode the Meral Current below the surface.

Parrol, out of his trousers and shoes, tightened the dive belt around his waist, groped about for the scattered rest of their diving equipment, cursing the darkness, the treachery of the *Attris* crew, his own stupidity. With an illegal source of drugs, that could make millionaires out of a thousand men, to exploit, Agenes would have had no difficulty in finding all the useful confederates it needed. Now he and Nile had one slim chance to outlive their blunder at least for a short while. They had to be out of the crippled car and away in the sea before the *Attris* got divers down to make sure they were finished off.

Nile lay doubled half across the slanted instrument board at his feet. There had been no time to find out how badly she was injured. She was certainly unconscious. But he could handle her in the water.

Parrol found the two sets of flippers behind the seat, had just finished slipping his on when there was a flicker of light in the blackness. He glanced around, startled, saw above and to the right what might have been a moving cluster of fireflies. Comprehension came instantly . . . the vision screen was showing him a group of jet divers approaching from the *Attris*.

Which left him perhaps thirty seconds to be away from here—

Swearing savagely, Parrol snapped the other set of flippers to his belt, squirmed around the front seat, picked up Nile and clamped her against him. His free hand groped about for the manual canopy release, found it. He pulled down the rear release first, instantly grasped the other and wrenched at it.

There was a roar, a momentary cold brutal pounding that smashed the air from his lungs, whirled him upwards.

He rolled over in water above the car, clutching Nile, came up against the rubbery trunk of a giant drift plant and straightened out. The fireflies were bigger and brighter here, turning toward the uprush of air from the PanElemental, moving closer through the great sodden underwater thicket in which it hung, gradually illuminating it. Parrol swung away from the lights, floated behind the car, saw a patch of empty blackness before and below him. He shifted Nile to his left arm, grasped the lower edge of the car's open section, reached down with his legs and gripped two of the plant trunks between his thighs. Locking himself to the plants, he hauled at the car. It swung around heavily, then began to turn, was suddenly sliding past him. In an instant, it had plunged out through the thicket and disappeared below.

Parrol turned around with Nile and went stroking steadily down at a steep slant into the chilled night of the Tuskason Rift.

✦   ✦   ✦

IV

It had been horribly hungry and weak; and now it was eating. Its memory and awareness covered almost nothing but that. There were blurred visual impressions—light, darkness, color—indicating other things out there which interested it not at all. There were booming, whistling, chirping sounds; and those it also ignored.

Taste and touch held interest, however. The eating process was a simple one. Something was put into its mouth, and it swallowed; and as soon as it had swallowed, something was put into its mouth again, and it swallowed again. Occasionally there would be a pause before something new came into its mouth; and then it had a feeling of anxiety. But the pauses were always short.

Its awareness of taste and touch was connected with whatever was brought into its mouth. There would be one kind of thing for a while, then another. There were variations in flavor, in saltiness, in slipperiness, degree of firmness. But it was all very good.

"I must have been nearly starved to death!" it thought suddenly. It wondered then what "I" was, but almost at once forgot the matter again.

A while later, it had another thought. It decided it didn't want to eat any more, at least not just now. Something was being pushed into its mouth, but it ejected the something and closed its mouth firmly. There was no impulse to do anything else. It remained exactly where it was, contentedly unmoving.

Now its other senses began to click in. It discovered the blue was gone from its vision and that there was a wide, colorful vista out there, full of individual details. There were things that moved, and many more things that stood still. It became aware of sounds again and for a while tried unsuccessfully to connect them to things it could see. Then there was a sudden awareness of buoyancy, of near-weightlessness. At once it knew what *that* meant!

"I'm under water . . . "

" . . . And I'm me, of course!" Nile Etland concluded, with a pleased sense of summing up the situation.

She was sitting here, upright, in the underwater ooze. Not quite upright—she was leaning back a little, against something hard.

Something moved. Nile tilted her head to look down at it. It was an arm. A repulsive arm-thick, mottled-gray, with corrugated, oily-looking skin. It was reaching around from behind her, and the cupped hand at its end held some bluish, sloppy oblongs, lifting them toward her face.

She realized that the hard thing she leaned against was the monster to which this arm was attached.

Nile jerked upward convulsively to get away from the thing. Somewhat to her surprise she succeeded. Next a powerful stroke of flipper-tipped legs that knocked up a cloud of ooze, and she was driving straight across the bottom towards an electric-blue stand of fan-shaped luminants.

Luminants! Where . . . ?

Memory blazed up. The stern deck of the *Attris*, ghostly clear in white moonlight, the sudden appearance of the gun. They'd been hit—

Nile twisted about, braking her forward momentum, got her legs under her and turned, looking back.

The gray thing which had to be Danrich Parrol was on its feet but making no attempt to follow. Nile's gaze went beyond him, to the dense, multihued ranks of a fire forest burning coldly in endless night on the floor of the Tuskason Rift.

Slowly—shocked, horrified, oddly fascinated—she brought up her hands and stared at them, twisted and turned briefly to inspect as much as she could of her body, ran palms like hard rubber over her rubbery face and head. The sense of shock drained away. Aesthetically she had nothing on Parrol; the pattern of modifications seemed much the same, was presumably identical. It still beat, by a long way, being dead.

He wasn't moving from where he stood, probably to avoid alarming her again. Nile went stroking back, stopped a few feet away, a little above him. The changed, ugly face turned toward her; otherwise he remained motionless. Armies of tiny luminous feeders darted about his trunklike legs, crept in the soft mud, swarming about the litter of a smashed shells, cracked carapaces and other remnants of their own ravenous feeding.

She studied him quickly, no longer repelled by what she saw. There were transparent horny sheaths over the eyes, bulging outward a little. She had them, too. The lids wouldn't close over them, but there was no discomfort involved with that. Their outer ears were covered by a bone-hard growth like a thick, curved sausage. Whatever the internal arrangement was, the growths were excellent sound conductors. Broadened noses with no indications of nostrils. When she tried to expand or compress her lungs, nothing happened. Lungs were out of the picture here. The shape remained humanoid if not human, thickened, coarsened, grotesque, but functional, at least temporarily, beneath more than a thousand feet of water. She felt strong and vigorous; the awkward-looking body had responded to her purpose with agile ease. It was better, miraculously so, than they could have had any reason to expect!

She drifted closer to Parrol, touched his shoulder with her hand. His face split in a rather grisly grin; then he turned, momentarily scattering the feeders, and crouched beside a creamy luminous globe protruding from the ooze a few feet away. Nile floated down to see what he was doing.

Parrol laid a fingertip on the plant-animal's surface. The luminant shuddered. A dark spot appeared where the finger touched it. The finger moved slowly up along the glowing surface, curved down again. A line of darkness followed it as the creature's surface cells reacted to the touch. Parrol was, Nile realized suddenly, writing on his living parchment. After a few seconds she read:

RATIONAL NOW?

She moved her head irritably up and down, telling herself it wasn't an entirely unreasonable question. The transformed Parrol produced his unpleasantly transformed grin again, detached something from his belt, held it up to her. With a shock of pleasure Nile recognized her gun. She clipped the sheathed UW to her belt while he resumed writing, then shifted to where she could read over his shoulder.

The two words of the question had almost faded out. New words appeared gradually:

OUR FRIENDS ARE HERE.

Nile gave him a startled glance. He nodded, motioned her to follow, turned and swam toward the thicket of brilliant-blue luminants for which she had headed when she broke away from him. Half crawling, half swimming, he moved into the thicket, Nile close behind. After some fifty feet they came into a less dense but much taller stand of a darkly red growth; here Parrol moved more cautiously. Presently he stopped, beckoned Nile up to him, pushed a few soggy armfuls of the red fronds apart.

Nile found herself looking down a sharply slanted rock slope at another section of the Rift floor a hundred yards below. The fire forest began again at the foot of the shelf, stretched away, clearly detailed nearby but blurring quickly as distance increased into a many-colored glow. Following Parrol's pointing finger, she could barely make out the long dark hull of a submarine harvester grounded along the towering wall of the side of the Rift on the right. Two other harvesters lay farther out among the luminants. Together the ships formed a rough triangle,

within which Nile now began to detect the moving
figures of men, bulky in deep-water armor.

There was no mistaking the nature of their activity.
The nidith was pale blue, a slender two-foot structure,
individually unobtrusive among the greater luminants. But
from the top of the shelf it was apparent that there must
be millions of them in the bed which stretched away up
the floor of the Rift, forming an unbroken carpet of
undergrowth among the thickets and groves of the fire
forest.

Parrol pointed to the right. About halfway between
their position and the harvesters, a single armored figure
sat astride a beam-gun floating just off the bottom, its
short snout pointed upwards.

Nile nodded comprehendingly. Of the myriads of creatures that crawled, walked and swam among the fire
forest's branches and over the ooze, almost all were
completely harmless from the viewpoint of a man in
underwater armor. But a few species were far from
harmless. As she looked, the beam-gun made an abrupt
half-turn, following something which slithered rapidly
through the fringes of darkness overhead, vanished upward
into the gloom again without attempting to descend.

She felt a brief inward shudder. One glimpse of that
flattened, rubbery twenty-foot disk had been enough to
identify it—a cloakfish, a rather small one but quite large
enough to be an immediate menace to any member of
the nidith harvesting gang outside of the ships. The
cloakfish ordinarily were found clinging to the walls of
the ocean rifts they inhabited, grinding into the rock with
the multiple sets of jaws lining their undersides to get
at a variety of burrowing wormlike creatures within. But
they put no strict limitation on their diet, frequently
attacked divers on sight, and had been known to saw open
a deep-water suit in less than a minute.

Parrol turned away, motioned with his head. She wasn't
sure what he intended but guessed he wanted to follow

the edge of the shelf to a point on the right where a cluster of luminants rose high enough to let them drop into the lower section of the Rift without being detected by the guard riding the beam-gun. She nodded agreement, followed as Parrol wound his way through the thicket, moving parallel to the open slope.

As they approached the stand of tall growth, a curious thudding sensation reached Nile through the water, followed within seconds by another. She puzzled over that a moment, decided that beam-guns stationed on the far side of the harvesters had opened fire on some assailant. The gang probably had been at work here for a week or two; by now the area would be swarming both with cloakfish and with other predators gathered to feed on cloaks the guns had crippled or killed.

Predators such as that twenty-foot snake shape which came eeling up over the edge of the shelf a few yards away! It might have picked up their scent in the water, for it darted at her instantly, jaws yawning wide.

Nile wasn't quite sure how it happened. She had pulled back slightly as the head struck past. Immediately afterwards, her legs were clamped about the slick, sinuous body, her arms locking her against it—

And her teeth were sunk into the thing! Not simply biting, but digging, slashing, cutting deeper through slimy hide that should have turned a knife, tearing the hide away and returning instantly to slice at unprotected flesh. The thicket of red luminants whirled about her, then open water; the section of snake body she gripped was knotting and twisting with monstrous strength. Bottom silt exploded in a dense cloud as they struck into it. For a moment, lifted high above her, she saw the thing's head, great jaws snapping wildly, Parrol leeched to its neck.

Those were blurred, remote impressions. The only clear impressions were the savage hunger that blazed up in her as the creature drove at them and the horrified delight with which she was satisfying it in quickly gulped bites of salty flesh until—almost as suddenly as it had awakened—the hunger feeling was gone. It was like a fog clearing from her mind.

She pushed away from the snakelike thing. It was still writhing, but for all practical purposes it was dead. The big head flopped loosely, seemed half torn from the body. They appeared to have rolled into the tall stand of luminants in the lower section of the Rift for which she had thought Parrol was heading when the creature attacked. Parrol floated a few yards away, looking at her. Nile glanced up the length of the sea thing again and saw that he had been feeding, too. His response must have been as immediate and violent as hers—they'd had their guns within reach and made no attempt to use them!

She looked at the mangled beast and tried to feel disgust for what had happened. But there was no disgust. Her changed body had demanded nourishment, and meeting the demand had been a wholly agreeable experience. When the hunger surge rose again, she would feed it again.

Three or four generations of children in the shallows settlements, Parrol thought, must have had stories of Nandy-Cline's sea hags recounted to them by their elders. In the version he had heard when very young, the sea hags were anthropomorphic ogres who lived in the depths of the ocean but came to the surface for the specific purpose of eating small boys who swam out farther than grownups thought they should go. The legend was supposed to have been created by the sledmen who had settled to live on the ocean world fifty or sixty years before the first Hub colonists arrived.

It seemed it hadn't been entirely a legend. When the sledmen began to follow the fraya packs, an uncounted number of them would have come unknowingly into contact with the chalot spores and undergone this weird transformation—some to be slaughtered by their horrified companions when they climbed back on the sleds, maddened by the change hunger, others meeting death in one form or another in the rifts and trenches where the chalot grew, their disappearance charged off to the giant predators that prowled the breeding grounds during the season. The last such occurrence—before this—might lie many decades in the past. The sledmen nowadays regarded it as extremely bad luck to swim about in rift waters when the frayas bred and carefully refrained from it, although they weren't aware of the specific danger that had created the superstition.

At the moment, however, the sea hag shape was the one great advantage he had. And he couldn't have asked for a better companion than another of those watery bogy-men beside him, controlled by Nile Etland's intelligence. Flattened out and buried to the eyes in flowing ooze, they were edging forward toward a group of tall, golden luminants standing some thirty feet back of the guard on the floating beam-gun. These were plant-animals with some rudimentary intelligence, known to students of the fire forest fauna as starbursts. For several more minutes they remained undisturbed, the clusters of tentacle arms at their tips fanning the water with slow, rhythmic motions.

Then, on the far side of the group, one individual began to move off toward the beam-gun. While it was capable of gliding slowly along the ooze on the widened base of its stem, it was not moving of its own volition now but being half carried, half pushed through the silt. The starburst was in a state of considerable agitation. Its tip had opened out into something like an inverted umbrella, and from the edges of this hood the gleaming tentacles flailed anxiously through the water.

Parrol let it down suddenly, jabbed Nile. Both settled a little deeper into the silt. The gun was swinging around toward them, then stopped, pointing in their general direction. The guard's face couldn't be seen behind the headpiece of his suit, but presumably he was staring a little suspiciously at the starburst. He might not remember how close the luminant had been to him, but the disturbed silt behind it indicated it had been moving.

However, it had stopped its advance now; and in spite of a vague resemblance to a fifteen-foot golden squid standing on end, starbursts were known to be utterly inoffensive creatures. The guard swung the gun around again, facing the nidith bed, to watch for cloakfish.

Parrol gripped the starburst, began climbing to his feet, lifting it clear of the mud. Nile rose with him. Together, in a plodding rush, they carried the writhing luminant up behind the guard. Its top end tilted forward and down, and an instant later the upper part of the guard's suit was enclosed in the widespread hood and thrashing arms of the alarmed creature. He was jerked out of the gun's saddle, pulled down into the ooze, the starburst knotting itself about him and clinging with grim desperation.

Parrol was immediately in the saddle, gripping the steering bar, while Nile swung herself into the lower part of the framework and found handholds there. The beam-gun swung around, darted off toward the rocky slope leading to the shelf from which they had come, up along it. Looking back, Nile saw guard and starburst roll together into another cluster of luminants where the entangled pair created considerable disturbance. No doubt the guard already was broadcasting his predicament over the suit communicator, but several minutes would pass before anyone could get over from the subs to release him.

❖   ❖   ❖

A few hundred yards beyond the edge of the shelf, Parrol turned the gun's snout up, steering it into the darkness pressing down toward the Rift's floor. They would assume back there that the guard had inadvertently knocked over the acceleration switch when he was hauled out of the seat by his strange attacker, and that the gun was now roaming about the Rift on its own. It was unlikely that they'd waste any time trying to find it again.

The magic gleanings of the fire forest faded below and the ocean night closed in. Parrol slowed the gun's ascent, checked their position carefully in the green glow of the instrument panel. Nile came clambering up, groped through the gun's tool pockets, pulled a spotlight out of one, a heavy-duty UW handgun out of another. She settled down on the edge of the panel, and Parrol heard a click through the water as she readied the gun. Cloakfish were welcome to show up any time now!

They exchanged sea hag grins, which somehow no longer seemed at all grotesque. Now they had the beamgun, there were several courses of action open. It wasn't merely a matter of trying to stay alive long enough to find out whether a human body which had undergone the chalot change could survive when the effect of the spores wore off. They should, Parrol thought, be able to do much better than that.

The nidith gang believed them drowned near the surface. The *Attris* wouldn't have opened fire on the PanElemental if they hadn't known who was in it and known, too, that if they disposed of Nile and Parrol their secret should still be safe. Which meant that Ilium Weldrow had succumbed to the big-money lure of the drug outfit, along with Captain Mace and the rest of the *Attris* crew. The assistant manager had been the logical one to buy to keep Giard from interfering with the operation. When the time came, he'd passed along the word that Parrol and Nile Etland had picked up the trail and were on their way to the Tuskason Rift to confirm their suspicions.

He and Nile almost had got killed because they hadn't thought of that possibility. But as a result, the nidith harvesters now felt secure and were open in turn to surprise attacks. Parrol steered the beam-gun up slowly, constantly checking his position and alert for signs of physical discomfort in himself or Nile. Others had returned alive to the surface in the sea hag form, long ago, but there were too many uncertainties about that to be at all hasty in their ascent. After a minute or two, Nile leaned forward, shaking her head, and moved the acceleration switch over. The gun surged upward. Parrol glanced at her, decided to go along with her judgment. He kept watching the depth gauge. When it showed them at a point four hundred feet below the surface, he halted the gun, brought it into a horizontal position, turning it slightly. The target-light above the muzzle stabbed out, disclosed a section of the Rift wall. Parrol played the beam up and along the wall. It sloped away here at an angle which indicated they might be approaching the top of the Rift.

Eighty feet farther up they were there. A dark sea floor stretched away before them to rise through a series of shelves toward the barely submerged shallows five miles to the east. Parrol began moving the machine horizontally back along the edge of the drop-off. When he stopped it again, it was at a point he calculated to be immediately above the submarine harvesters in the nidith bed.

Here might be the opportunity to strike the most telling blow of all. Nile knew by now what he was looking for. When he started forward again, gliding in slowly across the sea floor, she was leaning far out over the panel, head shifting this way and that, as she followed the sweep of the target-light. Suddenly she lifted a hand—

And this could be it, Parrol thought, excitement surging in him. A vertical dark ridge, some fifty feet high, perhaps three hundred yards up the sloping floor. The surface behind it was smooth, flat, level with the top of the ridge—a lake of sediment and sand, drifted down from the upper shelves, blocked off from the Tuskason Rift by a wall of rock.

A few minutes later, he was sure of it. He backed the gun away twenty yards, set the energy beam to full power, flicked it on. Something smashed into the ridge, began to move along it, water and rock boiling off in thick clouds at its touch. The gun bucked and danced as shock waves poured back at it. Parrol cut the beam, rode back another twenty yards, turned it on again. Now the gun was steady. The beam ate a fifty-foot gash slowly across the face of the ridge, returned along it.

A little over half the gun's charge was spent when the upper section of the ridge at last toppled ponderously forward. A river of mud and sand spilled down through the opening, flowed along the sea floor to the edge of the Rift, rolled thickly into it . . .

Enough there, Parrol thought, watching the dark slop stream by beneath the swaying gun, more than enough, to bury not only the harvester stationed against the wall, but the two other ships in the nidith bed with it. And burying any one of them with a nidith load on board was all that was necessary. Some of the divers outside might get away if they moved fast enough. The rest of the work gang was caught. They'd live because ships and suits were designed to preserve life even under the smashing blow of a deep-water muck avalanche; but they'd stay exactly where they were until somebody came along to dig them out.

❖   ❖   ❖

V

On the surface above the Tuskason Rift the cropper tender *Attris* rode the long, slow swells, anchor engines humming. Duse had set, and cloud banks were spread over half the night sky. To the north and west, fog was forming. For most of the past hour, the ship's communicator had been babbling excitedly. The *Attris'* captain looked distracted and harried.

From the edge of one of the nearby herds of pelagic croppers a single machine began moving toward the west, slowly at first but increasing speed as it drew farther away from the *Attris*.

Thirty minutes later, the wandering cropper reached a point eight miles west of the tender. In the *Attris'* chase-plane an automatic buzzer woke the pilot. He looked up at the glowing location chart above his bunk, saw the flashing red dot at the fringe of the eight-mile circle, swore sleepily, climbed out of the bunk and got on his direct line to the tender.

"What do *you* want?" his skipper's voice inquired hoarsely.

"Got a stray showing," the pilot began. "I—"

"Go after it, stupid! You know things are supposed to look right around here!" The line went dead.

The pilot scowled, yawned, sat down at the controls. The chase-plane slithered past the bow of the *Attris*, lifted into the air. Within a few minutes it was hovering above the cropping machine. The pilot directed an override beam at the cropper's engine shed, twisted the override control knobs and discovered that the cropper's automatic steering mechanisms were not responding. He muttered in annoyance. He'd have to reset them manually.

He brought the plane down, tethered the cropper to it, walked along a planking to the machine shed, opened the door and stepped inside. An instant later, there was a wild screech from within the shed, then a brief, violent splashing in the water beneath it. That ended, was followed presently by deep, croaking noises with odd overtones of human speech.

A sea hag appeared in the door of the shed, the unconscious and half-drowned pilot slung across its shoulder. Another hag came out behind it. They were breathing air with apparent difficulty, but they were breathing. The first one climbed into the plane with the pilot. The other detached the cropper, kicked it off, and joined its companion.

The plane swung about, rose from the surface and sped away, due west.

Shortly before daybreak, heavy fog rolled in over the shore ranches of the continental coast, drifted inland. The Giard Pharmaceuticals Station was thickly blanketed by it. Inside, most sections of the station were dark and deserted. But Parrol's office was lit; and in it a bulky figure with a grotesquely ugly, gray-mottled head, encased in a cloaklike garment which appeared to have been cut in haste out of a length of canvas, was painstakingly at work before a stenog machine. The screen above the machine showed the enlargement of a lengthy coded message. A number of minor deletions and revisions were being produced in it now. Finally, the cloaked shape switched off the machine. The screen disappeared, and a bloated-looking gray forefinger pushed at a tab on the side of the stenog. Two cards covered with microprint popped out on the table. The figure picked them up, glanced at them, came heavily to its feet.

From the open door to the office, a harsh, roughened voice, which nevertheless was recognizably the voice of Nile Etland, said, "I was finally able to contact Freasie, Dan. She's on her way to the hospital to set things up. Thirty minutes from now, we'll be able to get in quietly any time by the service entrance. Nobody but Freasie and Dr. Tay will know we're there or what condition we're in."

Parrol said, "Half an hour is about what it should take here." His voice was as distorted as hers but also recognizable. "I'll tell Fiawa, of course, that we'll be at the hospital."

"Yes, he should know."

"Did you explain to Freasie what happened?"

"Not in detail." Nile came into the room. She, too, wore a makeshift cloak covering everything but her head yet not adequately concealing the fact that the body beneath it was a ponderous caricature of her normal shape. "I told her we picked up the infection that hit the sea beef herds, and that when she sees us we'll look as if we'd been dead and waterlogged for the past two weeks."

Parrol grunted. "Not a bad description! We were prettier as deep-water sea hags than in this half-way state!"

"Do you still seem to be swelling?"

He held up his deformed fingers, studied them. "Apparently. I don't believe they looked as bad as that half an hour ago. I also feel as if most of my innards were being slowly pulled apart."

"I have that, too," Nile said. "I'm afraid we may be in for a very unpleasant time, Dan. But we definitely are changing back."

"Trying to change back?"

"Yes. No way of knowing exactly what will happen. But the sea beef may have been able to reverse the process successfully. Perhaps we can, too. And perhaps we can't." She looked across the room to an armchair in which the chase-plane pilot sprawled. His clothing, the chair, and the carpet beneath were soaked with water, and his eyes were closed. "How's our trigger-happy friend doing?"

"I don't know," Parrol said. "I haven't paid him any

attention since I dumped him there. He doesn't seem to have moved. I expect dragging him in through the shore swamps on the last stretch didn't do him much good."

Nile went over to the pilot, reached for his wrist, announced after a moment, "He's alive, anyway. I picked up some dope in the lab office. I'll give him a shot to make sure he stays quiet until the police come for him. Any immediate plans for Ilium Weldrow?"

"No," Parrol said. "I was hoping we'd find him still here. I would have enjoyed seeing his face when we walked in on him. But we'll leave him to Fiawa. Let's get out our reports and get the show on the road."

Nile brought a dope gun out from under her cloak, bent briefly over the pilot with it, replaced it and joined Parrol at the communicator. He was feeding the cards into the telewriting attachment.

"They're for Dabborn at Narcotics," he said. "I used his personal code. I've warned him there may be a leak in the office and that if he tries to talk to me from there, the higher-ups in the nidith business could get the word immediately and take steps to avoid being implicated. We'll talk to Fiawa at his home. He and Dabborn can get together then and work out the details of the operation."

Nile nodded. Parrol turned on the communicator, dialed a number. The connection light went on immediately. He depressed the transmission button on the telewriter.

A woman's voice said quietly, "Message received. Do you want to wait for a reply?"

Parrol remained silent. Some ten seconds later, the connection light went out.

"Dabborn's secretary," he said. "So he's in the office. Now let's get our chief of police out of bed, and things should start moving." He flicked out the cards, dropped them into a disposer, dialed another number.

It took Fiawa about a minute to get to the communicator. Then his deep, sleep-husky voice announced, "Fiawa speaking. Who is it?"

"For a man," Machon observed, "who's just put in seven weeks in the hospital—too deathly ill to see visitors—you seem remarkably fit!"

Parrol grinned across the dinner table at him.

"I had a few visitors," he said. "Dabborn and Fiawa dropped in from time to time to let me know how they were coming along with the nidith operation."

"They've done a bang-up job of rounding up the Agenes gang!" the secretary of the Ranchers Association assured him. "A couple of the big shots just might get off. The rest of them are nailed down!"

"I know it—and I'm glad I'll be there as a prosecution witness." Parrol hesitated, added, "Strictly speaking, neither Nile nor I have been ill. We were extremely uncomfortable for a while, but we could have received visitors any time after the first two weeks in the hospital. But Nile insisted no one should see us until we were ready to be discharged, and except for talking to Dabborn and Fiawa I've gone along with her in that. I think I can tell you about it privately now. She's prepared a paper for her xenobiological society covering the whole affair, and the paper will be out in a few weeks. But I warn you Nile still wouldn't want the details of our experience to become general knowledge."

"Don't worry—I can keep my mouth shut," Machon told him. "Go ahead."

"Well, I'll give you Nile's theory. It seems essentially correct. There's that fraya-chalot symbiosis pattern. Temporarily it's a complete symbiosis in every sense. The fraya has to be adapted to underwater living for a short period each year, then readapted promptly to surface living. And the frayas are pseudomammalian.

Their bodies are no more capable of rearranging themselves suddenly to such a drastic extent than the sea beef's or our own."

"Wait a minute!" Machon said. "The way I got it, you did adapt—fantastically! You and Nile literally turned into sea hags, didn't you?"

"We did—but *we* didn't actually change. The chalot was building on what was there. What we had to do was supply material for it to work with. In other words, we ate. When the changes are of a minor kind, you get hungry. When they're major ones, you find yourself periodically ravenous. The chalot builds its structures and maintains them. It has to be fed, or the structures collapse. If you don't supply it with extraneous food, it starts in on your body reserves. We found that out. You feel you're starving to death fast, which probably is exactly what would happen if you did nothing about it. So you eat compulsively.

"The chalot has to accomplish two things with its host animals. It has to enable them to get down into the fire forests and live there a time so they can eat the adult chalot plants and release the seeds of the plants by doing it. And it has to avoid killing or injuring the host, so the host can come back next year and repeat the process. It does nothing directly to the host body unless it has to draw on it for food. It turns itself into body supplements which combine with the host body to perform various functions. It's an unstable unit, but it's a unit which can exist for a while on the bottom of the ocean trenches.

"It remains a unit only as long as there is chalot around to keep it up. The frayas feed on the adult plants in the rifts, and they retain their underwater form throughout the breeding season. Then they've cleaned out the current crop of chalot and come back to the surface. The sea beef that got out into the Continental Rift here remained underwater breathers and feeders only for the days it took the cloud of chalot spores that had originated in the Tuskason Rift to pass through on the Meral. There are no chalot plants in the local fire forests, so up the beef came again. They were pretty plump animals when they were brought in, weren't they?"

"Yes," Machon said. "That fire forest diet didn't hurt them any. In fact, they seem to have thrived on it. But what they'd put on was mostly fat."

Parrol said wryly, "Uh-huh! Mostly fat . . . Nile and I picked up a load of the spores in one of the ranch farms here and probably another one in the water beyond the shelf. The spores added water-breathing equipment to our systems but nothing else, until we had to go down in the Tuskason Rift. We needed a complete change then and got it. We turned into the chalot's human deep-water variant—sea hags—on the way. But we stayed sea hags only a few hours because the spores we'd originally absorbed here were being used up in maintaining the change structures, and there was no live chalot left in the Tuskason Rift to replace them.

"The chalot evidently has had genetic experience with a wide variety of hosts. The fraya is the only native host left, but Nandy-Cline was swarming once with pseudomammals of that class. We can assume that many of them had a similar symbiotic relationship with the chalot the fraya still has, because the adaptations the chalot performs vary with the species and are according to the needs of the species. The sea beef really showed much less change than the fraya does in its underwater form.

"On the other hand, the change from an air-breathing human to a deep-water sea hag is an extremely radical one. The chalot went all out on us, and at intervals during those hours we had to eat ravenously to give it what it needed to maintain the form. Lord, how we ate!

"And then we were up on the surface again and began

to change back. Nile didn't mention it at the time, but she suspected what was happening when she saw the manner in which we were changing back."

"Yes?" said Machon.

"Fat," Parrol said. "When all that elaborate, dense chalot structure which keeps you alive and in action under a thousand feet of ocean begins to break down, it's converted into fat—the host body's fat! That's lovely if you're a fraya. For them, it's a kind of bonus they get out of their relationship with the chalot. They don't have to eat for a month afterwards. In the sea beef it wasn't too noticeable because the chalot hadn't added too much to them to start with.

"But Nile and I—!"

He shook his head. "I won't drag in all the grisly details, but Dr. Tay had to use plastiskin to hold us together. Literally. We were monstrous. He had us floating in tanks and kept whittling away at us surgically for the first ten days. After that, he figured a crash diet would see us through. It did, but it's taken almost two months to get back to normal—and it wasn't more than two weeks ago that Nile would let even me see her again.

"She's got that old figure back now, but her vanity's still hurt. She'll get over it presently. But if anyone happens to smile when they mention something overweight—like sea beef—to her for another month or so, my guess is they'll still be inviting a fast fist in the eye."

The Demon Breed

Chapter 1

As the pain haze began to thin out, Ticos Cay was somewhat surprised to find he was still on his feet. This had been a brutally heavy treatment—at moments it had seemed almost impossible to control. However, he *had* controlled it. The white-hot sensations, which hadn't quite broken through with full impact into consciousness, faded to something like a sullenly lingering glow. Then that faded too. His vision began to clear.

Cautiously he allowed himself to accept complete awareness of his body again. It was still an unpleasant experience. There were sharp twinges everywhere, a feeling of having been recently pierced and sliced by tiny hot knives; the residue of pain. The lasting damage caused by one of these pain treatments to the human nervous system and sensory apparatus was slight but measurable. The accumulative effect of a series of treatments was no longer slight; and there had been over twenty of them during the past weeks. Each time now, taking stock of the physical loss he had suffered during the process, Ticos wondered whether he would be forced to acknowledge that the damage had spread to the point where it could no longer be repaired.

However, it hadn't happened on this occasion. His mind was fogged over; but it always was for a short while after a treatment. Reassured, he shifted attention from his internal condition to his surroundings.

The big room had come back into focus. Most of it was dark because the demons had cut out all but a central section of the ceiling illumination. There remained a pool of light which enclosed most of the long worktable against which he leaned and the raised platform twenty feet away, from which they were watching him. The shelves and walls beyond, the rows of biological specimens, the arrays of analyzing and recording equipment, were in darkness.

Ticos Cay looked about, taking it in, drawing the trappings of reality back around him. He looked last at the demons.

"You succeeded again in avoiding the feeling of pain?" asked the small one of the three.

Ticos considered. The identity of the small demon was still blurred but coming clear. Yes, his name was Koll . . . the Great Palach Koll. One of the most influential among the leaders of the Everliving. Second in command of the Voice of Action. . . .

Ticos admonished himself: *Be very careful of Koll!*

He made a sound between what might have been a muttering attempt to speak and a groan. He could have replied immediately. But it wouldn't do to think foggily while being interrogated—and particularly not while being interrogated by Koll.

The three stared silently, unmoving. Their skins, harnesses and other equipment gleamed wetly as if they had come out of the sea only minutes before entering the room. Which might be the case; salt water was the demons' element, and they became sick and uncomfortable if they remained too long away from it. The one to the right of Koll held a device with a glowing blue eye. When the glow brightened, a pain treatment was about to begin. The one at the left of Koll had a weapon trained on Ticos. These two were squat heavy creatures hunkering on muscular hopping legs. Ticos had been obliged to watch one of their kind wrap his arms around the rib cage of a man and crush the man slowly to death without apparent effort.

It had been done at Koll's direction. The big demons were underlings; they were called Oganoon by the Palachs. Koll was of the same species but not large or heavy. Like many of the Great Palachs, he was a wrinkled miniature, not much more than a foot high. Cloaked and hooded, he looked like a shrunken mummy. But he could move like springing steel. Ticos had seen Koll leap eight feet to plunge a paralyzing needle into the eye of an Oganoon who had angered him. He struck five or six times, so quickly that the victim seemed to stiffen in death without understanding what had occurred.

Ticos strongly preferred not to anger Koll. But he needed as long a period of silence as Koll would permit to clear his head for the questions that would be directed at him. He had been maintaining a precarious balance between considerations on that order for some time. He waited until the speaking slit above Koll's eyes writhed open, then said unsteadily, "I could not avoid all the pain. But it remained tolerable."

"It remained tolerable!" the speaking slit repeated as if Koll were musing over the statement. Ticos was accustomed to the fact that many of the Everliving had an excellent command of human speech, but Koll's voice still seemed unnatural to him. It was a deep warm voice, rich and strong, which shouldn't be issuing from such a malevolent little entity. "These children are afraid of you, Dr. Cay," it told him. "Did you know that?"

"No, I didn't," Ticos said.

"At a tenth of the setting used here," Koll explained, "these instruments are employed to punish them for serious offenses. They are in terror of them. They are afraid of you because you seem able to bear agony beyond their comprehension. And there are other reasons. . . . Your communicator has recorded six call signals during the past two days."

Ticos nodded. "So I heard."

"You predicted that one of the so-called Tuvelas would attempt to contact you here."

Ticos hesitated, said, "The term Tuvela is yours. The person to whom you refer is known to me as a Guardian."

"Apparently the same class of creature," said Koll. "A creature assumed by some to possess abnormal qualities. Among them the quality of being invincible. Dr. Cay, what do you know of these remarkable qualities—if they exist?"

Ticos shrugged. "As I've told you, I've known of the Guardians and of their function in our civilization for a relatively short time. They operate very secretly. I've had personal contacts with only one of them. She appears to me to be an exceptionally capable human being. But if she or the Guardians generally have abnormal qualities, I don't know of them." He added, "Evidently the Everliving know more about the Guardians than I do."

"That is possible. You said they claim to be immortal."

Ticos shook his head. "I was told they've developed methods of restoring youthful health to an organism and maintaining it for a long period. I was not told they were immortal. To me the word does not have significant meaning."

"The concept of immortal entities is meaningless to you, Dr. Cay?"

Ticos hesitated again because this could become dangerous ground in speaking to a Palach. But he said, "Who can prove he is immortal before he's reached the end of time?"

Koll's dark face twitched. He might have been amused. "Who indeed?" he agreed. "Describe to me your relationship with these Guardians."

Ticos had described that relationship to Koll several times before. He said, "Two years ago I was asked whether I would enter their service. I accepted."

"Why?"

"I'm aging, Great Palach. Among my rewards was to be instruction in the Guardian's methods of obtaining longevity and regaining the advantages of youth."

"They've given you such instructions?"

"I've been instructed in some of the fundamental approaches. My progress evidently is satisfactory."

"In what way do you serve them, Dr. Cay?"

"I'm still undergoing a training process and haven't been told what my service is to be. I assume that my scientific background will play a part in it."

"The nerve controls you practice to distort the effects of the pain-giver were acquired through the longevity exercises?"

"Yes, they were."

A long pause followed his reply. Koll's speaking slit had closed and he remained unmoving. The lower sections of his double-lensed eyes were lidded; the upper sections stared with a kind of baleful blankness at Ticos. The hulking servitors had become equally immobile, probably as a sign of respect. Ticos wasn't sure what the pause meant. The same thing had occurred during earlier interrogations. Perhaps the tiny monster was simply reflecting on what had been said. But he appeared sunk in a remote trance. If he was addressed now he would ignore it, and he seemed unaware of motion about him. Ticos suspected there was the equivalent of human insanity in Koll. Even Great Palachs of his own rank seemed afraid of him, and he treated them with barely veiled contempt. His dark cowl and cloak were of utilitarian material and often indifferently clean, while they concealed their dwarfish bodies under richly ornamented garments, gleaming with jewels. Apparently they preferred to avoid Koll's company; but his influence on them was very strong.

The speaking slit above the eyes twisted open again.

"Dr. Cay," Koll's voice said, "I become increasingly inclined to add you to my museum of humanity. You have seen my collection?"

Ticos cleared his throat. "Yes," he said.

"Of course you have," Koll said, as if the fact had just occurred to him. "I showed it to you. As a warning not to lie to us. In particular, not to lie to me."

Ticos said warily, "I have been quite careful not to lie to you, Great Palach."

"Have you? I'm not at all certain of it," said Koll. "Do you believe that the person who is attempting to reach you by communicator is the Guardian of whom you told us?"

Ticos nodded. "Yes. The Guardian Etland."

"Why should it be she?"

"No one else has the call symbol of my communicator."

"Because you were to remain isolated here?"

"Yes."

"The Guardian Etland supervises your training?"

"Yes."

"You describe her as a young female," said Koll.

"I said she appears young," Ticos corrected him. "I don't know her age."

"You say that these Guardians or Tuvelas have developed a form of longevity which provides even the appearance of their species' youth. . . ."

"The Guardian Etland has implied that."

"And yet," said Koll, "you tell us the Guardians

assigned you the task of searching here for substances among the life forms of this world which promote longevity. What interest could the Guardians have in research which yields them no more than they possess?"

Ticos shrugged. "I know they're testing me in various ways, and it may be that this is their manner of testing my ability as a biochemist. But it's also possible that they're still interested in finding simpler or more dependable methods of gaining longevity than their present ones."

"What part does the use of chemicals play in their present methods?"

"I don't know. I've described the basic approaches I was told to practice. I've been given no hint of the nature of more advanced longevity procedures. My research is confined to the observation of effects in my test material."

"You've suggested that research at this level could be of value to the Everliving. . . . "

"I haven't suggested it," Ticos said. "I realize, of course, that a number of Palachs observe my test results and analyze the substances involved."

"Don't let yourself assume their scientific interest assures your continuing safety, Dr. Cay. Our methods of obtaining individual longevity require no improvement. I'm certain you are lying to us. I intend to determine in what manner you are lying. Why did you request permission to respond to the Guardian's call?"

"I explained my purpose to the Palach Moga," Ticos said.

"Explain it to me."

Ticos indicated the equipment and specimens in the darkened recesses of the room. "This project is the Guardian Etland's responsibility. I and my training are her responsibility. Until your arrival she came here at very regular intervals to inspect the progress I made. Since then she hasn't come here."

"What do you deduce from that?"

"It's possible that the Guardians know of your presence."

"I don't consider that a possibility, Dr. Cay."

Ticos shrugged. "It's the only explanation I see for the Guardian Etland's failure to maintain her schedule. The Guardians may prefer you to leave quietly before there is a general disturbance. If I'm permitted to turn on the communicator when she signals again, we may learn that the Guardian is on her way here to speak to the Everliving rather than to me. . . ."

"She would come knowingly into the area we hold?" said Koll.

"From what several Palachs have told me," Ticos remarked, "it would not be surprising conduct in a Tuvela. If it is true—"

"We'll assume it isn't true, Dr. Cay."

"Then," said Ticos, "I should still be permitted to take the call and attempt to divert her from visiting me at this time. If she does not know you are here and arrives, she will discover you are here. And even if you are able to prevent her from leaving again—"

Koll made a hissing sound. "If we are able to prevent her from leaving?"

"Your own records, as you've implied to me, indicate that Tuvelas are extremely resourceful beings," Ticos observed mildly. "But if you should capture or kill the Guardian, others will come promptly in search of her. Eventually your presence must be revealed." He shrugged. "I don't want these things to happen. As a servant of the Guardians, it is my duty to prevent them from happening if I can. As you're aware, I've been attempting to persuade some of the Everliving that your plans against my species must be abandoned before a general conflict becomes inevitable."

"I know that," said Koll. "You've had an astonishing—and shameful—degree of success. The Voice of Caution becomes increasingly insistent. Even the suggested use of your communicator is supported. Is it possible, Dr. Cay, that you are a Guardian who allowed himself to be captured in order to confuse the Everliving and weaken their resolution?"

"No," Ticos said. "I'm not a Guardian."

"You're a Hulon?"

"Since that's the name you give the general run of humanity, yes, I'm a Hulon."

"It was the name we had for a vicious and stupid creature we encountered in our past," Koll remarked. "We destroyed the creature, so the name was free to be bestowed again. Despite your efforts, our plans won't be abandoned, Dr. Cay. I know you're lying. Not too clumsily, but it will not be long before we put your story to the test. . . . Now attend to your collection here—and reflect occasionally on mine. . . . "

Ticos did not see him make any gesture, but the Oganoon on Koll's right snapped the nerve-torture instrument to one of the harness straps about its bulky body and half turned. The tiny cowled mummy made one of its startlingly quick leaps and was perched on the underling's shoulder. The group moved off the platform and along a raised walkway toward the exit door, the armed servitor bringing up the rear, backing off in short powerful hops, weapon still pointed alertly at Ticos Cay. The lighting brightened back to normal in the big room.

Ticos watched the three vanish through the door, heard the heavy click of its locks. He drew a somewhat shaky breath, picked up a boxed device from the worktable and fastened it by its strap to his belt. It was a complicated instrument through which he controlled temperature, humidity, radiation absorption levels and various other matters connected with his biological specimens in different sections of the room.

His hands were unsteady. The interrogation hadn't gone to his liking. Koll wasn't his usual savagely menacing self—and that in spite of some deliberate provocation. He'd made use of the pain-giver only once. Koll, for Koll, had been affable.

It seemed a bad sign. It indicated that Koll was as confident as he appeared to be that he could dispel the doubts Ticos was nourishing in other leading Palachs by proving their prisoner had misinformed them. And, as a matter of fact, Ticos had totally misinformed them. Over a course of weeks he'd created a carefully organized structure of lies, half-truths and disturbing insinuations designed to fill the Everliving with the fear of Man, or at any rate with the fear of Tuvelas. Who, as far as Ticos Cay knew, didn't exist. Sometimes he'd been hard put to remain consistent, but by now the pattern was so familiar that it held an occasional illusion of truth even for him.

It had been effective in restricting their plans until now. In spite of Koll, it might remain effective—but that depended on a large factor of chance. Ticos sighed inaudibly. He'd reduced the factor as much as possible, but it was still too large. Far too large!

He moved slowly about the room, manipulating the studs of his device now and then, tending to the needs of the biological specimens. He'd never been able to determine whether he was under visual observation or not, but it was possible, and he must not appear too concerned. Occasionally he felt the floor lift and sink under him like the deck of a great ship, and then there would be a heavy sloshing of sea water in the partitioned end of the room. His communicator was in there. A permanent post of Oganoon guards was also in there to make sure he didn't get near the communicator unless the Everliving decided to permit it. And the water covering most of the floor was there because the guards had to keep their leathery hides wet.

From the energy-screened ventilator window near the ceiling came dim sounds like the muted roaring of a beast. That and the periodic heaving of the floor were the only indications Ticos had been given for the past several days that the typhoons still blew outside. . . .

Rain squalls veiled half the sea below the aircar. It was storm season in the southern latitudes of Nandy-Cline . . . the horizon loomed blue-black ahead; heavy swirling cloud banks drove across the ocean to the south. The trim little car bucked suddenly in twisting torrents of air, was hauled about on its controls and, for the moment, rode steady again along a southeasterly course.

Inside the cabin, Nile Etland stabbed at a set of buttons on the panel communicator, said sharply into the transmitter, "Giard Pharmaceuticals Station—come in! Nile Etland calling . . . Giard, come in!"

She waited a moment, tanned face intent. A hum began in the communicator, rose to a wavering howl, interspersed with explosive cracklings. Impatiently, Nile spun the filter control right, then left. Racketing noise erupted along the scale. She muttered bitter comment. Her fingers flicked over the call buttons, picked out another symbol.

"Danrich Parrol—Nile calling! Come in! Dan, can you *hear* me? *Come in!*"

Silence for an instant. Then meaningless sound spat and spluttered again. Nile's lips twisted in angry frustration. She muted the speaker, glanced down at the animal curled in a thick loop of richly gleaming brown fur on the floorboards beside her. It lifted a whiskered head, dark eyes watching Nile.

"Dan?" it asked, in a high thin voice.

"No Dan! No anybody!" snapped Nile. "We keep hitting a soup of static anywhere beyond twenty miles all around."

"Soup?"

"Forget it, Sweeting. We'll try calling the sledmen. Maybe they can help us find Ticos."

"Find Tikkos!" Sweeting agreed. The furred shape shifted, flowed, came upright. Bracing short sturdy forelegs against the control panel, Sweeting peered at the sections of seascape and sky in the viewscreens, looked over at Nile. Seven and a half feet in length from nose to the tip of her muscular tail, she was the smaller of Nile's pair of mutant hunting otters. "Where's sledmen?"

"Somewhere ahead." Nile had swung the car fifteen degrees to the east. "Settle down."

The sled she'd sighted in the screens several minutes earlier presently came to view again, now only a few miles away. The car's magnification scanners showed a five hundred foot floatwood raft with flattened, streamlined superstructure, riding its runners twelve yards above the surging seas. The central heavy-weather keel was down, knifing through the waves between runners. On a day of less violence, the sled would have been drifting with an illusion of airy lightness over the water, keel withdrawn, sails spread. Now the masts were hauled flat to the deck, and it was the set of cannon drives along the sled's edges which sent it rushing toward the moving front of the storm. The rain-darkened afterdeck was emblazoned with a pair of deep-blue triangles—the Blue Guul symbol of the Sotira Fleet.

As the sled vanished below the next cloud bank, Nile switched the communicator to ten mile close-contact band, said into the transmitter, "Dr. Nile Etland of Giard Pharmaceuticals calling Sotira sled! Acknowledge, please!" Close-contact seemed to have stayed operational. And they should know her by name down there. The Sotira sleds did regular sea-harvest work for Giard.

The communicator said suddenly, "Captain Doncar of Sotira sled acknowledging. Go ahead, Dr. Etland. . . . "

"I'm in the air behind you," Nile announced. "May I come aboard?"

A moment of silence. Then Doncar's voice said, "If you wish. But we'll be running through heavy storm in less than fifteen minutes."

"I know—I don't want to lose you in it."

"Come down immediately then," Doncar advised her. "We'll be ready for you."

They were. Almost before Nile could climb out of the aircar, half a dozen men in swimming gear, muscular naked backs glistening in the slashing rain, had the small vehicle strapped securely against the sled's deck beside a plastic shrouded object which might be an oversized harpoon gun. It was a disciplined, practiced operation. As they stepped back, a brown-skinned girl, dressed down for the weather like the crewmen, hurried up from the central row of cabins. She shouted something almost lost in the din of wind and rain.

Nile turned. "Jath!"

"This way, Nile! Before the slop drowns us—"

They sprinted back to the cabins through the solid downpour. The otter loped easily after them, given plenty of room by the deck hands. Many of Sweeting's relatives preferred the unhampered freedom of Nandy-Cline's ocean to a domesticated life; and the seagoing mutant otters were known to any sledman at least by reputation. Nothing was gained by asking for trouble with them.

"In here!" Jath hauled open a door, slipped into the cabin behind Nile and the otter and let the door slam shut. Towels lay ready on a table; she tossed two to Nile, dabbed a third perfunctorily over her copper skin. Sweeting shook spray from her fur with a twist that spattered half the cabin. Nile mopped at her dripping coveralls, handed back one of the towels, used the other to dry hair, face and hands. "Thanks!"

"Doncar can't get away at the moment," Jath told her. "He asked me to find out what we can do for you. So— what brings you out in this weather?"

"I'm looking for somebody."

"Here?" There was startled surprise in Jath's voice.

"Dr. Ticos Cay."

A pause. "Dr. Cay is in *this* area?"

"He might be—" Nile checked momentarily. Jath, in a motion as quick as it was purposeful, had cupped her right hand to her ear, lowered it again.

They knew each other well enough to make the point of the gesture clear. Someone elsewhere on the sled was listening to what was being said in the cabin.

Nile gave Jath the briefest of understanding nods. Evidently there was something going on in this section of the sea which the Sotira sleds regarded as strictly sledman business. She was a mainlander, though a privileged one. An outsider.

She said, "I had a report from meteorological observers this morning about a major floatwood drift they'd spotted moving before the typhoons around here. The island Dr. Cay's been camping on could be part of that drift. . . ."

"You're not sure?"

"I'm not at all sure. I haven't been in touch with him for two months. But the Meral may have carried him this far south. I've been unable to get in contact with him. He's probably all right, but I've begun to feel worried."

Jath bit her lip, blue-green eyes staring at Nile's forehead. Then she shrugged. "You should be worried! But if he's on the floatwood the weather men saw, we wouldn't know it."

"Why not? . . . And why should I be worried?"

"Floatwood's gromgorru this season. So is the water twenty miles around any island. That's Fleet word."

Nile hesitated, startled. "When was the word given?"

"Five weeks ago."

Gromgorru . . . Sledman term for bad luck, evil magic. The malignant unknown. Something to be avoided. And something not discussed, under ordinary circumstances, with mainlanders. Jath's use of the term was deliberate. It was not likely to please the unseen listeners.

A buzzer sounded. Jath gave Nile a quick wink.

"That's for me." She started for the door, turned again. "We have Venn aboard. They'll want to see you now."

Alone with Sweeting, Nile scowled uneasily at the closed door. What the gromgorru business in connection with the floatwood islands was she couldn't imagine. But if Ticos Cay was in this ocean area—and her calculations indicated he shouldn't be too far away—she'd better be getting him out. . . .

Chapter 2

Ticos Cay had showed up unannounced one day at the Giard Pharmaceuticals Station on Nandy-Cline, to see Nile. He'd been her biochemistry instructor during her final university year on Orado. He was white-haired, stringy, bouncy, tough-minded, something of a genius, something of a crank, and the best all-around teacher she'd ever encountered. She was delighted to meet him again. Ticos informed her she was responsible for his presence here.

"In what way?" Nile asked.

"The research you've done on the floatwood."

Nile gave him a questioning look. She'd written over a dozen papers on Nandy-Cline's pelagic floatwood forests, forever on the move about the watery planet where one narrow continent and the polar ice massifs represented the only significant barriers to the circling tides of ocean. It was a subject on which she'd been acquiring first-hand information since childhood. The forests she'd studied most specially rode the great Meral Current down through the equatorial belt and wheeled with it far to the south. Many returned eventually over the same path, taking four to ten years to complete the cycle, until at length they were drawn off into other currents. Unless the polar ice closed about it permanently or it became grounded in mainland shallows, the floatwood organism seemed to know no natural death. It was an old species, old enough to have become the home of innumerable other species adjusted in a variety of ways to the climatic changes encountered in its migrations, and of temporary guests who attached themselves to forests crossing the ocean zones they frequented, deserting them again or dying as the floatwood moved beyond their ranges of temperature tolerance.

"It's an interesting subject," she said. "But—"

"You're wondering why I'd make a three weeks' trip out here to discuss the subject with you?"

"Yes, I am."

"It isn't all I had in mind," said Ticos. "I paid a visit to Giard's Central in Orado City a month or so ago. I learned, among other things, that there's a shortage of trained field biologists on Nandy-Cline."

"That's an understatement," said Nile.

"Evidently," Ticos remarked, "it hasn't hampered you too much. Your lab's held in high esteem by the home office."

"I know. We earn their high esteem by keeping way ahead of the competition. But for every new item we turn up with an immediate practical application for Giard, there are a thousand out there that remain unsuspected. The people who work for us are good collectors but they can't do instrument analysis and wouldn't know what to look for if they could. They bring in what you tell them to bring in. I still go out myself when I can, but that's not too often now."

"What's the problem with getting new hire?"

Nile shrugged. "The obvious one. If a man's a good enough biologist, he has his pick of jobs in the Hub. He'd probably make more here, but he isn't interested in coming all the way out to Nandy-Cline to do rough field work. I . . . Ticos, you don't happen to be looking for a job here with Giard?"

He nodded. "I am, as a matter of fact. I believe I'm qualified, and I have my own analytical laboratory at the spaceport. Do you think your station manager would consider me?"

Nile blinked. "Parrol will snap you up, of course! . . . But I don't get it. How do you intend to fit this in with your university work?"

"I resigned from the university early this year. About the job here—I do have a few conditions."

"What are they?"

"For one thing, I'll limit my work to the floatwood islands."

Why not, Nile thought. Provided they took adequate precautions. He looked in good physical shape, and she knew he'd been on a number of outworld field trips.

She nodded, said, "We can fit you up with a first-class staff of assistants. Short on scientific training but long on floatwood experience. Say ten or—"

"Uh-uh!" Ticos shook his head decidedly. "You and I will select an island and I'll set myself up there alone. That's Condition Two. It's an essential part of the project."

Nile stared at him. The multiformed life supported by the floatwood wasn't abnormally ferocious; but it existed because it could take care of itself under constantly changing conditions, which included frequent shifts in the nature of enemies and prey, and in the defensive and offensive apparatus developed to deal with them. For the uninformed human intruder such apparatus could turn into a wide variety of death traps. Their menace was for the most part as mindlessly impersonal as quicksand. But that didn't make them any less deadly.

"Ticos Cay," she stated, "you're out of your mind! You wouldn't last! Do you have any idea—"

"I do. I've studied your papers carefully, along with the rather skimpy material that's available otherwise on the planet's indigenous life. I'm aware there may be serious environmental problems. We'll discuss them. But solitude is a requirement."

"Why in the world should—"

"From a personal point of view, I'll be involved here primarily in longevity research."

She hesitated, said, "Frankly I don't see the connection."

Ticos grunted. "Of course you don't. I'd better start at the beginning."

"Perhaps you should. Longevity research . . . " Nile paused. "Is there some, uh, personal—"

"Is the life I'm interested in extending my own? Definitely. I'm at a point where it requires careful first-hand attention."

Nile felt startled. Ticos was lean but firmly muscled, agile and unwrinkled. In spite of his white hair, she hadn't considered him old. He might have been somewhat over sixty and not interested in cosmetic hormones. "You've begun extension treatments?" she asked.

"Quite a while ago," Ticos said dryly. "How much do you know about the assorted longevity techniques?"

"I have a general understanding of them, of course. But I've never made a special study of the subject. Nobody I've known has—" Her voice trailed off again.

"Don't let it embarrass you to be talking to a creaky ancient about it," Ticos said.

She stared at him. "How old *are* you?"

"Rather close to two hundred standard years. One of the Hub's most senior citizens, I believe. Not considering, of course, the calendar age of old-timers who resorted to longsleep and are still around."

Two hundred years was the practical limit to the human biological life span. For a moment Nile didn't know what to say. She tried to keep shock from showing in her face. But perhaps Ticos noticed it because he went on quickly, his tone light. "It's curious, you know, that we still aren't able to do much better along those lines! Of course, during the war centuries there evidently wasn't much attention given to such impractical lines of research."

"Impractical?" Nile repeated.

"From the viewpoint of the species. The indefinite extension of individual life units isn't really too desirable in that respect. Natural replacements have obvious advantages. I can agree in theory. Nevertheless, I find myself resenting the fact that the theory should also apply to me. . . ."

He'd started resenting it some two decades ago. Up to then he'd been getting by exceptionally well on bio-chemical adjustments and gene manipulations, aided by occasional tissue transplants. Then trouble began—so gradually that it was a considerable while before he realized there was a real problem. He was informed at last that adjustment results were becoming increas-ingly erratic and that there was no known way of balancing them more accurately. Major transplants and the extensive use of synthetics would presently be required. It was suggested that he get his memory stores computerized and transferred to an information bank for reference purposes—and then perhaps check in for longsleep.

Ticos found he didn't like any of the prospects. His interest level hadn't diminished noticeably, and he didn't care to have his activities curtailed by a progressively patched-up body or suspended indefinitely by longsleep. If he didn't take longsleep, he might make it past the two hundred year mark but evidently not by much. Previously he hadn't given a great deal of attention to regeneration research. Those problems were for other men—he had a large variety of pet projects of his own going. Now he thought he'd better start investigating the field and look for more acceptable alternatives to the prognosis offered him.

"You've been doing that for the past twenty years?" Nile asked.

"Very nearly. Some thousands of lines of research are involved. It makes for a lengthy investigation."

"I thought most of those lines of research were over on the crackpot side," she remarked.

"A great many are. I still had to check them out. One problem here is that nobody can prove his method is going to work out indefinitely—no method has been practiced long enough for that. For the same reason it's difficult to disprove the value of any approach, at least to those who believe in it. So egos and individualism run rampant in that area. Even the orthodox work isn't well coordinated."

"So I understand," Nile said. "You'd think the Federation would take a hand in it."

"You might think so," Ticos agreed. "However, there may be a consensus of opinion at Overgovernment levels that, because of economic and other factors, the unlimited prolongation of life in human beings would have questionable value. At any rate, while the Federation doesn't discourage longevity research, it doesn't actively support it. You could say it tolerates it."

"What about their own lives? They're human."

He shrugged. "They may be putting their trust in longsleep—some happy future in which all such problems will be solved. I wouldn't know. Of course, a good many people suspect that if you're one of the elect, you'll have treatments that work indefinitely. It seems a little improbable. Anyway I'm betting largely on biochemistry now. The individual cells. Keep them cleared of degenerative garbage, and other problems may no longer be too significant. I made some improvements in that area a few years ago. An immediate result was improvements in myself. As a matter of fact, I've been given to understand they're probably the reason I'm still operational."

"You've written that up?" Nile asked.

"Not under my name. The university handles that end of it. I've kept the biochemical research going, but I've also been working on new slants since. It struck me frequently in the course of all this that our instincts evidently aren't in favor of letting us go on indefinitely."

She frowned. "What gives you that impression?"

"For one thing, the fact that we generally won't put out very much effort for it. A remarkable number of my earlier associates dropped out on treatments simply because they kept forgetting to do, or refused to do, the relatively simple things needed to stay alive. It was as though they'd decided it wasn't important enough and they couldn't be bothered."

Nile said doubtfully, "You aren't exaggerating?"

"No. It's a common picture. The instincts accept the life and death cycle even when we're consciously opposed to it. They work for the species. The individual has significance to the species only to the point of maturity. The instincts support him until he's had an opportunity to pass along his genetic contribution. Then they start pulling him down. If a method eventually is developed to retain life and biological youth with no effort, it might be a different matter. Longsleep provides an illusion of that at present. But longsleep shelves the problem. I began to suspect longevity research itself is hampered by the instincts. And I'm not sure it isn't . . . we really *should* be farther along with it. At any rate, I decided to check with people who are interested in the less accessible areas of the mind. They're working in a major playground of the instincts, and they might have information. . . . "

He'd found two groups who were obtaining longevity and rejuvenation effects as a by-product of mental experimentation. One was the Psychovariant Association.

Nile knew as much about their work as they'd chosen to publish in the digests she followed. They used assorted forcing procedures to extend and modify mental experience. "Don't they make heavy use of synthetics?" she asked.

Ticos nodded. "Yes. Not only to replace failing organs but to improve on healthy ones. That's their view of it. I don't fancy the approach myself. But they have systems of basic mind exercises directed at emotional manipulation. Longevity's a secondary interest, but they've accumulated plenty of evidence that the exercises support it. . . ."

The other project was a branch of the Federation's Psychology Service. Its goal was a total investigation of the mind and the gaining of conscious controls over its unconscious potential. The processes were elaborate. In the course of them, deep-reaching therapeutic adjustments were required and obtained. Physical regeneration frequently was a result—again not as a primary objective but as a beneficial side-effect.

Ticos decided this approach also went beyond his own aims. His interests were outward-directed; his mind was an efficient instrument for that purpose, and he demanded no more of it. However, the goals of both organizations were as definitely bent on overcoming normal human limitations as longevity research. They were aware of the type of inherent resistances he had suspected and had developed methods of dealing with them.

"The matter of mind-body interaction," he said. "I can learn to distinguish and control instinctual effects both in my mind and in associated physical processes. And that's what I've started to do."

He'd presented his problem to members of the two groups, and a modified individual schedule of mind-control exercises was worked out for him. He'd practiced them under direction until his mentors decided he was capable of continuing on his own. Then he'd closed out the final phases of his university work. His search for more effective biochemical serums would continue; he was convinced now it was the basic key to success.

"Keep the instincts from interfering and who knows—we might have it made!"

"Immortality?" asked Nile.

He gave her his quick grin. "Let's try for a thousand standard years first."

She smiled. "You almost have me believing you, Ticos! And how does becoming a floatwood hermit fit in with it all?"

"Nandy-Cline evidently is a simmering hotbed of life. I know the general type of substances I'll be looking for next, and I think I'm at least as likely to find them here as anywhere else."

Nile nodded. "You might find almost anything here. Why make it a one-man job?"

"Planned solitude," said Ticos.

"What will that do for you?"

"The mind exercises. Does it seem to mean anything if I say that at the stages at which I'll now be working I step outside the standard mental patterns of the species?"

She considered. "It doesn't seem to mean much. Very advanced stuff, eh?"

"Depends on the viewpoint. The people I dealt with consider it basic. However, it's difficult work. There's seepage from other mind patterns about you, and if they're established human ones they jar you out of what you're doing. They're too familiar. It's totally disruptive. So until I become sufficiently stable in those practices, it's necessary to reduce my contacts with humanity to the absolute minimum."

Nile shrugged. "Well, that's obviously out of my line. Still, I'd think . . . you can't just go into a room somewhere and shut the doors?"

"No. Physical distance is required. Plenty of it."

"How long is it going to be required?"

"The estimates I've had range from three to four years."

"In the floatwood?"

"Yes. It's to be both my work place and my source of materials. I can't park myself in space somewhere and continue to do meaningful research. And I think that adequate preparations should reduce any risks I'll encounter to an acceptable level. A reasonable degree of risk, as a matter of fact, will be all to the good."

"In what way?"

"The threat of danger is a great awakener. The idea in this is to be thoroughly alert and alive—*not* shut away in a real or symbolical shell of some kind."

Nile reflected. "That makes a sort of sense," she agreed. She hesitated. "What's your present physical condition? I'll admit you look healthy enough. . . ."

"I'm healthier now than I was ten years ago."

"You don't need medical supervision?"

"I haven't needed it for several years. I've had one arterial replacement—the cultured product. That was quite a while ago. Otherwise, except for a few patches from around the same and earlier periods, my internal arrangements are my own. Nothing to worry about in that department."

Nile sighed.

"Well—we'll still have to convince Parrol it isn't suicide. But you're hired, Ticos. Make it a very high salary and nail down your terms, including your interests in anything that could classify as a longevity serum. After we've settled that, I'll start briefing you on the kind of difficulties you're likely to run into on your island. That can't be done in a matter of days. It's going to take weeks of cramming and on-the-spot demonstrations."

Ticos winked at her. "That's why I'm here."

She made it a very stiff cramming course. And Ticos turned out to be as good a student as he'd been an instructor. He had an alert, curious mind, an

extraordinarily retentive memory. Physically he proved
to be tough and resilient. Nile kept uprating his survival outlook, though she didn't mention it. Some things,
of course, she couldn't teach him. His gunmanship was
only fair. He learned to use a climb-belt well enough
to get around safely; but to develop anything resembling
real proficiency with the device required long practice.
She didn't even attempt to instruct him in water skills.
The less swimming he did around floatwood the better.

They moved about the Meral from one floatwood drift
to another, finally selected a major island complex which
seemed to meet all requirements. A shelter, combining
Ticos' living quarters, laboratory and storerooms, was
constructed and his equipment moved in. A breeding
group of eight-inch protohoms and cultures of gigacells
would provide him with his principal test material;
almost every known human reaction could be duplicated
in them, usually with a vast advantage in elapsed time.
The structure was completely camouflaged. Sledmen
harvesting parties probably would be about the island
from time to time, and Ticos didn't want too many contacts with them. If he stayed inside until such visitors
left again, he wouldn't be noticed.

He had a communicator with a coded call symbol.
Unless he got in touch with her, Nile was to drop by at
eight week intervals to pick up what he had accumulated
for the Giard lab and leave supplies. He wished to see
no one else. Parrol shook his head at the arrangement;
but Nile made no objections. She realized that by degrees
she'd become fiercely partisan in the matter. If Ticos Cay
wanted to take a swing at living forever, on his feet and
looking around, instead of fading out or sliding off into
longsleep, she'd back him up, however he went about it.
Up to this point he hadn't done badly.

And somewhat against general expectations then, he
lasted. He made no serious mistakes in his adopted
environment, seemed thoroughly satisfied with his life

as a hermit, wholly immersed in his work. The home office purred over his bi-monthly reports. Assorted items went directly to the university colleagues who had taken over his longevity project there. They also purred. When Nile had seen him last, he'd been floating along the Meral for eighteen months, looked hale and hearty and ready to go on for at least the same length of time. His mind exercises, he informed Nile, were progressing well. . . .

Chapter 3

There were three men waiting in the central cabin of the Sotira sled to which Jath presently conducted Nile. She knew two of them from previous meetings, Fiam and Pelad. Both were Venn, members of the Fleet Venntar, the sledman center of authority: old men and former sled captains. Their wrinkled sun-blackened faces were placid; but they were in charge. On a sled a Venn's word overrode that of the captain.

Doncar, the sled captain, was the third. Quite young for his rank, intense, with a look of controlled anger about him. Bone-tired at the moment. But controlling that too.

Jath drew the door shut behind Nile and the otter, took a seat near Doncar. She held a degree of authority not far below that of the others here, having spent four years at a Hub university, acquiring technical skills of value to her people. Few other sledmen ever had left Nandy-Cline. Their forebears had been independent space rovers who settled on the water world several generations before the first Federation colonists. By agreement with the Federation, they retained their independence and primary sea rights. But there had been open conflict between the fleets and mainland groups in the past, and the sleds remained traditionally suspicious of the mainland and its ways.

Impatience tingled in Nile, but she knew better than to hurry this group. She answered Pelad's questions, repeating essentially what she had told Jath.

"You aren't aware of Dr. Cay's exact location?" Pelad inquired. Ticos had become a minor legend among the sled people who knew of his project.

Nile shook her head.

"I can't say definitely that he's within four hundred miles of us," she said. "This is simply the most likely area to start looking for him. When I'm due to pay him a visit, I give him a call and he tells me what his current position is. But this time he hasn't responded to his call symbol."

She added, "Of course there've been intensive communication interferences all the way in to the mainland in recent weeks. But Dr. Cay still should have picked up my signal from time to time. I've been trying to get through to him for the past several days."

Silence for a moment, then Pelad said, "Dr. Etland, does the mainland know what is causing the interferences?"

The question surprised, then puzzled her. The interferences were no novelty; their cause was known. The star type which tended to produce water worlds also produced such disturbances. On and about Nandy-Cline the communication systems otherwise in standard use throughout the Federation were rarely operable. Several completely new systems had been developed and combined to deal with the problem. Among them, only the limited close-contact band was almost entirely reliable.

Pelad and the others here were as aware of that as she. Nile said, "As far as I know, no special investigation has been made. Do the sleds see some unusual significance in the disturbances?"

"There are two views," Jath told her quietly. "One of them is that some of the current communication blocks are gromgorru. Created deliberately by an unknown force. Possibly by an unnatural one. . . . "

Pelad glanced at Jath, said to Nile, "The Venntar has decreed silence in this. But young mouths open easily. Perhaps too easily. We may have reason to believe there is something in the sea that hates men. There are those who hear voices in the turmoil that smothers our instruments. They say they hear a song of hate and fear." He shrugged. "I won't say what I think—as yet I don't know what to think." He looked at Fiam. "Silence might have been best, but it has been broken. Dr. Etland is a proven friend of the sleds."

Fiam nodded. "Let the captain tell it to our guest."

Doncar grinned briefly. "Tell it as I see it?"

"As you see it, Doncar. We know your views. We shall listen."

"Very well." Doncar turned to Nile. "Dr. Etland, so far you've been asked questions and given no explanation. Let me ask one more question. Could human beings cause such communication problems?"

"By duplicating the solar effect locally?" Nile hesitated, nodded. "It should be possible. Is there reason to believe it's being done?"

"Some of us think so," Doncar said dryly. "We've lost men."

"Lost them?"

"They disappear. . . . Work parties harvesting a float-wood island—small surface craft and submersibles in the immediate vicinity of floatwood. Later no traces are found. Whenever this occurred, communication in the area was completely disrupted."

"To keep the men from reporting attackers?"

"That's what's suspected," Doncar said. "It's happened too regularly to make coincidences seem probable. You understand, Dr. Etland, that this isn't a problem which affects only the Sotira sleds. There have been similar disappearances near floatwood islands in many sea areas of late."

Nile asked for details, her mind beginning to race. She and Parrol were known as accomplished trouble shooters. They considered it part of their job; it was in Giard's interest to keep operations moving as smoothly as possible on Nandy-Cline. The sledmen had benefited by that in the past, as had the mainland. And trouble—man-made trouble—was always likely to arise. The planet's natural riches were tempting . . . particularly when some new discovery was made and kept concealed.

This then might be such trouble on a large scale. The pattern of disappearances had begun north of the equator, spread down through the Sotira range. It had started three months ago. And the purpose, she thought, presumably was to accomplish precisely what it had accomplished—to keep the sleds away from the islands. For a period long enough to let whoever was behind the maneuver clear out whatever treasure of rare elements or drugs they'd come across and be gone again.

No local organization was big enough to pull off such a stunt. But a local organization backed by a Hub syndicate could be doing it—

Gromgorru? Nile shrugged mentally. The deeps of Nandy-Cline were only sketchily explored; great sections of the ocean floor remained unmapped. But she had very little faith in unknown malignant powers. In all her experience, whenever there was real mischief afoot, human operators had been found behind it.

The others here were less sure. There was something like superstitious dread unspoken but heavy in the air of this cabin, with the deck shuddering underfoot and the typhoon howling and thudding beyond the thick walls. She thought Doncar and Jath weren't free of it. Jath had acquired a degree of sophistication very uncommon among the sledmen. But she still was a woman of the sea sleds, whose folk had drunk strangeness from the mysteries of ocean and space for centuries. Space life and sea life didn't breed timid people. But it bred people who would not go out of their way to pit themselves against forces they could not understand.

Nile said to Pelad, "You spoke of those who hear voices of hate when the communicators are blanked out."

The Venn's eyes flickered for an instant. He nodded.

"Do the other-seeing"—Nile used the sledmen term for psi sensitives—"connect these voices with the disappearances in the floatwood drifts?"

Pelad hesitated, said, "No. Not definitely."

"They haven't said this is a matter men can't handle?"

"They haven't said it," Pelad agreed slowly. "They don't know. They only know what they've told us."

So the witch doctors had suggested just enough to stall action. Nile said, "Then there may very well be two things here. One, what the other-seeing sense. The second, a human agency which is responsible for the present trouble in the floatwood. What if the sleds learn that is the case?"

Doncar said, "There're six spaceguns mounted on this sled, Dr. Etland, and men trained in their use."

"I myself," said Pelad, "am one of those men."

Fiam added, "There are two other Sotira sleds not far from here. Each armed with four spaceguns—very old guns but in excellent working order." He gave Nile a brief smile. "The mainland may recall them."

"The mainland does," Nile agreed. "You'll fight if you know you're not fighting gromgorru?"

"We'll fight men," Pelad said. "We have always fought men when necessary. But it would be unwise to challenge blindly an evil which may not be affected by guns and which might be able to wipe the sleds from the sea." His face darkened again. "Some believe there is such an evil at no great distance from us."

She must be careful at this point. Still, so far, so good.

In their minds the Venn were committed now to fight, if shown an enemy with whom weapons could deal. Too early to ask them to cooperate with mainland authorities in this. Their distrust was too deep.

Five minutes later she knew what she must do. Her immediate concern was to get Ticos out of harm's way. The big floatwood drift for which she had been looking was eighty miles south of this point. A Sotira seiner had been missing for several days, and the last reports from it indicated it might have moved too near the drift in the storm and become another victim of whatever menace haunted floatwood waters. Doncar's sled had been hunting for the seiner in the vicinity of the drift but found no clue to what had happened. The search had now been abandoned.

There were no other sizable floatwood islands within two hundred miles. Therefore the one on which Ticos had set up his project should be part of the drift. It was almost a certainty. If she took her aircar there at once, she could identify the island while daylight remained. The risk shouldn't be too great. Aircars hadn't come under attack, and the one she had was a fast sports model. If there was a suggestion of hostile action, she could clear out very quickly. If there wasn't, she'd try to wake Ticos up on the close contact channel and establish what the situation down there was. She might have him out inside an hour.

If that didn't work, she wasn't equipped to do much more by herself; and she needed reinforcements in any case before trying to determine who might have been turning the floatwood islands into death traps.

She asked, "Can you get a message through to the mainland for me?"

They nodded, the Venn warily. Jath said, "It may take a number of hours. But so far the fleets have always been able to relay messages through disturbance areas."

Fiam inquired, "What's the message, Dr. Etland? And to whom will it go?"

"It goes to Danrich Parrol," Nile told him. "The Giard Station will be able to locate him." She couldn't become too specific about gromgorru matters or the message would be blocked before it reached the mainland. "Give Parrol the location of the floatwood drift south of us. I'll wait for him there. Tell him I may have a problem getting Dr. Cay off his island, and that I'd like him to come out with full troubleshooting equipment—"

"*And* Spiff!" a thin voice interrupted emphatically from the corner of the room.

The sledmen looked around, startled. Sweeting blinked at them, began nosing her chest fur disinterestedly. People who didn't know Sweeting well frequently were surprised by the extent to which she followed the details of human discussions.

"And Spiff, of course," Nile agreed. "If we find out what's been happening around the floatwood, we'll try to get word to you at once."

Fiam nodded quickly. "Six hours from now we'll have a racing sled in the drift. Any close-contact messages should be picked up. Code Sotira-Doncar, on the sledmen frequencies. . . . "

"The Great Palach Koll," said the demon on the platform, "has persuaded the Everliving to permit him to test the Tuvela Theory."

Ticos Cay didn't reply immediately. His visitor was the Palach Moga, one of the Everliving, though of lower grade than the Great Palachs and somewhere between them and the Oganoon in physical structure, about Ticos' size and weight. Moga didn't squat but stood upright, long hopping legs stretched out, and walked upright when he walked, with short careful awkward steps. His torso was enclosed in an intricate close-worked harness of silver straps. In what was happening here he and Ticos Cay had become cautious allies. Ticos was aware that the alliance might be of very temporary nature.

"I was under the impression," he told Moga, "that the Voice of Caution was able to keep the reckless demands of the Great Palach from being given a hearing."

Moga's speaking slit twisted in agitation.

"We have done it until now," he said. "But the Great Palach has assumed control of the Voice of Action. He accused his predecessor of a Violation of Rules, and the Everliving found the accusation valid. The predecessor was granted the death of a Palach. You must understand that in his new position Koll's demands can no longer be silenced."

"Yes, I see . . . " Advancement usually came the hard way among the demons. Two favored methods were a ritualized form of assassination and having one's superior convicted of a Violation of Rules. They had the same practical result. Ticos swallowed. Bad—very bad. . . . He leaned back against the worktable to avoid revealing that his legs were trembling. "How does the Great Palach propose to test the Tuvela Theory?"

"The Guardian Etland is again attempting to contact you," Moga said.

"Yes, I know." The communicator in the partitioned end of the room had signaled half a dozen times during the past half hour.

"The signals," Moga explained, "are on the cambi channel."

The close-contact band! Ticos said thickly, "She already is in the area?"

"Could anyone else be seeking for you here?"

"No."

"Then it is the Guardian. There is a human airvehicle high overhead. It is very small but rides the storm well. It moves away, returns again."

"The island growth has changed since she was here last," said Ticos. "She may not have determined yet on which of these islands I should be." He added urgently, "This gives us a chance to forestall actions by Koll! I have the Guardian's call symbol—"

Moga gave the whistle of absolute negation.

"It is now quite impossible to approach your communicator," he said. "I would die if I attempted it unless it were under open orders of the Everliving. Koll will be allowed to carry out his plan. He has arranged tests to determine whether a Tuvela is a being such as the Tuvela Theory conjectures it to be. The first test will come while the Guardian is still in the air. At a selected moment the Great Palach will have a device activated which is directed at her vehicle. If she responds promptly and correctly, the vehicle will be incapacitated, but the Guardian will not be harmed. If she does not respond promptly and correctly, she dies at that point."

Moga stared at Ticos a moment. "The significance of her death, of course, will be the Everliving's conclusion that Tuvelas lack the basic qualities ascribed to them. The Great Plan is now in balance. If the balance is to shift again in favor of the Voice of Caution, the Guardian must not fail. Her class is being judged in her. If she fails, the Voice of Action attains full control.

"Let us assume she passes this first test. The vehicle will descend to a point where Koll's personal company of Oganoon await the Guardian. Unless she has weapons of great effectiveness, she must surrender to them. Note that if she does not surrender and is killed, it will be judged a failure. A Tuvela, as Tuvelas are assumed to be, will not make such mistakes. A Tuvela will surrender and await better opportunities to act to advantage."

Ticos nodded slowly. "I'll be able to speak to the Guardian if she is captured?"

"No, Dr. Cay. Only the Great Palach Koll will speak to the Guardian following her capture. The tests will continue at once and with increasing severity until the Guardian either dies or proves to the Everliving beyond all doubt that the Tuvela Theory is correct in all its implications—specifically, that the Tuvelas, individually and as a class, are the factor which must cause us, even at this last moment, to halt and reverse the Great Plan. Koll is staking his life on his belief that she will fail. If she fails, he will have proved his point. The Everliving will hesitate no longer. And the final stages of the Plan will be initiated."

"In brief," Ticos said slowly, "the Great Palach intends to discredit the Tuvela Theory by showing he can torture the Guardian to death and add her to his collection of trophies?"

"Yes. That is his announced plan. The torture, of course, is an approved form of test. It is in accord with tradition."

Ticos stared up at him, trying to conceal his complete dismay. There was no argument he could advance. This was the way they were conditioned to think. Before a Palach became a Palach he submitted to painful tests which few survived. As he progressed toward the ultimate form of existence which was a Great Palach, he was tested again and again. It was their manner of evaluation, of judgment. Ticos had convinced a majority of them that Tuvelas were at least their human counterpart. Some were convinced, however unwillingly, that the counterpart was superior to the greatest of the Great Palachs—opponents too deadly to be challenged. Koll's move was designed to nullify that whole structure of thought. . . .

"I'll keep you informed of what occurs, Dr. Cay," Moga concluded. "If you have suggestions which might be useful in this situation, have word sent to me immediately. Otherwise we now see no way to block Koll's purpose— unless the Guardian herself proves able to do it. Let us hope that she does."

The Palach turned, moved off down the walkway toward the exit door. Ticos gazed after him. There was a leaden feeling of helplessness throughout his body. For the moment it seemed difficult even to stir from where he stood.

He didn't doubt that Nile Etland was the operator of the aircar they were watching—and he had been hoping very much she wouldn't arrive just yet.

Given even another two weeks, he might have persuaded the Everliving through the Voice of Caution to cancel the planned attack on Nandy-Cline and withdraw from the planet. But Nile's arrival had precipitated matters and Koll was making full use of the fact. The one way in which Ticos could have warned her off and given her a clue to what was happening was closed completely.

Four words would have done it, he thought. Four words, and Nile would have known enough, once he'd switched on the communicator. He'd made preparations to ensure nobody was going to stop him before he got the four words out.

But now—without Moga's help, without the permission of the Everliving—he simply couldn't get to the communicator. It wasn't a question of the guards. He'd made other preparations for the guards. It was the devastatingly simple fact that the partitioning wall was twelve feet high and that there was no door in it. Ticos knew too well that he was no longer in any condition to get over the wall and to the communicator in time to do any good. They'd turn him off before he turned it on. He didn't have the physical strength and coordination left to be quick enough for such moves. . . .

If Nile had arrived a couple of weeks earlier, he could have done it. He'd counted then on being able to do it. But there'd been a few too many of their damned pain treatments since.

And if she'd delayed coming out by just two weeks, no warning might have been necessary.

But she was punctual as usual—right on time!

Well, Ticos told himself heavily, at least he'd arranged matters so that they wouldn't simply blast her out of the

air as she came down to the island. It left her a slim
chance. However, it seemed time to start thinking in
terms of last-ditch operations—for both of them. He had
his preparations made there too. But they weren't very
satisfactory ones. . . .

"Hungry," Sweeting announced from the aircar's floor
beside Nile.

"So starve," Nile said absently. Sweeting opened her
jaws, laughed up at her silently.

"Go down, eh?" she suggested. "Catch skilt for Nile,
eh? Nile hungry?"

"Nile isn't. Go back to sleep. I have to think."

The otter snorted, dropped her head back on her
forepaws, pretended to close her eyes. Sweeting's kind
might be the product of a geneticist's miscalculation.
Some twenty years before, a consignment of hunting otter
cubs had reached Nandy-Cline. They were a development
of a preserved Terran otter strain, tailored for an oceanic
existence. The coastal rancher who'd bought the consignment was startled some months later when the growing
cubs began to address him in a slurrily chopped-up
version of the Hub's translingue. The unexpected talent
didn't detract from their value. The talkative cubs, playful,
affectionate, handsomely pelted, sold readily, were
distributed about the sea coast ranches and attained
physical maturity in another year and a half. As water
hunters or drivers and protectors of the sea herds, each
was considered the equivalent of half a dozen trained
men. Adults, however, sooner or later tended to lose
interest in their domesticated status and exchanged it for
a feral life in the sea, where they thrived and bred.
During the past few years sledmen had reported encounters with sizable tribes of wild otters. They still spoke
in translingue.

Nile's pair, hand-raised from cubhood, had stayed. She
wasn't quite sure why. Possibly they were as intrigued

by her activities as she was by theirs. On some subjects her intellectual processes and theirs meshed comfortably. On others there remained a wide mutual lack of comprehension. She suspected, though she'd never tried to prove it, that their overall intelligence level was very considerably higher than was estimated.

She was holding the aircar on a southwest course, surface scanners shifting at extreme magnification about the largest floatwood island in the drift, two miles below, not quite three miles ahead. It looked very much like the one Ticos Cay had selected. Minor differences could be attributed to adaptive changes in the growth as the floatwood moved south. There were five major forest sections arranged roughly like the tips of a pentacle. The area between them, perhaps a mile across, was the lagoon, a standard feature of the islands. Its appearance was that of a shallow lake choked with vegetation, a third of the surface covered by dark green leafy pads flattened on the water. The forests, carrying the semi-parasitical growth which clustered on the floatwood's thick twisted boles, towered up to six hundred feet about the lagoon, living walls of almost indestructible toughness and density. The typhoon battering through which they had passed had done little visible damage. Beneath the surface they were linked by an interlocking net of ponderous roots which held the island sections clamped into a single massive structure.

The island was moving slowly to the south, foam-streaked swells running past it on either side. This might be the southern fringe of the typhoon belt. The sky immediately overhead was clear, a clean deep blue. But violent gusts still shook the car, and roiling cloud banks rode past on all sides.

Ticos Cay's hidden arboreal laboratory should be in the second largest section of the floatwood structure, about a third of the way in on the seaward side. He wasn't responding to close-contact communicator signals;

but he might be there in spite of his silence. In any case it was the place to start looking. There'd been no sign of intruders—which didn't mean they weren't there. The multiple canopies of the forests could have concealed an army. But intruders could be avoided.

Nile thought she might be able to handle this without waiting for Parrol. It was late afternoon now, and even if there were no serious delays in getting her message to him, it would be at best the middle of the night before he could make it out here. To drop down openly to the floatwood would be asking for trouble, of course, though there had been no reports of attacks on aircars as yet. But she could circle south, go down to sea level, submerge the car and maneuver it back underwater to the island through the weed beds which rode the Meral. If she'd had her jet diving rig with her, she wouldn't have hesitated. She could have left the car a couple of miles out, gone in at speed and brought Ticos out with her if he was in his hideaway, with almost no risk of being noticed by whoever else might be about. But she didn't have the rig along. That meant working the car in almost to the island, a more finicky operation.

But it could be done. The submerged weed jungles provided the best possible cover against detection instruments.

Nile checked course and altitude, returned her attention to the magnification scanners. Everything down there looked normal. There was considerable animal activity about the lagoon, including clouds of the flying kesters which filled the role of sea and shore birds in Nandy-Cline's ecological pattern. In the ocean beyond the floatwood at the left, two darkly gleaming torpedo-shaped bodies appeared intermittently at the surface. They were kesters too, but wingless giants: sea-havals, engaged in filling their crops with swarms of skilts. Their presence was another good indication that this was Ticos' island. There'd been a sea-haval rookery concealed in the forest section next to the one he'd selected—

An engine control shrieked warning, and a sullen roaring erupted about them. Nile saw a red line in the fuel release gauge surge up toward explosion as her hand flicked out and cut the main engine switch.

The shrieking whistle and the roar of energies gone wild subsided together. Losing momentum, the car began to drop.

"Nile?"

"We're in trouble, Sweeting." The otter was on her feet, neck fur erect, eyes shifting about. But Sweeting knew enough to stay quiet in emergencies that were in Nile's department.

Energy block . . . it could be malfunction. But that type of malfunction occurred so rarely it had been years since she'd heard of a case.

Someone hidden in the floatwood had touched the car with a type of weapon unknown to her, was bringing her down. The car's built-in antigrav patterns would slow their descent. But—

Nile became very busy.

When she next looked at the altimeter, it told her she had approximately three minutes left in the air. Wind pressure meanwhile had buffeted the car directly above the island, a third of the way out across the lagoon. That would have been the purpose of killing her engines at the exact moment it was done. When the car splashed into the lagoon's vegetation, she'd find a reception committee waiting.

She was in swim briefs by now for maximum freedom of action in water or in the floatwood. Fins and a handkerchief-sized breather mask lay on the seat. Most of the rest of what she was taking along had been part of the floatwood kit she'd flung into the back of the car on leaving the Giard Station. Various items were attached to a climb-belt about her waist—knife, lightweight UW gun, grip sandals, a pouch containing other floatwood gear she didn't have time to sort over. The otter caller she used to summon Sweeting and Spiff from a distance was fastened to her wrist above her watch. Her discarded clothing was in a waterproof bag.

"Remember what you're to do?"

"Yesss!" Sweeting acknowledged with a cheery hiss, whiskers twitching.

Sweeting would remember. They were going to meet some bad guys. Not at all a novel experience. Sweeting would keep out of sight and trouble until Nile had more specific instructions for her.

The bad guys hadn't showed yet. But they must be in the lagoon, headed for the area where the car seemed about to come down. It was rocking and lurching in the gusts toward a point some three hundred yards from the nearest floatwood. Not at all where Nile wanted it to go. But she might be able to improve her position considerably.

She sat quiet throughout the last moments, estimating the force of the wind, eyes shifting between the altimeter and a landing area she'd selected on the far side of the water. Then, at hundred yards from the surface, she pushed down a stud which slid out broad glide-vanes to either side of the car.

The fringes of a typhoon were no place for unpowered gliding. Like the blow of a furious fist, wind slammed the vehicle instantly over on its side. Seconds of wild tumbling followed. But she had the momentum now to return some control of the car's motion to her. To hostile watchers in the lagoon and the floatwood it must have looked like a futile and nearly suicidal attempt to escape— as it was intended to look. She didn't want them to start shooting. Twice she seemed within inches of being slammed head-on into the water, picked up altitude at the last instant. Most of the width of the lagoon lay behind her at that point, and a section of forest loomed ahead again. A tall stand of sea reeds, perhaps three hundred yards across, half enclosed by gnarled walls of floatwood, whirled by below.

Wind force swept the car down once more, too fast, too far to the right. Nile shifted the vane controls. The car rose steeply, heeled over, swung sideways, its momentum checked—and that was almost exactly where she wanted to be. She slapped another stud. The vanes folded back into the vehicle. It began to drop, antigrav effect taking over. Nile reached for the fins, snapped them on her feet. Green tops of the reeds whipped suddenly about the car. She drew the transparent breather mask over her face, pressed its audio plugs into her ears. Car door open, set on lock . . . dense vegetation swaying jerkily with wet crashing sounds on all sides as the car descended through it—

Thump and splash!

Sweeting slithered past Nile's feet, flowed down over the doorsill, vanished into the lagoon without a sound. Nile pitched the clothing bag through the door, swung about on the seat, slid out into cool water. Turning, she caught a handgrip on the side of the car, reached up, slammed the door shut on its lock.

She saw the bag floating beside her, caught its strap and went down. . . .

Chapter 4

The sea reeds, rising from layers of muck packed into the matted root system of the island thirty feet below, grew thick and strong. Almost in moments after leaving the car, Nile knew she was relatively safe from immediate pursuit. On her way across the lagoon she'd had a flashing glimpse of an enclosed boat coming about in a tight circle among the pads to follow her. It wouldn't be long before it reached the reeds, and it might have divers aboard. In open water a jet diver advancing behind a friction-cutting field would have overhauled her in seconds. But jet rigs gave little real advantage when it came to slipping in and out of slime-slick dense growth; and if one had been in operation within a hundred yards, her audio plugs would have distinguished its thin hissing through the medley of sea sounds. She moved on quickly toward the forest. Small life scuttled and flicked away from her gliding shape. A school of eight-inch skilts exploded suddenly about her in a spray of silver glitters. . . . Sweeting, out of sight but somewhere nearby, might have turned aside for a fast snack. Something large and dark stirred ahead; a dorashen, some five hundred pounds of sluggish ugliness, black armor half concealed by a rusty fur of parasites, was backing off from her advance, pulling itself up along the reed stems, multiple jaws working in menacing snaps.

Sudden darkening of the water told her she'd reached the base of the forest. The reed growth ended and thick twisted floatwood trunks appeared through murky dimness. She stroked up to them, paused to look back. A dim regular rumbling had began in the audio pickups. The sound of engines. But they weren't close.

Ticos Cay's hidden dwelling was less than a quarter-mile from here. Getting there unobserved would be the next move. A few minutes later, deep within the forest, in the maze of dark caverns formed by huge supporting trunks above the submerged roots, Nile lifted her head above the surging ocean surface, pulled off the breather. The otter's head appeared a dozen feet away.

"People here?" Nile asked.

"Smell no people."

"Boats?"

"Skilt boat. Coming slow."

"How big?"

"Big as three cars, heh."

No divers, and nobody upwind of them in the forest. Sweeting used nostrils in air, sensitive olfactories
in the lining of her mouth in water. What she couldn't
scent usually wasn't there. Skilt boat meant a submersible. It might have been the boat Nile had glimpsed
in the lagoon. When Sweeting saw it, it was approaching
the reed bed under water. Its crew should discover the
ditched aircar in not too many minutes.

"Kill?" the otter asked.

"Not yet. Go back and watch what they're doing till
I call you."

Sweeting vanished. Nile moved on through dark
shifting water, avoiding contact with the giant trunks.
They were coated with slime, heavily populated with
crawling things. Not a pleasant place to be; but this
level provided a quick route to the seaward side of the
forest, and she intended to make her ascent from
there. Presently she saw daylight flash intermittently
through the snaky tangles of floatwood ahead.

Far enough. . . . She found a place to get out of
the water, scrambled up to a horizontal perch and
knotted the strap of the bag containing her discarded
coveralls and other personal items around a spike of
wood. The fewer clues to the car's occupants left for
investigators, the better. She exchanged fins for grip
sandals, fastened the fins to her climb-belt, switched
the belt to its quarter-weight setting and stood up on
the trunk.

There was a partial gravity shield about her now.
Ordinary progress in a floatwood forest was an activity
somewhere between mountaineering and tree climbing.
With a climb-belt and sufficient practice in its use, it
became not much more arduous than motion along level
ground. Nile started up. The forest had no true floor, but

a thick carpet of parasitic growth, trailing drinking roots to the sea, stretched out overhead. She pushed through the stuff, came into a relatively open area.

She stood glancing about, letting senses and mind adjust again to what was here. It was long-familiar territory. She'd been born in one of the shallows settlements of Nandy-Cline, halfway around the globe from the mainland; and whenever one of the swimming islands moved near, her people had gone to harvest from it what was in season, taking their children along to teach them the floatwood's bounty and perils. Making the islands the subject of extensive studies later on had been a natural consequence.

Though this was less densely growth-infested than the central forest levels, vision was restricted to at most a hundred feet in any direction. In the filtered half-light, the host organism was represented by unbranched reddish-brown boles, sloping and twisting upward—enormously massive, as they had to be to support all the rest. Sprouting or hanging from the trunks, or moving slowly along their coarse-furred surface, was the many-shaped secondary growth, in the inhis and tacapu categories, with plant or plant-animal characteristics. Gliding and hopping through the growth, fluttering about it, were small specimens of the animal population.

Nile's eyes and nostrils took it all in with only superficial conscious responses. A definite conscious reaction would come if she encountered something she didn't know or knew might harm her—or if she detected any trace of the intruders who had forced her down from the sky. Listening was a waste of effort; the booming winds drowned minor sounds. She started up the ascending curve of the trunk by which she had climbed from the sea. Presently it branched, then branched again. Now the floatwood's great oblong leaves began to appear among the other growth, shifting green curtains which closed vision down to the next few dozen steps ahead. It was more to her advantage than not. In the constant stirring, her lean body, tanned almost to the tint of the floatwood branches, would be next to impossible to detect if hostile watchers were about.

She was nearly four hundred feet above the ocean before sunlight began to play through the forest in wavering flashes, filtered through the canopy above. By then Nile was moving along an interlaced network of lesser branches. She knew she was somewhat above Ticos' dwelling and had been watching for its camouflaged outlines in the vegetation below. It was a sizable structure, but anyone who didn't know it was there might stare at it for minutes and not realize what he saw. It had been built of the materials growing about it and blended into them.

A great wet mass of fernlike stuff, sadly bent and tattered by the typhoons, caught at Nile's memory. The hideout should be thirty feet below, off to the left.

She reached the soggy greenery, clambered through, found a spot where she could look down. Nothing but more waving growth beneath her. She jumped over to a sloping trunk, caught at it with flexing grip sandals and hands, moved along to a horizontally jutting branch and stepped out on it to look around the trunk.

A broad spear of sunlight blazed past her, directly into the concealed entrance of the hideout. A naked man sat cross-legged in the entrance, staring up, mouth stretched wide as if in a frozen shriek of laughter.

Nile's next awareness—at the moment it seemed a simultaneous one—was of the UW in her hand, stubby muzzle pointed down at the grotesquely distended mouth of the figure.

The figure didn't move. For seconds then, neither did she. The eyes seemed fixed on her and her skin crawled with something very close to superstitious terror. The sunlight winked out suddenly. The forest shook and groaned in renewed surges of wind.

She was looking at a dead man, her mind told her belatedly. Not Ticos; he didn't show the slightest resemblance to Ticos . . . but what had frozen this unknown dead man here in that position, head twisted back, facial muscles distorted into an expression of grisly mirth? Her eyes began to shift about, returning every few seconds to the seated shape, as if she expected it to gain sudden life and come leaping up at her. The forest boomed, danced, rustled and snapped in the wind. She saw and heard nothing else. The figure remained unmoving. It had been there unmoving, she decided, for a considerable time. Days, at least. It was streaked with dirt, as if rain had run down on it and it had dried while the storm whipped forest debris about it, and rain presently washed it again.

She stepped back behind the trunk, moved down along it. A minute later her left hand carefully parted the cluster of plants encircling the platform to let her look beyond the man-shape into the structure. The entrance door was gone. Not torn away by storm violence. Removed deliberately. The entrance had been widened, cut back on either side.

The interior was dim, but part of the wall lighting was on, and after a moment she could see enough. Except for a few tables and wall shelves, the place seemed to have been stripped. The partitions were gone; only the thick outer framework remained. But the structure wasn't empty. There might be between twenty and thirty of them inside. They crouched on hands and knees, squatted, lay about. Their rigid immobility said there was no more life in them than in the figure on the platform. Nile moved slowly forward, gun out before her.

She paused by the seated man in the entrance, prodded his shoulder with a finger. The skin was cool, gummy; the flesh beneath it unyielding as lead. She started past, checked again, stomach contracting. A wide gash laid open the figure's back. It appeared to have been gutted completely through the gash. She stared a moment, went inside.

The others weren't very different. Ticos wasn't one of them. Dead eyes stared at Nile as she moved among the bodies. Dead mouths snarled, pleaded, grinned. All were savagely mutilated in one way or another. A few had been women. One of the women had the Blue Guul symbol of the Sotira sleds etched on her forehead—a good luck charm. Several wall sections were still covered with Ticos Cay's scribbled work notations and sketches. Nothing else of his seemed here. Nothing else seemed to be here at all except what the wet winds had swept in through the entrance. . . .

Then her eyes checked on something the wind hadn't blown in. It sat in the shadows on a wall shelf to one side of what had been the main room. Puzzled, she went slowly over to it.

It looked like a featureless black cloth figure, a hooded lumpy little doll, less than fifteen inches high. It had been placed on a crumpled dark cloth spread along the shelf. As Nile came up, she saw that the hood and cloak were coverings. There was something beneath them. She pushed the hood back with the UW's muzzle, looked at the wrinkled blackish unhuman face which might have been carved out of wood, with considerable skill. The bulging heavy-lidded eyes were closed. A narrow mouth slit was the only other feature. In its miniature ugliness it was impressive. It was as if a small demonic idol had been set up to preside over what had become of Ticos Cay's laboratory. Nile let the hood fall into place, started toward the entrance.

One more discovery then . . . she saw something stir in the dirt piled against one wall and moved the dirt aside with her foot. Three of Ticos' protohoms lay in a pile, mutilated and slashed almost beyond recognition, still moving. As cruelty it was meaningless; they had no awareness and no sensitivity to pain. But it fitted the pattern of grotesque ugliness here. The UW hissed quickly three times, taking their semblance of life from them.

There seemed no reason to stay longer. The structure held a feeling of nightmare, heavy, almost tangible. At moments it seemed difficult to breathe and her head would begin to swim. But she had a recurrent nagging feeling of missing something. She glanced about once more. The dead shapes were there in their frozen postures. The dark little idol dreamed above them on its littered shelf. No . . . nothing else but unanswered questions.

In a thicket a hundred yards from the structure entrance, where she could watch the stretch along which she had come, Nile tried turning over the questions. Her mind moved sluggishly at first, blurred by fear and surges of pity and sick anger. She had to keep forcing all that to the back of her awareness. What she'd seen didn't fit the overall pattern she'd assumed. A very different type of mentality seemed involved. A mentality which systematically tortured human minds and bodies, leaving the victims degraded in death and carefully preserving their degradation, as if that were a goal in itself. . . .

It made no sense as yet. But the immediate situation hadn't changed. If Ticos had known about these intruders before they discovered his laboratory and converted it to the insanity in there, he might still be at large. He'd had a small boat with which he could have slipped away unnoticed to other sections of the island, or even to another island in the floatwood drift. He knew she'd be coming presently and would have tried to leave a message where she could find it, hoping she'd be able to escape capture in turn. Something to tell her what was going on, where he was.

A message where she could find it. Some place she'd associate naturally with Ticos . . . Nile shook her head. There were simply too many such places. She couldn't waste time checking them over at present. If Ticos was still in the island area, Sweeting might be able to pick up traces of him.

Her thoughts veered. The aircar. They'd have reached it by now, but door and engine keys were in the pouch at her belt. If they hadn't sunk the car or towed it away, they should still be busy around it. Watching them might tell her more about this group than she could get from Sweeting's reports. She set off quickly.

When she caught glimpses of the wind-whipped surface of the lagoon through the growth, she paused, calculating her position. The reed bed where she'd touched water should be on her right, not far away. She angled toward it, ran up a thick sloping branch stretching out above the water, turned and went on hands and knees along a lesser branch until she reached a point where sheaves of floatwood foliage overhung the lagoon. Here she straddled the branch, grasped two of the leaf stems, drew them cautiously apart and was looking down on the swirling reed tops two hundred feet below.

The area where she'd set down the car had been widened, the plants thrust aside and mashed down so that she could see a patch of open water. There were other indications that a surface craft had broken a way in from the lagoon. Nile saw nothing else, thought for a moment the car already had been destroyed or hauled off. But then she heard a series of clanging metallic sounds, partly muffled by the wind. Somebody was down there, perhaps engaged in forcing open the car's doors.

She waited, upper lip clamped between her teeth, heard no more. Then one end of the aircar edged into view, turning slowly as if it were being pushed about. A moment later all of it suddenly appeared in the open area—and on the canopy—

Nile's thoughts blurred in shock.

Parahuans. . . .

Some seventy years ago they'd come out of space to launch almost simultaneous attacks against Nandy-Cline and a dozen other water worlds of the Hub. They'd done considerable damage, but in the end their forces were pulled back; and it was believed that by the time the Federation's warships finished hunting them through space, only insignificant remnants had survived to return to their undiscovered home worlds. It had been the last open attack by an alien civilization against a Federation planet—even planets as far out from the Hub's center as Nandy-Cline.

And we became careless, Nile thought. *We felt we were so big no one would dare come again.* . . .

With a kind of frozen fascination, she stared at the two bulky amphibious creatures squatting on the car, thickly muscled legs bent sharply beneath them. A swarm of reflections based on various old descriptions of Parahuans went through her mind. The bluish-gray torsos and powerful arms were enclosed by webbings of straps, holding tools and weapons. The bulging eyes on the big round heads were double-lensed, the lower sections used for underwater vision and lidded in air, as they now were. A vocal orifice was connected to a special air system above the eyes. The two Parahuans below seemed to be gabbling at others outside her range of vision, though the wind drowned most of the sounds they were making.

Well, they had dared come again . . . and they already must be in considerable number on the unsuspecting planet, establishing themselves in and under the floatwood islands in recent months. The little figure in the gutted laboratory, the small devil brooding vengefully over the mutilated husks of human bodies, was made in their image.

It changed her immediate plans. In this storm-swept multileveled mountain of dense vegetation she'd felt reasonably safe from human searchers. But she could take no chances with these aliens until she knew their capabilities. She shifted back on the branch, then halted watchfully. In the water of the lagoon beyond the reeds something was moving. Nile couldn't make out details, but it was a very large creature, dirty white in color. As she stared, it sank slowly below the surface and was gone.

She scrambled back along the branch under cover of the leaves, got to her feet as soon as she reached more solid support, and retreated hurriedly into the forest. In their first campaign the Parahuans had brought a formidable creature along with them which took part effectively in the fighting. It was animalic in behavior, though there was some evidence that it was a gigantic adaptation of the Parahuan life form. Reportedly it had sharp senses, was equally agile on land and in water, and difficult to stop with ordinary weapons.

What she'd seen out in the lagoon just now was one of those creatures—a Parahuan tarm.

Eyes shifting quickly about as she moved on, she paused here and there for an instant. Her knife reached out, slashed stem, seed pod, blossom, fleshy leaf, chunky tentacle from one or another familiar tacapu or plant form. They bled tinted dust, tinted sap, quickly turning to streaks and blots of green, shadow blue, cinnamon, chocolate brown, gray and white on Nile's body, arms, legs, face, hair, equipment. Breaking outline, blending form into background . . . a trick used in stalking floatwood species wary and keen-sighted enough to avoid undisguised human hunters.

It might not be sufficient disguise now. Humans had a variety of life detection instruments. No doubt, Parahuans had them. For many such devices, one human being in the floatwood became simply one life form blurred among many life forms. But the distinctive human scent remained, and sharp senses read it as well as instruments. She could take care of that presently. To do it, she'd have to get back to the area of Ticos' laboratory. . . .

Her mind halted a moment. Ticos' laboratory! Nile made a sound of muted fury. If he'd left a clue for her anywhere, given any time to do it, he'd left it there! She'd felt she was overlooking something. She hesitated. If she hadn't been in partial shock because of what she'd come upon—

She returned along the route she'd followed from the laboratory to the lagoon, staying some thirty feet above what should be her actual trail.

And presently: a special minor area of agitation in the mass of wind-shaken growth below and ahead. A shimmer of blue-gray.

Nile sank smoothly to the floatwood branch she was crossing, flattened herself against it, then carefully shifted position enough to let her peer down.

The Parahuan was coming out of a thicket beneath her, following another branch. He crept along on all fours. It looked awkward, but his motion was fairly rapid and showed no uncertainty. He came to a parallel bough, paused, took a short hop over to it, went on. He seemed indifferent to the fact that he was several hundred feet above the sea. So they were capable climbers. As he reached a curtain of secondary growth, another Parahuan appeared, trailing the leader by twenty-five feet, and vanished behind him. Nile checked two minutes off on her watch. No more aliens had showed up—the pair seemed to be working alone. She went up twenty feet, hurried back in the direction of the lagoon.

It had startled her that they'd been able to pick up her trail so promptly in this vast green warren. The odds seemed all against that, but there was no question that they were following it. Both carried guns, heavy-looking thick-barreled devices fastened to the web of straps about their trunks. The one in the lead had a curved box attached to the top of his head, a number of tubes projecting from its sides and twisting about in the air with a suggestion of sentient searching. The second Parahuan carried a much smaller instrument directly above the vocal slit in the upper part of his head. That probably was a communicator.

Nile dropped back down, found a place to wait. There'd been a practical detail in the information contained in the old war records: the lower half of a Parahuan's head was the best point to aim at to put them out of action quickly. Second choice was the lower torso. . . .

The leading Parahuan came into sight again on a lower branch, edging out of a wind-tossed cluster of great leaves she'd been watching. He paused there, staring about and ahead. Nile held her breath, wondering what signals he was getting from his tracking instrument, until he started forward along the branch. She let him pass below. Parahuan Number Two showed up punctually in turn. As he came within twenty-five feet, Nile sighted along the UW, squeezed the trigger carefully. The big body turned sideways, rolled off the branch without a sound.

Nile twisted left, aimed again. The leader had noticed nothing. Moments later he too plunged down into the waving vegetation and was gone.

The buti was an unremarkable shrublike growth in the inhis category, with lacy fronds and thick woody stems, living as a semi-parasite on the floatwood. Its stems were hollow, and the creamy sap they oozed when cut had the quality of nullifying a wide variety of smells, though the sap had no pronounced odor of its own. Specifically, in this case, it nullified the scents of a human body. When floatwood had been hunted over enough to make some of its harvestible life shy of human visitors, anointing oneself with buti sap, if it was obtainable, was a common move among experienced collectors.

The buti stand Nile had remembered from earlier visits was not much more than a hundred yards from Ticos' laboratory, and somewhat above it. She let herself drop thirty feet into the center of the shrubs against the antigrav effect of the belt, then spent several minutes meticulously adding a coating of the sap to her color camouflage and to the various articles of her equipment. Her nerves were on edge; she did not like at all being in the immediate vicinity of the laboratory. They might know she'd been here before—the laboratory in fact was likely to be the point where their tracking instrument had picked up the fresh human trail and started them in pursuit. There might be a swarm of the creatures not far away at the moment.

But the job with the buti couldn't be hurried too much. Nile finished it at last, cut off a two foot section of the stem, seared its ends shut with the UW and added it to the items already attached to her climb-belt. Salt water dissolved the sap; and she should have swimming to do presently. Her scent trail ended now thirty feet above the buti shrubs. If they followed it that far and could not pick it up again, they might conclude she'd lost her footing and fallen through the forest into the ocean. At any rate, she'd become as nearly indetectable as she could be.

She moved out of the stand, approached the laboratory with quick caution, conscious of a growing urgency to be out of this area. When she reached the platform, nothing seemed changed. The interior looked undisturbed; she could make out no marks of webbed Parahuan feet in the debris on the floor.

She came in quietly, gun held out before her, eyes shifting about. The rigid human exhibits watched her walk past toward Ticos' former work area. As she went by the tiny hooded idol, dreaming its dreams on the shelf, she glanced over at it.

Two thoughts flashed simultaneously into her mind.

She was in abrupt motion almost before she became fully conscious of them—spinning around toward the shelf, dropping the gun. An instant later she had whipped up both ends of the leathery cloth on which the Parahuan manikin sat, brought them together with a twist over the hooded head, gripped them hard in both hands and swept the bundled figure from the shelf.

By then there was a great deal of activity inside the cloth, a furious jerking and twisting, carried out with such amazing vigor that it nearly tore the cloth from her hands. But she swung the bundle up, slammed it down hard against the floor, brought it up, slammed it down again. The bundle stopped jerking. Nile scooped up her gun, spilled the inert thing inside the cloth out on the floor. She stood gasping and shaking in fright and hate, staring down at it.

It had shifted its position on the shelf since she'd seen it last. Not much, perhaps three or four inches. As her mind had recorded the fact, memory brought up another datum from the old records. Some rescued human prisoners had reported that the Parahuan leaders were dwarfed creatures by comparison with their fellows.

She recalled no mention of their being dwarfed to this improbable extent. But if she hadn't killed it, she might have a useful captive.

She dropped to her knees, pulled off the hood. Something attached to the thing's chest—a flat dark disk with studs in it, metallic or plastic. Attached how? Nile gripped the disk in her fingers, tugged, then slid the point of her knife in sideways between the device and the Parahuan's body, pried upward. There was a momentary resistance. Then four prongs in the underside of the instrument pulled suckingly out of the wrinkled skin. A communicator? She turned it over quickly in her hand. That was how the first trackers had known how to start on her trail. And it probably had been used again as she appeared in the entrance a minute ago, to call other searchers back to the laboratory—

She opened the kit pouch with flying fingers. There was stuff in there ordinarily used to secure some vigorously active floatwood specimen which was wanted alive—and it should hold this specimen. She pulled out flat strips of tanglecord, taped the Parahuan's small wiry arms to the dumpy body, taped the webbed feet together, sealed the narrow vocal orifice above the eyes with a section of cord. She turned the midget quickly around, looking it over for other trick devices. Nothing but a few dozen brightly colored small jewels set in the wrinkled top of the head in what might be a symbol of rank or a decorative pattern. She bundled the captive back into the cloth, knotted the ends of the cloth together, spent another dragging minute nicking the buti stem and giving the bundle the sap treatment.

She left the bundle on the floor, went over to the section of Ticos' work area and found his message to her almost at once, scrawled blandly and openly among the many notations that decorated the wall:

Nile note. The sestran stand should be carefully studied.

Now out of here—fast!

She nearly, very nearly, was not fast enough. She pitched the communicator, wrapped in the midget's cloak, off the laboratory platform as she came out on it. The packaged midget himself rode her back, secured by a tanglecord harness. It was a minor nuisance; in the antigrav field his weight was nothing. . . . Less than a hundred yards from the laboratory, she ducked quietly into cover.

It was a good dense thicket. From where she crouched

she could see only a limited section of the forest above. She watched that, waited for indications of anything approaching the thicket itself. A group of three Parahuans moved presently through the area above the thicket—then two more.

After that, Parahuans were simply around for a while. It was a large search party, congregating now on the laboratory. Nile kept on the move herself as much as she could, edging in the opposite direction. Most of them were climbing up from below, so she couldn't simply drop down through the forest to get out of their way. They came close enough so that she heard their voices for the first time: an oddly mellow modulated hooting, interspersed with hissing sounds. Two swarmed up the line of a grapple gun a dozen feet from her. Then she saw none for a while. By that time she had worked the green blanket of an intermediate forest canopy between herself and the main body of the searchers. She decided she was clear of them and began to climb more quickly.

Something crashed down from the upper levels ahead—a great broken branch, accompanied by assorted litter torn loose in its descent. Nile looked up, and her mind went bright with terror. She took one slow step to the side, thumbed the antigrav up high. Nothing beneath her feet now . . . she was falling limply, bonelessly, turning over slowly, toward the shelter of the canopy below. No human motions. No voluntary motions of any kind. Be a leaf, an undefinably colored uninteresting small dead dropping part of the forest. She reached the canopy, settled through it, went drifting down until she touched a solid branch and motion stopped. She huddled there, clutching the growth on either side of her. Fear still stormed along her nerves.

The tarm had been like the tip of a fog bank swirling into sight around a floatwood bole above her. It was rushing by overhead as she dropped, so close that it seemed almost impossible she'd remained unnoticed—

close enough, she thought, for one of its pale tentacles to have reached down and plucked her from the air. But it had moved on. She listened to the receding sounds of its passage through the forest long enough to make sure it wasn't returning, then set off hastily, still shaking. She wasn't nearly as far from the laboratory as she should be before the search fanned out again. They must have discovered by now that their midget was missing. Nile told herself they were least likely to come back to an area already hunted over by the tarm.

She might have been right. Ten minutes passed without further signs of her pursuers, and her nerves steadied again. If they'd shifted to the eastern areas of the forest, it could keep them futilely occupied until nightfall. Flashes of fading sunlight began to reach her. She wasn't far now from the forest roof on the seaward side and should not be far either from the sestran stand to which Ticos Cay's note had directed her. Eight months before, they'd brought sestran shoots from another part of the island and established them here for his studies. He'd known his use of the term would tell her exactly where to look.

She discovered the stand presently—and discovered also that chaquoteels had built a colony nest above it since she'd been here last. The tiny kesters greeted her with a storm of furious whistlings. Nile ducked quickly into the sestran, but not quickly enough. The chaquoteels were on her in a darting rainbow swarm, and her back smarted from dozens of jabs before they decided she'd been sufficiently routed and left her alone in the vegetation. Then the racket quieted quickly again.

Her search was a short one; Ticos had done what she'd expected. The tiny script recorder was in weatherproof sealing, taped to the side of one of the thickest sestran stems. Nile freed herself of her prisoner and laid the bundle down where she could watch it. The midget hadn't stirred yet, but that didn't mean he wasn't awake.

She considered briefly. There was cover all about. If Parahuans, or the tarm, showed up, she could fade away in any direction without stepping into the open. And with a few hundred bad-tempered chaquoteels scattered around the vicinity, she couldn't be taken by surprise.

Yes—as good a place as any to find out what Ticos had to tell her. . . .

Nile settled down, fitted the recorder to her eye, and started it.

Chapter 5

Long before she put the recorder down for the last time Nile had decided that Ticos Cay ranked among the great liars of history.

He was still alive. At least he'd been alive less than a week ago when he left the last of the four recorder disks which contained his report here for her.

She sat still, sorting over the information.

Some seventy years ago the Parahuan leadership had been smarting in defeat and trying to understand how defeat could have been possible. In their minds they were the race which had achieved perfection at all levels, including individual immortality for those with the greatness to attain it. They were the Everliving. None could match them. The water worlds of the galaxy which met their requirements were destined to be their own.

Since they first moved out from Porad Anz, their home world, the Sacred Sea, they had encountered nothing to contradict that assumption.

But now an inferior land-dweller which was in possession of a number of such worlds had flung back and almost completely destroyed the Parahuan forces sent to occupy them. The experience stunned the Everliving. It affronted logic.

Before the attack they had made what seemed a sufficiently comprehensive study of the Federation of the Hub. This human civilization was huge. But it was a heterogeneous, loosely organized, loosely governed mass of individuals quite normally in serious conflict among themselves. The analysis of captured humans confirmed the picture.

That muddled, erratic, emotionally swayed creature had routed the disciplined Parahuan forces. Something was wrong—it simply shouldn't have happened.

What had been overlooked?

They went back to studying the enemy in every way they could. The creature was blocking the orderly procession of the goals of Porad Anz. That was intolerable. The secret of its ability to do it must be found—and then means devised to destroy the ability.

Presently, in the creature's relatively recent history, a clue was discovered.

It developed into the Tuvela Theory. . . .

Nile made a snorting, incredulous sound. Not much more than two centuries ago—not many decades before Ticos Cay was born—the Hub still had been one of the bloodiest human battlegrounds of all time. It was the tail end of the War Centuries. A thousand governments were forming and breaking interstellar alliances, aiming for control of the central clusters or struggling to keep from being overwhelmed.

The Tuvelas belonged in the later part of that pre-Federation period. They were a sophisticated equivalent of ancient warlords. Some believed they arose from well-defined genetic strains at a high genius level. Legends clustered about their activities. But the fact was that the records of those muddled times were contradictory and thoroughly unreliable. In any event, the Tuvelas were long gone.

The Parahuan Palachs, searching for an explanation of their own defeat, decided they weren't long gone.

The mysterious superhuman Tuvelas not only were still around, they were now the true secret rulers of the Federation of the Hub. They had organized and guided the operation which resulted in the defeat of the Parahuan expeditionary forces.

The Everliving, or at least a majority of them, didn't intend to let the matter rest there. They now had a rationalization of the past disaster, and it restored to some extent their shattered pride. To have been bested by a foe of abnormal ability whose existence hadn't been suspected, that could be accepted. The human species as such was inferior to Porad Anz. Its apparent strength lay in the fact that its vast masses were directed and controlled by these freakish monsters.

To even the score with the Tuvelas, to bring them down and destroy them, became an abiding obsession with the Everliving—or again, at least with a majority of them. Some evidently felt from the beginning that the Tuvelas might be such dangerous opponents that it would be better not to come into conflict with them a second time. The view never became popular, but it was agreed that all reasonable precautions should be taken to avoid another debacle. The majority opinion remained that since a Parahuan Great Palach was the ultimate development of life, the human Tuvela could not possibly be his superior. The advantage of the Tuvelas had been solely that the Everliving hadn't known they were there—and naturally hadn't considered such a remote possibility in preparing the first attack.

Out of this situation grew the Great Plan, aimed at the ultimate destruction of the Hub's rulers and the Hub as a civilization. The conflicting opinions were represented by the groups known as the Voice of Action and the Voice of Caution. Between these opposed factions, the uncommitted ranks of the Everliving maintained the wisely flexible Balance.

The Voice of Caution had determinedly dragged its

heels from the start and continued to drag them for seventy years. In spite of such resistance, the Great Plan gradually matured. The Parahuans found allies—the Hub had more enemies with long memories among the stars than it might know. But they were wary enemies. If the Parahuans could take and hold a number of Federation worlds and engage a major portion of the Federation's forces . . . *then* a score of alien civilizations would attack other points in the Hub simultaneously, splitting and weakening the human defenses until they were shattered. But only if the Parahuans succeeded.

The Voice of Action argued that this was good enough. The Voice of Caution argued that it wasn't. In the Balance between them an initial test was decreed—a potential invasion force was maneuvered with careful secrecy into the seas of Nandy-Cline.

This force was regarded as expendable. On the face of it, it should be able to take Nandy-Cline with relative ease in a coordinated surprise attack. Careful study had established the fact beyond a doubt. But its primary purpose was to flush the Tuvelas to view and test their alertness and ability. If it should be established that they were indeed entities against whom the Everliving were outmatched—if, for example, the invasion force, in spite of its apparent superiority, again was destroyed or obliged to retreat, the most disconcerting aspects of the Tuvela Theory must be considered proved. Then the Great Plan would be canceled and Porad Anz would resign itself to a future of circumspect obscurity.

But if Nandy-Cline fell as scheduled, the Tuvelas could be dealt with, now that their influence on humanity was known; and the Voice of Action would receive full authority to proceed with the further operations designed to end in the destruction of the Hub.

In the course of preparing for the attack on the planet, the hidden invasion force ran head-on into Dr. Ticos Cay. . . .

◆   ◆   ◆

Ticos had been tracked to his laboratory and taken by surprise. A study of the lab's equipment told his captors that here was a human with advanced scientific knowledge who might have useful information. He was treated with care, questioned at length. Many Palachs had acquired a faultless command of translingue as an aid to their understanding of the enemy. They interrogated Ticos under drugs and with the application of calculated pain. His acquired level of mental control enabled him to withstand such pressures; and the Palachs considered this to be of great interest. No other human prisoner had shown a similar ability.

They were further intrigued to discover he had been working, among other things, at the development of longevity drugs. All reports indicated that humans had never attained an unlimited life span; the lack of an overall immortality program was in fact the most definite indication that the Hub's civilization, in spite of its accomplishments in other fields, stood basically at a low level. Among themselves, the science of immortality in all its branches was held sacred, its study restricted to Palachs. Evidently it was at this point they decided Ticos might belong to a class of humanity which knew at least something about the Tuvelas. Earlier prisoners had been totally ignorant even of the existence of their anonymous rulers.

Ticos was puzzled at first by the new direction the interrogations were taking. He framed his replies very carefully in a manner designed to draw more revealing questions. Presently his concept of the Palachs' Tuvela Theory grew clear—and now he was able to suggest possibilities which seemed to confirm the worst fears of his inquisitors. He could claim convincingly that the specific information he had was quite limited, but the implications in what he said matched to a disturbing degree the blackest calculations made concerning the nature of Tuvelas. The majority of the Everliving connected with the expeditionary force found their faith in themselves again shaken. Endless bitter debates were unleashed between the opposed groups, while the Balance, temporarily at least, shifted toward the views of the Voice of Caution. The invasion was not actually called off, but all immediate attack plans were stalled for the time being.

Ticos meanwhile had been in an anxious quandary of his own. Nile's next scheduled visit was some weeks away; but she was bound to come then, and that he would have been able to persuade the Palachs to abandon the planet before she arrived seemed hardly possible. If he did nothing, she either would be killed out of hand as she came down from the air or captured and put to death in some very unpleasant manner. The Parahuans were not at all gentle with ordinary prisoners. As far as he knew, he was the only one picked up on Nandy-Cline who had lived more than a few days in their hands.

So he'd turned Nile into a Tuvela. It made one thing certain: the Palachs wouldn't kill her while they saw a chance of taking her alive—and knowing Nile as he did he felt that might very well give her an opportunity to escape into the forests. Parahuan scientists were studying the results of his longevity experiments; and he was allowed to go about the floatwood under guard at regular intervals to collect the materials he wanted. On such occasions he would deposit the significant information he had gathered where she should find it. After reading this report, she should do what she could to get away from the island and alert the planet. However, if she was captured, they might still be able to maintain the Tuvela bluff together and bring about a withdrawal of the alien forces. Success was questionable; but it was the best course he could suggest. . . .

Nile inhaled shakily, blinking at the knotted cloth

containing a Parahuan Palach. A *Great* Palach, she corrected herself. She'd better have her information well memorized in case events made it necessary to attempt to play the role of Tuvela Ticos had bestowed on her. Going by the descriptions he'd given of his principal interrogators, she thought she could even call this particular Great Palach by name.

She pursed her lips, thinking it over. She already had plans for escaping from the island presently, with Danrich Parrol's help. But the plans didn't make provision as yet for getting Ticos out, and she didn't intend to leave without him.

Besides, the general situation had evidently become one which could take an unpredictable turn at any time. The Everliving, already sufficiently overwrought as a result of Ticos' machinations, had tipped their hand in trying to take her alive and failing to do it. If they suspected she could get away from the island again and warn Nandy-Cline, it might stampede them into launching the overall attack immediately, before they lost the advantage of surprise. At best that would cost a great many human lives. . . .

Lives that would be saved if the aliens could be talked into withdrawing.

Nile's reflections checked there a moment. She didn't like the line they were taking—but the line was an inevitable one. As things had worked out, the Palachs had reason to believe that in her they were dealing with a genuine Tuvela. If Ticos had come close to persuading them to retreat from the planet, a genuine Tuvela should be able to finish the job.

But that meant putting herself voluntarily in the power of those creatures. And the thought was enough to dry her mouth. . . .

A chaquoteel whistled a dozen feet away, and Nile started violently, then cursed her jittering nerves. It hadn't been an alarm call. Nothing of significance to the chaquoteels, and therefore to her, had come near the sestran stand since she'd been sitting here.

She looked at the bundled Great Palach again. He was awake. There'd been occasional cautious stirrings under the cloth. One question was simply whether she could play the part of a Tuvela-Guardian well enough to keep the aliens deceived. The midget in there was a highly aggressive representative of the Voice of Action. If she could sell *him* the idea that Porad Anz was doomed if it persisted in challenging the Tuvelas, there was a good chance she could bluff the Everliving as a whole.

Why not find out?

She'd have to believe it herself first. Quit being Nile Etland and *be* a Tuvela. The more outrageously, the better. No small lies—big ones. Keep the creature surprised.

She moistened her lips, fished the tanglecord's release key from her pouch, placed her gun on the chunk of floatwood supporting the thicket. The tanglecord strips securing the cloth about the Parahuan came away at the touch of the key. She dropped them in the pouch, unknotted the cloth and drew it cautiously from the captive.

The atmosphere sections of the Parahuan's eyes were open. They watched her steadily. The tanglecord clamped about his arms and feet was tight and in place. Nile pulled the strip away from the vocal slit, set him upright against a clump of sestran, backed away eight or nine feet, and sat down, holding the gun loosely before her. She studied the alien for some seconds.

He didn't look too formidable, but Ticos' caution against underestimating Palachs of any grade probably was well founded. Their approach to immortality involved a progressive induced metamorphosis. The muscular structure became condensed and acquired extreme efficiency. Most of the thinking apparatus was buried inside the chunky torso; presumably it did not undergo physiological changes. Reduced to essentials, Ticos had said. Very well, she'd watch this Great Palach. . . .

What did he see in her? A Tuvela? Nile had a mental picture of herself—lean, next to naked, smeared with colorful plant sap. Hardly the most impressive image. But it couldn't be helped. She was a Guardian of the Federation of the Hub, a Tuvela. To him, she was gromgorru. A mysterious, powerful being, with information sources beyond her captive's knowledge. The last, at any rate, she had.

She said, "I believe I am addressing the Great Palach Koll."

The manikin stared a long moment. At last the vocal slit moved. "And I believe" a voice like golden velvet told her, "that I address a Hulon named Etland."

Hulon—Parahuan term signifying low-grade human. There'd been no suggestion of alien inflection in the words. They *had* studied humanity in patient detail.

"You have another name for us," the Tuvela said indifferently. "Call me Hulon if you wish. Where are you holding Dr. Cay at present?"

"Not far from here. What is your interest in Dr. Cay?"

"Our interest in Dr. Cay," Nile said, "is less than it was. He has not performed well in this test."

"Test?" Koll's voice had thinned. Nile regarded him a moment.

"Surely you must have wondered from time to time," she remarked, "why no one came here to inspect Dr. Cay's activities. Yes, a test. Not that it's your concern, Great Palach, but Dr. Cay was a candidate for the true-life. I'm not sure he will remain one. When we saw you had discovered him, we waited to observe how capably he would handle this unexpected situation. I'm disappointed in him."

Koll's vocal slit opened and closed silently twice. The Tuvela scowled absently.

"However, I'm more than disappointed in the Everliving," she resumed. "If you didn't find Dr. Cay sufficiently persuasive, very moderate intelligence alone should have told you to be long gone from here . . . and glad to be away! Haven't you felt the snare this world represents waiting about you? Has the Sacred Sea grown senile instead of immortal?"

She shrugged. A Tuvela, after all, was not greatly interested in the limitations of Porad Anz.

"You'll be told to go now," she stated. "You've been butchering the ones you call Hulons a little too freely. That disgusts me. It seems you fear even the human shape so much you revert to your animal beginnings when you meet it. We don't choose to see our people wasted— and Dr. Cay has had time enough to demonstrate his present lack of satisfactory potential."

Silence. Long silence. The sestran shrubs rustled. Wind roaring rose and ebbed in the distance. The air was darkening quickly. The wizened manikin sat motionless, staring.

Gromgorru, Nile thought. It had been weighing on both sides. It should weigh heavily on the Parahuans now. A Tuvela was about, an invisible ghost in the floatwood. It had plucked the Great Palach Koll from his grisly command post. Bear down on those fears. Yes, it might very well work. . . .

The velvet voice said suddenly, "I see and hear a creature lying in clever desperation to conceal its helplessness. You can't escape and you can't contact your kind. You did not come here to tell the Everliving they must leave. You're here because you were trapped."

Nile's lips curled. "The sken beam? If the technicians who examined my car understood what they saw, they must know I could have blocked such a device. And by the true-life, I believe I can play the hunting game against a mob of Oganoon and stupid animals! Great Palach Koll, Voice of Action—look around! Who is trapped here, and who is helpless?"

She leaned forward. "The stupidity of Porad Anz! It tampered with our worlds and was thrown out. All it learned was to look for allies before it tried to come back. No doubt you'd need allies—more than you can find. But you've already found too many to make the Great Plan possible! Even if we'd had no other methods of information, your secret was spread too far to remain a secret—"

She broke off. Koll was quivering. The vocal slit made spitting sounds.

"We'd been minded to spare you," the Tuvela began again. "But—"

"Guardian, be silent!" The voice was squeezed down to an angry whine. "Lies and tricks! The Everliving will not listen!"

The Tuvela laughed. "When I come to them with a Great Palach tied in a rag, dangling headdown from my belt, they won't listen?"

Koll squealed—and became a blur of rubbery motion.

The long legs swung up, brought the fettered feet to his shoulder. Something projected in that instant from the shoulder, a half-inch jet of fire. It touched the tanglecord, and the tanglecord parted. The webbed toes of one foot gripped one of the jewels on Koll's head, pulled it free. The other leg was beneath him again; it bent, straightened; and he came toward Nile in a long, one-legged hop, quick and balanced. The jewel-handled needle gripped in his foot leveled out. . . .

Nile was in motion herself by then, dropping back, rolling sideways—

The needle spat a thread of pink radiance along her flank as she triggered the UW.

And that was that. The UW's beam was hot, and Koll

was in mid-jump, moving fast, as it caught him. His lumpy
torso was very nearly cut in two.

Nile got up shakily, parted the sestran stems through
which he had plunged, and looked down from the
floatwood branch. Nothing but the waving, shadowy
greenery of the vertical jungle below . . . and no point
in hunting around for the body of the Great Palach down
there. Ticos had neglected to mention that the thick
Parahuan hide could be used to conceal an arsenal, but
after seeing the communicator Koll carried grafted to
himself, the possibility should have occurred to her.

Why had he attacked at that particular moment? She
hadn't convinced him Porad Anz faced destruction unless
the invading force withdrew—or else he had such a
seething hatred for mankind that the fate of his own race
was no longer of sufficient consideration. But apparently
she *had* convinced him that a majority of the Palachs
would accept what she said.

He should know, Nile thought. She'd lost her prisoner,
but the Great Palach Koll dead, silenced, vanished,
remained an impressive witness to the Tuvelas' capability
and stern ruthlessness.

Let the Everliving stew in the situation a while. She'd
give them indications presently that she was still around
the island. That should check any impulse to launch a
hasty military operation. Meanwhile she'd try to find out
where Ticos was held, and prepare to carry out other
plans . . . And now it was time to check with Sweeting
and learn what her water scouting had revealed.

Nile dropped quietly down out of the sestran thicket
to lower branches to avoid arousing the chaquoteels, and
slipped away into the forest.

Back down at the water's edge, she looked out from
a niche between two trunks at the neighboring island
section. It was the largest of the five connected forests,
a good half wider and longer than this one and lifting

at least a hundred yards farther into the air. From the car she'd seen thick clusters of a dark leafless growth rising higher still from a point near the forest's center, like slender flexible spear shafts whipping in the wind. Oilwood it was called. Weeks from now, when the island rode into the electric storm belts of the polar sea, the oilwood would draw lightning from the sky to let its combustible sheathing burn away and the ripened seeds beneath tumble down through the forest into the ocean.

Set ablaze deliberately tonight, it should provide a beacon to mark the island for Parrol and let him know where she was to be found.

The water between the two forests wasn't open. The submerged root system extended from one to the other; and on the roots grew the floatwood's aquatic symbiotes, pushing out from the central lagoon, though their ranks thinned as they approached the rush of the open sea. The Parahuans wouldn't have stopped hunting for her, and ambushes could easily be laid in that area. The sea south of the forest seemed to offer a safer crossing, now that evening darkened the sky and reduced surface visibility. The Meral Current carried weed beds: dense moving jungles which provided cover when needed.

Nile gave the otter caller on her wrist another turn. Sweeting should be here quickly. A receiver embedded in her skull transmitted the signals to her brain, and she homed in unerringly on the caller.

"Nile—"

"Over here, Sweeting!"

Sweeting came up out of the water twenty feet away, shook herself vigorously, rippled along the side of the floatwood bole and settled beside Nile.

"These are *new* bad guys!" she stated.

"Yes," said Nile. "New and bad. They don't belong on our world. What can you tell me about them?"

"Much," Sweeting assured her. "But found two Nile-friends. They tell you more."

"Two—" Nile broke off. In the surging sea five yards below, two dark whiskered heads had appeared on the surface, were looking up at her.

Wild otters.

Chapter 6

The wild otters were a mated pair who'd selected the floatwood lagoon as their private preserve. The male would nearly match Spiff in size. The female was young, a smaller edition of Sweeting. They might be three or four generations away from domestication, but they used translingue as readily as Sweeting and much in her style. Interspersed were unfamiliar terms based on their independent oceanic existence, expressing matters for which no human words had been available. Usually Nile could make out their sense.

When the Parahuans arrived, the curious otters had made a game of studying the unfamiliar creatures and their gadgetry. There was a ship anchored to the island under the floor of the lagoon. It was considerably bigger than the average human submersible, chunky and heavily built—evidently a spaceship. Its lock was always open on the water. A second ship, a huge one, was also in the vicinity. Normally it stayed deep in the sea, but at times it had moved up almost to the island. Ticos had said that the headquarters ship of the Parahuan expedition seemed to be accompanying this floatwood drift.

Above sea level the Parahuans had set up ten or twelve posts in the forest. Most of them were small, probably observation points or weapon emplacements. The exception was in the island section to which Nile wanted to go. "Big house," Sweeting said. It was set near the edge of the lagoon, extending well back into the floatwood and completely concealed by it. Perhaps a fifth of the structure was under water. Nile got the impression of something like a large blockhouse or fort, a few hundred yards beyond the rookery of the sea-havals. She wouldn't have selected the giant kesters as neighbors herself—the rookery was an evil-smelling and very noisy place—but alien senses might not find that disturbing.

The immediately important thing about the blockhouse was that it told her exactly where Ticos could be found, unless he'd been taken away after her arrival. He'd said his captors had shifted him and his equipment to such a structure and described its location.

The wild otters knew nothing of Ticos, but they did know about the tarm. When the Parahuans first came, there'd been two of the pale monsters in the lagoon from time to time. One of them evidently had been taken away again shortly afterward. The description they gave of the other one matched that of the records. It was an aggressive beast which fed heavily on sea life and made occasional forays into upper forest levels.

"Have you had any trouble with it?" Nile asked.

The question seemed to surprise them. Then they gave her the silent otter laugh, jaws open.

"No trouble. Tarm's *slow!*" Sweeting's small kinswoman explained.

"Slow for you," Nile said. Hunting otters had their own notions about water speed. "Could I keep away from it in the water?"

They considered.

"Jets, heh?" the big male asked.

"Sadly, no jets!" Sweeting made a stroking motion with her forelegs, flipped hind feet up briefly. "Human swim . . ."

"Human swim! Tarm thing eat you!" the female told Nile decisively. "You hide, keep no-smell, Nile! How do the no-smell? Trick, heh?"

"Uh-huh. A trick. But it won't work in the water."

The male grunted reflectively. "Tarm's back under big house. Might stay, might not." He addressed the female. "Best poison-kill it soon?"

Poison-killing, it developed, involved a contraption put together of drift weed materials—hollow reeds and thorns chewed to fit the hollows and smeared with exceedingly poisonous yellow bladder gum. Wild otter tribes had developed the device to bring down flying kesters for a change of diet. The female demonstrated, rolling over on her back, holding an imaginary hole-stock to her mouth and making a popping noise through her lips. "Splash come kester!" They'd modified the technique to handle the occasional large predators who annoyed them too persistently—larger thorns, jammed directly through the hide into the body. Big sea animals didn't die as quickly as the fliers, but they died.

"Many thorns here," the male assured Nile. "Stick in ten, twenty, and the tarm no trouble."

She studied him thoughtfully. Sweeting could count . . . but these were wild otters. Attempts had been made to trace the original consignment of laboratory-grown cubs to its source. But the trail soon became hopelessly lost in the giant intricacies of Hub commerce; and no laboratory was found which would take responsibility for the development of a talking otter mutant. The cubs which had reached Nandy-Cline seemed to be the only members of the strain in existence.

For all practical purposes then, this was a new species, and evidently it was less than fifty years old. In that time it had progressed to the point of inventing workable dart blowguns and poisoned daggers. It might have an interesting future. Nile thought she knew the yellow bladder gum to which they referred. It contained a very fast acting nerve poison. What effect it would have on a creature with the tarm's metabolism couldn't be predicted, but the idea seemed worth trying.

She asked further questions, gathered they'd seen

the tarm motionless under the blockhouse only minutes before Sweeting got the first caller signal. It was the creature's usual station as water guard of the area. Evidently it had been withdrawn from the hunt for the Tuvela. Groups of Parahuans were moving about in the lagoon, but there was no indication they were deployed in specific search patterns. . . .

"Waddle-feet got jets," remarked the male.

"Slow jets," said the female reassuringly. "No trouble!"

But armed divers in any kind of jet rigs could be trouble in open water. Nile shrugged mentally. She could risk the crossing. She nodded at the dark outlines of the distant forest section.

"I've got to go over there," she said. "Sweeting will come along. The waddle-feet have guns and are looking for me. You want to come too?"

They gave her the silent laugh again, curved white teeth gleaming in the dusk.

"Nile-friends," stated the male. "We'll come. Fun, heh? What we do, Nile? Kill the waddle-feet?"

"If we run into any of them," said Nile, "we kill the waddle-feet fast!"

A few minutes later the three otters slipped down into a lifting wave and were gone. Nile glanced about once more before following. A narrow sun-rim still clung to the horizon. Overhead the sky was clear—pale blue with ghostly cluster light shining whitely through. High-riding cloud banks to the south reflected magenta sun glow. Wind force was moderate. Here in the lee of the forest she didn't feel much of it. The open stretch of sea ahead was broken and foaming, but she'd be moving below the commotion.

In these latitudes the Meral produced its own surface illumination. She saw occasional gleams flash and disappear among the tossing waves—colonies of light organisms responding to the darkening air. But they wouldn't give enough light to guide her across. Time to shift to her night eyes. . . .

She brought a pack of dark-lenses from the pouch, fitted two under her lids, blinked them into position: a gel, adjusting itself automatically to varying conditions for optimum human vision. An experimental Giard product, and a very good one.

She pulled the breather over her face, fitted the audio plugs to her ears, and flicked herself off the floatwood. Sea shadow closed about her, cleared in seconds to amber half-light as the dark-lenses went into action. Fifteen feet down, Nile turned and stroked into open water.

Open but not empty. A moving weed thicket ahead and to the right . . . Nile circled about it, a school of small skilts; darting past, brushing her legs with tiny hard flicks. She brought her left wrist briefly before her eyes, checked the small compass she'd fastened to it, making sure of her direction. The otters weren't in view. If the crossing was uneventful, she shouldn't see much of them. They were to stay about a hundred feet away, one of the wild pair on either side, Sweeting taking the point, to provide early warning of approaching danger.

A cloud of light appeared presently ahead; others grew dimly visible beyond it . . . pink, green, orange. The Shining Sea was the name the sledmen gave the Meral as it rolled here down the southern curve of the globe toward the pole. Nile began to pass thickets in which the light-bearers clustered. Each species produced its own precise shade of waterfire. None were large; the giants among them might be half the length of her forearm, narrow worm bodies. But their swarms turned acres of the subsurface to flame.

The fins moved her on steadily. She listened to the sea through the audios, sensed its changing vibrations against her skin. Amber dimness of open water for a while; then she went turning and twisting through a soggy dark forest of weed. Beyond it, light glowed again. She avoided the brightest areas—too easy to be spotted there.

Sweeting came to her once, circled about, was gone, a flicking shadow. Not an alarm report; the otter had checked on her position.

Then there was a sound which momentarily overrode the myriad other sounds of the Meral. A deep, distant booming. Half a minute later it was repeated. Closer now.

Nile held her course but moved toward the surface, scanning the areas below and ahead of her. The giant sea-havals were hunting. An encounter with one of the great creatures in the open sea ordinarily brought no risk to a human swimmer or, in fact, to anything but a sizable skilt. Sea-havals hunted by scent and sight; and skilts were their only prey. But when they made that sound, they were driving a major school. To avoid accidents, it was best to keep well out of the way of such a school. . . .

If possible, Nile added mentally.

And there came the first indications of trouble!

A dozen big torpedo shapes hurtled toward her, coming from a line of light-thickets ahead. Skilts—approximately in the three hundred pound class. Preferred size for a sea-haval.

Nile checked, moved quickly to the side, lifted farther toward the surface near enough to feel the tugging surge of the swells—

The sea boomed like the stroke of a tremendous bell.

And the string of light-thickets exploded as the van of the skilt school bulleted through them. Coming at her in a straight line. They were harmless creatures in themselves, but their panic, speed and weight made them deadly now. The impact of any of them would break her body apart. And the sea seemed an onrushing mass of thousands.

The scene was blotted from Nile's vision as she broke the surface. She rolled herself into a tight ball. There was nothing else she could do. A great wave lifted her. Then came a vast, thudding sensation from below, streaming past, a racing river which threatened to drag her down. Skilts exploded from the sea in frantic thirty foot leaps all about, came smashing back to the surface. Then two final tremendous surges of the water beneath her. A pair of sea-havals had gone past.

Sweeting was there an instant later. The wild otters arrived almost as promptly.

"Nile here, heh? . . . Fun, heh?"

Nile had no comments. She'd pulled off the breather, was gulping long lungfuls of storm air. Dim and remote, more sensed by her nerves than heard, came an echo of the sea-havals' booming. The hunt had moved on.

Moments later, she and the otters were underway again. For the next two hundred yards, weed beds were ripped and shredded by the passage of the fleeing school. Cleanly sectioned skilts, chopped by the big kesters, drifted about. Then things began to look normal. . . .

Suddenly Sweeting was back, moving past Nile's face in a swirl of water, dropping a dozen feet, checking to turn, turning again and gliding toward a great limp tangle of weeds below her. Nile followed instantly in a spurt of speed. *Come fast!* was what that had meant.

She slipped into the rubbery slickness of the thicket. The otter was there, waiting. Far enough, apparently. . . . Nile turned, took out the UW, parted the weeds enough to see anything coming toward her. When she glanced aside again, Sweeting was gone.

She waited. A light-thicket hung twenty yards to her left; about her was dimness. Small skilt shadows slipped past, and something big and chunky drifted up, slowly turning head-on as it came opposite her to stare in at her among the weeds. It paused, moved off. A large weed skilt, perhaps three times the weight of the

maddened projectiles which had made up the school.
A carrion eater by preference. It should do well in the
wake of the sea-havals' hunt tonight—

Abrupt violent commotion—swirling of water, lifting
and sinking of the weed fronds, thudding sensations
which suddenly stopped. . . . Nile knew the pattern of
an underwater death fight; and this had been one, not
many yards away. It was over now. She slipped forward,
gun held out, peering up. Dark smoky veils floated down
and something bulky came settling through them, grazing the weed tangle. The Parahuan's head seemed nearly
detached from the squat body, blood pumping out
through the gashes. Typical otter work.

Sweeting reappeared from above. Together they hauled
the unwieldy thing by its harness straps into the weeds.
Fastened to the broad back was the Parahuan version of
a jet rig. Nile studied it a moment, gave up the notion
of converting the device to her own use; she would lose
more time over that than it should take her to get back
into the floatwood. They left the big rubbery body
wedged in the center of the tangle. As they turned away,
the first scavenging weed skilt was nosing up toward it
from the other side.

A hissing had begun in the audio pickup and was
growing louder. Nile halted Sweeting in the trailing
fringes of the thicket. Then two other bulky figures
were slanting down swiftly through open water toward
them, trailed by thin jet tracks. The Parahuans' guns
were in their hands. Possibly they had picked up traces
of the brief commotion and were looking for their
dead companion. At any rate, they were hardly twenty-
five feet away when Nile saw them, and their faces
were turned toward her, semicircular water eyes staring. The UW couldn't miss on such targets, and didn't.

The immediate vicinity of a sea-haval rookery at
night was not for the nervous. Monstrous rumblings

and splashings came from within the floatwood walls surrounding it, as the adult kesters left the rookery by a diving hole hacked through the forest's subsurface root floor, returned presently, beak-spears holding up to a ton of mangled skilts, to be greeted by the roars of their gigantic young.

Upwind of the racket, on the lagoon side, Nile finished recoating herself and her equipment with buti sap. She was down among the massive boles near the water, waiting for Sweeting to return and report. While they were dealing with three members of the Parahuan sea patrol, the wild otters had found and dispatched another three. That seemed to have left no survivors. But the patrol should have been missed by now; and what she did next would depend at least in part on what the Parahuans were doing as a result.

The tarm had been found still at its station beneath the blockhouse. Nile was thankful for that. The sudden near-encounter in the other forest with the pallid sea thing had rammed fear deep into her nerves; the thought of it hadn't been far from her mind since. The early reports that the Parahuans might have developed the monsters out of their own kind somehow made the tarm more horrible. After seeing what their biological skills had done in creating the form of a Great Palach, Nile thought it was possible. She told herself the buti and reasonable caution would keep the creature from noticing her if she met it again, but she wasn't at all sure of that. And the buti would be no protection if it came near her in the water.

Her wild allies might presently free her of that particular fear. They'd gone to get a supply of the poisoned thorns and seemed confident that in the underwater tangle of floatwood beneath the blockhouse they could plant a lethal dose into the tarm's huge body without too much trouble. Sweeting was prowling the lagoon, looking for signs of alien activity there or in the forest near Nile.

"Found Tikkos, Nile!"

"Where?"

Sweeting slipped up along the bough out of the lagoon, crouched beside her. "In boat," she said. "With little waddle-feet."

"*Little* waddle-feet?" Palachs?

"Half-size," said Sweeting. "Five, six. Tikkos talking to Guardian Etland. Then waddle-feet talking to Guardian Etland. Loud-voice. You Guardian Etland, heh?"

"The waddle-feet think so." Loud-voice was a loud-speaking device. "Let's get this straight! First, where's the boat Ticos and the waddle-feet are in?"

The otter's nose indicated the eastern end of the forest. "Boat's coming into lagoon. Coming this way. Got lights. Got loud-voice. Talking to forest. They think Guardian Etland's in forest. Tikkos say waddle-feet talk, not fight. You talk and maybe they go away. Waddle-feet say they sorry about fighting. No guns in boat. You come talk, please." Sweeting paused, watching her. "Kill them, get Tikkos now, heh?"

"No," Nile said. "No, we don't kill them. I'd better hear what they have to say. You say the boat's coming in this direction—"

"Coming slow. You don't listen to waddle-feet, Nile! Trick, heh? You come close, they kill you."

"It may not be a trick. Stay here."

But she felt shaky as she climbed quickly back into the forest toward the sea-haval rookery. The theoretical Tuvela, totally self-confident, certainly would be willing to talk to the aliens at this point, press the psychological advantage she'd gained. On the other hand, the Tuvela presumably would know what to do if it turned out she'd stepped into a Parahuan trap. Nile wasn't sure she would know what to do.

She caught her breath briefly as the wind backed up and assorted rookery stenches billowed around her. Far enough from the lagoon. . . . She opened the pouch, took out the roll of tanglecord, added the otter caller to the other items, closed the pouch and shoved it into one of the fins, the buti stick into the other. She taped the fins together. They made a compact package which she wedged into a floatwood niche and secured further with tanglecord, leaving the roll stuck to the package. She was keeping the climb-belt and the UW.

She looked around a moment, memorizing the place, started back to the lagoon. Sweeting was hissing with alarm and disapproval when she got there. Nile calmed the otter, explained the situation as well as she could. The boat lights hadn't yet appeared around the curve of the forest to the east. They set off in that direction, Nile moving through the floatwood not far from the edge of the lagoon, Sweeting in the water slightly ahead of her. If a trap had been laid, they should spot it between them before they were in it. . . .

Going by Ticos' descriptions, the six Parahuans in the boat with him were Palachs. Concealed at a point some fifty feet above the water, Nile looked them over. Two were about his size; four ranged down from there, though none came near the midget level. In the boat lights they displayed odd headgears and elaborate harness arrangements . . . and, of course, they might be carrying concealed weapons.

She studied Ticos more carefully than his companions. There was a stiffness in the way he moved which showed he wasn't in good physical condition. But his amplified voice was clear; and if his phrasing had more than a suggestion of obsequiousness about it, that fitted the role he was playing: an inferior addressing the Guardian. A role of his own choosing; not one he had been forced to assume.

She was convinced that so far there was no trap. But there were other considerations. . . .

The loudspeaker began booming about her again. It was set to penetrate high and deep into the forest, overriding the surging winds, to reach the attention of the Guardian Etland wherever she might be. Ticos and one of the Palachs used it alternately. The others squatted about the boat as it moved slowly through the lagoon along the forest.

The message was repetitious. She'd been listening to it for the past few minutes, keeping pace with the boat. Her talk with the Great Palach Koll had been monitored by the Everliving. The transmitting device presumably had been another of the jewels fixed to Koll's head; and the idea might have been Koll's—to let the other Great Palachs and Palachs follow his interrogation of the captured human, witness the collapse of her pretensions as Guardian and Tuvela. If so, the plan had backfired. Everything said, the fact that Koll was the prisoner, the Tuvela's evident knowledge of Porad Anz's secrets, was designed to further undermine the Everliving's confidence. It explained Koll's sudden furious attack. He felt she had to be silenced then and there to preserve the goals of the Voice of Action. Oganoon trackers had found his body an hour later.

Nile gathered that the ranks of the Everliving had been in turmoil since. The loss of the sea patrol did nothing to calm them. They didn't suspect she had nonhuman assistants, so it appeared to them that the patrol had encountered the Tuvela on her way over from the other forest and that she'd wiped it out single-handedly before it could get out an alarm. Then a short while ago they'd begun getting reports that a small fast surface vessel was maneuvering elusively about the Drift—the Sotira sleds had kept their promise to provide her with a message courier. The Everliving naturally associated the presence of the ship with that of the Tuvela. But they didn't know what its purpose was. . . .

They'd been under psychological pressure since she'd first avoided what had seemed inevitable capture. With each move she'd made thereafter the pressure increased. That the moves were forced on her they didn't realize. All of it would seem part of the Tuvela's developing plan . . . a plan they didn't understand and seemed unable to check. They didn't know to what it would lead. Fears they'd nourished and fought down for over half a century fed heavily on them again.

So they, the proud Palachs of Porad Anz, had sent out Dr. Ticos Cay and a delegation of the Voice of Caution to offer the Tuvela a cessation of hostilities and the opportunity to present the Guardians' terms to them in person. No doubt some of Koll's adherents remained ragingly opposed to the move.

Could she risk talking to them?

As things stood, she had a very good chance of getting away from here presently. Then she could warn her kind that there was an enemy among them and that they must prepare for attack. If she walked into the enemy's camp and couldn't maintain the Tuvela bluff, she'd have thrown away the chance. If Ticos had understood that, he mightn't be urging her now to reveal herself.

But if she didn't respond and remained concealed, the pressure on the Everliving wouldn't let down. They'd interpret silence to mean that they were no longer being offered an opportunity to withdraw. How would they react? They might feel it was too late to attempt retreat. They'd had many weeks to prepare the strike against Nandy-Cline from their hidden floatwood bases. If they decided to launch it before countermoves began, how long would it be before space weapons lashed out at the mainland? Hours? Her warning would come too late in that case.

The real question might be whether she could risk *not* talking to them.

Abruptly, Nile made up her mind.

The Parahuan boat came slowly around the curve of
the forest. The loudspeaker began to shout again. After
a few words it stopped. The Palach Moga, standing beside
Ticos Cay, lowered the instrument carefully and turned
it off with an air of preferring to make no sudden moves.
There was a burst of sibilant whisperings behind Ticos.
They ceased. The boat's engines cut out and it drifted
up against a tangle of lagoon weeds. The man and the
six aliens stared at the motionless figure standing at the
forest's edge ten yards away.

The Tuvela's voice said crisply, "Dr. Cay!"

Ticos cleared his throat. "Yes, Guardian?"

"Have that craft brought over here and introduce the
Parahuan officers to me—"

Stepping down into the boat was like crossing the
threshold of a grotesque dream. They stood erect on
long legs, abandoning the natural posture of their kind,
balanced not too certainly on broad feet. Parahuan
heads inclined in obeisance to the Guardian as Ticos
introduced them in turn. She knew the names of the
Palach Moga and one of the others from his report.
Along with half a dozen Great Palachs, Moga was the
most influential member of the Voice of Caution. He
retained his place beside Ticos. The others stood well
to the back of the boat as it turned out again into the
lagoon.

Moga spoke briefly into a communicator, said to Nile,
"The Everliving are assembling to hear the Guardian. . . ."

She didn't ask where they were assembling. A
Tuvela would show no concern for such details. An
angry whistling came for an instant from farther out
in the lagoon. Sweeting still didn't approve of this
move.

The sound seemed to jar all along Nile's nerves. She
was frightened; and knowing that now of all times she
couldn't afford to be frightened simply was making it that

much worse. For moments her thoughts became a shifting blur of anxieties. She tried to force them back to what she would say to the Everliving, to anticipate questions to which she must have answers. It didn't work too well. But the physical reactions faded gradually again.

Stocky Oganoon figures, weapons formally displayed, lined the sides of the water-level entrance to the block-house. The boat moved a few yards along a tunnel, was moored to a platform. She followed Moga up into the structure. Ticos stayed a dozen steps behind, effacing himself, playing his own role. After the introductions, she hadn't spoken to him. On the next level, she realized he was no longer following.

The Palach Moga paused before a closed door.

"If the Guardian will graciously wait here . . . I will see that the Assembly is prepared. . . . "

Nile waited. After moments the door reopened and the Palach emerged. He carried something like a jeweled handbag slung by a long strap over one shoulder. Nile had the impression he was ill at ease.

"If the Guardian permits . . . There are Great Palachs beyond this door. They are unarmed. They would prefer it if the Guardian did not address them with a weapon at her hand."

If she couldn't convince them, Nile thought, she would die behind that door. But a Tuvela would not need to draw courage from a gun at this stage—and the UW by itself was not going to get her back past the clusters of guards in the passages behind them. She unclipped the holster from her belt, held it out. Moga placed it carefully in the bag and drew open the door. Nile went inside.

For a moment she had the impression of being in the anteroom to a great, dimly lit hall—too large a hall by far to be part of this structure in the floatwood. Then she knew that the whole opposite wall of the room was

a viewscreen. There were upward of a dozen Great
Palachs in the room with her, squatting along the wall
to either side . . . creatures not much larger than Koll,
in richly colored stiff robes and an assortment of equally
colorful hats. The remainder of the Everliving, Palachs
and Great Palachs of all degrees, were arranged in rows
along the hall, which must be a section of the headquarters ship below the sea. Shallow water shifted and
gleamed here and there among the rows. Motionless and
silent, the massed amphibians stared up at her from the
dimness.

Nile heard the door through which she had come
close quietly at her back. And curiously, with the tiny
click her uncertainties were gone. A cool light clarity
seemed to settle on her mind, every thought and
emotion falling into place. . . . She discovered she had
moved forward and was standing in the center of the
chamber, facing the big screen.

Selecting her words with chilled precision, the Tuvela
began to speak.

Chapter 7

The outstanding feature of the big room in the blockhouse structure the Parahuans had assigned Ticos Cay
as his working laboratory was its collection of living
specimens. The floatwood island's life forms lined three
of the walls and filled long shelf stands in between.
Neatly labeled and charted, they perched on or clung
to their original chunks of floatwood, stood rooted in
the pockets of forest mold or in victimized life forms
in which they had been found, floated in lagoon water,
clustered under transparent domes. They varied from
the microscopic to inhis organisms with a thirty foot
spread. For the most part, they were in biological

stasis—metabolism retarded by a factor of several million, balance maintained by enzyme control and a variety of other checks. Proper handling would otherwise have been impossible.

The Guardian was able to find little fault with the progress Dr. Cay had made in his work projects. "In this respect you have not done badly," she acknowledged, for the benefit of whatever ears might be listening. She tapped the charts he'd offered for her inspection and dropped them into the file he'd taken them from. "It's disappointing, however, that it became necessary at last for me to intervene directly in a matter we had expected you to handle without our assistance."

"Given more time, I might have done it!" Ticos remonstrated humbly. "I was opposed by a number of intractable beings, as you know."

"I do know—having encountered one of those beings. But it was hardly a question of time. The issues were clear. If they had been presented with clarity, a rational majority of our uninvited guests would have drawn the correct conclusions and acted on them. We must count this a failure. You needn't let it concern you unduly. The excellent thoroughness of your work on the basic assignment, under somewhat limiting conditions, will offset the failure, at least in part."

Ticos mumbled his gratitude, went back with evident relief to additional explanations about his project. Nile checked her watch.

Forty-two minutes since she'd been escorted with careful courtesy from the assembly chamber to the lab and left there with Ticos. No word from the Everliving since then, and the Palach Moga hadn't shown up with her gun. Good sign or bad? While she was talking to them, she'd almost *been* a Tuvela. She'd blasted them! She'd felt exalted. There'd been no questions. The Great Palachs closest to her in the chamber had edged farther back to the walls before she was done, stirred nervously again whenever she shifted a glance in their direction.

Afterward, brief sharp letdown. No Tuvela, no Guardian. Simply a scared human in a potentially very bad spot, with much too much at stake. If she'd fumbled this in any way, made the slightest slip—

Now she was somewhere between those states, back to normal, worried enough but again busily balancing possibilities, planning as much as could be planned here.

One of the factors she'd been considering was this room itself. It was long, wide, high, located somewhere near the top of the overall structure—she'd come up another level after leaving the chamber. It had a door at either end, probably locked now. The last could make no real difference since there was bound to be a gaggle of armed Oganoon outside each door to make sure the Guardian and her scientist didn't walk out on the conference. From the door at the left a raised walkway led to a platform some four feet above the floor near the center of the room. The Palachs, Ticos had explained, customarily stood there when they'd come to have dealings with him. Lighting came from conductor rods in ceiling and walls, primitive but efficient. Ventilation arrangements, while equally simple, met the lab's requirements perfectly. There was a large shadowy rectangle enclosed in a grid up on one of the walls just below the ceiling. Behind the grid was an unseen window, a rectangular opening in the wall. The salty-moist many-scented freshness of the floatwood forest swirled constantly about them. Enclosed without it, many of Ticos' research specimens would have died in days. But the storm gusts which occasionally set the blockhouse structure quivering were damped out at the window, and almost no sound came through.

So the shadowy rectangle was a force screen. It would let out no light, and certainly it was impenetrable to solid objects such as a human body. The screen controls must be outside the room, or Ticos would have indicated them to her. But there was a knobby protrusion on either side of the grid which enclosed the rectangle. And beneath those protrusions were the screen generators. . . .

Which brought up the matter of tools, and weapons or items which could serve as weapons. Her UW would be hard to replace in either capacity. But one could make do. Ticos had left a small cutter-sealer on the central worktable back of them. A useful all-around gadget, and one that could turn into a factor here. Another potential factor was the instrument studded with closely packed rows of tiny push-buttons, which Ticos carried attached to his belt and through which he regulated various internal balances and individual environmental requirements of his specimens.

The only obvious weapons around were the guns in the hands of three Parahuan guards who squatted stolidly in two feet of water in the partitioned end of the room at the right. From the platform, Nile had looked in briefly across the dividing wall at them. Two were faced toward the wall; one was faced away toward a long table near the second exit. None of them moved while she studied them. But they looked ready to act instantly. The guns appeared to be heavy-duty short-range blasters, made to be used by hands four times larger than hers. On the table stood Ticos Cay's communicator.

The guns weren't factors, except as they could become negative ones. But with a Sotira racing sled moving within close-contact band reach, the communicator was a very large factor. The Everliving in their nervous ambivalence had decreed it should be available at a moment's notice in case they were forced to open emergency negotiations with the Tuvelas through Dr. Cay. The guards were there to blast death into anybody who attempted to use it under any other circumstances.

Ticos Cay himself was, of course, an important

factor. Physically he could become a heavy liability if matters didn't develop well. He'd lost his wiry bounciness; be was a damaged old man. His face looked drawn tight even when he smiled. He'd been holding pain out of his awareness for weeks; but as an organism he'd been afflicted with almost intolerable strains and had begun to drift down towards death. Of course be knew it.

Mentally he didn't seem much impaired. His verbal responses might be a trifle slowed but not significantly. Nile thought she still could depend on him for quick and accurate reaction, as she might have to do. Because the final factor in the calculation here was Ticos Cay's collection of floatwood life. On the worktable, next to the cutter-sealer she'd mentally earmarked, lay several objects like hard-shelled wrinkled gray fruits, twice the size of her fist. Ticos had taken them out of a container to explain the purpose they were to serve in his research, left them lying there.

They were called wriggler apples and the shells showed they had ripened. The thing to know about ripe wriggler apples was that they remained quiescent until they received the specific environmental stimulus of contact with salt water. At that moment they split open. And the wrigglers came out. . . .

At best, the apples were a dubious research item. And they were not at all the only specimens in that category here. At a rough estimate, one in fifty of the life forms which cluttered the shelf stands and walls had caused Nile to flinch inwardly at first glimpse or whiff of identifying odor. Floatwood stuff she'd been conditioned against almost since she was big enough to walk. It wasn't all small or unobtrusive. Dominating the center of the room was a great purple-leafed inhis, the pale blue petals of its pseudoflowers tightly furled. A rarity, to no one's regret. In the forests, Nile wouldn't have come willingly within thirty feet of one. By classification it was a plant form. A vegetable, with lightning reactions. The sledmen, with good reason, had named it the Harpooneer. For some weeks it had loomed above and just behind the Palachs who had come and squatted on the platform, staring down at the human prisoner. . . .

It was dormant now, as were most of the other unreliable specimens—totally innocuous, metabolism slowed to a timeless pulse. In biological stasis. It would remain innocuous until it was given the precise measured stimulus, massive enzyme jolt or whatever, that broke the stasis.

And who could produce such stimuli? Why, to be sure, Dr. Cay with his push-button control device. He'd made certain that when it came time to die, he should have the means of taking some of the enemy with him.

Which might not be a detached scientific attitude but was certainly a very human one. . . .

Nile flicked another glance at her watch. Forty-three and a half minutes.

The door at the left clanged open.

The Palach Moga came first along the walkway. The bag into which the UW had disappeared swayed at his side, its strap slung over his shoulder. That detail might have been reassuring if the group behind him had looked less like an execution squad.

Nile stood with her back to the worktable, feeling tensions surge up and trying to show nothing. Ticos gave her an uncertain, questioning look, then turned and moved off slowly along the table, stopping a dozen feet away to watch the Parahuans. The fingers of his right hand fiddled absently with the control device. Moga was approaching the central platform in his grotesquely dainty upright walk, webbed feet placed carefully for each step. Two Oganoon guards came behind him, staring at Nile, massive short-barreled guns held ready for action. Two unfamiliar Palachs followed, moving in an uncompromising Parahuan waddle. Their strap harnesses were an identical crimson; and each carried two sizable handweapons, one on either side, grips turned forward. Another pair of guards concluded the procession. These had their guns slung across their backs and held items like folded black nets. A fifth guard had stopped inside the door, which had closed again after the party passed through. He had another kind of gun with a long narrow barrel, attached to a chunky tripod. He set the tripod down with a thump on the walkway, squatted behind it. The gun muzzle swung around and pointed at Nile.

She didn't move. She'd given them some reason not to trust her.

The group reached the platform, spread out. Moga stood near the platform's edge. The red-harnessed Palachs flanked him, hands clamped on their gun grips. The guards with the guns took up positions to either side of the Palachs. The guards with the black nets remained a little to the rear, at the left side of the platform. There were, Nile thought, indications of as much nervous tenseness as she was able to make out in a Parahuan visage—silently writhing speech slits, blinking atmosphere eyes. And all eyes were fixed on her, on the Tuvela. Nobody looked at Ticos Cay.

"Guardian, I shall speak first for myself," Moga's voice said suddenly.

Nile didn't answer. The voice resumed. "I am in great fear for Porad Anz. . . . When you agreed to address the Everliving, I was certain that your mission would succeed and that the Balance would shift to reason. And the response of the Assembly was strongly favorable. Your logic was persuasive. But there has been an unforeseen development. By violence the Voice of Action has assumed control of our forces. It is against all custom, an unprecedented Violation of Rules—but that appears to be no longer important. Here, on the

Command Ship and elsewhere on this world, many Great Palachs and Palachs lie dead. Those who survive have submitted to the Voice of Action which now alone speaks for the Everliving. I have come to inform you of what has been decreed. And having spoken for myself, I shall speak now with the words of the Voice of Action."

Silence.

The group on the platform remained tautly motionless. Nile watched them; they stared at her. So the redharnessed Palachs represented the Voice of Action. . . . The thought came suddenly that these must be very courageous creatures. They'd entered the laboratory to confront a legend. They were braving gromgorru. They waited now to see what the Tuvela might do in response to Moga's statement.

The Tuvela also stayed silent and motionless.

The Palach to Moga's right began speaking abruptly in a series of fluctuating Parahuan hootings, eyes fixed on Nile. After perhaps half a minute he stopped. Moga promptly began to translate.

"Whatever you call yourself, you are a Tuvela. We know this now. You have threatened Porad Anz in the name of your kind. That cannot be tolerated. You have told us that in any hostile encounter with the Guardians the Everliving must be defeated. Once and for all, that lie shall now be disproved. . . . "

Moga's voice ended. The red-harnessed Palach spoke again. His fellow turned his head for an instant, addressed the two Oganoon holding the nets. The two took the nets from their arms, shook them out. Black straps dangled from their rims. . . .

Moga took up the translation.

"The Voice of Action offers you and Dr. Cay the death of Palachs. It is painful but honorable. If you accept, you will submit to being enclosed by the confinement nets. If you attempt to resist, you will be shot down and die here like Hulons. In either case, Tuvela, your defeat and death signal the beginning of the hour of our attack on your world. And now, if it is within the power of a Tuvela to defy our purpose, show what you can do."

Beyond the group, the Parahuan at the door sagged silently forward over the gun, head and upper body obscured by the curling green fog lifting from a specimen on the wall beside him. The armed guards on the platform had pointed their guns at Nile. The red-harnessed Palachs drew their weapons. A dozen or so of the Harpooneer's pseudoflowers behind the platform quivered and unfurled in a flick of motion like great yellow-blue eyes blinking open. Nile dropped flat.

There had been at least two guns aimed directly at her in that instant; and fast as the Harpooneer was, it might not be fast enough to keep the guns from going off.

They didn't go off. There were other sounds instead. Something landed with a thump on the floor not far away. With a brief shock of surprise her mind recorded the bag Moga had been carrying. She was coming back up on her feet by then, scooped two of the gray-shelled wriggler apples from the worktable, lobbed them across the partitioning wall into the flooded section of the room. She heard them splash. A detached part of her awareness began counting off seconds. She looked around.

They were dead up there, nervous systems frozen, unlidded double-lensed eyes staring hugely. Embedded in their backs were bone-white spikes, tipping the thick coiled tendrils extended from the pseudoflowers. Four still stood swaying, transfixed, long legs stretched out rigidly. Three had been lifted from the platform, were being drawn over to the Harpooneer. Nile upended Moga's bag, shook out the UW, had it clipped to her climb-belt as the part of her mind that was counting seconds reached thirty and stopped. There'd been a few violent splashings from beyond the partition, but she heard nothing now. Ticos, holding the control device in both hands, face taut and white, gave her a quick nod.

The climb-belt was at half-weight as she reached the partition wall. She jumped, clapped her hands to the top, went up and over.

Seven years before, she'd seen a wriggler swarm hit a human diver. It was largely a matter of how close one happened to be to the apple when it tumbled down out of the floatwood forest, struck salt water and split. In the same moment thousands of tiny writhing black lines spilled from it and flashed unerringly toward any sizable animal bodies in the immediate vicinity, striking like a cluster of needle drills, puncturing thick hide or horny scales in instants.

The three guards lay face down, partly submerged, in the water that covered the floor. Two were motionless. The third quivered steadily, something like a haze of black fur still extending along his torso below the surface. All three were paralyzed now, would be dead in minutes as the swarms spread through them, feeding as they went.

And the passage was safe for Nile. The wrigglers were committed.

She reached the stand with Ticos' communicator on it, flipped switches, turned dials, paused an instant to steady her breath.

"Sotira-Doncar!" she said into the speaker then. "Sotira-Doncar! *Parahuans here! Parahuans here!*" And cut off the communicator.

No time to wait for a reply. No time at all—

"Can you needle the stink-fogs into action?"

"Of course. But—"

"Hit them!" Nile drew the climb-belt tight around his waist, clipped the UW to the top of her trunks. "If we can get out, we'll be out before it hurts us."

Ticos glanced up at the force-screened window

oblong, grunted dubiously. "Hope you're right!" His finger tapped a control. "They're hit. Now?"

Nile bent, placed her hands together. "Foot up! Try to keep your balance. You're minim-weight—you'll go up fast. Latch on to the grid and drop me the belt. I think I can make it to your ankles."

She put all her strength into the heave. He did go up fast, caught the grid and hooked an arm through it. The climb-belt floated back down. Greasy clouds boiled about the aroused stink-fogs near the entrance door on the left as Nile snatched the belt out of the air and fastened it around herself. Ticos was hanging by both hands now, legs stretched down. She sprang, sailed up along the wall, gripped his ankles and swarmed up him, the antigrav field again enclosing both of them. Moments later she'd worked her knees over a grid bar, had the belt back around Ticos. Breathing hard, he pulled himself up beside her and reached for the control device.

"Fogging up down there, all right!" he wheezed. "Can't see the door. Might alert a few more monsters, eh?"

"Any you can without killing us." Somebody outside the room *must* know by now that the execution plans had hit a snag. Clinging by knees and left hand, Nile placed the UW's muzzle against one of the grid casings that should have a force screen generator beneath it, held the trigger down. The beam hissed and spat. The casing glowed, turned white. An incredible blending of stenches rose about her suddenly, closing her throat, bringing water to her eyes. She heard Ticos splutter and cough.

Then the casing gave. Something inside shattered and flared. Wind roared in above Nile, salty and fresh.

"Up and out, Ticos! Screen's gone!" She hauled herself up, flung an arm across the ledge. Her shoulder tingled abruptly. Nerve charge! Parahuans in the lab. . . . Below her, Ticos made a sound of distress. Straddling the ledge, she squinted down, saw him blurrily. He'd dropped the control gadget, was clinging to the grid with both hands, shaking in hard convulsions. Heart hammering, Nile reached for him, caught his arm, brought the low-weight body flopping over the ledge and into the growth outside the window. He grasped some branches, was steadying himself, as she turned back.

Half the lab below was obscured by stink-fog emissions, whirled about by the wind. There was an outburst of desperate hootings—one or more Parahuans had run into a specimen which wasn't bothered by smells. She had glimpses of bulky shapes milling about, blinded by the fog. They should also be half-strangled by it. But at least one of them had seen Ticos up here long enough to take aim with a nerve gun. . . .

The greasy mist swirled aside from a section of floor where four glassy containers stood on a low table. Nile had seen what was inside them when she came into the lab. The top of the nearest container splintered instantly now under the UW's beam. She shifted aim. The startled organism in the shattered container already was contracting and expanding energetically like a pump. A second container cracked. As Nile sighted on a third one, a Parahuan reeled out of the stink-fog cloud, swung a big gun up at the window.

She ducked back behind the ledge. No time for gun duels. And no need. Two of the containers were broken and she'd seen jets of pale vapor spurting from both. The specimens in them were called acid bombs, with good reason. Nobody in the lab at present was likely to leave it alive—and certainly no one coming in for a while was going to get out again in good enough condition to report that the captives had fled by way of the force screen window.

She aimed along the room's ceiling to a point where the central lighting bars intersected. Something exploded there, and the lab was plunged into darkness.

Nile swung back from the window, the stink-fog's reek wafting about her. Ticos was leaning against branches, clinging to them, making abrupt jerking motions.

"How badly are you hit?" she asked quickly.

He grunted. "I don't know! I'm no weapons specialist. What *did* hit me? Something like a neural agitator?"

"In that class. You didn't stop a full charge, or you wouldn't be on your feet. With the climb-belt, I can carry you. But if you can move—"

"I can move. I seem able to hold off some of the effects. If I don't slow you down too much."

"Let's try it out," Nile said. "They shouldn't be after us immediately. Let me know if it gets too difficult. . . . "

Her bundle was in the niche of floatwood where she'd left it. She opened it hastily. Ticos stood behind her, clinging to the vegetation, bent over and gasping for breath. Nile was winded enough herself. They'd scrambled straight up from the roof of the blockhouse into the forest, cut across south of the sea-haval rookery, clambered down again toward the lagoon. It hadn't been a lightweight dance along the branches for her this time. Her muscles knew they'd been working. Even so, Ticos, supported by the climb-belt, had been pushed very hard to keep up with her. He wasn't equipped with dark-lenses, wasn't sufficiently skilled in the use of the belt; and at intervals the nerve gun charge he'd absorbed set off spasms of uncontrollable jerking and shaking. There were antidotes for the last, and no doubt the Parahuans had them. But there was nothing available here. He'd have to work it out. Another five or ten minutes of climbing might do it, Nile thought. It had better do it: she knew now Ticos had lost half his reserves of physical energy since she'd seen him last. If the effects of the alien weapon corresponded at all closely to those of its humanly produced counterparts, a more central charge should have killed him quickly.

The load he'd stopped might still do it, though that seemed much less likely now.

She fished the pack of dark-lens gel from the pouch, handed it to him. "Better put on your night eyes."

"Huh? Oh! Thanks. I can use those."

A series of shrill whistles rose from the lagoon. Ticos' head turned quickly.

"Sounded almost like one of your otters!"

"It was. Sweeting." Nile had heard intermittent whistling for the past several minutes, hadn't mentioned it. The wind still drowned out most other sounds. She pried the end of the buti stem open with her knife. "Got the lenses in place?"

"Yes."

"Then let's see how fast you can put on a coat of buti. We might have a problem here rather soon."

Ticos took the stem, began rubbing sap hurriedly over his clothes. "Parahuans?" he asked.

"Perhaps. Something seems to be coming this way along the lagoon. That was Sweeting's warning signal. Did you know your friends had a tarm here?"

"I've seen it." Ticos' tone held shock, but he didn't stop working. "You think that's what's—"

"It's more likely to be the tarm than Parahuans."

"What can we do, Nile?"

"Buti seems to be good cover if it doesn't see us. The thing got close to me once before. If it comes this far, it probably will find our trail. I'll go see what Sweeting has to tell. You finish up with the buti. But don't smear the stuff on your shoe soles yet."

"Why not?"

"I think we can lose the tarm here. It may not be too healthy by now anyway."

He looked up briefly, made a sound that was almost a laugh.

"More Tuvela work?"

"This Tuvela has little helpers." Nile switched on the

otter-caller, moved quickly toward the lagoon. At the edge of the water she stood glancing about, listening. Nothing significant to be seen. The blurred snarling of engines came for a moment from the general direction of the blockhouse. Then Sweeting broke the surface below her.

"Nile, you watch out! Tarm's coming!"

Nile rejoined Ticos moments later. The tarm was approaching through the floatwood above water level. It might be casting about for their trail, or might be on the move simply because it was beginning to feel the effects of the wild otters' weed poison. They'd succeeded in planting a considerable number of the thorns in it under the blockhouse. Sweeting reported its motions seemed sluggish. But for a while it could still be dangerous enough.

She postponed further explanations, and Ticos didn't press for any. They hurried down to the lagoon together. If the tarm didn't turn aside, it should come across their human trail. Then the lagoon must be where the trail seemed to end. If it began searching for them in the water, the otters would try to finish it off. Evidently the tarm didn't realize that the small elusive creatures might be dangerous to it. After it found it couldn't catch them, it hadn't paid them much attention.

They rubbed buti sap into the soles of their shoes, waves lapping a few feet below. Nile thought the last coating she'd given herself should be adequate otherwise. Her stock of the sap was running out; she might need some later and didn't know whether she could find another stand. By the time they finished, otter whistling had begun again, not far off. She led the way back into the forest, moving upward. Ticos crowded behind her, tarm fear overriding his fatigue. Perhaps a hundred feet on, Nile suddenly checked.

"Down, Ticos! Flatten out!"

She dropped beside him on the bough along which

they had been moving. There was a disturbance in the forest below that wasn't caused by the wind. Vegetation thrashed heavily. The noise stopped for some seconds, then resumed. It seemed to be approaching the area they'd left. They watched, heads raised, motionless.

Then Nile saw the tarm for the third time. Ticos stiffened beside her. He'd detected it too.

Even with the dark-lenses she couldn't make out many details. There was growth between them. The great thing moving among the boles of the forest looked like a fat gliding worm. Its nearness had an almost numbing effect on her again. She stared at it in fixed fascination; and it was some moments then before she realized it had stopped—about at the point where they had gone down to the water, where the human scent lay and where it should end, blotted out by the buti.

They both started at an abrupt series of loud sucking noises. The pale mass seemed to swell, then flattened. It had turned, was flowing up into the forest. Ticos swallowed audibly.

"It's—"

"Going back the way we came. It isn't following us."

He sighed with relief. They watched the tarm move out of sight. Long seconds passed. Finally Ticos looked over at Nile. She shook her head. Better not stir just yet. . . .

And then the tarm reappeared, following the line of their trail back to the water's edge. Now it slid unhesitatingly down into the lagoon and sank below the surface. Otter whistles gave it greeting.

They got to their feet at once, hurried on. The wind noises had become allies, covering the sounds of their retreat. Nile selected the easiest routes—broad boughs, slanted trunks. Ticos simply wasn't up to much more; he stumbled, slipped, breathed in wheezing gasps. At last she stopped to let him rest.

"Huh?" he asked. "What's the delay?"

"We don't have to kill you at this stage," Nile told him.

"They may not even know yet that we aren't lying dead in the laboratory. They've probably sealed the doors to keep half their fort from becoming contaminated."

He grunted. "If they haven't searched the lab yet, they soon will! They can get protective equipment there in a hurry. And someone should have thought of that window by now."

Nile shrugged. The tarm could chill her, but she was no longer too concerned about Parahuan trackers. "We have a good head start," she said. "If they trail us to the lagoon, they won't know where to look next. We could be anywhere on the island." She hesitated. "If they have any sense left, they won't waste any more time with us at all. They'll just get their strike against the mainland rolling. That's what I'm afraid they'll do."

Ticos made a giggling sound. "That's the one thing they can't do now! Not for a while."

"Why not?"

"It's the way their minds work. The only justification the Voice of Action had for what it's done was the fact that it could deliver your head. Proof of the argument— Tuvelas can be destroyed! They've lost the proof and they'll be debating for hours again before they're up to making another move. Except, of course, to look for you. They'll be doing that, and doing it intensively. We'd better not wait around. They might get lucky. How far is it still to the incubator?"

Nile calculated. "Not much more than four hundred yards. But it includes some pretty stiff scrambling."

"Let's scramble," Ticos said. "I'll last that far."

Chapter 8

The incubator was a loosely organized colony-animal which looked like a globular deformity of the floatwood bough about which it grew. The outer surface of the globe was a spiky hedge. Inside was a rounded hollow thirty feet in diameter, containing seed pods and other vital parts, sketchily interconnected. The hedge's spikes varied from finger-long spines to three foot daggers, mounted on individually mobile branches. Only two creatures big and powerful enough to be a potential threat to the incubator's internal sections were known to have found a way of penetrating the hedge. One of them was man.

The other was no enemy. It was a flying kester, a bony animal with a sixteen foot wingspread, at home among the ice floes of the south, which maintained a mutually beneficial relationship with the incubator organism. Periodically it flew northward to meet float-wood islands coming along the Meral, sought out the incubators installed on them, left one of its leathery eggs in a seed pod on each, finally returned to its cold skies. In the process it had distributed the incubators' fertilizing pollen among the colonies, thereby carrying out its part of the instinctual bargain. When the young kester hatched, the seed pod produced a sap to nourish the future pollinator until it left its foster parent and took to the air.

Man's energy weapons could get him undamaged through the hedge. The simpler way was to pretend to be a polar kester.

"It's right behind these bushes," Nile said. She indicated a section of the guard hedge curving away above the shrubbery before them. "Don't get much closer to it."

"I don't intend to!" Ticos assured her. Their approach had set off a furious rattling as of many dry bones being beaten together. The incubator was agitating its armament in warning. Ticos stood back watching as Nile finished trimming a ten foot springy stalk she'd selected to gain them passage through the hedge. Another trick learned in childhood—the shallows settlers considered incubator seeds and polar kester eggs gourmet items. Spiky fronds at the tip of the stalk were a reasonable facsimile of the spines on the kesters bony wing-elbow. Confronted by an incubator's challenge, the kester would brush its elbow back and forth along one of the waving hedge branches. A number of such strokes identified the visitor and admitted it to the globe's interior.

Nile moved up to the shrubs standing across their path on the floatwood bough, parted them cautiously. The rattling grew louder and something slashed heavily at the far side of the shrubs. She thrust out the stalk, touched the fronds to an incubator branch, stroked it lightly. After some seconds the branch stiffened into immobility. Moments later, so did the branches immediately about it. The rattling gradually died away. Nile continued the stroking motion. Suddenly the branches opposite her folded back, leaving an opening some five feet high and three wide.

They slipped through, close together. Nile turned, tapped the interior of the hedge with the stalk. The opening closed again.

Unaided human eyes would have recorded blackness here. The dark-lenses still showed them as much as they needed to see. "Over there," Nile said, nodding.

The interior of the colony-animal was compartmentalized by sheets of oily tissue, crisscrossed by webbings of fibrous cables. In a compartment on their left were seven of the big gourd-shaped seed pods. The caps of all but two stood tilted upward, indicating they contained neither fertilized seeds nor an infant kester.

"We settle down in those?" It was Ticos' first experience inside an incubator.

"You do," Nile said. "They're clean and comfortable if you don't mind being dusted with pollen a bit. The whole incubator has built-in small-vermin repellents. We could camp here indefinitely."

"It doesn't object to being tramped around in?"

"If it's aware of being tramped around in, it presumably thinks there's a kester present. Go ahead!"

He grunted, gripped one of the cables, stepped off the bough to another cable and swayed over to the nearest pod. Nile came behind, waited while he scrambled up the pod, twisted about, let himself down inside and found footing. "Roomy enough," he acknowledged, looking over the edge at her. He wiped sweat from his face, sighed. "Here, let me give you back your belt."

"Thanks." Nile fastened the climb-belt about her. "Where's yours, by the way?"

"Hid it out in my quarters when I saw the raiding party come up. Thought I might have use for it later. But I never got an opportunity to pick it up again. It's probably still there."

"How do you feel now?"

Ticos shrugged. "I've stopped twitching. Otherwise physically exhausted, mentally alert. Uncomfortably alert, as a matter of fact. I gather you've had experience with nerve guns?"

"Our kinds," said Nile. "The Parahuan item seem to produce the same general pattern of effects."

"Including mental hyperstimulation?"

"Frequently. If it's a light charge, a grazing shot—which is what you caught. The stimulation should shift to drowsiness suddenly. When it does, don't fight it. Just settle down in the pod, curl up and go to sleep. That's the best medicine for you at present."

"Not at present!" Ticos said decidedly. "Now that we've hit a lull in the action, you can start answering some questions. That ship you may have contacted—"

"A sledman racer. It was waiting for a message from me."

"Why? How did it happen to be there?"

Nile told him as concisely as possible. When she finished, he said, "So nobody out there has really begun to suspect what's going on. . . . "

"With the possible exception of Tuvelas," Nile said dryly.

"Yes, the Tuvelas. Gave you quite an act to handle there, didn't I?"

"You did. But it kept me from being clobbered in the air. The Parahuans have been creating the recent communication disturbances?"

"They've been adding to the natural ones. Part of the Great Plan. They're familiar with the comm systems in use here. They worked out the same general systems on their own water worlds centuries ago. So they know how to go about disrupting them."

"What's the purpose?"

"Testing their interference capability. Conditioning the humans to the disturbances. Just before they strike, they intend to blank out the planet. No outgoing messages. Knock off spaceships attempting to leave or coming in. Before anyone outside the system gets too concerned about the silence, they intend to be in control."

Nile looked at him, chilled. "That might work, mightn't it?"

"Up to that point it might. I'm no trained strategist, but I believe the local defenses aren't too impressive."

"They aren't designed to deal with major invasions."

"Then if the Voice of Action can maintain the previous organization—coordinate the attack, execute it in planned detail—I should think they could take Nandy-Cline. Even hold it a while. The situation might still be very much touch and go in that respect. Of course the probability is that they killed too many dissenting Palachs tonight to leave their military apparatus in good working condition. And in the long run the Great Plan is idiotic. Porad Anz and its allies don't have a reasonable chance against the Hub."

"Are you sure of that?"

"I am. Take their own calculations. They've studied us. They've obtained all the information they could, in every way they could, and they've analyzed it in exhaustive detail.

So they wound up with the Tuvela Theory. A secretly maintained strain of superstrategists. . . . "

"I don't see how they ever got to the theory," Nile said. "There isn't really a shred of evidence for it."

"From the Palachs' point of view there's plenty of evidence. It was a logical conclusion when you consider that with very few exceptions they're inherently incapable of accepting the real explanation: that on the level of galactic competition their species is now inferior to ours. They've frozen their structure of civilization into what they consider a pattern of perfection. When they meet conditions with which the pattern doesn't cope, they can't change it. To attempt to change perfection would be unthinkable. They met such conditions in their first attempt to conquer Hub worlds. They failed then. They'd meet the same conditions now. So they'd fail again."

"They've acquired allies," Nile said.

"Very wobbly ones. Porad Anz could never get established well enough to draw them into the action. And they're showing sense. Various alien civilizations tried to grab off chunks of the Hub while the humans were busy battling one another during the War Centuries. All accounts indicate the intruders got horribly mangled. How do you account for it?"

Nile shrugged. "Easily enough. They got in the way of a family fight, and the family had been conditioned to instant wholesale slaughter for generations. It isn't surprising they didn't do well. But frankly I've begun to wonder how prepared we'd be generally to handle that kind of situation now. The nearest thing to a war the Hub's known for a long time is when some subgovernment decides it's big enough for autonomy and tries to take on the Federation. And they're always squelched so quickly you can hardly call it a fight."

"So they are," Ticos agreed. "What do you think of the Federation's Overgovernment?"

She hesitated. One of the least desirable aftereffects

of a nerve gun charge that failed to kill could be gradually developing mental incoherence. If it wasn't given prompt attention, it could result in permanent derangement. She suspected Ticos might be now on the verge of rambling. If so, she'd better keep him talking about realities of one kind or another until he was worked safely past that point. She said, "That's a rather general question, isn't it? I'd say I simply don't think about the Overgovernment much."

"Why not?"

"Well, why should I? It doesn't bother me and it seems able to do its job—as witness those squelched rebellious subgovernments."

"It maintains the structure of the Federation," Ticos said, "because we learned finally that such a structure was absolutely necessary. Tampering with it isn't tolerated. Even the suggestion of civil war above the planetary level isn't tolerated. The Overgovernment admittedly does that kind of thing well. But otherwise you do hear a great many complaints. A recurrent one is that it doesn't do nearly enough to control the criminal elements of the population."

Nile shook her head. "I don't agree! I've worked with the Federation's anticrime agencies here. They're efficient enough. Of course they can't handle everything. But I don't think the Overgovernment could accomplish much more along those lines without developing an oppressive bureaucratic structure—which I certainly wouldn't want!"

"You feel crime control should be left up to the local citizenry?"

"Of course it should, when it's a local problem. Criminals aren't basically different from other problems we have around. We can deal with them. We do it regularly."

Ticos grunted. "Now that," he remarked, "is an attitude almost no Palach would be able to understand! And it seems typical of our present civilization." He paused. "You'll recall I used to wonder why the Federation takes so little obvious interest in longevity programs, eugenics projects and the like."

She gave him a quick glance. Not rambling, after all? "You see a connection?"

"A definite one. When it comes to criminals, the Overgovernment doesn't actually encourage them. But it maintains a situation in which the private citizen is invited to handle the problems they create. The evident result is that criminality remains a constant threat but is kept within tolerable limits. Which is merely a small part of the overall picture. Our society fosters aggressive competitiveness on almost all levels of activity; and the Overgovernment rarely seems too concerned about the absolute legality of methods used in competition. The limits imposed usually are imposed by agreements among citizen organizations, which also enforce them."

"You feel all this is a kind of substitute for warfare?"

"It's really more than a substitute," Ticos said. "A society under serious war stresses tends to grow rigidly controlled and the scope of the average individual is correspondingly reduced. In the kind of balanced anarchy in which we live now, the individual's scope is almost as wide as he wants to make it or his peers will tolerate. For the large class of non-aggressive citizens who'd prefer simply to be allowed to go about their business and keep out of trouble, that's a non-optimum situation. They're presented with many unpleasant problems they don't want, are endangered and occasionally harassed or destroyed by human predators. But in the long run the problems never really seem to get out of hand. Because we also have highly aggressive antipredators. Typically, they don't prey on the harmless citizen. But their hackles go up when they meet their mirror image, the predator—from whom they can be distinguished mainly by their goals. When there are no official restraints on them, they

appear to be as a class more than a match for the predators. As you say, you handle your criminals here on
Nandy-Cline. Wherever the citizenry is making a real
effort, they seem to be similarly handled. On the whole
our civilization flourishes." He added, "There are shad-
ings and variations to all this, of course. The harmless
citizen, the predator and the antipredator are ideal con-
cepts. But the pattern exists and is being maintained."

"So what's the point?" Nile asked. "If it's maintained
deliberately, it seems rather cruel."

"It has abominably cruel aspects, as a matter of fact.
However, as a species," said Ticos, "man evolved as a
very tough, alert and adaptable creature, well qualified
to look out for what he considered his interests. The
War Centuries honed those qualities. They're being even
more effectively honed today. I think it's done deliberately. The Overgovernment evidently isn't interested
in establishing a paradisiac environment for the harmless citizen. Its interest is in the overall quality of the
species. And man as a species remains an eminently
dangerous creature. The Overgovernment restricts it no
more than necessity indicates. So it doesn't support the
search for immortality—immortality would change the
creature. In what way, no one can really say. Eugenics
should change it, so eugenics projects aren't really
favored, though they aren't interfered with. I think the
Overgovernment prefers the species to continue to
evolve in its own way. On the record, it's done well.
They don't want to risk eliminating genetic possibilities
which may be required eventually to keep it from
encountering some competitive species as an inferior."

Nile said after a pause, "Well, that's mainly speculation,
Ticos."

"Of course it is. But it's no speculation to say that the
Hub still has its Tuvelas and that they're as thoroughly
conditioned to act at peak performance as they ever were
in the pre-Federation days. Further, there's now a relatively

huge number of them around. That's what makes the position of the Parahuans and their potential allies impossible. They aren't opposed by a narrow caste of Guardians. They'd hit automatic Tuvela strategy again wherever and whenever they tried to strike. A few, a very few, of the Palachs realized that. Moga was one of them. That's why he killed himself."

"Moga killed himself?"

"At the crucial moment in the lab," Ticos said, "you rather cravenly dropped flat on your face. Since nobody was pointing a gun at me, I remained standing and watched. Moga couldn't foresee exactly what would happen, but I knew he'd been aware of the purpose of my specimens for some time. He understood that he and the group which came into the lab with him would have to die if we were to escape. We had to escape to keep the Voice of Action checked. When the moment came, Moga was quite ready. The others didn't find time to squeeze their gun studs. He found time to pitch that bag at you so you would get your gun back. You see, he knew you were a very competent but still very vulnerable human being. He didn't believe at all in the legend of the invincible Tuvela. But he had to do what he could to help preserve the legend. He had a cold, hopeless hatred for humanity because he had realized it was the superior species. And, as he said, he was in deathly fear for Porad Anz. The Everliving as a whole were simply unable to understand that mankind could be superior to them. The concept had no meaning. But they could be persuaded to withdraw if they became convinced that the freakish supermen who ruled humanity were truly invincible. So, in effect, Moga conspired with me, and later with you, to produce that impression on them. . . . "

He paused, shook his head, yawned deeply. Nile watched him.

"You see, I . . . uh, what . . . " His voice trailed off.

His eyes were half closed now, lids flickering. After a moment his head began to sag.

"How do you feel?" she asked.

"Huh?" Ticos raised his head again, shook it. "I don't know," he said hesitantly. "There was—mental confusion for a moment . . . swirling bright lights. Don't quite know how to describe it." He drew a deep breath. "Part of the nerve charge effect, I suppose?"

"Yes, it is," she said. "Neural agitators are dirty weapons. You never know what the results will be. The particular kind of thing you're experiencing can build up for hours. When it does, it may cause permanent brain damage."

Ticos shrugged irritably. "What can I do about it? I've been blocking the stuff, but it seems to be leaking through to me now."

"Sleep's indicated. Plenty of sleep—preferably not less than a day or two. After that you should be all right again."

"The problem there," Ticos said, "is that I don't believe I'll be able to sleep without drugs. And we don't—" He glanced at her. "Or do we?"

"We do. I saw balath seeds on the way here and brought a few along."

He grunted. "Think of everything, don't you? Well, I'll be no good to the cause in the shape I'm in; that's obvious. Better give me the balath and get on about your Tuvela business. Try to make it back here though, will you?"

"I will." The natural end to the balath sleep was death. For the human organism, in about a week. Ticos knew that if she couldn't get him to the mainland and to antidotes presently, he wouldn't wake up again.

He took three soft-shelled seeds from her hand, said, "Hold your breath—good luck!" and cracked them between his fingers, close to his face. Nile heard him breathe deeply as the balath fumes drifted out from the seeds. Then he sighed, slumped back and slid down out of sight into the pod. After a few seconds, the pod cover closed over the vacated opening. . . . Well, he'd be as safe in there for a while as he could be anywhere in this area.

She reset the belt, checked her gear. Then paused a moment, head turned up. Something—a brief muffled thudding, as much body sensation as sound. It seemed to come from the sky. She'd heard similar sounds twice before while Ticos was talking. Evidently he hadn't heard them. They might have been the rumble of thunder, but she didn't think it was thunder.

Lightweight again, she moved back quickly along the living cables to the floatwood bough which intersected the incubator and on to the barrier hedge. She laid her hands for a moment against the hedge's branches. They opened quietly for her, and she slipped out into the forest.

For a minute she stood glancing about and listening. The thudding noise hadn't been repeated and there were no other indications of abnormal activity about. A great racket was starting up in the sea-haval rookery; but the sea-havals, young and old, needed no abnormal activities to set them off. Nile descended quickly through the forest until she heard water surge and gurgle below, then moved back to the lagoon.

The sky was almost cloudless now, blazing with massed starshine. She gazed about the lagoon from cover. At the base of the forest across from her a string of tiny bright-blue lights bobbed gently up and down. Were they looking for her over there? She twisted the otter caller.

Sweeting appeared, bubbling and hunting-happy, eager to be given fresh instructions. The tarm was dying or dead. The otters had rammed a fresh battery of poison thorns into it when it came out into the water, and shortly afterward it sank to the lagoon's root floor, turned on its side and stopped moving. Next they discovered a large group of armed Parahuans prowling about the floating pads and other vegetation in the central area of the lagoon. The otters accompanied them in the water, waiting for opportunities to strike. Opportunities soon came. By the time the search party grew aware of losses in its ranks, eight lifeless Oganoon had been left wedged deep among the root tangles. . . .

"You didn't let yourselves be seen?"

Sweeting snorted derisively.

"Waddle-foot jumps into water. Doesn't come up. Is sad, heh? Sea-haval eat him? Guardian Etland eat him? No otters there then."

Nile could picture it. A subsurface swirl in the dark water, three or four slashes, another flopping body hauled quickly down toward the roots . . . and no slightest indication of the nature of the attacker. The remaining Parahuans had bunched up together on the pads, keeping well away from the water. When lights began to flash and several boats approached, bristling with guns, Sweeting and her companions moved off. From a distance they watched the boats take the search party away.

Presently then: "Bloomp-bloomp! Big gun—"

Which explained the thudding noises Nile had heard. Great geysers boiled up suddenly from the area where the Parahuans had been waylaid. The fire came from a hidden emplacement on the far side of the lagoon. Sweeting described pale flares of light, soft heavy thumps of discharge. A medium energy gun—brought into action in hopes of destroying what? The Tuvela? The Palachs would have no other explanation for what had happened out there. And if they'd realized by now that their great tarm was also among the dead or missing . . .

"What were they shooting at later?" she asked.

Sweeting tilted her nose at the sky, gave the approximate otter equivalent of a shrug. "Up here! Kesters. . . ."

"Kesters?"

Kesters it seemed to have been. Perhaps the gun crew had picked up a high-flying migratory flock in its instruments and mistaken it for human vehicles. In any case, some time after the discharge a rain of charred and dismembered kester bodies briefly sprinkled the lagoon surface.

Nile chewed her lip. Parrol couldn't possibly be about the area yet, and that some other aircar should have chanced to pass by at this particular time was simply too unlikely. It looked like a case of generally jittery nerves and growing demoralization. Ticos had questioned whether the Voice of Action would be able to maintain the organization of the forces which were now under its sole control.

"And this last time?" she asked. Water stirred at her left as she spoke. She glanced over, saw that the wild otter pair had joined them, lifted a hand in greeting. They grinned silently, drifted closer.

"Wasn't us," Sweeting told her. The fire had been directed into the lagoon again, near the western end of the island. The otters hadn't been anywhere near those waters. Another panic reaction?

"What are they doing over there?" Nile asked. She nodded to the north, across the lagoon. The pinpricks of blue light had continued to move slowly along the base of the forest.

The otters had investigated them. A flotilla of small submersibles had appeared, presumably dispatched by the great command ship in the depths. Each was marked by one of the lights—purpose unknown. They were stationing sentries in pairs along the edge of the forest.

Nile considered it. The beginning of a major organized drive to encircle the Tuvela in the lagoon, assuming the energy gun hadn't got rid of her? It seemed improbable. Sentries normally were put out for defensive purposes. They had at least one gun emplacement over there, perhaps other posts that looked vulnerable to them. They might be wondering whether the Tuvela would presently come out of the water and start doing something about those posts. . . .

How open were the sentries to attack?

The otters had been considering the point when Sweeting picked up Nile's signal. The Parahuans were stationed above water level, at varying heights. One pair squatted on a floatwood stub not much more than fifteen feet above the lift of the waves. There was no visual contact between most of the posts.

Nile had seen Spiff and Sweeting drive up twenty-five feet from the surface of the sea to pluck skimming kesters out of the air. . . .

"If you can pick off that one pair before they squawk," she said, "do it. It will keep the rest of them interested in that side of the lagoon for a while. Stay away from there afterward . . . and don't bother any other waddle-feet until you hear from me."

They agreed. "What you doing now, Nile?" Sweeting asked.

"Getting a fire started so Dan can find us."

Chapter 9

She moved steadily upward. The ancient floatwood trunks swayed and creaked in the wind; lesser growth rustled and whispered. The uneasy lapping of the ocean receded gradually below.

When she had come high enough, she turned toward the sea-haval rookery. The thickest sections of the oilwood stand rose somewhat beyond it. A swirl of the wind brought the rookery's stenches simmering about her. Vague rumblings rose through the forest. The area was quieter than it had been in early evening, but the gigantic feedings and the periodic uproar connected with them would continue at intervals through the night. She kept well above the rookery in passing. It was like a huge dark cage, hacked and sawn by great toothed beaks out of the heart of the forest. Intruders there were not viewed with favor by the sea-havals.

She was perhaps three hundred feet above the rookery and now well over toward the southern front of the forest when she came to an abrupt halt.

Throughout these hours her senses had been keyed to a pitch which automatically slapped a danger label on anything which did not match normal patterns of the overall forest scene. The outline which suddenly impressed itself on her vision was more than half blotted out by intervening thickets; but her mind linked the visible sections together in an instant. The composite image was that of a very large pale object.

And that was enough. She knew in the same moment that another tarm had been brought to the island by the Parahuans.

Nile stood where she was, frozen with dismay. There was no immediate cover available here; the slightest motion might bring her to the tarm's attention. The massive latticework of the forest was fairly open, with only scattered secondary growth between her and the clusters of thickets along the great slanted branch where the giant thing lay. The wild otters had reported seeing two of the creatures when the Parahuans first arrived. This one must have been kept aboard the big headquarters ship since then; it had been taken back to the surface to be used against her, had approached the island through the open sea to the south—

What was it doing in the upper forest levels? . . . Had it already discovered her?

The answer to the first question came immediately. The wind carried the scent of all life passing through the area to the west and along the lagoon up to the tarm.

It was lying in wait for an indication that the human enemy was approaching the big blockhouse. A defensive measure against the Tuvela . . . and it was possible that it had, in fact, made out her shape, approaching along the floatwood branches in the night gloom, but hadn't yet defined her as human because she didn't bring with her a human scent.

Nile took a slow step backward, then another and a third, keeping her eyes fixed on what she could see of the tarm. As she reached the first cluster of screening growth, the great body seemed to be hunching, shifting position. The bushes closed behind her. Now the tarm was out of sight . . . and it was difficult to avoid the thought that it had waited only for that instant to come swinging cunningly through the floatwood in pursuit, grappling branches with its tentacle clusters, sliding along the thicker trunks. She ran in lightweight balance toward a huge central bole, rounded it quickly, clutching the gnarled surface with hands and grip-soles, hesitated on the far side, eyes searching the area below.

Forty feet down was a twisted branch, thickets near its far end. Nile pushed off, dropped, landed in moments, knees flexing, ran along the branch and threaded her way into the thickets. From cover, she looked back. Nothing stirred above or behind her. The tarm hadn't followed.

She moved on less hurriedly, stopped at last to consider what she could do. She was still stunned by the encounter. Scentlessness would have been no protection if she had come much closer to that lurking sea beast before she discovered it. And how could she get to the oilwood now? The tarm lay so near it that it seemed suicidal recklessness to approach the area again. She scanned mentally over the weapons the floatwood offered. There was nothing that could stop a great creature like that quickly enough to do her any good. The UW's beam would only enrage it.

She had an abrupt sense of defeat. The thing might

very well lie there till morning, making it impossible to start the beacon which was to identify the island to Parrol. There *must* be something she could do to draw it away from its position.

Almost with the thought, a vast bellowing erupted about her, seeming to come from inches beneath her feet, jarring her tight-drawn nerves again. . . . Only a sea-haval from the rookery below.

Nile's breath caught.

Only a sea-haval? From the rookery below—

She went hurrying on down through the forest.

Presently she returned, retracing her former route. But now she gave every section of it careful study—glancing ahead and back, planning it out, not as a line of ascent but of a headlong descent to follow. When she came back along it, she would be moving as quickly as she could move, unable to afford a single misstep, a single moment of uncertainty about what to do, or which way to turn. A good part of that descent would be low-weight jumping; and whenever one of the prospective jumps looked at all tricky, she tried it out before climbing farther.

She reached a point at last where she must be within a minute of sighting the tarm . . . if it had stayed where it was. For it might have been having second thoughts about the upright shape which had been coming toward it and then backed away, and be prowling about for her now. Nile moved as warily and stealthily as she ever had in her life until she knew she was within view of the branch where the tarm had lain. She hadn't approached it from the previous direction but had climbed up instead along the far side of the great bole which supported most of the floatwood and other growth in the area.

When she edged around the bole, she saw the tarm immediately where she had judged it would be—flattened out on the branch, the head end of the big worm body turned toward her. A great lidless pale eye disk seemed fixed on the bole. Something thick and lumpy—the mass of retracted tentacles—stirred along the side. There was a deceptively sluggish heavy look about the thing.

Nile glanced back and down along her immediate line of retreat. Then she took the UW from its holster and stepped out on a branch jutting from the massive trunk. Weaving tips lifted abruptly from the tarm's clumped tentacles. Otherwise it didn't move. Nile pointed the gun at the center of the horny eye lens and held down the trigger.

The tarm's body rose up. Nile snapped the gun into the holster, slipped back around the bole. Turned and sprang.

There was a sound of something like tons of wet sand smashing against the far side of the bole as she darted through a thicket thirty feet down. She swung out below the thicket, dropped ten feet, dropped twenty-five feet, dropped again, descending a stairway of air. . . .

A deep howling swept by overhead, more like the voice of the storm than that of an animal. Nile turned, saw the tarm, contracted almost to the shape of a ball, hurtle through smashing growth a hundred feet above, suspended from bunched thick tentacles. She pulled out the UW and held the beam centered on the bulk, shouting at the top of her lungs. The awesome cry cut off and the big body jerked to a stop, hung twisting in midair for an instant, attached by its tentacles to fifty points of the floatwood. Then the tarm had located her and swiftly came down. Nile slipped behind a trunk, resumed her retreat.

She was in and out of the tarm's sight from moment to moment, but the next series of zigzagging downward leaps did not draw her away from it again. She heard its crashing descent, above and to this side or that, always following, cutting down distance between them—then stench and noise exploded about. Strain blurred her vision, but there was a wide opening among the branches below and she darted toward it. A horizontal branch came underfoot—a swaying narrow bridge, open space all about and beneath. Sea-haval stink roiled the air. Heavy stirrings below, angry rumble. . . .

A great thump behind her. The branch shook violently. The tarm's howl swelled at her back, and furious bellowings replied. The branch creaked. Ahead to the right were the waving thickets she remembered—

Nile flung herself headlong off the branch into the growth, clutching with arms and legs. An explosively loud crack, not yards away—another. Then, moments later, a great thudding splash below.

Then many more sounds. Rather ghastly ones. . . .

Nile scrambled farther into the thicket, found solid foothold and stood up, gripping the shrubbery. She fought for breath, heart pounding like an engine. The racket below began to settle into a heavy irregular thumping as the beaks of the sea-havals slammed again and again into the rubbery monster which had dropped into their rookery, gripping a branch of floatwood . . . a branch previously almost cut through at either end by the beam of Nile's gun. The tarm was finished; the giant kesters wouldn't stop until it had been tugged and ripped apart, tossed in sections about the evil-smelling rookery, mashed to mud under huge webbed feet.

Nerves and lungs steadying gradually, Nile wiped sweat from her eyes and forehead, then looked over her gear to make sure nothing of importance had been lost in that plunging chase. All items seemed to be on hand.

And now, unless she ran into further unforeseen obstacles on the way, she should be able to get her oilwood fire started. . . .

There were no further obstacles.

❖   ❖   ❖

For the fourth or fifth time Nile suddenly came awake, roused perhaps by nothing more than a change in the note of the wind. She looked about quickly. A dozen feet below her, near the waterline, an otter lifted its oval head, glanced up. It was the wild female, taking her turn to rest while her mate and Sweeting patrolled.

"Is nothing, Nile . . . " The otter yawned, dropped her head back on her forelegs.

Nile turned her wrist, looked at her watch. Still about two hours till dawn. . . . She'd been dozing uneasily for around the same length of time at the sea edge of the forest, waiting for indications of Parrol's arrival. Current conditions on the island had the appearance of a stalemate of sorts. On the surface, little happened. The Parahuans had withdrawn into their installations. An occasional boat still moved cautiously about the lagoon, but those on board weren't looking for her. If anything, since the last developments, they'd seemed anxious to avoid renewed encounters with the Tuvela. There was underwater activity which appeared to be centered about the ship beneath the lagoon floor. If she'd had a jet rig, she would have gone down to investigate. But at present the ship was out of her reach; and while the otters could operate comfortably at that depth, their reports remained inconclusive.

In spite of the apparent lull, this remained an explosive situation. And as she calculated it, the blowup wouldn't be delayed much longer. . . .

It must seem to the Voice of Action that it had maneuvered itself into an impossible situation. To avoid the defeat of its policies, it had, by its own standards, committed a monstrous crime and dangerously weakened the expeditionary force's command structure. Porad Anz would condone the slaughter of the opposed Great Palachs and Palachs only if the policies could be successfully implemented.

And now, by the Voice of Action's own standards again,

the policies already had failed completely to meet the initial test. The basis of their argument had been that Tuvelas could be defeated. Her death was to prove it. With the proof at hand, the fact at last established, the attack on the planet would follow.

Hours later, she not only was still alive but was in effect disputing their control of the upper island areas. They must have armament around which could vaporize not only the island but the entire floatwood drift and her along with it. But while they remained here themselves, they couldn't employ that kind of armament. They couldn't use it at all without alerting the planet—in which case they might as well begin the overall attack.

Their reasoning had become a trap. They hadn't been able to overcome one Tuvela. They couldn't expect then that an attack on the Tuvelas of the planet would result in anything but failure. But if they pulled out of Nandy-Cline without fighting, their crime remained unexpiated, unjustified—unforgivable in the eyes of Porad Anz.

Nile thought the decision eventually must be to attack. Understaffed or not, their confidence shaken or not, the Voice of Action really no longer had a choice. It was simply a question now of when they would come to that conclusion and take action on it.

There was nothing she could do about that at present. At least she'd kept them stalled through most of the night; and if the Sotira racer had caught her warning, the planet might be growing aware of the peril overhanging it. Nile sighed, shifted position, blinking out through the branches before her at the sea. Starshine gleamed on the surging water, blended with the ghostly light of the luminous weed beds. Cloud banks rolled through the sky again. Fitful flickering on the nearby surface was the reflection of the oilwood. If Parrol would only get here . . .

She slid back down into sleep.

Something very wet was nuzzling her energetically. She shoved at it in irritation. It came back.

"Nile, wake up! Spiff's here!"

Grogginess vanished instantly. "Huh? Where are—"

"Coming!" laughed Sweeting. "Coming! Not far!"

She'd picked up the tiny resonance in the caller receiver which told her Spiff was in the sea, within three miles, homing in on her. And if Spiff was coming, Parrol was with him. Limp with relief, Nile slipped down to the water's edge with the otter. Almost daybreak, light creeping into the sky behind cloud cover, the ocean black and steel-gray, great swells running before the island.

"Which way?"

Sweeting's nose swung about like a compass needle, held due south. She was shivering with excitement. "Close! Close! We wait?"

"We wait." Nile's voice was shaky. "They'll be here fast enough . . . " Parrol had done as she thought—read the oilwood message from afar, set his car down to the south, worked it in subsurface toward the floatwood front. He'd be out of it now with Spiff, coming in by jet rig and with equipment.

"Where are your friends? Has anything been happening?"

"Heh? Yes. Two ships under lagoon now. Big one."

"Two—Has the command ship moved up?"

"Not *that* big. Waddle-feet carrying in things."

"What kind of things?"

Sweeting snorted. "Waddle-feet things, heh? Maybe they leave. Ho! Spiff's here. . . . "

She whistled, went forward into the water. Nile stood watching intently. Against the flank of a great rising wave two hundred yards out, two otters appeared for an instant, were gone again. . . .

"You look something of a mess, Dr. Etland!"

She'd jerked half around on the first low-pitched word, had the gun out and pointing as his voice registered on her consciousness. She swore huskily. "Thought you were a—forget it!"

On the surface twenty feet to her right, straddling the saddle of a torpedo-shaped carrier, Parrol shoved black jet rig goggles up on his forehead, reached for a spur of floatwood to hold his position. A UW rifle was in his right hand. He grinned briefly. "Dr. Cay?"

"All right for the moment," Nile said. She replaced her gun, hand shaking. "Did you run into trouble coming in?"

"None at all. The immediate area's clear?"

"At present."

Parrol had left the mainland in response to Nile's first call for help nine hours previously. Most of the interval he'd spent being batted around in heavy typhoon weather with a static-blocked communicator. He was within two hours of the island when he got a close-contact connection with sledman fleet units and heard for the first time that Dr. Etland meanwhile had got out another message. The Sotira racer had received her chopped-off report about Parahuans, carried it within range of other sleds. It was relayed through and around disturbance areas, eventually had reached the mainland and apparently was reaching sled fleet headquarters all about Nandy-Cline. Parrol's informants couldn't tell him what the overall effect of the warning had been; if anything, communication conditions had worsened in the meantime. But there seemed to be no question that by now the planet was thoroughly alerted.

They speculated briefly on the possibilities. There might or might not be Federation warships close enough to Nandy-Cline to take an immediate hand in the matter. The planet-based Federation forces weren't large. If they were drawn into defensive positions to cover key sections of the mainland, they wouldn't hamper the Parahuans much otherwise. The mainland police and the Citizens Alert Cooperative could put up a sizable fleet of patrol cars between them. They should be effective in ground and air encounters, but weren't designed to operate against heavily armed spacecraft. In general, while there were weapons enough around Nandy-Cline, relatively few were above the caliber required to solve personal and business problems.

"The sleds have unwrapped the old spaceguns again," said Nile. "They'll fight, now they know what they'll be fighting."

"No doubt," Parrol agreed. "But the Navy and Space Scouts are the only outfits around organized for *this* kind of thing. We don't know if they're available at present, or in what strength. If your web-footed acquaintances can knock out communications completely—"

"Evidently they can."

Parrol was silent a moment. "Could get very messy!" he remarked. "And in spite of their heavy stuff, you figure they're already half convinced they'll lose if they attack?"

"Going by their own brand of logic, they must be. But I don't think it will keep them from attacking."

Parrol grunted. "Well, let's talk with the otters again . . ."

The wild otters had joined the group. They confirmed Sweeting's report of the arrival of a second ship beneath the lagoon. It was more than twice the size of the first, anchored directly behind it. Parahuans were active about both. Parrol and Nile asked further questions and the picture grew clear. The second ship seemed to be a cargo carrier, and the Parahuans apparently were engaged in dismantling at least part of the equipment of their floatwood installations and storing it in the carrier.

"So they're clearing the decks," Parrol said. "And not yet quite ready to move. Now, if at this stage we could give them the impression that the planet was ready—in fact, was launching an attack on them—"

Nile had thought of it. "How?" she asked. "It would

have to be a drastic demonstration now. Not blowing up their blockhouse. Say something like hitting the command ship."

"We can't reach that. But we can reach the two under the lagoon. And we can get rather drastic about them."

"With what?"

"Implosion bombs," Parrol said. "Your message suggested I should bring the works, so I did. Three Zell-Eleven two pounders, tactical, adherent." He nodded at the equipment carrier in the water below them. "In there with the rest of it."

"Their ship locks are open," said Nile, after a moment. "Two should do it. One in each lock."

"Spaceships. It may not finish them. But—"

They glanced over at Spiff. He'd been watching them silently, along with the other three.

"Like to do a little bomb hauling again, Spiff?" Parrol inquired.

The big otter's eyes glistened. He snorted. Parrol got to his feet.

"Brought your rig," he told Nile. "Let's go pick up Dr. Cay and get him out to the car. He'll be safest there. Then we'll take a look at those ships. . . . "

Trailing Parrol and the carrier out to the aircar, Nile darted along twenty feet below the surface, the twin to his UW rifle clasped against her, luxuriating in the jet rig's speed and maneuverability. They'd left the otters near the floatwood; fast as they were, Sweeting and her companions couldn't have maintained this pace. It was like skimming through air. The rig's projected field nearly cancelled water friction and pressure; the rig goggles clamped over Nile's eyes pushed visibility out a good two hundred yards, dissolving murk and gloom into apparent transparency. Near the surface, she was now the equal of any sea creature in its own element. Only the true deeps remained barred to the jet rig

swimmer. The Parahuan rigs she'd seen had been relatively primitive contrivances.

Parrol, riding the carrier with Ticos Cay asleep inside,
was manipulating the vehicle with almost equal ease. It
too had a frictionless field. He slowed down only in
passing through the denser weed beds. By the time they
reached the aircar, riding at sea anchor in the center of
a floating thicket, a blood-red sun rim had edged above
the horizon.

They got Ticos transferred to the car, stowed the carrier
away, locked the car again, made it a subsurface race back
to the floatwood and gathered up the otters. Spiff and
Sweeting knew about tactical bombs by direct experience;
their wild cousins knew about human explosives only by
otter gossip and were decidedly interested in the operation. Roles were distributed and the party set off. Spiff,
nine foot bundle of supple muscle, speed, and cold nerve,
carried two of Parrol's implosion devices strapped to his chest
in their containers. He'd acted as underwater demolition
agent before. Parrol retained the third bomb.

And shortly Nile was floating in a cave of the giant
roots which formed the island floor, watching the open
locks of the two Parahuan spaceships below. A fog of
yellow light spilled from them. Two points of bright
electric blue hovered above the smaller ship, lights set
in the noses of two midget boats turning restlessly this
way and that as if maintaining a continuous scan of the
area. There were other indications of general uneasiness.
A group of jet-rigged Oganoon, carrying the heavy guns
with which she had become familiar, floated between the
sentry boats; and in each of the locks a pair of guards
held weapons ready for immediate use.

All other activities centered about the lock of the larger
ship. Parahuans manipulating packaged and crated items
were moving into it from the sea in escorted groups,
emerging again to jet off for more. Like the guards, they
carried guide lights fastened to their heads.

Nile glanced around as Spiff came sliding down out
of the root tangles above. The otters had returned to the
surface to saturate themselves with oxygen before the
action began. Spiff checked beside her, peering out
through the roots at the ships, then tilted his head at her
inquiringly. His depth-dark vision wasn't equal to hers but
good enough for practical work. Nile switched on her rig
speaker. "Dan?"

"I read you."

"Spiff's back and ready to go."

"My group's also on hand," Parrol's voice told her.
"We'll start the diversionary action. Sixty seconds, or any
time thereafter—"

Nile's muscles tightened. She gave Spiff a nod, watched
him start off among the roots. Resting the barrel of the
UW rifle on the root section before her, she glanced back
and forth about the area below. Her position placed her
midway between the two ship locks; Spiff was shifting
to the right, to a point above the lock of the cargo carrier,
his first target. Where Parrol and the other three otters
were at the moment she didn't know.

A group of Oganoon approached the cargo lock again,
guiding a burdened transport carrier. As they moved into
the lighted area, the one in the lead leaped sideways
and rolled over in the water, thrashing violently. The
next in line drifted limply upward, long legs dangling.
The ripping sound of Parrol's UW reached Nile's audio
pickup a moment later.

There was abrupt milling confusion around and within
the lock. The rest of the transport crew was struggling
to get inside past the guards. Thumping noises indicated
that a number of Parahuan weapons had gone off. A
medley of watery voice sounds filled the pickup. Then one
of the little boats was suddenly in purposeful motion,
darting at a slant up from the ships toward the root floor
of the island. The other followed.

"Boats have a fix on you and are coming, Dan!"

"I'm retreating."

The boats reached the roots, edged in among them. The patrol above the smaller ship had dispersed, was now regrouping. Somebody down there evidently was issuing orders. Nile waited, heart hammering. Parrol's rifle snarled, drew a heavier response, snarled again. Among the roots he had a vast advantage in mobility over the boats. A swarm of armed Parahuans jetted out from the smaller ship's lock. One of them shifted aside, beckoned imperiously to the patrol above. They fell in line and the whole group moved quickly up to the roots. Their commanding officer dropped back into the lock, stood gazing after them.

"The infantry's getting into the act," Nile reported.

"Leaving the ships clear?"

"Clear enough."

The transport crew had vanished inside the carrier. Its two guards floated in the lock, shifting their weapons about. The pair on duty in the other lock must still be there, but at the moment only the officer was in sight. Nile studied him. Small size, slight build—a Palach. He might be in charge of the local operation. . . . Parrol's voice said, "I've given the otters the go-ahead. They're hitting the infantry. Move any time!"

Nile didn't answer. She slid the rifle barrel forward, sighted on one of the carrier guards, locked down the trigger, swung to the second guard as the first one began a back somersault. In the same instant she saw Spiff, half the distance to the carrier already behind him, doubling and thrusting as he drove down in a hunting otter's awesomely accelerating sprint. He'd picked up his cue.

Now the Palach at the smaller ship floated in the rifle's sights, unaware of events at the carrier. Nile held fire, tingling with impatience. The two guards there hadn't showed again; she wanted them out of the way before Spiff arrived. The Palach glanced around, started back into the lock. She picked him off with a squeeze of her finger—and something dark curved down over the hull of the ship, flicked past the twisting body and disappeared in the lock.

Nile swallowed hard, slipped forward and down out of the cover of the roots. There were thumping sounds in the pickup; she couldn't tell whether some of them came now from the ship. Her mind was counting off seconds. Parrol's voice said something, and a moment later she realized she hadn't understood him at all. She hung in the water, eyes fixed on the lock entrance. Spiff might have decided his second implosion bomb would produce a better effect if carried on into the spaceship's guts—

A Parahuan tumbled out of the lock. Nile's hand jerked on the rifle, but she didn't fire. *That* Parahuan was dead! Another one. . . .

A weaving streak emerged from the lock, rocked the turning bodies in its passage, seemed in the same instant a hundred feet away in the water, two hundred—

Nile said shakily, "Bombs set, Dan! *Jet off!*"

She swung about, thumbed the rig's control grip, held it down, became a glassy phantom rushing through the dimness in Spiff's wake.

Lunatic beast—

Presently the sea made two vast slapping sounds behind them.

There was light at the surface now. Sun dazzle shifted on the lifting waves between the weed beds. The front of the floatwood island loomed a quarter of a mile to the north. Flocks of kesters circled and dipped above it, frightened into the upper air by the implosions which had torn out a central chunk of the lagoon floor.

"Can you see me?" Parrol's voice asked.

"Negative, Dan!" Nile had shoved the rig goggles up on her head. Air sounds rolled and roared about her. "Too

much weed drift! I can't get far enough away from it for
a clear look around."

"Same difficulty here. We can't be too far apart."

"Nobody seems to be trailing us," Nile said. "Let's keep
moving south and clear this jungle before we try to get
together."

Parrol agreed and she submerged again. Spiff and
Sweeting were around, though not in view at the
moment. The wild otters had stayed with Parrol. There
was no real reason to expect pursuit; the little gun-
boats might have been able to keep up with them, but
the probability was that they'd been knocked out
among the roots by the bombs. She went low to get
under the weed tangles, gave the otter caller a twist,
glanced at her rig compass and started south. Parrol
had a fix on the aircar. She didn't; but he'd said it
lay almost due south of them now.

Sweeting and Spiff showed up half a minute later,
assumed positions to her right and left . . . then there
was a sound in the sea, a vague dim rumbling.

"You getting that, Nile?"

"Yes. Engine vibrations?"

"Should be something of that order. But it isn't
exactly like anything I've ever heard. Any impression
of direction?"

"No." She was watching the otters. Their heads were
turning about in quick darting motions. "Sweeting and
Spiff can't tell where it's coming from either." She added,
"It seems to be fading at the moment."

"Fading here too," Parrol said. "Let's keep moving."

They maintained silence for a minute or two. The
matted canopy of weeds still hung overhead. The strange
sound became almost inaudible, then slowly swelled,
grew stronger than before. There was a sensation as if
the whole sea were shuddering faintly and steadily about
her. She thought of the great spaceship which had been

stationed in the depths below the floatwood drift these
months. If they were warming up its drives, it might
account for such a sound.

"Nile," Parrol's voice said.

"Yes?"

"Proceed with some caution! Our wild friends just
showed up again. They indicate they have something
significant to report. I'm shifting to the surface with them
to hear what it is."

"All right," said Nile. "We'll stay awake."

She moved on, holding rig speed down to her companions' best traveling rate. The dim sea thunder about
them didn't seem to change. She was about to address
Parrol when his voice came again.

"Got the report," he said. "There's a sizable submersible moving about the area. Evidently it is not the
source of the racket we're hearing. It's not nearly large
enough for that. The otters have seen it three times—
twice in deeper water, the third time not far from the
surface. It was headed in a different direction each time.
It may not be interested in us, but I get the impression
it's quartering this section. That seems too much of a
coincidence."

Nile silently agreed. She said, "Their detectors are
much more likely to pick up your car than us."

"Exactly."

"What do we do, Dan?"

"Try to get to the car before the sub does. You hold
the line south, keep near cover if you can. Apparently
I'm somewhere ahead of you and, at the moment, closer
to the sub. The otters are out looking for it again. If we
spot it on the way to the car, I'll tag it."

"Tag it?"

"With bomb number three," Parrol said. "Had a feeling
it might be useful before we were through. . . . "

Nile gave Spiff and Sweeting the alert sign, indicating the area before them. They pulled farther away on

either side, shifted to points some thirty feet ahead of her. Trailing weed curtains began limiting visibility and the overhead blanket looked as dense as ever. The rumbling seemed louder again, a growing irritation to tight nerves. . . . Then soggy tendrils of vegetation suddenly were all about. Nile checked rig speed, cursing silently, pulled and thrust through the thicket with hands and feet. And stopped as she met Sweeting coming back.

Something ahead. . . . She followed the otter down through the thicket to the edge of open water. Other drift thickets in the middle distance. Sweeting's nose pointed. Nile watched. For an instant then, she saw the long shadow outline of a submersible glide past below. Her breath caught. She cut in the rig, came spurting out of the growth, drove after the ship—

"Dan!"

"Yes?"

"If you see that sub, _don't_ try to tag it!"

"Why not?"

"Because it's _ours_, idiot! I was looking down on it just now. It's a Narcotics Control boat! And at a guess the reason it's been beating around here is that it has its detectors locked on the Parahuan command ship—"

The receiver made a muffled sound of surprise. Then, quickly: "It's probably not alone!"

"Probably not. How far do you register from your car?"

"Nine hundred yards," Parrol's voice said. "By the time we get together and make it there, we might—"

"We might be in the middle of a hot operation!"

"Yes. Let's get back upstairs and see what we can see."

Nile jetted up through the water, trailed by darting otter shapes, broke surface in a surging tangle of drift growth, began splashing and crawling out of the mess. Morning sun blazed through wind-whipped reeds about and above her.

"Nile," snapped the intercom, "their ship's here!"

"Their ship?"

"It's got to be the Parahuan. Something beneath me—lifting! Looks like the bottom of the ocean coming up. Keep out of the way—that thing is *big!* I'm scrambling at speed."

The intercom went silent. Nile stumbled across a pocket of water, lunged through a last tangle of rubbery brown growth, found open sea before her. The drift was rising sluggishly on a great swell. She shoved the goggles up on her head. Something shrieked briefly above. An aircar swept past, was racing back into the sky. Higher up, specks glinted momentarily, circling in the sun. A chain of patrol cars, lifting toward space, cutting through the aliens' communication blocks—

The swell had surged past; the weed bed was dropping toward its trough, shut off by a sloping wall of water to the south. Nile knifed into the sea, cut in the rig, swept upward, reached and rode the shifting front of the wave. View unobstructed.

"Sleds coming, Dan! Three of them."

His voice said something she didn't catch. Off to the right, less than half a mile away, the black hull of the Parahuan command ship lifted glistening from the sea. Rounded back of a giant sea beast. Nile tried to speak again and couldn't. Wind roar and sea thunder rolled about her. Out of the west, knifing lightly through the waves like creatures of air, the three sleds came racing in line on their cannon drives. On the foredeck of the one in the lead, the massive ugly snouts of spaceguns swiveled toward the Parahuan ship, already a third clear of the water and rising steadily. Pale beams winked into existence between the sled's guns and the ship, changed to spouts of smashing green fire where they touched the dark hull. The following sleds swung left, curving in; there were spaceguns there too, and the guns were in action. About the spaceship the ocean exploded in steam. Green fire glared through it. A ragged, continuous thundering rolled over Nile. The ship kept lifting. The sleds' beams clung. There was no return fire. Perhaps the first lash of the beams had sealed the ship's gunports. It surged heavily clear of the sea, fled straight up into the sky with an enormous howling, steam and water cascading back from it. The beams lifted with it, then winked out in turn, ceasing their thunder.

Nile's ears still rang with the din. Lying back in the water, she watched the ship dwindle in a brilliant blue sky.

Run, Palachs, run! But see, it's too late!

Two thin fire lines converged in the blue on the shrinking dot of the Parahuan ship. Then a new sun blazed in white fury where the dot had been. The fire lines curved away, vanished.

Federation warships had come hunting out of space. . . .

She swung about in the water, saw a section of a broken floatwood bough twenty feet away, caught it and clambered aboard. A wave lifted the bough as she came to her feet, sent it rushing south. Nile rode it, balanced against a spur, gaze sweeping the sea . . . a world of brilliance, of dazzling flashes, of racing wind and tumbling whitecaps. Laughter began to surge in her, a bubbling release. One of the great sleds knifed past, not a hundred yards away, rushing on humming drives toward the island. A formation of CA patrol cars swept above it, ports open. Jet chutists would spill from the ports in minutes to start cleaning the abandoned children of Porad Anz from the floatwood.

Details might vary considerably. But as morning rolled around the world, this was the scene that was being repeated now wherever floatwood drifts rode the ocean currents. The human demon was awake and snarling on Nandy-Cline. . . .

"Nile—"

"Dan! Where are you?"

"On the surface. just spotted you. Look southwest. The aircar's registering. Dr. Cay's all right. . . . "

Flick of guilt—*I forgot all about Ticos!* Her eyes searched, halted on a swell. There he was.

She flung up an arm and waved, saw Parrol return the salute. Then she cut in the rig, dived from the floatwood, went down and flashed through the quivering crystal halls of the upper sea to meet him.

Chapter 10

"You are *not*," said the blonde emphatically, "Dr. Ticos Cay. You are *not* Dr. Nile Etland. There are *no* great white decayed-looking monsters chasing you through a forest!"

Rion Gilennic blinked at her. She was an attractive young creature in her silver-blue uniform; but she seemed badly worried.

"No," he told her reassuringly. "Of course not."

The blonde brightened. "That's better! Now, who are you? I'll tell you who you are. You're Federation Council Deputy Rion Gilennic."

"Quite right," Gilennic agreed.

"And where are you?"

He glanced about. "In the transmitter room."

"Anybody can see that. Where's this transmitter room?"

"On the flagship. Section Admiral Tatlaw's flagship. Oh, don't worry! When I'm myself, I remember everything. It's just that I seem to slide off now and then into being one of the other two."

"You told us," the blonde said reproachfully, "that you'd absorbed recall transcriber digests like that before!"

"So I have. I realize now they were relatively minor digests. Small doses."

She shook her head. "This was no small dose! A double dose, for one thing. A twenty-six minute bit, and a two minute bit. Both loaded with emotion peaks. Then there was a sex crossover on the two minute bit. That's confusing in itself. I think you've been rather lucky, Deputy! Next time you try out an unfamiliar psych machine, at least give the operators straight information. On a rush job like this we had to take some things for granted. You *could* have stayed mixed up for weeks!"

"My apologies," said Gilennic. Then he made a startled exclamation.

"Now what?" the blonde asked anxiously.

"What time is it?"

She checked her watch. "Ship or standard?"

"Standard."

She told him. Gilennic said, "That leaves me something like ten minutes to get straightened out before Councilman Mavig contacts me."

"I can give you a shot that will straighten you out in thirty seconds," the blonde offered.

"Then I won't remember the digests."

"No, not entirely. But you should still have the general idea."

Gilennic shook his head. "That's not good enough! I need all the details for the conference."

"Well, I understand the Councilman's absorbed the digests too. He may not be in any better shape."

"That'll be the day!" said Gilennic sourly. "Nothing shakes the Councilman."

She reflected, said, "You'll be all right, I think. You've been coming out of it fast. . . . Those two subjects had some remarkable experiences, didn't they?"

"Yes, remarkable. Where are they at present?"

She looked concerned again. "Don't you remember? They left ship almost an hour ago. On your order. Dr. Etland wanted to get Dr. Cay back to the planet and into a hospital."

Gilennic considered. "Yes, I do remember now. That was just before this stuff began to take effect on me, wasn't it? I suppose—"

He broke off as the entrance door slid open. A trim young woman stepped in, smiled, went to the transmitter stand, placed a sheaf of papers on it, and switched on the screen. She glanced about the other items on the stand and looked satisfied.

"These are the reports you wanted for the conference, Mr. Gilennic," she announced. "You'll have just time enough to check them over."

"Thanks, Wyl." Gilennic started for the stand.

"Anything else?" Wyl asked.

"No," he said. "That will be all."

Wyl looked at the blonde. "We'd better be leaving."

The blonde frowned. "The Deputy isn't in good condition!" she stated. "As a Psychology Service technician, I have a Class Five clearance. Perhaps—"

Wyl took her arm. "Come along, dear. I'm Mr. Gilennic's confidential secretary and have a Class Two clearance. That isn't good enough to let me sit here and listen."

The blonde addressed Gilennic. "If you start running hallucinations again—"

He smiled at her. "If I do, I'll buzz for help. Good enough?"

She hesitated. "If you don't put it off too long, it will be. I'll wait beside the buzzer." She left the room with Wyl, and the door slid shut.

Rion Gilennic sighed and sat down at the stand. His brain felt packed—that was perhaps the best way to describe it. Two sets of memories that weren't his own had been fed in there in the time span of fifty seconds. He gathered that the emotional effects they contained were damped out as far as possible; but they remained extraordinarily vivid memories as experienced by two different sensory patterns and recorded by two different and very keen minds. For the next several hours, a part of him would be in effect Dr. Ticos Cay, able to recall everything that had occurred from his first realization of a search party of alien beings closing in stealthily on the floatwood hideout to the moment consciousness drained from him in the incubator pod. And another part would be Dr. Nile Etland, scanning at will over the period between her discussion with the Sotira sledmen and her return to the mainland with Danrich Parrol, Dr. Cay, and a pair of mutant otters.

By now Gilennic's mind seemed able to recognize these implants for what they were and to keep them distinct from his personal memories. But for a while there'd been confusion and he'd found himself running colorful floatwood nightmares in a wide-awake condition, blanked out momentarily on the fact that he was not whichever of the two had experienced that particular sequence. He'd really been much less upset about it than the two transcriber technicians who evidently blamed themselves for the side-effects. A recall digest, in any case, was the fastest and most dependable method known to get *all* pertinent information on a given set of events from a person who'd lived through them; and a few hours from now the direct impressions would fade from his mind again. No problem there, he decided. . . .

He flicked through the reports Wyl had left. Among them was one from the surgeon's office on the condition of Dr. Ticos Cay—a favorable prognosis. In spite of his age Dr. Cay's recuperative ability remained abnormally high. He'd been near total exhaustion but should recover in a few weeks of treatment. Gilennic was glad to see the memo; he'd been worried about the old man.

The latest report on military developments had nothing of significance. Most of the fighting had been concluded five hours ago, almost before the Etland party reached the mainland. Space pursuit continued; but the number of targets was down to twelve. Gilennic considered. Call Tatlaw and tell him to let a few more get away? No, two

shiploads were enough to carry the bad word to Porad
Anz. Too many lucky escapees would look suspicious—
the Parahuans had learned the hard way that Fed ships
could run them down. Some eight hundred Oganoon,
holed up in a floatwood island, had been taken alive. The
Palachs with them were dead by suicide. No value to that
catch—

The other reports weren't important. The Psychology
Service was doctoring newscast sources on Nandy-Cline.
He'd hear more about that in the conference.

Gilennic sat a moment reflecting, smiled briefly. Not
a bad setup, he thought. Not bad at all!

"Ship's comm section to Deputy Gilennic," said the
screen speaker.

"Go ahead," he told it.

"Transmission carrier now hot and steady, sir! Orado is
about to come in. When I switch off, the transmission
room will be security-shielded."

"Double check the shielding," Gilennic said and
pushed down the screen's ON button.

"What decided you to give the order to allow two
Parahuan warships to escape?" Federation Councilman
Mavig asked.

Gilennic looked at the two men in the screen. With
Mavig was Tolm Sindhis, a Psychology Service director—
publicity angles already were very much a part of the
situation, as he'd expected. The discussion wasn't limited
to the three of them; Mavig had said others were attending
on various extensions on the Orado side. He hadn't given
their names and didn't need to. Top department heads
were judging the Federation Council Deputy's actions at
Nandy-Cline. Very well. . . .

Gilennic said, "Section Admiral Tatlaw's fleet detachment was still approaching the system when we picked
up a garbled report from Nandy-Cline indicating the
fighting had started there. Tatlaw went in at speed. By

the time the main body of the detachment arrived, Parahuan ships were boiling out into space by twos and threes. Our ships split up and began picking them off.

"It was clear that something drastic had happened to the enemy on the planet. The colonial forces were in action, but that couldn't begin to account for it. The enemy wasn't in orderly retreat—he was breaking from the planet in absolute panic. Whatever the disaster was, I felt it was likely to be to our advantage if Porad Anz were permitted to receive a first-hand account of it by informed survivors.

"The flagship had engaged the two largest Parahuan ships reported so far, approximately in our cruiser class. It was reasonable to assume they had high-ranking Parahuans on board. We know now that except for the headquarters ship, which was destroyed before it could escape from the planet's atmosphere, they were in fact the two largest ships of the invasion. There was no time to check with Orado, even if it had been possible in the infernal communication conditions of the system. We were in a running fight, and Tatlaw would have cut the enemy apart in minutes. I was the leading representative of the civilian government with the detachment. Therefore I gave the order."

Mavig pursed his lips. "The Admiral didn't entirely approve of the move?"

"Naturally not," said Gilennic. "From a tactical point of view it made no sense. There were some moments afterward when I was inclined to doubt the wisdom of the move myself."

"I assume," Mavig said, "your doubts were resolved after you absorbed the digest of Dr. Etland's recall report."

"Yes. Entirely so."

Mavig grunted.

"Well, we know now what happened to the invasion force," he remarked. "Its command echelons were subjected to a concentrated dose of psychological warfare, in singularly appalling form. Your action is approved, Deputy. What brought Dr. Etland and her companions to your attention?"

"I went down to the planet at the first opportunity," Gilennic said. "There was still a great deal of confusion and I could get no immediate explanation for the Parahuan retreat. But I learned that a warning sent out by a Dr. Etland from one of the floatwood islands had set off the action. She reached the mainland at about that time, and I found her at the hospital to which she'd taken Dr. Cay. She told me in brief what had occurred, and I persuaded her to accompany me to the flagship with Dr. Cay. She agreed, on condition that Dr. Cay would remain under constant medical attention. She took him back to a mainland hospital a short while ago."

Mavig said, "The people who know about this—"

"Dr. Etland, Dr. Cay, Danrich Parrol," said Gilennic. "The two recall transcriber technicians know enough to start thinking. So does my secretary."

"The personnel will be no problem. The other three will maintain secrecy?"

"They've agreed to it. I think we can depend on them. Their story will be that Dr. Etland and Dr. Cay discovered and spied on Parahuans from hiding but were not seen by them and had no contact with them. There'll be no mention made of the Tuvela Theory or of anything else that could be of significance here."

Mavig glanced at the Psychology Service director. Sindhis nodded, said, "Judging by the personality types revealed in the recall digests, I believe that's safe. I suggest we give those three people enough additional information to make it clear why secrecy is essential from the Federation's point of view."

"Very well," Mavig agreed. "It's been established by now that the four other water worlds which might have been infiltrated simultaneously by Parahuans are clear. The rumored enemy action was concentrated solely on

Nandy-Cline. We're proceeding on that basis." He looked at Tolm Sindhis. "I understand your people have begun with the publicity cover work there?"

"Yes," Sindhis said. "It should be simple in this case. We're developing a popular local line."

"Which is?"

"That the civilian and military colonial forces beat the fight out of the invaders before they ever got back to space. It's already more than half accepted."

Gilennic said thoughtfully, "If it hadn't been for Dr. Etland's preparatory work, I'm inclined to believe that's what would have occurred. Not, of course, without very heavy human casualties. The counterattack certainly was executed with something like total enthusiasm."

"It's been a long time between wars," Mavig said. "That's part of our problem. How about the overall Hub reaction, Director?"

"We'll let it be a three day sensation," said Sindhis. "Then we'll release a series of canned sensations which should pretty well crowd the Nandy-Cline affair out of the newscasts and keep it out. I foresee no difficulties."

Mavig nodded. "The follow-up then. I rather like that term 'gromgorru.' We can borrow it as the key word here."

"Gromgorru and Tuvela-Guardians," said Tolm Sindhis.

"Yes. The two escaped cruisers reach Porad Anz. The sole survivors of the invasion present their story. The top echelons of the Everliving have a week or two to let new Tuvela-fear soak through their marrows. There is no word of a significant reaction in the Federation. What happens then? Deputy, you've shown commendable imagination. How would you suggest concluding the matter?"

"How would Tuvela-Guardians conclude it?" said Gilennic. "Dr. Etland set the pattern for us, I think. The attitude is not quite contempt, but not far from it. We've taken over a thousand low-grade prisoners for whom we have no use. Guardians don't kill purposelessly. In a week or two the prisoners should be transported to Porad Anz."

"By a fleet detachment?" Mavig asked.

Gilennic shook his head.

"One ship, Councilman. An impressive ship—I'd suggest a Giant Scout. But only one. The Guardian Etland came alone to the floatwood. By choice, as far as the Parahuans know. The Guardians would not send a fleet to Porad Anz. Or more than one Guardian."

"Yes—quite right. And then?"

"From what Dr. Cay was told," Gilennic said, "there are no surviving human captives on Porad Anz. But we'd make sure of that, and we'd let them know we're making sure of it. Half dead or insane, we don't leave our kind in enemy hands."

Tolm Sindhis said, "The Service will supply a dozen xenotelepaths to the expedition. They'll make sure of it."

Mavig nodded. "What else, Deputy?"

"Men were murdered on Nandy-Cline," said Gilennic. "The actual murderers are almost certainly dead. But the authorities on Porad Anz need a lesson—for that, and simply for the trouble they've made. They're territory-greedy. How about territorial restrictions?"

Mavig said, "Xeno intelligence indicates they've occupied between eighteen and twenty water planets. They can be told to evacuate two of those planets permanently—say the two closest to the Federation—and given a limited time in which to carry out the order. We'll be back presently to see it's been done. Would that sum it up?"

"I think," said Gilennic, "a Guardian would say so." He hesitated, added, "I believe the terms Tuvela or Guardian should not be used in this connection by us, or in fact used by us at all. The Everliving of Porad Anz can form their own conclusions about who it is that issues them orders in the name of the Federation. As far as we're concerned, the superhumans can fade back now into mystery and gromgorru. They'll be more effective there."

Mavig nodded, glanced aside. "I see," he remarked, "that meanwhile the selection of the person who is to issue the Council's orders to Porad Anz has been made." He pressed a button on the stand before him. "Your transmission duplicator, Deputy—"

Rion Gilennic slid a receptacle from the stand duplicator, took a card from it, saw, without too much surprise, that the name on the card was his own. "I'm honored by the assignment," he said soberly.

"You can start preparing for it." Mavig shifted his gaze to Tolm Sindhis. "We should expect that some weeks from now there'll be individuals on Nandy-Cline taking a discreet interest in the backgrounds of Dr. Etland and Dr. Cay. It might be worth seeing what leads can be developed from them."

The director shrugged. "We'll watch for investigators, of course. My opinion is, however, that if the leads take us anywhere, they'll show us nothing new. . . ."

Conclusions of the Evaluating Committee of the Lords of the Sessegur, Chiefs of the Dark Ships

Subject: The Human-parahuan Engagement of Nandy-cline

The committee met in the Purple Hall of the Lord Ildaan. Present besides the Lord Ildaan and the permanent members of the Committee were a Wirrollan delegation led by its Envoy Plenipotentiary. The Lord Ildaan introduced the Envoy and the members of the delegation to the Committee and referred to the frequently voiced demands of Wirrolla and its associated species that the Alliance of the Lords of the Sessegur should agree to coordinate and spearhead a unified attack on the Federation of the Hub. He explained that the conclusions to be expressed by the Committee might serve as a reply to such demands. He then requested the Lord Toshin, High Ambassador of the Alliance to the Federation of the Hub, to sum up intelligence reports compiled in the Federation following the Parahuan defeat.

The Lord Toshin: The overall impression left in the Federation by the attempted Parahuan conquest of the world of Nandy-Cline is that it was an event of almost no significance. In the relatively short period before I left Orado to confer in person with other members of this Committee, it appeared that the average Federation citizen had nearly forgotten such an attempt had been made and certainly would have found it difficult to recall much more than the fact. We must understand, of course, that this same average citizen in all likelihood never before had heard of the planet of Nandy-Cline. The sheer number of Federation worlds blurs their individual significance.

On Nandy-Cline itself the conflict with the Parahuans naturally has remained a topic of prime interest. While we may suspect that the bulk of the Parahuan force was destroyed in space by Federation military, the continental population takes most of the credit for its defeat. No opinions have been obtained from the sizable pelagic population known as sledmen, who appear to be secretive by habit and treat Federation news personnel and other investigators with such scant civility that few attempt to question them twice.

There has been no slightest public mention in the Federation of the Parahuan Tuvela Theory. The person referred to in the reports of Parahuan survivors to Porad Anz as "the Guardian Etland" and believed by them to be a member of a special class of humans known as

Tuvelas, does exist. Her name is Dr. Nile Etland and she is a native of Nandy-Cline. My office had a circumspect but very thorough investigation made of her activities and background. Most of you are familiar with the result. It indicates that Dr. Etland is very capable and highly intelligent, but in a normally human manner. She is a biochemist by training and profession, and there is nothing to suggest overtly that she might be one of a group of perhaps mutated humans who have made themselves the secret rulers and protectors of the Federation. A simultaneous investigation made of her associate, Dr. Ticos Cay, believed by the Parahuans to be possibly another Tuvela, had similar results. We have no reason to think that Dr. Cay is more or other than he appears to be.

Of particular interest is the fact that there is no public knowledge in the Federation of the role ascribed to these individuals by Parahuan survivors in bringing about the evidently panic-stricken retreat from Nandy-Cline. On the planet Dr. Etland and Dr. Cay are generally credited with having given the first warning of the presence of alien intruders, but it is assumed that this is all they did.

Under the circumstances, I felt it would be unwise to attempt to have Dr. Etland questioned directly. It would have been impossible in any case to question Dr. Cay. After a period of hospitalization, he appears to have returned to his research on one of the many floating jungles of that world; and it is believed that only Dr. Etland is aware of his current whereabouts.

The Lord Ildaan: The Lord Mingolm, recently the Alliance's Ambassador to Porad Anz, will comment on discrepancies between the Federation's publicized version of the Parahuan defeat and the account given by Parahuan survivors.

The Lord Mingolm: As the Committee knows, only two of the Parahuan invasion ships escaped destruction and eventually returned to Porad Anz. Aboard those ships were eighty-two Palachs and Great Palachs, twenty-eight of whom had been direct witnesses of the encounter between the Everliving and the female human referred to as the Guardian Etland.

All of these twenty-eight were members of the political faction known as the Voice of Action and under sentence of death for their complicity in the disastrous revolt of the faction on Nandy-Cline. All were questioned repeatedly, frequently under severe torture. I attended a number of the interrogations and on several occasions was permitted to question the subjects directly.

Their stories agreed on every significant point. Both Dr. Cay and Dr. Etland had stated openly that Dr. Etland was a Guardian of the Federation and that the designation of Tuvela applied to her. Such statements would not have convinced the Voice of Action, which had argued vehemently against the implications of the Tuvela Theory in the past, and particularly against the claim that Tuvelas appeared to have supernormal powers. However, the chain of events which began with the arrival of Dr. Etland in the area where they were holding Dr. Cay did convince them. There seemed to be nothing they could do to check her. She came and went as she chose, whether in the sea or in the dense floating forests, and was traceless as a ghost. Moreover, those who had the misfortune of encountering her did not report the fact. They simply disappeared. The list of the missing included an advanced Great Palach, renowned as a deadly fighter and the leader of the Voice of Action, and two battle-trained tarms, which are most efficiently destructive giant beasts. When a majority of the Everliving voted to parley with the Guardian, she came voluntarily into their forest stronghold, spoke to them and ordered them off the planet. The Voice of Action realized the nerve of their colleagues had broken and that the order would be obeyed. In frenzy and despair they struck out at the yielding majority and gained control of the invasion forces.

But now the situation simply worsened. The Voice of Action had made its move under the assumption that the Guardian Etland, in her willingness to speak to the Everliving, had allowed herself to be trapped. At the time she was still in a guarded compartment of the stronghold, disarmed and in the company of Dr. Cay. But when a detachment was sent to execute her there, it was destroyed in a horribly vicious attack by native life forms which until then had appeared completely innocuous. Deadly fumes infested other sections of the fort; and there was so much confusion that considerable time elapsed before it was discovered that the Guardian had left the stronghold, evidently unharmed, and had taken Dr. Cay with her.

Neither of the two was seen thereafter, but there were continuing manifestations of the Guardian's presence in the area. The Great Palachs and Palachs of the Voice of Action, now in furious dispute among themselves as to what might be the best course to follow, retreated to the expedition's command ship and to two other space vessels in the vicinity. The ships were stationed at depths below the surface of the sea which seemed to place them beyond the reach of the Guardian, but presently the command ship received a fragmentary report that she was attacking the two other vessels. This was followed by violent explosions in which the two ships evidently were destroyed.

It was enough. The command ship broadcast an order to all divisions on Nandy-Cline to withdraw at once from the planet. As we know, this belated attempt to escape was not successful. The general human attack already had begun. The command ship apparently was annihilated in the planet's atmosphere, and in a short time the entire expeditionary force was virtually wiped out.

I must emphasize strongly the oppressively accumulating effect these events produced on the Parahuans during the relatively short period in which they occurred. As related by the survivors, there was a growing sense of shock and dismay, the conviction finally of having challenged something like an indestructible supernatural power. At the time they were questioned, the survivors still seemed more disturbed by this experience than by the practical fact of their own impending demise on orders of Porad Anz, of which they were aware. It is not only that at the end there were no Parahuan disbelievers in the Tuvela Theory on Nandy-Cline but that the Tuvelas seemed to have proved to be monstrously more dangerous even than had been assumed. The impression was strengthened by the fact that the Guardian Etland appeared to be a young female. The Parahuans are aware that in the human species as in many others it is the male who is by biological and psychic endowment as well as by tradition the fighter. What a fully mature male Tuvela might have done to them in the circumstances staggered their imagination. Evidently the Guardians had considered it unnecessary to employ one of their more formidable members to dispose of the invasion forces; and evidently their judgment was sound.

I must conclude that the account of the surviving Parahuan witnesses was objectively correct. What they reported did occur. The interpretation we should put on these events may be another matter. But the reports circulating in the Federation obviously were distorted in that the true cause of the Parahuan rout at Nandy-Cline—that is, the appearance and actions of Dr. Etland—was not made public. I offer no opinion on the possible reasons for the falsification.

The Lord Ildaan: The Lord Toshin will comment.

The Lord Toshin: I agree with the Lord Mingolm's conclusion. We can assume that the Parahuan survivors told the truth as they knew it. We must ask, then, why the Federation's official version of the Parahuan defeat did not refer to the Tuvela Theory, why Dr. Etland's name was barely mentioned, and why she is credited only with having warned of the enemy presence.

The simplest explanation might seem to be that she is in fact, as she claimed and as Dr. Cay claimed, a Tuvela-Guardian. But that confronts us with the other question of why a Guardian should reveal her most secret identity and expose her group to the enemy. To that question there is no reasonable answer.

Further, I see no room in the structure of the Federation's Overgovernment for a class of hidden rulers. It is a multilayered complex in which the Federation Council, though popularly regarded as the central seat of authority, frequently appears to be acting more as moderator among numerous powerful departments. That all these organizations, led by very capable beings, should be the unwitting tools and pawns of Tuvela-Guardians may not be impossible but is highly questionable.

Therefore, I say we should not accept the possibility that Dr. Etland is a Guardian as a satisfactory explanation. I ask the Lord Ildaan to poll the Committee.

The Lord Ildaan: I poll the Committee and the Committee agrees. The Lord Toshin will resume comment.

The Lord Toshin: The second possible explanation is that Dr. Etland, while not a Guardian and not in the Parahuan sense a Tuvela, has paranormal abilities and employed them to terrorize the invasion force to the point of precipitate retreat. I refer to what is known as the Uld powers. To this, I can say only that there is nothing in her record or reputation to indicate she has such abilities. Beyond that, lacking sufficient information on the human use of Uld powers, I shall offer no opinion.

The Lord Ildaan: The Lord Gulhad will comment.

The Lord Gulhad: At one time I made an extensive

investigation of this subject in the Federation. My purpose was to test a theory that the emergence of a species from its native world into space and the consequent impact of a wide variety of physical and psychic pressures leads eventually to a pronounced upsurge in its use of Uld powers. The human species, of course, has been in space for a very short time in biological terms. Because of the recent acute disturbances in its political history, I was unable to obtain confirmation of the theory. The available records are not sufficiently reliable.

However, I could establish that the humans of our day make use of Uld powers more extensively than most other intelligent species now known to us. Humans who do so are called psis. There is little popular interest in psis in the Federation, and there is considerable misinformation concerning them. It is possible that several branches of the Overgovernment are involved in psi activities, but I found no proof of it. It is also possible that the Federation has advanced the non-biological harnessing of Uld powers to an extent considerably beyond what is generally known, and is therefore relatively indifferent to its usually less exact control by living minds.

The question is then whether Dr. Etland, either directly or with the aid of Uld devices, could have used Uld powers to produce the disconcerting manifestations reported to the Committee by the Lord Mingolm. Did she incite normally harmless lower life forms to attack the Parahuans? Did she make herself invisible and generally untraceable? Did she cause opponents to disappear, perhaps into the depths of the sea, into space—even into dimensions presently unknown to us? Did she madden the minds of the Voice of Action, forcing them into their disastrous revolt? Was the explosion of the two submerged ships which triggered the abrupt retreat brought on by a manipulation of Uld powers?

All this is possible. We know or suspect that human

psis and other users of Uld have produced phenomena which parallel those I listed.

However, it is improbable. In part because there is no record that any one Uld user could employ the powers in so many dissimilar ways. Even if we assume that Dr. Cay was also an accomplished psi and that the two worked together, it remains improbable.

It is further improbable because we cannot say that Dr. Etland could have achieved what she did only through the use of Uld power. Considered individually, each reported event might have had a normal cause. And since the deliberate control of Uld to a significant extent remains exceedingly rare also among humans, its use should not be assumed when other explanations are available.

The Lord Ildaan: I poll the Committee and the Committee agrees. The Lord Toshin will comment.

The Lord Toshin: There remains, as the Lord Gulhad indicated, a third possibility. I find it perhaps more disquieting than the two we have considered. It is, of course, that Dr. Etland is precisely what she seems to be—an exceptionally capable human, but one with no abnormal qualities and no mysterious authority. Our investigation indicated that she is thoroughly familiar with the floating forests of her world and the life forms to be found there, is skilled with weapons and on a number of occasions has engaged successfully in combat with her kind. Dr. Cay was a Parahuan captive long enough to have gained detailed information on the Tuvela Theory. It is difficult to see how he could have transmitted this knowledge to Dr. Etland. But if we assume he found a way of doing it, it seems we should accept, as the most probable explanation of the events reported by the Parahuan survivors, that Dr. Etland used the information and her familiarity with the area and its tactical possibilities, along with physical competence and ordinary weapons, to demoralize and eventually rout the enemy.

Of course, we cannot prove this. And evidently that is precisely what the Federation's Overgovernment intends, in seeing to it that no mention was made of Dr. Etland's role or the Tuvela Theory in the accepted reports on the Parahuan invasion. Any investigators who were aware of the Parahuan version of the affair would know something was being concealed but could only speculate, and perhaps speculate uneasily, on what was concealed. For note that it is not of major significance which of the possibilities considered here contains the answer. To an enemy, the individual we know as Dr. Etland would be as deadly in one aspect as in another. We should regard the silence of the Federation's authorities on the point as a warning directed to those who might base their actions on too definite a conclusion—such as the one made by Porad Anz. It implies that a hostile intruder cannot know in what shape disaster may confront him among humans, that if he comes he will face the unexpected—perhaps the uncalculable.

The Lord Mingolm: Still, we must calculate. We have established only that Dr. Etland was a dangerous individual. What information does the Parahuan mistake give us about the species?

The Lord Toshin: It confirms that the species is extremely variable. The Parahuan evaluation was based on the study of a few thousand individuals, plucked secretly from space over a long period of time and tested to destruction. No doubt Porad Anz learned a great deal about these humans in the process. Its mistake was to generalize from what it learned and to calculate from the generalizations. To say that *the* human is thus and so is almost to lie automatically. The species, its practices and philosophies remain unpredictable. Individuals vary, and the species varies with circumstances. This instability seems a main source of its strength. We cannot judge it by what it is today or was yesterday. We do not know what it will be tomorrow. That is the cause of our concern.

The Lord Ildaan: It is, indeed, the cause of our

concern. And it seems from what has been said that the human Overgovernment must be considered now as a prime factor. The Lord Batras will comment.

The Lord Batras: The function of the Overgovernment is strategy. In part its strategies are directed at the universe beyond the Federation. But that is a small part.

Regard the Federation as the object of an invader's plans. It covers a vast area of space. Its inhabited worlds appear almost lost among the far greater number of worlds which support no human life. Below the central level, its political organization seems tenuous. Federation military power is great but thinly spread.

The area of the Federation would thus appear open to limited conquests by a determined and well prepared foe. But we are aware that during many star periods every such attempted thrust has failed. We have seen more subtle plans to weaken and cripple the human civilization fail as completely, and we still do not know specifically why some of them failed. However, on the basis of what we have observed, we can say in general now that the Federation is a biological fortress armed by the nature of its species. The fortress may be easily penetrated. When this occurs, it turns into a complex of unpredictable but always deadly traps.

This being true, we must ask why the Overgovernment persists in acting in a manner which appears almost designed to conceal the strength of the Federation's position. We have seen that its policy is to treat hostile activities as being of no importance and that it provides no more information concerning them than it can avoid. We may assume it genuinely believes its present galactic neighbors do not constitute a serious military threat. However, the great restraint it shows in retaliating for planned attacks must have a further reason. In the latest instance, it has not even forced Porad Anz to disarm, as it easily could have done.

I believe we have amassed sufficient information at

last to explain the matter. The Overgovernment's main concern is with its own populations. What plans it has for the species we do not know. As yet, that defies analysis. But we know what plans it does not have for the species and the means it employs to keep it from turning into directions regarded as undesirable.

Consider the creature again as the Lord Toshin described it. Individuals vary in attitude and behavior, but the creature as a class is eminently dangerous. It is, of course, inherently aggressive. Before the structure of the Federation was forged, humans fought one another for many star periods throughout that area with a sustained fury rarely observed in other species. Since that time they have remained technically at peace. But the aggressive potential remains. It expresses itself now in many ways within the confines of the human culture.

I said that we know what the human Overgovernment does not want. It does not want its unstable, variable, dangerous species to develop a philosophy of space conquest from which it could gain nothing it does not already have, and through which it might return eventually to the periods of interhuman conflict which preceded the Federation. Possibly the Overgovernment is influenced by additional considerations in the matter. We do not know that. We do know that the human species is oriented at present to deal with other intelligent beings in a nonhostile manner. There are criminal exceptions to that rule—we and others have clashed with them. But those exceptions are regarded as criminals also by their kind.

This general attitude could change if the present humans of the Federation gained the impression they were being seriously challenged by outside enemies. So far, they have been given no reason to believe it. The Parahuan invasion was a serious challenge only in the minds of Porad Anz. We anticipated its failure but believed we could gain information from it—as we have done.

I submit to the Committee that we now have gained information enough. The Overgovernment has shown it is afraid of the effects continuing irritations of the kind might have on its species. We too should be wise enough to be afraid of such effects. If the Federation is launched on a pattern of retaliatory conquests, the pattern might well become an established habit. That is the real danger.

The Lord Ildaan: The Committee agrees. I speak then as the Lord Ildaan, representing the Alliance of the Lords of the Sessegur, Chiefs of the Dark Ships. I address the Wirrollan delegation and all those they represent. To the ends of the area through which the influence of the Alliance extends there will be no further hostile action prepared or planned against the human Federation. The Alliance forbids it, and the Dark Ships enforce our ruling as they have done in past star periods. Be warned!

The Committee concurs. The meeting is closed.

AFTERWORD

by Eric Flint

With this volume, we conclude the project of re-issuing all of James H. Schmitz's stories set in his Federation of the Hub universe. I hope the readers have enjoyed these stories as much as I always have.

Happily, the series has met with a very favorable response from the audience. As a result, Baen Books has decided to re-issue more of Schmitz's writings.

Two more volumes are planned:

In the next, we will turn to the other common setting, besides the Hub, which James Schmitz used for several of his stories. That is his universe of the Confederacy of Vega, in which he wrote four long stories: "Agent of Vega," "The Illusionists," "The Truth About Cushgar," and "The Second Night of Summer." Taken as a whole, that quartet is the length of a novel, and we will be re-issuing it in its entirety.

Along with the Vega stories, we will also include a

number of the best Schmitz stories which are not part of any common setting. That includes such relatively well-known tales as "The Custodians," as well as some excellent stories which have never been re-issued since their original magazine publication back in the 50s and 60s: "Beacon to Elsewhere," "Gone Fishing," and "The End of the Line," just to name some of them.

We will then re-issue, in a separate volume, Schmitz's longest novel and best-known work, *The Witches of Karres*.

So if you've enjoyed the Hub stories, don't go away. There's plenty more of James H. Schmitz to come.

RECURRING CHARACTERS IN THE HUB SERIES

by Guy Gordon

For those readers who are interested in following the adventures of the various characters who appear in more than one Hub story, we have compiled the following list. The stories are listed in chronological order for that particular character.

Telzey Amberdon	*Novice*	Volume 1
	Undercurrents	"
	Poltergeist	"
	Goblin Night	"
	Sleep No More	"
	The Lion Game	"

Got questions? We've got answers at
BAEN'S BAR!

Here's what some of our members have to say:

"Ever wanted to get involved in a newsgroup but were frightened off by rude know-it-alls? Stop by Baen's Bar. Our know-it-alls are the friendly, helpful type—and some write the hottest SF around."
— **Melody L** *melodyl@ccnmail.com*

"Baen's Bar . . . where you just might find people who understand what you are talking about!"
— **Tom Perry** *perry@airswitch.net*

"Lots of gentle teasing and numerous puns, mixed with various recipes for food and fun."
— **Ginger Tansey** *makautz@prodigy.net*

"Join the fun at Baen's Bar, where you can discuss the latest in books, Treecat Sign Language, ramifications of cloning, how military uniforms have changed, help an author do research, fuss about differences between American and European measurements—and top it off with being able to talk to the people who write and publish what you love."
— **Sun Shadow** *sun2shadow@hotmail.com*

"Thanks for a lovely first year at the Bar, where the only thing that's been intoxicating is conversation."
— **Al Jorgensen** *awjorgen@wolf.co.net*

Join BAEN'S BAR at
WWW.BAEN.COM
"Bring your brain!"